A COURT of BLOOD & BONE

THE IRONWORLD SERIES

BOOK TWO

Candace Osmond

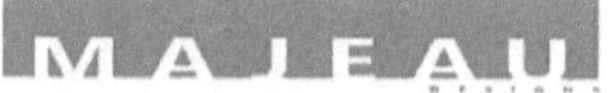

Dedication

To anyone who has ever lost
somone they love.

Acknowledgements

Thanks to coffee and chocolate...
and my husband.

Sol
Beach
Tower
Hollows
Summer
Territory
Three Sisters
Malton Forest
Frozen
Pass
Winter
Territory
The
Eternal
Sea

Seelie Court
Ruined Lands
The Grove
Territory of Dreams
Faerie Lake
Haven
Territory of Nightmares
Isle of Serene
The Dark Forest

Chapter One

"Again."

"What?" I huffed as my tired arms slacked at my sides, knowing I looked worse than I felt. I was grateful for the din of night. The darkness was a noise that could hide anything. "Moya, we've been doing this for weeks. I'm not getting any better."

"You've mastered water travel and Calling." She leaned against a large rock and examined her nails. "You'll master this, too."

"Mastered is a loose term for what I've been able to do."

Yes, I could travel to the Sanctuary or to Oliver's cottage by water from Ironworld. That was easy enough, but it was also the extent of what I could do. I managed to Call a few times like Julie had done to summon Moya to our living room that night. But only if the person was in Ironworld…and nearby.

I groaned.

There was still so much I had to learn. I couldn't wisp for the life of me, and my own powers were wild and chaotic. A burning beneath my skin. At first, after my impromptu trip to the Temple of Dreams, when I reached deep inside my soul and plucked my powers off the bare stone floor…I'd had control of it. It was almost…small. Manageable.

I cringed inwardly.

The image of my bare skin against Cillian's as I held a blade of sunlight to his throat flashed through my mind. I wouldn't dare attempt that now. Not when my magic had practically grown beyond my control. It seemed the more I used it, the stronger *it* got.

"What's the matter?" she asked.

I'm worried I'll kill my boyfriend. A sigh raked through me. "I don't know."

The depths of her sea-green hair were pulled back and hung down her back as she paced around me. "Again. I know you can do it."

I chewed at my lip. "But… what if I hurt you?" The image of all those vampires—nothing but ashes—circling me screamed across my vision. I shuddered at the memory I'd managed to block out until now.

I was a danger to everyone and everything.

Moya's enchanting grin made the corners of her beautiful, bottomless eyes pinch. "I'm not a vampire and am privy to the burn of the Summer sun." She grinned to herself.

"You mean magic." I rolled my eyes. Magic that I couldn't even control. I was fantastical, just like them, like all those creatures I walked amongst each day… and I was useless.

A ticking time bomb.

"Everything in Faerie derives from magic," she replied. "The clouds in the sky, the grass beneath our feet. Even the sun. Try again. Summon the sunlight."

My eyes followed her fingertip toward the dense forest that lay ahead. We'd been standing there for over two hours now, and I failed to even grow the light in my hands, let alone illuminate the forest. From fear or lack of ability…I had no idea.

But I tried anyway.

I closed my eyes and braced my legs as I worked through calming my breaths, focusing on the glow that hummed in my veins. A dormant thing, all sleepy and warm. A little too warm. I could already feel the static of magic building in my hands, crackling over the heat. *Chaos.*

I steadied my breathing and slowly widened the space between my palms as I opened my eyes. The light grew and grew, expanding until I was consumed by it. When I moved, *it* moved. All I ever got was a taste of control before it dissipated.

But this time, it lingered. I willed the light to move and form until I was confident it would go where I directed it.

I glanced at Moya with a giddy but tired smile, and she beamed proudly.

My hands stretched toward the forest. With a deep breath, I channeled the light to fill the darkness between the trees until I illuminated every crack and crevice as the day would. But that familiar tinge of static returned, and a cold, stark chill struck me just as the glow turned and flickered and… set fire.

"Oh, my god!" I gasped and shook my hands at my sides, extinguishing the source.

Moya didn't miss a beat. She lunged forward and swung her arms, her fingers clenched into clawed fists as she called upon her own magic with such ease it made me cringe with jealousy. Water seemed to pull from the air and the very pores of the Earth, forming a wave that splashed down on the fire I'd started. Wet, sizzling bark crackled in my ears, and night fell upon us again.

"I'm sorry," I said, my fingers numb with panic. "I don't know what that was."

She turned from the doused fire as if it were no big deal and crossed her arms. "That was the best you've done yet.

I call that progress." When I didn't reply, she continued with a sigh. "Look, Avery, you're mortal. It's going to take some practice to wield your powers." I sat on a large rock, and she followed. "But, even mortal, you possess a power unlike anything I've ever seen outside of a High Fae."

"You mean, Summer Fae don't all have this light?"

She shook her head and crossed her arms. The leather of her deep teal trench coat groaned. "No, not like yours. Not for a long time."

"What do you mean?"

"There were old families of Higher Fae that had tapped into the power of the Summer sun, but that was hundreds of years ago. Bits trickled down into the following generations, but nothing like I've witnessed in you. And we've only just cracked the surface of your magic. I suspect it's ancient."

I guffawed. "Yeah, maybe the Summer Lord snuck into Ironworld for a few nights on the town with a mortal woman."

She didn't laugh or smile at my comment. "Don't be fooled. It's a possibility."

I swallowed dryly. "Would it be so bad if that's who my father is?"

She managed a half smile that didn't reach her eyes. "No, it wouldn't. Kheelan's a decent Lord, for the most part. A little selfish and pompous." Her sandaled foot toed the dirt at our feet. "Obsessed with war tactics and protecting the border." She sighed. "But I doubt it would have been him. Kheelan was only crowned a few decades ago. It would have been his father or grandfather if it were any from his bloodline." Her eyes sparkled as she looked at me. "But that's assuming it was even Kheelan's bloodline."

"What do you think?"

She pressed her lips together in thought, and I wondered if she was keeping something from me. "No, I don't think so. Only a handful of families wielded the Summer sun, which wasn't his."

"Will… will we ever find out?" As much as I tried to keep them out, I was constantly worried about who my true parents were. And I wasn't entirely sure what to expect from Oliver's blood mapping.

"Yes," she said stonily and stared at the ground. But I knew she wasn't so sure. "Possibly. We just have to wait and let Oliver work his magic."

I let it go as I chewed at the inside of my lip. "Where are your sisters tonight?"

Moya grinned. Even in darkness, she radiated otherworldliness. Like the invisible burn of the sun when reflecting off the waves. Just… the *feeling* of it. Moya's magic was unlike anything I'd felt from any Fae yet. Not more powerful, but not less, either. Just… different. Like the gold crayon.

"Helping Oliver," she replied.

Aya and Brie had been teaching me all about poisons, tiny weapons, where to hide them on my body, and even a few lessons on stealth. Regardless of their skills, they claimed to not be fighters, and the more I learned from the sisters, the more I believed them. They were all about observing, gathering information, and using your opponent's strength against them.

I gobbled up everything they could teach me while they took turns asking me questions about Ironworld. Their fascination with the mundane was endless.

I leaned back and gripped the rock behind me as I stared at the moon. It slowly crawled out from behind a tuft of cloud. "Can I ask you something?"

She shrugged. "Anything."

"What are your sisters?"

"Didn't Julie tell you?"

I tipped my head from side to side. "A little. I mean, not enough to really get it."

Her bound hair, dark in the moonlight, fell over her shoulder and hung down the other side of her face. "Shades, wraiths, ghosts." Another shrug. "Whatever you wish to call them, I suppose. It's all the same."

"Why aren't you like them?"

Moya's breath hitched. But she replied, her eyes distant. "I'm the eldest of three daughters to the King of the Seas."

She waited for a beat, letting it sink in for me. "And…he cursed every one of us."

"What?" I gasped. "Why?"

"He'd made an… *arrangement* for me, and I wouldn't comply."

My throat ran dry. "Marriage?"

She shook her head. "Worse. Ruler." To my widened eyes, she continued. "Of half the seas. After our mother died, all seven seas were too much for him to bear alone. He needed me–was forcing me to take my mother's throne. But I wanted nothing of it. I saw what that power did to my mother. It drove her mad. I watched her turn her own people into bottom-feeding slugs at even the smallest slight. The power twisted and deformed her and drove her to her eventual death. You see…she was the raging sea, while my father was its calm. Perfect balance. When she died, he couldn't stand it."

I finally took a breath. "So, he killed your sisters?"

"At first, he banished me to land. Never to step foot in the sea again. Not as I once was, anyway. The moment I step foot in the ocean again, I'll be trapped and forced to rule them." Moya remained calm as she spoke. I guess the years since must have made it easier. "Eventually, when he grew tired of waiting for me to give in and return, Aya and Brie were removed from their bodies, and their souls banished with me. They cannot return without me, nor can they fully be here, either." Her eyes went distant again, but this time laced with pain. "Trapped in death. With the sea constantly screaming in your head, and the only way to make it stop is if I take them back."

"I'm…." My mouth just gaped as I struggled for words. I couldn't imagine carrying that sort of guilt and expectation. "I'm so sorry."

She smiled and tipped her head. "It's okay. We've adjusted, and my sisters understand why I won't return. We have a purpose on land; we've found friends." She stretched her long shimmery arms and jingled the dozens of metal bangles on her wrists. "I've grown quite fond of life here, actually. The food, the clothes."

I couldn't help but smile. The twins were always clad in elegant fighting leathers and silks, while Moya's preferred style was more modern.

"So, what did you look like? You know, before?"

She laughed and gestured to herself. "Pretty much like this but more… watery. Creatures of the ocean are *of* the ocean. We're part of it, waves that crashed against the shores. The dark blue depths. We have no true form until we come on land. Well, not a physical form like *this*." She swayed her magnificent body. "This is a manifestation of what our other selves are."

Part of me settled, knowing that I wasn't alone. That I wasn't the only… outsider. Moya and the twins were born

of the sea. And they'd adjusted to life on land, in a different form, no less. It gave me hope that I could gain control
of my own abilities and life. That I'd one day settle into my
role, a hybrid being existing in two worlds at the same time.

I had a lot to learn about myself, and part of me was
thrilled and excited. But the other part of me, that dark
spot at the back of my mind that saw visions of Dark
Lords and festering wounds, constantly whispered *what-ifs*
in my ear. But only one stood out among the rest…

What if I didn't like what I found?

Chapter Two

Tomas sipped from his coffee cup. "Okay, so I'll start on the plans for the lighting. But I'll need your visual details to start the audio."

I nodded and wrapped both hands around my drink, letting the warmth soak in. Fall was in full swing as we sat by the wall of windows in the school canteen, and the chill almost seemed to seep through the glass. "I'll work on that this weekend then."

I had a massive end-of-semester project to present for one of my classes, and it just so happened that what I needed Tomas' expertise for–lighting and audio–would count as *his* end-of-semester project. It couldn't have worked out any better. Plus, I got to work closely with a friend.

I smiled as he explained his ideas and scribbled notes on the pad between us. When I reached the dregs of my coffee, I checked my phone for the time.

"I gotta get to my next class." I scooped my stuff into a pile and began stuffing it all in my leather bag.

Tomas did the same, but he cleared his throat nervously. "So, what have you guys been up to lately?"

I stopped and looked at him, noting the slight pink that flushed in his cheeks. "What do you mean?"

"You and Julie," he replied and met my gaze, rubbing the back of his neck. "I've hardly seen you two around."

I blinked, not knowing what to say. "Didn't–I thought you and Julie were…hanging out?"

"We were," he said as we got off our stools. "But she's been pretty distant lately."

I'd been so wrapped up in my own drama that I hadn't paid much attention to Julie's movements. Aside from the couple of shifts we shared at the café each week, and the time we both spent at Oliver's cottage, learning magic. She was determined to master wisping. A task I ultimately failed at and abandoned immediately.

Water travel would have to be good enough. As long as there was a natural water source, I could go to Oliver's or the Sanctuary.

"I'm sure she's just busy with school." I rolled my eyes sarcastically. "You know, those academic types. Not as carefree as us creatives." He chuckled lightly, but I could sense hesitation all over him. I touched his arm, and we stopped in the hall. "I think she's just prepping for some big test. We all could use a breather. Let's hang out this weekend."

Tomas's dark hair fell over the crinkle at the corner of his eye. "Sounds good."

"I'll see you later."

We split off, and I headed to my next class. The prof shut the door just as I took my seat, and I immediately noticed the empty one next to me. I glanced around the room, searching for her ebony hair and a permanent look of disdain. But she wasn't here. Max was never *not* here. In fact, she'd never missed a class and was always the first to arrive.

As class began and everyone settled in, I couldn't shake the tangibly bad feeling that spread through my chest. My eyes kept darting to Max's empty seat. The hour passed slowly, and by the end, when my knee bounced in place, and the nagging feeling of dread whispered over my skin, I shoved from my seat the second we were dismissed and made a beeline for the bathroom.

I threw myself into an empty stall and locked the door behind me. My bag fell to the floor as I plopped down on the toilet seat and closed my eyes. I had to tap into my Oracle ability. I had to see why I felt weighted with this feeling. I didn't know what to do or how to do it, so I focused on each breath. *In and out.*

My thoughts began to wander, but I had control. I

steered myself through the maze that was my mind until I saw her or…*felt* her. I stood in murky blackness, just like in my nightmares, but I could feel Max's energy. Could smell her expensive perfume.

And sense her feelings.

Something familiar coursed through me. A sense of being a fly on the wall, but I couldn't see. I could only *feel*, and it was a feeling that had been haunting me for days. Evaine. Rage and fear twirled at the back of my throat as I slowly opened my eyes. The din echo of the empty bathroom rang in my ears.

Was Max in trouble?

***

I left three messages on Max's cell before giving up.

"Do you have those receipts from the Mitchel showing?" Celadine asked over my shoulder as I sat hunched over my hovel of paperwork at the front desk.

I stopped what I was doing—budgeting for a small upcoming show—and fanned through a basket of Zip-loc bags, each marked in Sharpie with their corresponding event. I found the Mitchel bag and handed it to her.

Celadine eyed the basket with an arched brow. I sighed and smiled. "It's the best method for keeping track of things until I get a moment to log it all."

She crossed her slender, tattooed arms across her chest. So stark and pale against the midnight black sleeveless jumper she wore. The hint of a smile teased her mouth. "Is the workload too much for you?"

I straightened. "No, I swear. It's not too much. In fact," I smiled, and Celadine relaxed against the edge of the desk. "This job is the easiest part of my life. I love it. I need it."

"And you're staying on top of things at school? If your classes are suffering so you can manage this job—"

"They're not," I blurted and took a calming breath. "They're not. School is fine, too. Easy. Not nearly distracting enough." We shared a tired laugh. "Actually, I have a favor to ask."

Celadine brightened. "Yes?"

"I have this end-of-semester project coming up that's worth a huge chunk of my grade," I said. "A vignette series."

"Would you like to use the gallery?"

I raised my brows. I hadn't expected her to just offer it. "If it's alright with you?"

Celadine nodded. "Of course. It's at your disposal. You know the gallery schedule just as well as I do. Pencil yourself in. Use whatever you need. It's all good business for the gallery, anyway."

I chewed at the corner of my lip. "And good…energy for you?"

She smiled coyly and adjusted her cat-eye glasses. "Yes. Does that bother you?"

I shook my head without hesitation. "Not at all. I think it's fascinating. I mean, who am I to judge? I don't even know what I am. Not truly."

She leaned toward me with delight. "How lucky I am to witness you discover it." I couldn't help but mirror her smile, and the knots in my stomach loosened just a little. Celadine straightened and smoothed out the wrinkles on her jumper. "Anyway, I wanted to let you know I've hired someone part-time to take care of the menial day tasks for you."

"What? Why?"

"This journey you're about to embark on," she replied. "Learning magic, discovering who you are… you'll need time. But I'd very much like it if you'd continue our evening apprenticeship."

I gave her a nod. "I'd like that, too."

Celadine sucked in a deep breath. "Do you want to see it?"

"She what?"

"The gallery." She gestured around us. "The energy. How I do it."

My eyes bulged. "I would *love* to see that. But isn't it…a private thing?"

My boss chuckled. "Maybe for some. But not the way

I do it. And–" She shrugged. "I've got a feeling you'll be around for a while if my brother has anything to do with it." She motioned to the floor. "The entire building is lined with quartz, marble, and marble inlay."

I watched as she reached out, her hand hovering over the floor beneath us. And I felt it. A deep hum that seemed to crawl over every inch of the room. From the stone, clear waves radiated toward Celadine. Like the air above the black pavement on a hot summer day.

She closed her eyes and sucked in a sharp breath, and then everything stopped. The humming, the vibrations in the air. Celadine looked at me with half a grin, and I could see it. The slight change. Her alabaster skin beneath the tattoos radiated with the pulse of energy.

Of life.

I shook my head with an impressed chuckle. "You never cease to amaze me."

"It's too bad you don't have an aptitude for witch magic," she replied. "I could show you a thing or two."

I sighed and thought about the nightmarish visions that haunted me at night. Just one of the many things I was facing. "One overwhelming thing at a time."

She closed her hands in front of her and tilted her head. "How are things going? With your newfound powers?"

"I'm learning to control them the best I can, but it doesn't feel like enough, and there's only so much Moya can teach me. Especially with this weird bind in my blood." I rubbed my arms. "It makes my flimsy control seem chaotic. Like a wild animal at times." I stared into her violet eyes. "And it terrifies me."

A pause held the echoey room.

"Cillian worries for you," Celadine admitted. He'd been gone all week on some work thing overseas. "He won't say it, but I feel his worry for you."

I stared at a spot on the floor. "And what else do you feel?"

She laughed. "Nothing like what you're thinking. My feelings toward you are strictly platonic."

"Thank God for that," Cillian chuffed as he entered the gallery, strutting toward me like a god down a runway.

"You're back!" I exclaimed, my heart clawing to get out and reach for him.

He stopped at the desk and curled a finger at me. "I owe you a proper date."

My forehead pinched together. "Wait, what?"

"A date?" he said, brows raised, ready for a sarcastic reply. "One where I don't leave before the end."

Celadine adjusted her glasses and swung her thick beaded braid over her shoulder. "I'll see you later," she said, barely containing a grin as she waved the receipts. "Thanks for these."

I turned to Cillian and gestured to my grungy t-shirt

and day three jeans. "I'm a mess."

He offered his elbow. "We'll stop by your place first, then. We have an hour before our reservation."

"Reservation?" I stood and grabbed my jacket. "Sounds fancy." I stuffed my arms in the sleeves and looped one through Cillian's waiting elbow.

He reached out and brushed his hand across my face as his lips touched mine. The taste of mint, the smell of cool leather; I let him envelop me, and I melted in his arms.

When he finally pulled away, I had to will my heart to calm. But I played it cool. "So, are we walking or flying?"

We strolled toward the front doors. "What do I look like, a taxi service?"

I shrugged. "It's just awfully convenient." Cillian playfully shoved me but gripped a hand over my arm that dangled off his. "I mean, I bet you're never late for anything."

We stepped into the crisp chill of the late fall air, and Cillian laughed as he secured an arm around my waist. I knew what was coming and held my breath in wait. But time seemed to slow as dark tendrils crawled off him and cocooned us in shadow. His eyes locked on mine in a silent warning, and I hugged him tightly as we bolted into the sky.

We were on my balcony in a single breath, and my heart struggled to catch up as Cillian set me down.

"Is that how you do it?" I asked. "Flying without being

spotted? The shadows?"

He stuffed his hands in the pockets of his black jeans as the moon shone in the inky sky behind his head. "Yes. I'm not sure where the ability came from. I discovered it a few years after being Made. I can render myself and anything I touch practically invisible."

And like with every scrap of him he reveals to me, Cillian stood with a sense of hesitancy. As if readying himself for my evident running and screaming. But he wasn't the monster he thought himself to be. Not in my eyes, anyway.

I flashed a smile. "That's handy."

He shook his head with a laugh of relief and slipped an arm around me, pulling me close. As his lips brushed my mouth, a deep hum turned over in his chest, and he pressed his forehead against mine. "Go get ready."

I rolled my eyes and slid open the patio door before entering the apartment. A yelp came from the kitchen, and I found Julie standing there, clutching a frying pan to her chest.

"Christ, guys!" she gasped and braced her hands on the counter. "A little warning next time?"

"Sorry," I replied and turned toward my room. "Just popping in to get changed."

As I closed the door, I heard Julie say something to Cillian, and he strode to the kitchen. I scrambled about my room, searching for some semblance of a clean outfit. I seriously needed to do laundry.

I settled on a pair of black leggings and an old olive-green sweater Tess handed down to me and tossed my hair into a ponytail. I threw on a pair of gold hoops, hoping it would help the outfit pass as reservation worthy, and tossed a pink lip gloss in a small brown purse before heading back out to the apartment.

Julie and Cillian stood close to each other, and he turned to face me with a pleased grin. His eyes scanned me up and down, and a heavy sigh erupted from him. "You look gorgeous."

I rolled my eyes. "Flattery will get you nowhere."

Julie chewed on a carrot stick as she carefully studied our behavior, and I walked to Cillian's side.

"What about honesty?" he asked cheekily. I just laughed in response, and he offered his elbow again. "We can walk the rest of the way. It's just down the street."

I looped my arm through his and said goodbye to Julie. When we were strolling down the street below, I looked up at him and asked, "What were you and Julie talking about?"

The corner of his mouth curved. "She said if I ever hurt you, she'd magically fry my balls off."

***

The fancy restaurant was inside one of the most

prestigious hotels in Halifax, The Prince George. Nestled in the heart of downtown, in a massive, gorgeous brick building. Cillian held the front door as I stepped inside and marveled at the breathtaking lobby. Mostly white with a space divided by two front desks where a woman waited with a smile.

"Good evening, Mr. Danes," she said as she handed him a tiny flat envelope. "Here's your key. Stefan is in the kitchen preparing your meal for the night, and dinner should be served around nine."

Cillian nodded once and tucked the key card into the inside pocket of his jacket. "Thanks, Marlene. And the space?"

She folded her hands in front of her. "Ready as per your instructions." She looked at me. "Enjoy your time here."

I thanked her and glanced around, noticing how we were the only people to be seen. Cillian ushered me toward the elevator doors with a hand at my back. As we waited for them to open, I glanced up at him with a curious look.

"We're staying the night?"

His perfect, pale pink lips widened, and he flashed those white teeth at me. "Have somewhere else to be?"

I rolled my eyes and gestured to my lack of an overnight bag. "You could have prepared me for it. Maybe I'd have packed some pajamas or something."

A gentle *ding* chimed in the air, and the elevator door

opened. "And ruin the surprise?" He took my hand and led me inside, his thumb brushing against my palm. "Plus, I have no intention of letting you wear anything tonight, let alone pajamas."

The drop in his tone and the profound raspy promise sent a rush of heat searing through my body, and I had to cross my legs to keep my knees from buckling. Cillian lifted my hand to his mouth as those blue eyes sparkled with devious delight.

The doors opened, and he led me into the well-lit hallway with a beautiful, modern gray carpet. We passed a few rooms until we reached a door at the end of the grand hallway, and I waited at his side as he fetched the room key from his pocket.

All the while, my ears were listening for the sounds of other guests. But the hotel was eerily silent as Cillian opened the heavy door and led me inside. My breath froze in my chest at the sight before me. The room was like something fit for modern royalty. A bedroom, living room, dining room, kitchen, and bathroom. This wasn't a hotel room; it was an apartment.

"This is insane," I said and laid my purse on the black marble island top. "We're staying here?"

Cillian's long arms wrapped around me from behind, and I leaned back into him. His lips brushed my ear.

"For as long as you want."

I twisted in his grasp and stared up at his face, those striking blue eyes never failing to take my breath away. "As much as I'd love to hide away in a hotel room with you for the rest of time, I think one night is all my busy schedule can allow."

He made a show of rolling his eyes before planting a kiss on my mouth. His lips lingered there, seeping the warmth from my own, and I wrapped my arms around his neck, holding him closer. The tip of Cillian's nose brushed against my face, down the side of my nose, and trailed gently across my cheek.

"Hungry?" he whispered, his breath tickling my skin.

Goosebumps peppered over me, pooling at my core, and I couldn't help it as my eyes went to the clean edge of his teeth. "Are you?" I lifted my hand and brushed the pad of my thumb over his lip, just grazing the gleaming white.

Just one word, so many implications.

Yes, I was hungry. I could always down a few tacos, but I also hungered for something else. Cillian. It was constant, my need for him. The fresh desire that bound me to him, I followed it like a starving dog, desperate to discover more. He invaded my every thought, even my dreams, but not… not my nightmares. So different from my visions, these dark landscapes haunted me at night—the nightmares lingered on my skin for days. All my worries bound into one.

Cillian held me tightly, but I slowly pushed away. Hiding

my sudden unease with half a laugh. I tucked my hair behind both ears and smiled. "Aren't you…"

His brows pinched in the middle. "What?"

"Do you think…" I wrung my hands together. "Are we maybe moving too fast?" When his eyes widened, I quickly added, "Not that it's a bad thing. I just, I've never really done this before. And with us, things are just so—"

"Intense?"

Our eyes met; a sigh pressed from me as I nodded.

He stalked toward me, one hand in his jacket pocket. The other with a finger to his lips as he thought. "You're some sort of semi-mortal being. We've got all the time in the world, Avery." His knowing grin made my heart flutter. "Let's take this as fast or as slow as you want. I'm not going anywhere."

He stopped a foot away, and a lock of that silky black hair flopped across his forehead. I gravitated toward that cool, crisp allure that only a predator of the night could emit. But Cillian wasn't a predator at all.

"But you're right," he almost whispered, and I leaned into him with my hand against his hard chest. "Perhaps we are moving fast. But how many truly get to feel this, the impossible burning urge in the bottom of your gut that *screams* for the other person?" I laid my cheek on his shoulder and stared up at his perfect face. His hum was almost a purr as he smiled down at me. "Most could only hope to taste a fraction of it. So, yes, we may get a few lifetimes on this earth, but why waste a single day of feeling like that? Why turn away happiness? It's such a rarity in this world as it is."

A chuckle snorted from me. "I can't believe I was ever afraid of you."

Cillian tensed and let his grip around me fall as that soft pink mouth formed a straight line. "You had every right mind to be afraid of me." But I just rolled my eyes. Cillian loosed a deep breath and checked his watch before offering me his palm.

I looked at it. "What's this? You wanna dance?"

He laughed, and it warmed my heart to see it chase away the flicker of sadness. "No, I want to go eat."

I slipped my hand into his. "I fear this place is a bit too fancy for the likes of me."

"See, I knew you'd say that," he replied in a way that made me second guess all my doubts from a moment ago and hauled the door open with his free hand. "So, I arranged something different for us." The grin that followed those words had me leaning into his arm as we exited the room.

I let him lead me to a large metal door and followed him into a stairwell. We climbed up two flights of stairs before Cillian shoved open yet another metal-clad exit, and we stepped out onto a rooftop terrace that overlooked the city.

The chill of Fall kissed my skin, and I brushed off a little shiver as I stepped toward the ornate wrought iron railing that lined the perimeter. The city stretched out before us like a million little fireflies, and I inhaled deeply as I cast my face to the ebony sky above, drinking in the moonlight that beamed down.

Cillian cleared his throat, and I looked to my right, where he stood around the corner of a partition wall, surrounded by hanging twinkle lights as he leaned against the edge of a bistro table with an array of familiar black and purple flowers in the middle. From his sister's garden.

My eyes burned as they glossed over, and I tore my awed gaze from the quaint display and stared at him. "What's this?"

Cillian circled the table and hauled a chair, gesturing for me to sit. "It's dinner."

I sat down and immediately noticed how warm it was. A quick peek under the table told me an outdoor heater was to thank, but Cillian still slunk out of his leather jacket and draped it over my shoulders before taking his seat across from me.

"Aren't you cold?" I asked him.

"No." He smiled, rolled the sleeves of his black shirt up to his elbows, and leaned them on the table.

Those cerulean eyes stared at me, admiring…examining…I wasn't sure, and my cheeks warmed at the look. This was a date. Like an actu*al* date, something I'd never really had before. Tiny lights illuminated the space, and the muffled sounds of the city serenaded us. I thought he might say something as his lips parted, but he only shifted and took the domed lid off a metal platter. The smell of fresh sushi coated the air.

"Bon appetit."

I laughed, scooped up a set of chopsticks near my plate, and plucked a few pieces onto it. I popped a dragon roll into my mouth and relished the taste. I'd been so busy these last few weeks I couldn't remember the last time I'd had a decent meal that wasn't Julie's leftovers or something I grabbed from the café.

"So, has Oliver found anything?"

I shoved everything to the side of my mouth. "No, not yet." I swallowed. "But I don't want to talk about that right now."

Cillian poured two glasses of white wine and handed one to me before he replied, "What do you want to talk about then?"

"I'd like to learn more about you."

He sipped from his glass as his brows rose. "Oh? I believe I told you quite a bit about what I am."

"Yes, I mean, I know you and your sister are basically ancient–"

"Hey," he cut in cheekily, and I chuckled.

"And I know you guys came from some Viking heritage before you were Made," I continued. "And the whole psychic sharing thing you share is cool, but…." I swirled my glass around as I thought. "I want to hear what it's like."

Cillian stuffed some sashimi in his mouth. "What do you mean?"

I shrugged. "Like, you can obviously eat. But do you need to? Do you like it?"

"I do. Like it, that is. I don't *need* to eat food." He squared his jaw nervously, cautiously. "Blood gives me everything I truly need to survive." I made sure not to let so much as a muscle move at that, assuring him it didn't bother me. "But it grows tiring. I enjoy eating mundane food for its variety of texture."

I nodded, filing away the bits of info as I lobbed off the end of gyoza.

"My turn?" he asked, and I motioned for him to proceed as I chewed. "Did you truly grow up alongside someone who is Fae and not know who or what she really was?"

"I met Julie when I was ten," I replied and washed down my food with another sip of wine. "I was a kid. Even if she'd told me, I'm not sure it would have fully registered, you know? Like, I spent my whole life immersed in imaginary things, painting them, drawing them. I lived in a thatched roof stone cottage surrounded by gardens fit for a fairy tale." I laughed to myself. "I'm not sure I would have even noticed the signs if there were any. Julie was… good at hiding it." I raised my brows. "My turn?"

"By all means." He leaned back in his chair, draping one arm over the back as he watched me.

"Tell me a story," I said.

"A story?"

"Yeah. I mean, you've been on this earth for thousands of years. I bet you've got a few crazy tales."

He shook his head as he seemed to rummage his mind for something. "I spent some time on a pirate ship in the seventeen hundreds."

"What?" I chortled as I dipped a dynamite roll in sriracha. "Like a real pirate ship?"

Cillian laughed. "Yes, on and off the coast of Newfoundland with a ship called The Queen, captained by Charlotte Roberts, the daughter of Red Jack Roberts. We sailed up and down the coast, looking for relics and objects of power." An endearing smile spread over his mouth as his eyes filled with the distant memory. "Lottie wasn't your typical pirate; she never pillaged or stole. We were a crew of treasure hunters."

"How did you deal with the whole sunlight issue?"

"Oh, I worked in the kitchen below decks during the day. She knew what I was," he replied and took another sip of wine. "It was the main reason she recruited me. She sought this one relic, an orb that could summon the soul of anyone who'd passed. But it was apparently buried at the bottom of the ocean."

His eyes sparkled teasingly, urging me to put the pieces together. I gnawed at the end of a tempura shrimp tail as our eyes locked, and I pondered for a moment. Then it hit me, and I let out a little chuckle.

"And you don't need air to breathe."

Cillian's answering grin tickled my heart. "I'm also an exceptional swimmer."

"So, what did you get out of it?" I asked. "Aside from the obvious epic adventure."

Startled sadness flickered across his expression, but Cillian whisked it away with a cheeky grin. "Adventure was my only reward."

The sarcasm made my eyes roll. Clearly, it was a subject he wasn't ready to breach. So, I let it be. For a long moment, all I could hear was the distant croon of the city below and our chewing.

"So," I cleared my throat, and Cillian almost looked relieved that I said something. "What do you do during the day? I mean, here, now. In the city."

He arched a wicked brow. "Wouldn't you like to know?"

"Isn't that the point here?"

He gave me a look that said, *touché*. "I work out, read, watch TV, study various languages, and work the stock market."

"The stock market?" I leaned back and folded my arms, giving my food time to settle. "With a few lifetimes of practice, I bet you're pretty good at that."

Cillian gave me a wink. "Especially when you're friends with a psychic. A kooky old lady over on Gottingen. She's never been wrong, though."

"Don't you spend time with other vampires?"

Those dark brows lowered, and a slight growl turned over in his chest. "They don't–Cellie and I aren't considered *their* kind."

"Because of your souls?" I asked but immediately regretted it as Cillian's eyes snapped to me. I made a point to focus on the fine gold detailing around the edge of my plate. My heart pumped nervously in my chest.

But he took a deep, calming breath. "We don't know if that's…." He shifted in his seat. "I don't have a soul, Avery. Souls are for the living." The weight of regret and sadness that dragged on every word broke my heart, and I met his gaze across the table. "We don't want to be associated with them anyway. We've long accepted it."

Yeah, but it must still hurt, I thought, but I didn't dare say. To be rejected by your own kind, like Julie and Moya were.

Another calm silence hung between us before Cillian spoke again. "Is it my turn now?"

I smiled and nodded.

He leaned forward and rested his chin on his hands as those blue eyes raked over me. "Tell me about your childhood."

A sort of protectiveness I never knew was there sparked to life in my chest. A possessiveness over a life that now felt foreign to me. My chest expanded as I sat back and inhaled deeply with thought.

"Well, you know about my parents. Tess became my mother, my aunt, and my best friend. She was…" I shook my head. "She was my everything. And now, I think about that part of my life, and it feels like a hundred years ago, like someone else had lived it, and I'm just left with the memory of it." My cheeks warmed, and I cleared my throat nervously. "Um, maybe let's start with some easy questions."

Cillian's answering chuckle settled my nerves, and I held up my empty glass as he replenished it. "Favorite food?"

I motioned to the table. "I think that's obvious. But I hate meatloaf. And salmon," I added with a grimace.

"Noted," he replied. "Dating life?"

"What is this, twenty questions?" My shoulders bunched to my ears. But his expression was staid, waiting for an answer. I tried to stifle the groan that crawled up my throat. "Well, I wasn't exactly a virgin when we met if that's what you're asking."

"It's not."

"Even so, my dating history is…pretty grim."

Cillian's forehead crinkled as his brows rose. "You're kidding me? I find it hard to believe. I can't imagine there was much competition in a small-town high school, but even if there were, they'd be no match for–"

"I didn't go to high school," I cut in before he could inflate my ego. "Tess home-schooled me."

He nodded as if that explained so many of his questions. "Do you miss it? Your old life?"

I considered it for a moment. "No. I was a different person then. Maybe part of me changed the moment I found out magic was real. Or maybe…maybe this is what becoming an adult is all about. Everything gets hard and scary. Complicated."

"I hope I'm none of those things. And if I am–"

"You'll be the first to know," I assured him. Amongst all the craziness that was my life, Cillian was the one thing I was so sure of. I wanted to be with him, regardless of the risks or dangers. But as our gazes locked from across the bistro table, and he reached for my hand–our fingers entwining–only one thought filled my mind.

The only risk or danger to us was…*me*.

Chapter Three

Despite the nightmares that plagued me every night–flashes of darkness, my flesh being sliced open, blackness oozing from the wounds–my days went by in a pleasant blur. School, work, training.

But one thing constantly clung to me. The worry that something was wrong with Max. She hadn't been to class in two days, returned any of my texts, or answered her phone.

The visions–nightmares–of her hung over my shoulders for hours upon waking, but Cillian chased away the shadows with good morning texts and phone calls throughout the day.

The mere sound of his voice soothed my nerves and grounded me. During daylight hours, I immersed myself in school. But as the sun dipped beyond the horizon, my nights belonged to him. When I wasn't at the gallery, that is.

Classes had ended over an hour ago, but I stayed behind to work on my big project until the pangs of hunger beckoned me home. I wove through the near-empty halls of the campus and stepped out onto the bustling city streets, only to be met with a woman who walked directly into my view. Her large brown eyes—heightened by her ebony complexion—locked on mine, and a familiar aura held me in place.

"Avery Quinn?" she asked, and I fixated on her blood-rep lips, past the perfectly manicured black curls that hung to her shoulders. *Had I met her before?*

"Yes," I replied hesitantly and zipped up my jacket.

She reeked of expensive perfume. The woman held out a red-leather gloved hand. "Vivian Carmichael."

Oh. My stomach soured. I could taste fleeting memories of nightmares on my tongue. She was Max's mother. I shook her hand politely. "Can I help you with something?

"I was wondering if you knew where Maxine is. She hasn't been seen for days."

"Max?" I questioned with confusion, trying not to note how her cheek twitched at my use of Max's preferred name. I shrugged, hoping to mask the fact that my skin had broken out with a zest of sweat. "All I know is that she hasn't been to class for a few days. Could she be with friends?"

Vivian stifled a chortle and tightened the sash on her ankle-length red trench. "Maxine doesn't have friends."

"I'm her friend," I replied quickly, surprised by my sudden urge to defend Max.

Vivian's face twisted as if she'd caught a whiff of a bad smell. "Funny you should say that since her Jeep was found on the street outside your apartment."

My mouth gaped, but I had no reply. I hadn't even noticed. Our street was always filled with overnight parkers and vehicles from people who worked within walking distance. Also…how did this woman know where I lived?

A black town car pulled up to the sidewalk where we stood, and Vivian plucked a red business card from her pocket. She handed it to me before strutting over to the car, her brown boots clicking on the pavement.

"If you see or hear from her, be a dear and call me."

She didn't give me a second glance as she slipped into the backseat and sped away. I was frozen in place as my mind filled with the horrors of the vision I'd had about Max. The…*feeling*. I had ignored it until now, chalking it up to anxiety.

It wasn't until the car disappeared around a corner that I took off for home. My chest burned with quickened breaths as I barged into my apartment. Julie stood in the kitchen, brows raised as she finished pouring herself a drink.

"Hard day?"

Lattie flew over and fluttered next to her, sniffing and trying to poke her long fingers inside her drink. Julie swatted her away.

I let my bag slide from my shoulder and fall to the floor. "I need your help."

Julie's body tightened with concern as she exchanged a glance with Lattie. "Are you okay?"

"Help me break into Max's apartment."

"Um," she carefully set her glass down, "*what?*"

"Max's mother just side-lined me outside of school. Looking for her. And normally, I wouldn't care, but I induced some kind of vision about her the other day, and… something is wrong."

"Wrong?" Lattie crossed her long, spindly arms. "What do you mean? What kind of vision?"

I inhaled slowly, but it did nothing to settle my nerves. "I–I don't know. She wasn't in class, which I found strange. It's not like her to miss a class. So, I went to the bathroom and tried to…I dunno…like, tap into something. I just pictured her, and then suddenly, I *felt* her, could *smell* her. And she was scared."

"Why didn't you say anything?" Julie asked.

I shrugged. "It was so quick and scrambled. I just thought…maybe I'd done it wrong, or maybe I'd just imagined it. Created it in my mind." Julie just stared at me, a calculating look in her eyes. "Jules, I *know* something is wrong. And her mother just confirmed it."

A jittered breath ran through her as her chest expanded. "Okay, so Max is possibly missing." She paced the floor as Lattie zipped around in the air between us. "Her mother somehow knows who you are, and you want to break into her apartment."

"Yes."

But then another thought spilled into my mind. How *did* Vivian know who I was and that I knew her daughter? The sound of that dark lord's voice suddenly rang in my ears. *I want to know how to undo her, inside and out.*

Did Evaine do something to Max? We weren't exactly friends, but if someone were spying on me, they'd have seen me with her enough; at school, the gallery, or when she gave me a ride home.

Was this my fault? Guilt toiled in my gut.

"Do you know where she lives?" Julie asked as she grabbed her coat. I could have kissed her for jumping in head first, and my heart raced. But I had no idea where Max actually lived. My cheeks warmed, and Julie rolled her eyes. "I can do a tracking spell, but I'll need something of hers."

I rummaged through my thoughts. "All I have are notes from that project we did."

"It'll have to do, I guess."

I ran to my room as Lattie followed me, watching as I grabbed a pile of books and papers from my desk and tossed them on the bed.

"Are you certain of this, Avery?" Lattie's eerie musical voice chimed as I rifled through the papers. "Meddling in the affairs of mortals can lead to more trouble."

I found Max's notes and clutched them in my hand as I looked at my tiny blue friend. Her giant black eyes blinked with concern. "I feel… No, I *know* this is my fault. I think Evaine might have done something, so I have to be sure. I have to know if she's okay."

Lattie just stared at me, and her tiny breaths turned to a moan as her gangly limbs hung from her body. Her wings fluttered wildly to keep her in the air. "Fine," she said. "Let's go meddle with the angry human's life. I'm sure she won't mind."

***

The three of us trailed the streets through town, wisping from alley to alley as Julie followed her tracking spells to Max's place, a basement apartment of some old fancy brownstone fronted by a black metal door with rivets on all the sides.

Julie's knee-length white trench coat glowed in the moonlight as we descended the brick staircase that led to

Max's front door. I noted the tiny narrow garden to the left, filled with flowers and herbs of all kinds. It reminded me slightly of Celadine's.

I gave three hard knocks on the dark metal, and we waited, but there was no reply, and no one came to the door. Julie pulled some pins from her pocket and squatted as she picked the lock. Lattie and I watched for a few seconds, my chest tight with nerves. But I smiled as Julie pushed to her feet and turned the old iron knob.

She halted in the open doorway and looked at me, eyes wide. "You feel that?"

"What?"

She yanked on my sleeve, and I stumbled toward her. We stood in the doorway, and I did indeed feel it. Magic. Humming in the air and touching my tongue with a metallic, staticky taste.

"It's…different," I said as I tasted the air. My brows pinched together. "Not like Fae magic."

"No," she replied quietly, her skin ghostly white as she peered around. "It's not."

Julie had a knowing look on her face, and for a moment, I thought she might leave. But she stepped further into Max's apartment, and I followed without a word. Lattie clung to my shoulder, sniffing loudly at the smatter of scents all over the studio apartment.

Lavender, jasmine, wormwood, and other plants I

couldn't name hung from a row of hooks above the slate-topped island in the galley kitchen. A basket of cinnamon sticks sat on a round walnut table. Various candles sat half-melted in trays and in candle holders.

Walls of dark stone surrounded us. The only natural light came from the left, through a single small window above an emerald, green velvet couch. Flanked by rows and shelves of varying labeled jars, boxes, and tins. Everything from bone dust to newt eyes and even…Fae blood.

"Holy shit," Julie gasped as she leaned over Max's bed. It was a queen draped in never-ending layers of black sheets and duvets, topped with a heap of pillows. A spread of weathered parchments and open scrapbooks laid across it all. And Julie's jaw hung open as she read them over. "Max is a witch."

"What?" My stomach clenched.

She spun on her heel. "We need to leave."

"Why?" I asked. "We haven't even looked for clues to where she is."

Julie glanced around one more time in disbelief. "If Max is a witch, she's involved in some deep shit."

I shook my head and shrugged. "But it's all just magic, isn't it?"

"No," she said as she chewed at the corner of her mouth. "It's different. Being born with magic is wildly different than forcing it into a mortal body. Over centuries, witches experimented with Fae blood to alter themselves to withstand the power. But when the Therians came to Ironworld, they spent centuries hunting them down, eradicated the lot of them, and stole their secrets. Witches have been extinct for decades. The Therians made sure of it and still do. They'll come for her if they haven't already and come for us if we're involved. We need to get out of here."

"What do I tell Max's mother?" My heart raced in my chest.

Julie turned at the door and sighed. "My guess? Either Max has been taken by Therians, or she's out with her coven, and she'll show up when she wants to. There's nothing we can do. If her mother approaches you again, just tell her the same thing. You haven't seen Max."

***

Thoughts of Max plagued me. I couldn't shake her, couldn't let go of the idea that it might be something else. Not the Therians, not some witchy getaway in the woods. I'd sensed Max in that dark vision, and she was scared.

"Av'?" Julie's voice crackled through my distant resolve. I blinked a few times as my eyes focused on her raised brows. "*Hellooo?*"

I shook my head. "What?"

She tipped her chin at Moya standing across from us on

Oliver's vast front lawn. "What do you want to practice?"

Moonlight mixed with the glow of the firepit and shrouded us all in a strange light against the dark background of trees. Even Moya's sisters who lazed about on a swinging bench. Their legs draped over the crooked wooden arms.

"Uh, wisp," I replied and crossed my arms tightly. Julie had mastered it within Ironworld's limits and was already working at crossing the border. "I want to practice more wisping." No one mentioned anything about my magic. They must have known, could sense that I was leery. Hesitant to use my powers for fear of…I didn't even know. Myself? I glanced at the twins and forced a chuckle. "Or maybe some combat training. I'm sure you guys could teach me to fight, right?"

Aya and Brie exchanged a cheeky grin before one of them peered back at me. "We could. But we told you, we're not really fighters."

The other added, "We're more spies and protectors of our sister. The true Queen of the Sea."

Moya hissed at them as she slipped on a pair of teal silk gloves, the sea raging in her eyes. "Shut up."

For a moment, I saw a flicker of madness flash across her face like a storm on the water. But she blinked it away.

"Not real fighters?" Moya steered the conversation as she settled the storm in her deep gaze. "I've watched you both behead a coven of selkies in total darkness with nothing more than a sharpened stick."

The twins shrugged modestly but shared a sly grin. "We have our skills."

The front door of Oliver's cozy cabin creaked open, and he stomped out onto the rickety porch. It moaned beneath his troll-sized weight, the stairs bowing as he descended toward us. Oliver's sheer size and girthy shoulders always amazed me. Especially when watching him handle dainty tools and elements between fingers the size of corndogs. He could pinch the exact amount of some powdery ingredient and get every spec into a tiny vial before stuffing a cork in the top.

A gentle giant.

I smiled at him, and he nodded as he walked over to the open fire. We watched him hang an iron pot on a spit and stir the contents with a large wooden spoon.

"How goes the mapping?" I asked as I stepped to his side.

He grumbled and straightened. "Something's wrong. I can't finish it."

Everyone else took a step closer to the fire. I shook my head. "What do you mean?"

"Your blood," he replied. "There's a strange marker in it I've only ever seen in Summer. I'm headed there in the morning to meet with Lord Kheelan. To get his help."

At my wide-eyed expression, he added, "I assure you the Summer Lord can be trusted. Besides, I've told him nothing of you, so nothing will be traced back to you. I swear." He cupped a massive palm over my upper arm. "Not to worry, child, I'll map your blood yet. We'll figure this out."

My friends all offered promising smiles. I couldn't show the worry that stirred in my gut. I feared letting someone else in on my secret, even if it was a Lord. I didn't know Kheelan. But I had to trust that Oliver knew what he was doing. Had to trust that Moya or Julie would have stepped in and said something.

So, I managed a weak smile. Because—between threats of Evaine, Max's disappearance, and my petulant powers—I couldn't afford to let any more worry fill my mind.

✳✳✳

Cillian's shadows enveloped us as he cradled me in his arms and flew through the cool night air. We caught a late-night movie, and I was grateful for the distraction for a couple of hours. I let my head rest in the crook of his neck and inhaled his lovely scent—leather and mint and a crisp breeze.

Cillian was my anchor, my iron rock in my life's mess. Hunted by Evaine, a missing friend—who was apparently a witch—learning to trust my budding powers, school, work… It was all too much, and the weight of it all was almost too hard to bear at times.

But being with Cillian cleared my head. I could breathe, close my eyes, and not be bombarded with flashes of all my fears and anxieties. I sometimes wondered if it was part of his vampire charm, that predatory lure and spell to lull their prey.

We began to slow and descend. My feet gently hit the earth as his grip loosened on me, and I stepped out of his embrace. A chill brushed over me, and I zipped up my favorite emerald leather jacket.

Cillian took my hand and smiled as we walked the boardwalk by the harbor. "Cold?"

I shook my head. "No, I'm fine. Just wish I brought a pair of mittens or something."

Late Fall was in full swing. We'd already had a few sprinkles of snow, but they'd melted before the day was done. I could feel it in the air, though. The crisp threat of winter in the Maritimes. Cold and wet and unforgiving. It was coming.

"I thought you could summon the sun?" he asked.

My other hand balled inside my pocket. "No, I don't like using my magic lately." His mouth gaped with a question, but I quickly added, "Plus, summoning the sun when I'm with a vampire? Probably not a great idea."

We strolled a few feet in silence. "I thought…you

seemed so in control of it. You know, before."

When we made love, and I held a blade of sunlight to his throat? Yeah, that seemed like a lifetime ago. Since then, my magic had grown almost past the point of control. It lived in me. Doing as it pleased. Wanting to be set free.

And it terrified me.

I dropped my gaze to the weathered, frost-covered boards beneath our feet. "How does it not bother you?" He shrugged, all cool and collected, and I hated him for it. "It bothers the shit out of *me*. I don't...."

"Don't what?" He stopped and spun to face me.

Uncertainty possessed me, and I took a deep breath. "I don't want it anymore. My powers. It's too much. Every time I use it, it's stronger."

Cillian's chest rose as he raked his fingers through that jet-black hair and sighed. "You don't scare me. You don't bother me. And if that day ever comes, I promise to be honest with you." He stuffed both hands in his pockets and cocked his head to the side. "I'm not worried about your magic or the burn of the Summer sun. You're learning and practicing every day and getting better, right?"

It wasn't enough.

My clammy hands balled at my sides, but I nodded with a smile. I had to believe him. Because the alternative was succumbing to the crippling weight of it all. It felt like I wasn't learning or honing anything with Moya. She was doing her best, but the bottom line was that I couldn't do it. I couldn't wield power as old as she once suggested. There was a disconnect between me and…*it*.

But all that aside, there were still vivid dreams and visions. The stormy gray eyes of that Fae Lord seared into my brain and haunted me every day. I needed to tell someone, had to get it out and off my chest.

I'd shared the vision of Max with my friends and the occasional nightmare of Evaine. But I'd told no one of the dream about the Dark Fae Lord and his conversation with Evaine about a girl I had no doubt was me.

I opened my mouth to speak, but something rustled in the dark bushes.

My throat tightened with a breath. Cillian was at my side immediately, his hands gripping my upper arms, holding me close to him. But I leaned forward, squinting and peering into the void as the strange, dark figure slowly inched toward the treeline. Two eyes glowed in the shadows.

My heart thrummed in my chest, sending a scalding sensation searing through my veins.

Cillian tensed, his knees slightly bending, ready to take off into the skies. "We should go."

But something held me in place, begging me not to leave. This wasn't Evaine. Her shadows didn't behave this way, like a beast fumbling in the dark, cracking branches and moving earth. She *was* the dark, and she *never* fumbled.

Finally, the creature emerged, clawing at the partially frozen earth as it shakily pushed to stay on its four feet, and my eyes widened in disbelief.

Cillian's fingers dug into my arms. "Avery, we need to leave *now*."

My eyes locked on the giant, black wolf before us. A slight whimper escaped the beast as its long, muscular legs nearly buckled where it stood.

"Wait." I put my hand to his chest, "I think it's hurt."

I'd never seen a wolf of this size, not even in movies. The silver moonlight shone over its slick, black fur, glistening where it was soaked in red. *Blood.* I stared into its pure black eyes, eyes that rang with an air of familiarity. I took a cautious step toward it.

"Avery…" Cillian whispered through clenched teeth.

But he didn't stop me.

The wolf locked on my unblinking gaze and took a few hobbled steps toward me. Every movement seemed like a pained struggle for the animal. Another series of whimpers spilled into the air, and I reached for the creature just as its legs buckled completely. The beast collapsed into a half-frozen puddle as mud and blood splashed over my boots.

I turned and glanced at Cillian over my shoulder, but he wasn't looking at me. He stared at the wolf, seemingly unsure what to do, but with a knowing look.

I shrugged helplessly. "What do we do—"

The wolf began to convulse, and Cillian immediately hauled me back. I gawked at the creature, tears stinging my unblinking eyes as I watched in horror. Black fur moved like wet silk, morphing over the giant frame, disappearing in places to leave behind smooth, ebony skin. The sounds of crunching bones and flesh filled my ears, and I covered them, my stomach threatening to heave with every moist rip and tear.

The beast continued to shiver and spasm on the ground until it was done. Until all signs of a wolf disappeared and all that remained was the slender shape of a human woman, curled into a trembling fetal position. A human woman with skin like the night and a head of long dark curls. The impossibility of it held me in place as shock possessed me.

I slowly wriggled from Cillian's embrace and dropped to my knees in the puddle of dirt, blood, and frost. With trembling fingers, I smoothed the damp curls away from her face, confirming my suspicions as she looked at me with pained-filled, blood-shot, half-conscious eyes.

"Oh my god, *Max*?" But she was gone. The pain and trauma took her deep into the void. I whipped my head around and found Cillian standing a few feet away. "Give me your coat."

He didn't move.

"*Cillian?*"

He shrugged off his leather jacket and tossed it to me with a sigh. I covered Max's exposed and beaten body and checked for a pulse. I sighed in relief when the faint thrum of life beat against my fingertips.

"Can you help me get her back to my place?" When he hesitated, I shot to my feet. "What's wrong?"

"She's a Therian," he said as if that was supposed to mean something to me.

"So?" I shook my head. "Is this some kind of vampire-werewolf rivalry thing?" I was half kidding, but his serious expression made me guffaw. I pointed down at my friend's body on the ground, rage toiling in my gut. "Help me get her back to my place, *please*." The last word ground against my teeth.

Cillian didn't say a word as he bent down and scooped Max into his arms with ease.

"Fly her there now," I said. "I'll run back and meet you there in a few."

Curse my failure to wisp.

Again, not a word of a reply as he bolted into the night air and disappeared. My chest burned when I reached the stairs in the alley, and it took everything in me to climb them. Finally, I burst through my front door. Cillian was standing in the living room, arms crossed, and motioned with his chin toward my room.

"She's sleeping."

I worked to calm my heaving breaths. "Were you *really* not going to help her?"

"I'd do whatever you asked of me." His arms slacked at his sides.

"No," I shook my head, "That's not what I asked." He didn't say anything, only looked at me apologetically. My eyes widened. "Are you shitting me?"

"Therians are nothing but monsters," he said. "They take, and they take until there's nothing left, and they don't care who gets hurt along the way." I just stood frozen in anger and disbelief. "Avery–"

"Just leave, please," I snapped. I couldn't blame him for feeling that way towards them, not after all their kind had done to vampires and witches. But I couldn't bring myself to accept it. So, I stomped down the rage. "I can't–I have to check on Max."

"Avery, please, let me explain."

Cillian reached for me, but I swatted his arm away as a ball of emotions exploded in my chest. For a split second, the sear of the Summer sun glared at the contact, and he winced away.

"Oh, my God!" I darted toward him but immediately pulled myself back, sticking both hands under my arms. "A-are you okay?"

Cillian adjusted the sleeve of his jacket to cover the burn I knew was there. "I'm fine, I swear. It was an accident."

Tears burned my eyes. "Yeah, it's an accident until it's not." *Until I outright kill you.*

Pain and confusion pinched his face. "What's that supposed—"

"Just…you have to go, Cillian," I said defeatedly. "I have to make sure Max is okay, and I'm *exhausted*. I can't deal with this, too. I can't walk on eggshells, worried I'll burn your arm off while my friend, who is quite obviously a…*werewolf*," the word came out like a question, "lies unconscious, naked, and beaten in my bed."

He nodded solemnly. "No, I get it. I get it." His nostrils flared as he inhaled deeply and slowly eased toward me to place a kiss on my forehead. "I'll go. But call me if you need anything." Those blue eyes glanced at my bedroom door over my shoulder. "And be careful?"

I chewed at my lip as wetness brimmed my eyes. My arms remained crossed as I nodded.

It wasn't until Cillian was gone that I crumbled to the floor and completely fell apart.

Chapter Four

After a long cry, I pulled myself together as best I could and cracked open my bedroom door to peek inside. Max was on her back, covered in a small, knitted throw I kept at the foot of my bed. She looked like a corpse, lying there, still as death.

I held a breath as I eased inside the dim room. The only light was my small bedside lamp, casting a warm, yellowy glow over the darkness. I stared unblinkingly at Max's chest, waiting for it to rise and fall. I caught the faintest movement and finally released the air stifling my lungs.

I didn't know what to do. So, I just stood near the closed door and waited. For what? I had no idea. To wake up from this nightmare? For someone to come and tell me everything will be alright?

The slight sound of moist, open flesh caught my attention, and I inched closer. A gash across Max's chest was closing on its own, and I leaned forward in awe. The wound disappeared beneath the blanket, and my hand gravitated toward it.

"What the fuck are you doing, Quinn?" Max rasped, eyes still closed. Unmoving.

I fisted my hand and straightened, my heart racing from the fright. "Jesus, you're terrifying in every sense of the word, you know."

The corner of her mouth twitched as her dark eyes opened. Only a look of disdain stared at me. "Am I naked?"

"Yes."

She closed her eyes and sighed. "Do you have any clothes?"

Without a word, I turned to my closet and fished out the first thing I touched—a red romper. It reminded me of her mother's lipstick. "Your, uh, mom stopped me outside school."

Her eyes widened as she slipped the spaghetti straps over her toned shoulders. She looked way better than I ever did in that thing. "What did you tell her?"

I shrugged. "Nothing. I mean, I had no idea where you were at the time."

"Good." She stood hovering in the middle of the room, seemingly unsure whether to stay or go.

"Max…what *are* you?"

"You know what I am." She crossed her long arms.

"A Therian?" My brow arched in question. I'd never seen one before. Had no idea what to expect. "A shape-shifter?"

She tilted her head at the term. But her eyes were suddenly vacant. "Wolves."

"Wolves." The word came out in a breath, and I pressed my rear end against the dresser. When an awkward silence hung too long, I said, "I'm–"

"Fae," she said curtly and then nodded. "Well, partly, anyway."

"How did you know?"

Max feigned a shrug. No sign of her recent wounds. "I could tell. Not what, exactly. Not at first. But I knew there was something off with you."

Off. Not different or special. Just off. It felt…appropriate.

I hugged myself tightly to ward off the chill that always came after an adrenaline rush. The evening had taken a drastic turn. "I'm also an Oracle of some kind." Max's eyes widened with a mix of panic and concern. "But not a very good one. I haven't quite figured out how it all works. But I knew there was something wrong with you. I went to your apartment to check on you–"

"If my mother doesn't already know that fun little fact, I'd keep it under wraps. Vivian Carmichael has a penchant for magical things."

"Is she that bad?"

Max finished wrestling her thick curls into an elastic she plucked from my bedside table and looked me square in the eye. "My mother is the Alpha of the North American pack. Thousands of Therians are under her deployment, and many…others."

I pushed off the dresser when she stepped toward the door. "Do you know anything about Therians and vampires working together to harvest Fae blood?"

She hesitated, her lips forming a line. "Just stay out of my mother's affairs as much as possible. And…stay away from me. It's for the best."

"I thought we were friends?" She stared blankly at a spot on the floor, so I pressed. "Max, you have Fae blood in your apartment."

She cringed and reached for the doorknob. "I bought that at the market." She swung open my bedroom door.

"Wait," I said, and Max glanced over her shoulder with those dark eyes. "Will you tell me what happened to you tonight?"

She sighed impatiently. "Some kind of fairy I'd never encountered before. She reeked like death…." Her gaze glistened. "And made me beg for it."

My mouth gaped with a hollow echo claiming my throat. "W-why?"

Max's expression hardened. "Because of you. She pried me for information about *you*."

She slipped away. It wasn't until I heard the apartment door slam shut that I dared move. I slammed to the floor just as my stomach heaved its contents into the toilet. I lurched until my body slumped against the side of the cool bathtub.

Evaine was starting to come after people who knew me. Only luck had it that Max was otherworldly and could defend herself. But what if Evaine came for Tomas? Or Tess?

A chill possessed me, and I lay shaking on the bathroom floor as I thought only one thing. I had to master my abilities before she came for someone else.

***

When Cillian didn't answer his phone, I jogged to Celadine's house, the frosty sidewalk threatening to take me down. I slowed as I neared the short, iron gates and spotted her immediately.

She sat on the vast covered porch, staring at the moon as she sipped from a large wine glass. Her braids and dreads were in a tight beehive. White silk pooled around her feet from the oversized kimono she wore—every inch of tattoos covered—and the moonlight made it glow like stardust.

She sensed me approaching several feet away, I could tell from the way her peaceful expression became alert, and she craned her neck to where I stood on the lawn, breath burning in and out of my chest.

"He's not here," she said in a kind tone.

"Did you know?" I asked, my throat raw from the brisk jog. "What Max was." When her dark eyebrows pinched together, I added. "You interviewed her. Did you know… could you tell she was a wolf?"

Celadine patted the spot next to her, and I dropped my ass on the step.

"Yes," she finally said. "I could tell *something* was off, diff–otherworldly." She grinned at my chosen word for all of them. I guess I was included in that group now. "But I couldn't quite tell. At best, I figured she might have been half human, half wolf."

My leg brushed against hers as I sighed. "I don't think she's half anything. She said her mother was the North American alpha or something."

Celadine went ramrod straight at that. I gawked at that vast, violet stare. "Vivian Carmichael is the Therian alpha?"

I nodded, chewing at my lip. "How could you not know? She's a benefactor at the gallery."

"I'd never actually met her face to face. Only over the phone and through her people." Celadine guffawed. "Who are clearly human. She hid it carefully. Which leaves me to believe she might have known what I was."

"The Botwood guy," I said. "He seemed awfully desperate

to get you guys to join their council."

She shook her head. "No, Botwood has his own reasons for us joining. He thinks we have…souls. He wants to create a race of vampires with souls, himself included. He thought I could change them all with magic."

"But you can't?"

"No, not without my mother's grimoire, which was lost to our people hundreds of years ago."

I thought about it all. What Celadine said as well as Max's words. She'd warned me to stay away from her mother when I told her about my Oracle abilities. And the Therians were believed to have eradicated all witches. Maybe they stole their magic for themselves.

"No, I don't think it has anything to do with your vampirism. I think she wanted a line to you for your magic, the gifts from your mother."

I couldn't look away from the smile that spread across her face. "No one's ever called them gifts before."

"That's what it is, though. A gift."

"I would think the same of yours."

I shrugged, suddenly fascinated with the grass beneath the toe of my boot. "I think mine's more like a curse."

"The power of the sun?" She raised her brows as she leaned into my view. "I should think not."

"I'm worried I'll hurt Cillian." The words came out in a dry whisper. When she didn't reply, I looked up, and awkward energy passed between us. I groaned. "He already told you."

She pressed her lips together for a moment. "His pain shot through the bond. I asked him about it." I flung my head to my lap, raking my fingers through my hair with a groan. Celadine put a hand on my back. "I assure you, the only part of Cillian that's hurt is his pride. You have nothing to worry about. He's a man. Just give him time to lick his wounds. You see, my brother left that world a long time ago. It's hard for him to face it again."

"What do you mean? Why?"

"After we were turned…." She wiggled her hand in the air with a shrug. "Give or take a few thousand years ago, our own people shunned us, and we were forced from our village. For centuries, we roamed the Earth, searching for our place. Humans were terrified of us, and vampires rejected us—whether from jealousy or something else, I'll never know. And the Therians…" She heaved a sigh. "Well, they would reject anyone who's not a wolf. We watched them fall from grace and get shoved into Ironworld. Watched how they fought for space alongside the vampires and the witches of this world. How they eradicated the entire witch community, what little there was of it…even my mother's. All the while, Cillian and I were never welcome."

I weighed the scope of that. *Thousands of years.* Cillian had told me just how old he and his sister were several times before. But it hadn't truly sunk in until now. The grandness of it.

They were like gods.

"Are you happy now, after all this time?"

Something like sadness flickered in her deep, purple eyes behind the thick coal surrounding them. "Happy?" she questioned, and part of me wondered if she even knew the answer. "Perhaps that's too strong a word. I can't speak for Cillian, but after thousands of years roaming this planet, he's still…restless. Myself, I've found comfort in the small stuff. But I'm tired, Avery." Celadine sighed. "I'll never have anything I truly want out of life, and I've yet to find the answer."

"What answer?"

She waited a long moment to reply. "If the scraps of contentment I've been granted are enough."

"*Enough?*" A chill crept down my spine. "Celadine… what are you–"

My phone beeped, and I plucked it from my pocket. It was Julie.

Late-night training? =)

I put it away with a sigh. "I have to go." I gave her a hug. "Will you be okay?"

She nodded and smiled. "Yes, of course. I've been okay for years." When a laugh chuffed from her, I chuckled, too. "I'll let him know you came."

"Thanks."

***

We trained for a couple hours. Julie was wisping–which she now did like a pro–and I learned the best ways to choose, hold, and wield knives of all sorts with the twins. Aya had her long, dark hair pulled into a tight bun as she had me practice with a set of small hand knives. For once, she wore something different than her sister.

Brie was brown leather from head to toe and a charcoal blouse beneath her gear. But Aya donned a navy pair of slacks, held up with matching suspenders over an even darker blue long-sleeved shirt. She somehow made suspenders look badass. Especially when I realized just how stocked she was, even in a casual outfit.

Aya's wrists were bound in cuffs of antique gold. And, while stylish, I soon learned the bracelets held metal spikes that shot out at the click of a button. A gold locket dangled from her chest, filled with poison. In her pocket was a small metal cylinder, no bigger than a lighter, but it transformed into a staff instantly.

She let me play with all her killer gear before Brie took over and showed me a few things with a long dagger. Primarily defensive stuff involving hiding behind trees and using the landscape to my advantage.

The three of us now lay on the grass under the stars outside Oliver's cabin–with Lattie fluttering about–just as Julie and Moya made their last trip back from wherever they'd wisped.

Julie collapsed with a smile at my side and took a few deep breaths as she stared up at the stars. "I can wisp anywhere within Ironworld. And the same goes for here, in the In Between. But I can't get from here to the apartment."

"Have you tried in Faerie?"

A grin tugged at the corner of her mouth, and she turned to look at me. Those crystal blues sparkling in the moonlight. "Yeah, our magic is heightened the closer we are to Faerie, and everything comes easy. It's almost intoxicating."

"Ahem," Brie purposely cleared her throat on my other side, and I laughed.

We'd been in a game of twenty questions, the twins nailing me with curiosity after curiosity about the mundane world.

"Right," I said. "Where were we?"

Moya passed on the idea of lying on the ground and sprawled across the wooden bench swing with a cat-like smile. A glass of wine appeared from somewhere, and she balanced it with two fingers. Lattie perched close by as she wiped at her tiny mouth and licked the remains of her last kill from her fingers.

Aya said, "What's a self-watering plant? Is it magic?"

"No, I mean, it's science."

"Alchemy?"

I sat up and wrestled my hair into a messy bun. "Yeah, I guess you could say that. Partly, anyway."

"What's a shoe horn?" Brie asked.

"It's a curved stick to help get your shoes on."

Aya propped herself up on an elbow. "What's a yoga mat?"

"It's for doing yoga," I told them as Julie and Moya stifled a shared laugh. The twins were quiet for a moment.

"What's yoga?" Aya followed up, and the rest of us roared in laughter.

A bright light formed in the distance, and a portal opened. Oliver stepped through, and we all sat upright as he neared, the portal closing behind him.

"What was that?" I asked.

Oliver's clunky brown boots stopped just a few feet away, a weary look on his face. "A private portal," he replied. "I didn't want to wisp and risk being tracked by anyone who might be watching our circle."

My heart warmed at the words. *Our circle.* A group of friends, a family I never knew I needed. Even though I didn't live at Oliver's cabin, it felt like home.

Julie pushed to her feet and wiped off her white jeans—

not a grass stain in sight. "So, did you do it? Did you figure out the map in Avery's blood?"

His warm brown eyes locked on mine. "I did. The Summer Lord recognized the marker immediately."

I exchanged a wide-eyed look with my friends and gave Oliver a tense shrug. "So? Who did it?"

He inhaled deeply. "Me." My heart sprang faster as I watched him walk inside the cabin with solemn, hunched shoulders.

The five of us rushed after him as Oliver headed over to a rickety, worn red china cabinet. He plucked a wooden box from the top and wiped the caked dust from the surface before placing it on the table. He flung the hinged lid open, filling the room with a warm glow, and my jaw hung.

A ball of pure fiery sunshine sat in a bed of emerald silk. Its light flooded the cabin and poured outside.

"Oliver, what is this?" Moya asked, her eyes fixated on the orb.

He sat down with a harumph. "I once stripped away every ounce of magic, of…Fae-ness from a newborn Summer elf. She couldn't have been more than a few months old when a frantic hooded woman knocked at my door in the middle of the night. She begged me to do it and paid me well. I'd never heard desperation like that in all my years, and I lived through the Great War. So, I took all I could manage and put it in that orb. All except one drop."

I stared at the ball, enthralled by the pulsating hum of it, like a heartbeat that matched my own, calling to me. I yearned to reach out and touch it.

Oliver cleared his throat. "The woman who came to my door that fateful night was the Lady of Summer." Gasps filled the room. "I helped her strip away the Fae from the baby to make her nearly human."

Julie's hand covered her mouth. "Wait…wasn't her name…."

"Tessana," Moya finished for her. But her tumultuous stare was on me. "Lady Tessana of Summer."

Chapter Five

I stormed over to the coat rack and grabbed my jacket. Winter was in full swing in Ironworld.

Julie paced behind me as the others filed out onto the
porch. "It's late, Av'. You're not driving over an hour on
the highway on that Vespa."

I looked her square in the eyes as I plucked a pair of
green mittens from my pocket and shoved them on. "I'm
not driving there." I tipped my chin toward the open door
and the small pond that sat near the edge of the property.

"Do you want me to come with you? I can wisp you
from Ironworld."

"No." I shook my head, fists balled at my sides. I was
nothing but a ball of nerves contained within a fleshy pris-
on. My limbs were stiff with adrenaline I didn't want. "This
is between Tess and me. Having you there, even for a moment, would escalate the situation. Plus, we don't know if

she has wards against wisping. I'm betting she might."

She stood between me and the door, concern wrought in her crystal blue eyes. Her glamor completely dropped. She was like fresh snow glittering in the sun but without the wintery chill.

Our breathing fell in sync, and we just stared at each other with a deeper understanding of one another. The roots of our friendship constantly deepened and twisted.

She crossed her long arms. "How do you know she doesn't have wards against water travel, too?"

I chewed my lip in thought. My mind wandered to that night in Tess's garden before we moved to the city. I'd fallen into the fountain, and voices filled my ears. I fell forever into a swirl of whispers and nothingness.

I pressed my lips together. "I just know."

Everyone walked with me to the water's edge and waited as I steeled my nerves. Lattie fluttered over, wringing her long, boney blue fingers.

"I'm sorry," she said in her musical voice.

"You have nothing to be sorry for," I told her. But I understood what she meant. Sorry that I had to find out the truth of my past on my own, turning over stones I didn't even know were stones, only to be left with more questions. I nodded to my friends. "I'll be back soon. I just need to talk to Tess myself."

Moya's arms were crossed tightly over her chest, her

sandaled feet firmly in place. She was the only one who didn't speak, who didn't wish me farewell and good luck.

I said nothing as I knelt and touched the water. I closed my eyes as I brought forth the image of Tess's garden, the heavy aroma of satsuma and lilacs, and the gentle breeze that always seemed warm on my face. When I opened my eyes, my fingers remained dipped in water, but that of the old stone fountain basin I grew up playing around.

Tess cleared her throat, and I found her in the darkness. Dim, yellow light spilled out of the patio doors behind her, catching on the strands of yellow hair that had escaped her messy side braid. The sight of her twisted my guts every which way. I pushed to my feet and wiped my hand on my pants as we stared at one another in silence.

Finally, she crossed the large flaps of her green knitted sweater over her chest and spoke with a sigh. "Come inside. I guess we have a lot to talk about."

My stomach swirled with nerves, but I kept calm as I followed her inside my childhood home. It felt both warm and foreign at the same time, and I viewed everything with new eyes. I stood by the dining table as Tess nervously piddled about in the kitchen, filling the kettle and placing it on a burner.

"I didn't come here for tea, Tess," I said calmly. "Or should I say, Lady Summer?"

She froze, and those deep blues bore into me. Her

oversized sweater hung off her body, revealing her pale, lithe frame. Her human frame. *What did she really look like?* "It seems you know more than I thought."

"And yet, I know nothing at all. Do I?"

"Everything I did was to protect you," she said with such certainty that I believed her. Wanted to believe her, anyway.

"From what? Why?"

Tess rubbed a hand over her face and covered her mouth as she thought. She motioned to the table, inviting me to sit with her. So, I did.

"Why don't...." She took in a shuttered breath. "Tell me what you do know."

My shoulders moved tensely. "I know I'm not human. Or that I wasn't born one, anyway. I know you stole me from my home in Faerie and begged Oliver to strip away all that made me Fae. I know I have power—a drop of it— and that the Dark Lord of Nightmares and his assassin have been spying on me." I blew out and quirked a brow. "Am I missing anything?"

She chortled and caught a tear that I had noticed escaped. "You have no idea."

"Enlighten me, then." I leaned forward and reached across the table. But she just stared at my hand. "Why did you take me? Who am I? Who are you to me? Why is the Dark Lord after me?"

Her mouth opened to speak, but her head cocked toward the patio doors. As if something caught her ear, something my near-human ones couldn't pick up. Tess's eyes suddenly widened, and she sprung up from the chair.

"Move!" she ordered frantically and hurried me toward the linen closet. "Move it! Faster. Get in there."

"Why?" I asked as I crammed myself inside the closet. "Tess, what's happening—"

"Shhh!" She clamped a hand over my mouth and whipped a glance over her shoulder. When she turned back to me, her eyes were full of pleading. "Whatever you see, whatever you hear, do not come out of this closet. Understand?"

"Tess—"

"*Do you understand?*" I just nodded. Her eyes glossed over as if she seemed to be taking in the sight of me for the last time. "Stay in Ironworld. You're safe there. And just know that I love you more than anything in this world and beyond. You are my everything—"

The house filled with the sound of glass shattering, and Tess slammed the closet door shut. A scream died in my throat as I peered through the crack in the wooden slats and witnessed four golden armored men—Fae—storm into our wrecked living room. But they didn't go for Tess.

Two other heavily armored Fae males marched in behind them, but their gear was made of silver, and their helmets were horned. Gold and steel clanged together as the soldiers destroyed our home, and Tess suddenly had a sword in her hand.

It looked like it belonged there. She drove it through the neck of one silver fighter before slicing it through the head of the other. When their bodies fell to the ground, I expected the clamor of armor, but they disintegrated into nothing.

I clamped both hands over my mouth to stifle a cry.

"Lady Tessana," one of the golden soldiers greeted with a deep rasp.

She waved off his attempt to detain her. "No need, Sparis. I'll come willingly." Her voice was different. More regal and laced heavily with authority.

I watched through the narrow line of sight the closet door allowed, and my throat threatened to close off with the onslaught of tears that wanted to spill from me. But I kept dead silent until they were gone. Slowly, I pushed open the door, and it moaned on its hinges.

Our home was destroyed. The patio doors crashed in, and glass littered the floor in tiny squares and jagged bits. The dining room table I loved so much smashed to bits. The couches were torn and scattered to one side of the space.

I forced my legs to move over the rubble, careful not to fall or trip. When my sneakers hit the grass outside, I sprinted for the fountain–the one the soldiers no doubt used–and shoved my hand in the freezing water. I was on Oliver's property in seconds and jogged to the cottage. I'd only been gone a short while, but my world had flipped upside down. Again.

Lattie and the twins were gone, but Moya remained, and Julie was at the door with her jacket, ready to head home. She balked at the sight of me.

"Shit, what the hell happened?"

All words suddenly froze in my throat, and I counted my breaths. "Tess… They came."

"Who came?" Moya demanded, bolting to her feet.

"Soldiers. Gold and silver. They…destroyed *everything* and took her."

They all exchanged a look before Moya came closer, her body tense, her eyes wide with worry. "Avery, listen to me. It's imperative you tell me which color soldiers took your aunt."

"Wha–" I shook my head. "Uh, it was the golden ones. Tess," I swallowed dryly, "killed two silver soldiers."

The white's around Julie's eyes expanded.

Moya turned to Oliver. "That's Summer soldiers. Kheelan finally took her back."

"Will she be punished for abandoning her throne?" I asked. A hole burned in my stomach.

No one answered. Finally, Oliver spoke up from his

big chair. "We don't know. Kheelan's father was tyrannical. We don't know much about Kheelan. The throne has only been his for a few decades. He's yet to have the chance to prove himself as a High Lord."

"Except for flaunting his armies," Moya added with distaste. "He's hell-bent on protecting Summer's borders because Summer is the most accessible to Ironworld."

"Those guys were pissed, though," I said.

Julie sighed. "Well, she kinda did screw them over. The whole Territory. With Tess—*Tessana* as his wife, his Lady, Kheelan would have been able to access enough power to make his kingdom a Court."

That's right. Lattie once told me something about that. How the Lady of Summer disappeared the night of their wedding. They must not have finished the ceremony or something. I nodded slowly. "So, Kheelan got gypped." I steeled my nerves. Her last words to me were those of love. "I can't take the chance that Tess is in trouble. I'm going to see her."

"You can't," Oliver said. "Summer's borders are solid on a normal day. They just found the lost Lady of Summer and returned her to the throne. And, if silver-clad soldiers fought Summer's men for her...." His beady brown eyes met Moya's deep-sea gaze, and they exchanged a sense of knowing with a defeated sigh before he looked back at me. "Those would have been from the Seelie Court. Someone tipped off Mabry, and she clearly wanted to snuff out the possibility of Kheelan rising to the same level as her. He'll have everything on lockdown. There's no way into Summer right now. I can promise you that."

"Well, that's not entirely true," Moya spoke up, and Oliver shot her a grumpy look that said *shut it*.

Hope bubbled in my chest. "Please, tell me. If there's a way in, I have to go. I can't leave things like this. Tess could be hurt or in trouble, all because of me. And I need answers. If she knows the secrets of my past, of my existence… If she has any information about why Evaine is after me…I need to talk to her."

I was desperate for a way to control my magic. When no one replied, I continued to press. "The Lady of Summer is clearly not my mother, but I ended up in her care anyway. Tess knows who and what I really am, and I deserve to know the truth."

Moya gave Julie a terse nod, and my best friend looked me square in the face. "I'm coming."

Oliver stood with a grumble and stomped off to where the bedrooms were. Muttering something about *damn fools*.

"I can get us in," Moya said and slipped into a long copper-colored jacket. It brought out the brassy tone in her hair, catching the light of the hearth fire as she turned. "Being Summer Fae, I should be able to bypass the wards. I was just there today." She stole a worried glance out the open door toward the waiting waters across the property. "We should probably hurry, though."

We raced to the water's edge, and Moya offered her hand to Julie, who took it and then tightly gripped mine. We formed a connected trio as Moya knelt and touched the pond's surface. I closed my eyes as the air around us changed, becoming denser, and a soft satsuma breeze washed over me. The ground beneath my feet firmed, and I knew we were already there.

I opened my eyes to find the blaring Summer sun shining on us, making the luscious tropical landscape glimmer like diamonds. Birds of all sorts and colors wove through the air, carrying melodies I'd never heard of before, yet… felt familiar. The grass—a strange shade of teal—billowed in the breeze.

I spun around in awe just as a pair of giant hands grasped me by the upper arms and yanked my wrists together at my back. Moya and Julie faced me as two soldiers bound them the same.

Julie dropped her glamour, stunning them momentarily with her radiant, stark white glow. Her long snowy hair cascaded down over her tethered arms. Magic hummed over her, building, ready to strike, but one of the guard's elbows hammered into her face, and she slumped into his grasp.

"Julie!" I screamed.

Moya struggled. "We're here to see Tessana, you fools!"

"Did the Queen send you?" one of them bellowed inside the golden armor.

"No," I replied. "I swear. We're friends of hers." I couldn't think of another word. She wasn't my family, clearly. I had no real idea what she was to me other than a lie.

Moya fought against the thick golden cuffs they chained around her wrists. "Sparis! You know damn well who I am! I'm no traitor! Unbound me!"

He only tightened the chains in response while the other two dutifully held Julie and me. "All I know is that you appear to have known where Lady Summer has been all these years and didn't tell our Lord. That sounds like treason to me."

Our plan was foiled before we'd even had a chance to execute it.

My chest heaved with scorching breaths as my nerves frayed all along my limbs. I had to find Tess. I had to make sure she was okay. I *needed* answers, and I couldn't let them get in the way of that. Reluctantly, I called to my magic, buried deep inside. It didn't respond, but I knew it was there. I could feel it like a petulant child refusing to look at me.

I'm sorry, I said in my mind. *I'm sorry…I'm afraid of you. But I need you. Help me. Help us.*

Nothing.

Please, I begged as the guard's grip on my wrists loosened. His attention was on Moya, the angry maiden of the sea, as she grunted. The cuffs clearly stifled her powers somehow. They must have known what a threat she could be…but not me. To them, I was a lowly human. *Please*, I begged once more. *This is my only chance.*

And there it was, like an animal shaking off a crust of early morning snow. It purred in my ear.

Are you suurrrre?

Yes, I replied. *Please, help us. I need you.*

That was all it needed. My stomach filled with an unwanted sense of delight, and my veins thrummed with heat, burning until they glowed like molten metal. The chains around my wrists softened like warm silk, dripping down over my skin, and I knew it was only a matter of seconds before my magic broke the surface.

Sharp, blinding pain at the back of my neck sent me reeling, and the ground came rushing up before everything went black.

✳✳✳

The room spun as I slowly sat up and blinked away the fuzz that lined the edges of my vision. No, not a room—a dungeon cell. Sand crunched beneath my weight, and I moaned as my stomach swirled.

"Av'," Julie whispered and scooted across the floor toward me. "You okay?"

I rubbed the back of my neck. "Yeah, just sore. A little dizzy." I searched inside for my power, but it was as if it'd locked itself in a closet again. I glanced around. Details of the rough-hewn stone were barely visible in the dim torchlight that spilled in through the thick metal bars, and the slow drip of water could be heard echoing in the distance.

"Where are we?" I asked.

Moya stood in the corner, slouched against the wall with her arms crossed. She stared at the floor. "In the dungeons beneath the Summer castle." Her words were low and hoarse.

Julie helped me to my feet. Dried blood was smeared across her mouth and chin. "Are you alright?" I asked her.

She wiped her alabaster face—almost gray in the dim light, but the blood had long dried. "I'm fine," she said disgruntledly and tipped her head back so I could get a better look. "Did I set it right? I had to do it the old-fashioned way since none of us can use magic."

My mind spun as I noted three pairs of binding gold cuffs. "Av'?"

"What—" I shook my head and examined her bloody nose. "It's perfectly straight. You're good."

"Thank the gods," she said and stomped over to a heap of straw on the floor and plopped down. "Now that we're all awake, what do we do?"

Moya shifted in place; her arms still tightly wound around herself. I thought it was sadness when I'd first glanced at her, but I saw what it really was that brewed in her eyes. Rage. It stirred in her distant gaze like the ocean's depths in a storm. Whorls of black and emerald and jade. I looked back at Julie when I could have sworn the maiden swiped away a tear.

I willed myself not to say anything. Now was not the time. I stared down at the thick cuffs around my wrists. "How do we get these off?"

"We don't," Julie replied. "I've never seen them, but I've heard of them. These cuffs were apparently once used by Egyptian gods, gifted by the first to come here from the stars."

My forehead scrunched together. "Egyptian *gods*?" My widened eyes shot to Moya, but she only nodded solemnly. I ran my fingers through my hair. "What—how did the Summer Lord get them? How are they connected?"

"I have no idea," Julie said and shrugged. "Faerie and Ironworld have been linked since anyone can remember. The creatures of both sides are always crossing paths in some way."

"So, that's it then?" My arms flapped at my sides before I plunked down next to her. "We just give up? Just stay here, no magic, no way out, locked in by a giant padlock—"

The hinges. They were just iron pins. My breathing quickened as I bolted about the cell, kicking and scuffing at the piles of dirt and straw in the corners.

"Avery, what are you doing?" Julie sat up straight.

My heart skipped a beat as the toe of my shoe met a loose rock. I fetched it from the floor and stalked over to the cell door, peeking as far down the corridor as possible to ensure the coast was clear. Then I banged the rock against the bottom of a hinge pin. It only took four hard strikes to pop it out and three for the top.

Julie gasped with delight as Moya failed to stifle a laugh.

"Goddess!" She shot to her feet and yanked Moya along as we left the cell and headed down the hallway of hewn stone.

It seemed to never end. We took several turns, my throat raw with rapid, heavy breaths, before we rounded a corner and found two golden-clad guards. My heart climbed up my throat, and I cursed the chains that bound our wrists. I couldn't even properly defend myself.

But it didn't matter. Moya moved with lightning speed as she jumped and wrapped her legs around one guard's neck, gripping it. She leaped from him to the next before he even hit the ground. The second guard joined him a moment later. Moya gawked at us as she panted, clearly not used to relying on her physical strengths.

I just stared at her.

"I keep forgetting what a badass you are," Julie said gleefully.

"The gods above," a startling echo shot down the hall. My stomach dropped when I saw Tess, unharmed, unchained, unaccompanied…her ears now slightly pointed and poking out from her platinum hair. She stormed over to us, still wearing her teal Lululemon tracksuit. Her new eyes, still green but now multi-faceted like genuine emeralds, looked at me with worry. "What are you *doing* here? I told you you'd be safe in Ironworld."

"Tessana," Moya said through a swallow, unblinkingly.

My aunt spun on her. "How could you bring her here?"

"Gods above, Tessana, I thought you were *dead* all these years! Excuse me for overreacting when I discover you're not only *alive* but suddenly taken against your will. I thought you might be in danger."

Tess's hands balled at her sides. "You know it's not like that. That…*he's* not like that."

"Our home is destroyed, Tess. I would say otherwise." My throat was raw with emotion.

"You don't understand. It wasn't just Kheelan's men. Someone in Summer tipped off Mabry immediately." She swallowed dryly and straightened. "Also, Kheelan is—he thought…I would resist."

"You're nothing but a pawn to him," Moya gritted. "A power tool."

Tess just stared at her and crossed her arms. "Kheelan cares for me."

Moya chortled. "He cares for you about as much as his soldiers care for their swords."

I looked at the person I thought was my aunt for eighteen years. She was a total stranger to me now. "You're not in danger?" My eyes filled with tears.

The wrinkles in her forehead softened, and she tipped her head to the side. "Oh, sweetheart, no—"

"Was my entire life a lie?"

Tess's mouth gaped soundlessly, but she froze the moment she noticed who else was with us. "Julie…"

My best friend wavered in the background, hugging her torso as if trying to hide her striking appearance of near-complete white. Half of her mouth turned up in a nervous smile. "Hey, Tess."

I grabbed Tess's wrist, demanding her attention back to me. "*What. Happened?*"

"It's complicated, it's," she shook her head, "there's so much to explain."

I grit my teeth. "Try me. That story about my parents being murdered. That was a lie, wasn't it?"

She tilted her head, those emerald eyes sparkling with the reflection of torchlight. "It was the only way I could keep you from the city. I knew Ironworld was flooded with Fae and Therians, even vampires. I knew you'd be drawn to them. So, I hid you from it all."

"Why?" I pleaded.

She took both my hands in hers, bringing them together. Emotions and words boiled to the surface as she fought back the tears. "You were just a baby, an orphan. I had to protect you."

"Oh my God, Tess," I yanked my hands away. "*Why?* I want to know why I, an *orphan*, needed to be protected. From *what?* From *who?* By the Lady of Summer, of all people?" I swallowed through the lump in my throat. "Are you my real mother?"

She inhaled a long, deep breath through her nose. "No."

"Then *why?*" The words rasped from me with the last of my energy.

Tess had no reply, just a blatant look of guilt smeared across her grim expression. A gasp from Moya made our heads whip in her direction, and she gawked at me with an awe of curiosity and a hint of disbelief. She began mouthing numbers, counting on her fingers, and her face paled.

"My gods above…."

"What?" Julie and I asked in unison.

Moya quickly glanced at Tess before stepping closer to me, like someone approaching a baby bird. "Eighteen years." She studied my face, scanning all the lines and features, and leaned back as she took in my long red hair. She plucked a lock of it in her hands and let it slowly fall through her fingers. "You're the missing heir."

Terror iced my veins. "What? No–"

"I don't know how I didn't see it before," Moya added in almost a whisper.

Julie capped a hand over her mouth as she mumbled, wide-eyed, "holy shit."

I stared at Tess, and my eyes stung as they filled with tears of betrayal. "Is it true? Am I...*Mabry's* daughter?"

She hesitated but then gave a solemn nod. "Yes, sweetie. You are. But not–"

"Don't call me sweetie!" I yelled and backed away from them all, my fists balled at my sides as the world tilted. The hallway began to spin, and my stomach twirled in knots, threatening to rise. I could already taste bile in my throat and tried to focus on the floor beneath me, desperate for everything to stop rolling.

"It's a long story," Tess replied carefully. "But I couldn't exactly turn around and leave the moment I returned to my kingdom after being missing for nearly two decades. Kheelan had to make sure no one followed from the Seelie Court. I was about to send word, I swear. But I knew you'd be safe in the city, in the apartment. With my wards–"

"The wards?" My lip trembled. "*You* placed those wards around our apartment."

Moya and Julie moaned an *ohhh* as they realized the truth of it.

"Oh my god, my entire life is a lie." My breaths came hard and rapid. I reached for the rough stone wall to find balance, but it didn't help. I needed air. "I can't breathe."

"Avery," Tess stepped toward me.

I threw out an arm to stop her, to stop any of them. I needed air desperately. I needed to get out of the darkness of the dungeons of this place. My feet moved with a will of their own. I darted between Tess and Moya as I bolted down the hall in search of an exit.

I had no idea where I was going. Every corridor was like the last, dimly lit by torchlight and walls that scratched at my exposed skin as I frantically rounded each corner. I could hear the faint cries of my friends behind me as they called my name.

Suddenly, a hazy streak of sunlight spilled across the floor, and I followed it to a random exit flanked by crates stacked on either side. Some sort of servant's wing, I assumed but didn't care. I leaped through the door and sucked in a deep breath of fresh Summer air. Notes of satsuma and honey filled my nose.

When my breathing calmed enough to think, I glanced around. Thick forests surrounded this part of the castle, but I bet I could find a water source there. A pond, a creek, maybe even a small lake. Anything that would get me out of here.

I bolted through the trees, stumbling over roots and

stones. Unfamiliar sounds of animals howling and cawing from the depths of the forest. Everything threatened to take my feet out from under me, but I finally found myself in the middle of a small clearing, where I spotted a tiny brook trickling into a pond. A sigh of relief flooded me.

I fell to my knees at the water's edge and reached for the surface. But my fingertips hovered as I caught my reflection. Pale, dirty, disheveled. Eyes wide and crazed. I hardly recognized myself.

As if I even know who I am at all.

I wanted to cry. I wanted to scream into the living forest around me. But there was nothing. I was empty. My mother was one of the most horrible creatures to walk this Earth. Her own people were fleeing in terror, choosing a short life of constant agony in Ironworld over her rule.

I couldn't stay here a moment longer. I reached for the water again just as clawed, blackened fingers threaded through mine and locked my hand in an iron grip. I stared into the face of pure evil as Evaine leaned into my view, fear possessing me.

She grinned widely, revealing a set of rotting teeth. Worn and chipped horns curled from her head. "So, good of you to finally visit."

"Avery!" My head whipped in the direction of my best friend's voice, my heart beating wildly. But it was no use. She'd never reach me in time.

Evaine's grip tightened, the bones of my hand cracking, but she had me locked in some sort of hold. I couldn't move, couldn't scream, couldn't even blink. She stood and hauled me to my feet just as Julie broke through the tree line.

"Oh my god, *Avery!*"

Evaine flung her other arm around me, holding me tight to her chest, and we wisped away, leaving behind a trail of distant cackles.

Chapter Six

We tore through the fabric of space and time and broke into a different kind of darkness. A canopy of night sky hung above us as our feet hit the dirt ground. Thick cherry trees line the property, leading up to a structure of wood and stone, and glass. Gothic peaks cut the sky, and modern wood covered parts of the exterior, mixing with windows and rock. Several chimneys piped smoke into the air.

"Where are we?" I demanded as thunder rolled in the distance.

"Where you belong," she replied with a level of finality. As if this were the last task on her long to-do list. She reached for my arm, and I scrambled backward.

"I'm not going anywhere with you!"

Her tar-molten eyes flashed with anger and impatience. "You'll come, willingly or not."

Trees, nothing but dark cherry trees as far as the eye could see. Nowhere to run, no bodies of water. Just a dense forest and a creepy castle at the end of a very long path. I cursed my inability to wisp.

Or defend myself.

Evaine kicked my feet out from under me, and I hit the ground like a sack of meat, the air puffing from my lungs. I gasped to fill them as Evaine jumped on top of me and hastily tied my hands together. My legs kicked fruitlessly at her back, and she delighted in my failure, cackling under her raunchy breath.

"Let me go!"

Her clawed and blackened fingers pulled the rope tight when my wrists were bound and secure, and she stood over me. "I'd suggest you hold on."

"What–"

Faerie's assassin yanked, and my wrists screamed in pain. As Evaine dragged my writhing body up the log dirt path, I struggled and floundered to no avail. It was a good hundred yards to the stone beast in the distance, and my wrists would surely break by then, so I fought to grab the rope as the gravel tore through my clothes. I could already tell where it had worn completely through. My skin burned.

Finally, we reached the castle. But Evaine never let me get to my feet. She entered a narrow archway, and I welcomed the change of torture from jagged gravel to smooth stone, but my grip on the rope began to weaken.

Around a few turns and directly through the middle of several dimly lit rooms, Evaine finally gave one last haul on the rope and tossed me to the center of an ample space lined with open arched windows to the night outside. Thunder rolled again, followed by a bolt of lightning that crackled through the sky.

I shimmied into a sitting position and glanced around frantically. One way in, one way out. No—there were two doors behind a platform where a throne of obsidian held a man with pointed ears, long hair like the driven snow, and grey eyes so cunning they almost sucked you in, like staring into the eye of a storm.

The Dark Lord of Nightmares.

He gripped a long, black cane topped with some sort of bone carving. He stood up, adjusted his fitted black suit of leather and silk, and stalked toward where I sat on the floor. He towered over me with a look of disdain and sighed as he dragged his gaze toward Evaine.

"This is how you treat my special guest?" His baritone voice vibrated deep in my chest.

She only made some sort of wet sound with her mouth and sneered at me.

"What am I doing here?"

He arched a silvery brow as his pure white hair fell over his shoulder like a silky drape. "I would think it's obvious."

"Obvious?" I chortled and struggled with the ropes to no avail. "All I know is that bitch has been following me for weeks with unwarranted threats and even attacked one of my friends for no reason. And now I'm here–" I waved my bound hands in the air. "Against my will."

He gave me a surprised look of bemusement. "Is it now?"

I shook my head in confusion. "What?"

"Is that *all you know?*"

The Dark Lord grabbed the knotted rope and hauled me to my feet with such ease. As if I weighed nothing at all. And I felt it, the thrum of his power. He exuded it. It rolled off his shoulders like a building storm, and I had to force myself not to get lost in his stare, so I fixated on his cane. The carving was clearly the head of a dragon.

He slid the tip across my neck and raised my chin until I looked into his eyes. They flashed with a warning and a promise, and I swallowed dryly. He held my stare for a moment too long for comfort and gently dragged the dragon's head across my cheek.

"Show me," he said calmly.

Confused, I replied, "show you what?"

"Your powers." He grinned like a cat. "Let me see how beautiful they are. I've heard so much about them." His cane continued to trail down my body, hugging my hip.

"I-I'm not a damn show pony."

I felt something change in the air, almost a lessening. As if he turned down his power a few notches. The Dark Lord took a step back and examined me thoroughly, from head to toe. His expression was that of disbelief.

"Evaine, dear, you've brought me the wrong woman."

"I assure you," she said with an annoyed rasp. "This is her."

I wanted to kill her for this and for what she did to Max.

His stormy eyes raked over me once again as he seemed to ponder. A breath solidified in my chest as he reached for me and pinched my hair between his fingers. He grinned to himself as if recalling a pleasant and funny memory and tossed it over my shoulder.

"This is her, milord," Evaine assured him again. "She surrounds herself with the sea witch, Moya. The healer, Oliver, and other Solitary miscreants. Even a Therian bitch."

"You take their names out of your disgusting mouth!" I yelled and spat. Evaine gave me a look that said, *how dare you*, while the lord chuckled off to the side. My skin warmed, building, and burning. My powers snowballed in anger, and this time…I let it.

That's it, come on, I said to it. *I won't hold you back.*

My sunlight blossomed in my chest, spreading through my veins and limbs, filling every inch of my body. I stared down at the thick rope around my wrists, and they burst into flame—a flame that didn't mar my skin—and the fibers turned to ash. I shook it all to the floor as my power continued to grow.

I raised my stare toward Evaine as the Dark Lord observed from the sidelines. She almost looked bored, but I'd wipe that look off her face in two seconds—

Gone. It was all gone. Every ounce of my magic snuffed out like a candle. Panic flooded me, and I shook my hands, desperate for any remaining spark. But there was nothing. I whipped my head toward a low, raspy chuckle and froze as the Dark Lord stalked toward me again, slowly circling where I stood, sizing me up and down as he tapped a finger against his lips.

"W-what did you do to me?"

"If you don't demand full control of your power, then someone with a greater power will," was his reply. He wiggled his fingers, and I felt a gentle tug, a tether.

My magic, it *listened* to him like an obedient cat. *Traitor,* I hissed at it.

"I appreciate the little show," he added and stuffed one of his hands in the pocket of black velvet slacks. "Evaine, be a dear and show our guest to her quarters."

Evaine moved toward me, and I clumsily kicked at her, missing widely. "My *what*? You're crazy! I'm not staying here!"

Her bare feet padded against the cold stone floor as she

advanced. She stood between me and the exit and slowly pushed me deeper into the room, closer to the Dark Lord. Panic took over, and I immediately dove into a fight or flight mode. I needed my magic.

Come on, I begged it. *Why are you listening to him?* It was there; I could sense it. As if it waited behind a glass wall, taunting me. So easily accessible and yet…just beyond my reach. I closed my eyes and placed a hand of my mind against the cool glass. *Please.*

Just reach out, it spoke back to me in a musical voice, reminding me of the strange vision Solenna had induced in the Temple of Dreams. *Take me, claim me. Set me freee…*

I can't, I replied as I sensed Evaine within inches of where I stood. My heart pounded in my ears. *I don't know how.*

Just let go…

I can't! Evaine's claws wrapped around my arm.

Just let go!

My mind filled with the screeching sound of glass shattering as something broke through the wall, and my magic slammed back into me like a taut elastic, finally letting go. My eyes flew open, and the room was illuminated with my glowing sunlight. My heart raced from fear and exhilaration as my powers grew beyond my control and filled the room until it exploded from me.

The floor beneath me shook. Massive fissures split the

walls, crawling upward. A giant chunk of the vaulted ceiling fell, trapping the Dark Lord behind it. More debris began to fall, and I dove out of the way, closer to Evaine, and she snatched me by the neck. Her black eyes were crazed.

"What have you done, you little shit?" she gritted between rotten teeth.

I kicked her shin, and her grip loosened. An elbow to her gut was enough to let me go, and I ran for the exit. But it was too late. The castle was crumbling; I was surrounded by shards of glass, heaps of jagged rock, and splintered wood. The exit was blocked.

Clumps of stone, wood, and glass continued to fall around us so fast I could hardly think. Everything was collapsing. But it didn't stop the Dark Lord from coming for me. He blasted through the blockage and dodged falling debris unblinkingly, his stormy gaze fixated on me across the room.

I spun around, searching for another way out, just as a massive block of stone broke away from the cathedral ceiling and hurdled right for me. I closed my eyes and threw my arm out, but my magic didn't respond.

Some other force slammed into me, and I flew through all the falling refuse, narrowly missing every piece until I skidded across the dewy lawn.

I gasped for breath and watched, wide-eyed in terror, as an entire wing of the castle crumbled to nothing but a hovel of everything it was made of. The Dark Lord and his assassin were trapped underneath.

It all happened so fast. One minute I was inside, flanked by two impossible threats, the next...I was on the lawn outside, where the painful silence of night fell on me like a heavy blanket. I didn't know this place, but I couldn't stick around to see if there were survivors.

I had to find water.

"Damnit!" I clenched my fists. *If only I could wisp.* A promise solidified in my mind. A commitment to myself. If I somehow made it out of this hell alive, I'd figure it out.

With a deep breath, I hobbled into the thick expanse of cherry trees. The aroma was a strange delight as I traipsed through the root-ridden forest where things rustled in the bushes and sprung from branches above, whispering in the distance. A cluster of different voices, too far for me to hear what they were saying.

No sound of footsteps followed behind, but I kept my head down and marched along. I only tripped once, but it was enough to cover half my body in the juices of fallen, half-rotten cherries. After a while, the ground dipped and turned, changing to an even denser bouquet of trees. Ferns and shrubs, pine, and other types I couldn't name all twisted together in a creepy sort of harmony, like walking through a Tim Burton film.

It felt like hours had passed, and I was no closer to a

body of water. But there had to be something. The forest was alive with…things. I could hear them bristling about, watching me, observing the strange new creature entering the woods. Those things had to drink water, didn't they?

Something slashed across my arm, and I winced as I cupped my hand over the gash. But nothing was there. No cut, no blood.

"What the…"

Another painful sensation slit across the exposed skin of my thigh that poked out through torn jeans. I choked on the cry of pain as my stomach suddenly cramped, and I keeled over. My knees wobbled before I finally fell to them, and nausea swirled through my head as sweat broke out all over my body.

What was happening?

I felt clawed fingers crawl up my curved spine as I hunched over myself on the ground and managed a gurgled scream. Invisible hands, reaching from every which way, held me in place, stuffing my body with jolts of pain and sickness. I wanted to weep and scream and die all at the same time. I wanted forgiveness. I wanted closure, even revenge. For what? For things I didn't even know or understand.

The darkness crawled over my skin, finding ways to seep in and burrow inside my fragile chest. But something else was there to greet the foreign emotions. Something dormant, petulant, and far more chaotic than anything this dreaded forest could throw at me.

My power.

Sunlight exploded from me, banishing the emotions and invisible creatures that leaked into me. Shadows skittered across the forest floor as the air filled with sounds of hissing and quiet shrieks. And just like a bomb imploding on itself, it was gone. Every last shred of warm, powerful sunshine snapped back into my body like an elastic band, and I was again in darkness.

Shakily, I stood up and fought to regain a steady breath.

A dense black shadow moved over the deadened bark of a tree. Followed by another. And another. And another. Fluidly, they curled around branches, crawled up and down trunks, and finally circled the ground where I stood. Trapping me in place. A puddle of blackness enclosed me, and my breath froze in my chest as I watched figures erect from the soil. They were solid, featureless, and ebbed like a pulse.

A little far from home, she is.
Returned home to us, she did.
Not returned…arrived.
Does her mother know?
She'll shred her to ribbons and lace the great halls of the Seelie castle with her entrails.

Pity, such a pretty thing.

An invisible finger caressed my cheek. I spun around at the whispering–and strangely familiar–voices, searching for a way out.

"Who are you?" My jaw jittered. I stomped forward, and the figures pulsed as one, moving with me, giving me a berth but not an escape. "Get out of my way!"

Feisty, she is.
A fine queen, she'll be.
A queen, she is not. Not yet.
A girl, she is. Knows nothing, she does.

The voices, they finally clicked in the deepest corner of my memories. I'd heard them before, in Tess's garden… when I fell in the fountain.

Something slashed at my arm again, but this time it drew blood. Warm and sticky, it trickled down my skin, and I shook it off just as another gash sliced across my cheek. Hot blood slid downward as the sensation of a cold tongue swept upward.

Taste her.
The Lord won't be happy.
The Dark Lord has plans for her. Plans for the queen.

Kill the queen.
Kill the queen.
Kill the queen.

The voices chanted in my ears, filling my mind and buzzing like a swarm of bees. I closed my eyes as the world spun and struggled to keep my footing, but it was no use. As my back hit the ground and the wind knocked from my lungs, the dirt turned to water, and I continued to fall.

Down, down, down.

The water seemed to never end. My limbs kicked and clawed for the surface, but there was only darkness all around. I refused to give up. With the last drop of oxygen in my lungs, I swam and reached for any shred of hope until my fingers felt the cool caress of air.

I broke through the surface and gasped for breath as I crashed against a hard, concrete ledge of something. I slung an arm over it to steady myself. A fountain. No... I was in Tess's garden.

I'd wisped.

The night sky hung above, and the deadening sound of nothingness ebbed in my ears. The house—what was left of it—stared back at me like an injured animal. I couldn't bear to see it. The reality of what I'd done hit me again. I'd wisped from one realm to another. Julie couldn't even do that yet.

How did I do it?

I crawled over the ledge, and my drenched body hit the ground with a hard thwomp. My lungs protested, and I coughed water as my breathing settled. I had to get home.

Closing my eyes, I tried to recreate what I'd done, but it was no use. Nothing happened. I couldn't even sense my powers. I was alone, injured, and stranded in the middle of nowhere with no way back.

I glanced at the fountain and heaved a defeated sign as I dipped my hand inside and concentrated. When I opened them, I knelt at the edge of the quiet duck pond in the Public Gardens—the Ironworld façade for the Sanctuary.

I was running on fumes, but I couldn't afford to hang around if Evaine or the Dark Lord were already searching for me. Tess—I cringed at the thought of her name—had said I'd be safe at home, in the apartment under her wards. So, I used the last of my energy to run home.

The short journey was a blur as my mind threatened to go under, but I somehow found myself climbing the rickety stairs in the alley and burst through the door. I was met with my friends' muffled concern as their hands reached for me, and the cold, unforgiving floor rushed upward.

***

Something warm and moist touched my forehead, moving gently to my cheek in quick blots. I tried to place it as my mind swam to the surface, and my eyes fluttered open. The dimly lit room slowly became focused as I blinked away the remnants of sleep and the faces of my friends hovered over me.

Julie breathed a long air of relief as she patted my clammy skin with something. A moist cloth, I noted as she wrung it out in a bowl on the coffee table. Moya sat at my feet, spreading her hands over the space above my thigh. She gave me a kind smile.

"Av'," Julie spoke calmly. "What the hell happened to you? Where did you go?"

Lattie fluttered about and came to sit on my chest, blinking with those massive, black eyes. A moan forced itself from me as I struggled to sit up.

Moya stood. "Perhaps you should continue to rest. Your wounds are fairly extensive."

I glanced down at my arms and legs. No marks to be found. "No, I only had a couple scratches… I think…" I shook my head, and it spun inside. I braced my palm against it, only to find a half-dried gash across my forehead. "What–" I couldn't remember getting a head injury.

"You fell on your face when you burst through the door," Julie said. "You nearly gave me a heart attack from the sight of you. Torn and soaked clothes, cuts, and scrapes all over you. I thought you were covered in blood, but it's just…." She pinched and tugged at my white t-shirt and leaned forward to sniff. "I think it's berries or something."

Everything came flooding back, and I groaned as I sunk back onto the sofa. "Cherries."

"Can you tell us what happened after you fled the Summer castle?" Moya asked. Since I last saw her, she'd changed into a shimmery teal jumper, barely held up with thin straps.

"Tess…"

Julie put a hand on my shoulder. "She's fine. We sent word that you're okay and home."

Lattie crawled around on my chest, sniffing at my skin and clothing. "You were in the Dark Forest?"

Their eyes widened as the air seemed to suck out of the room.

I guffawed. "That's a fitting name for a forest from hell."

"Gods above." Moya pinched the bridge of her nose. "What were you doing in the Dark Forest? How did you even get out in one piece?"

I shrugged, but it killed my neck. "Not without great difficulty. There was no way to get home, no source of water to be seen around the castle–"

"Wait, what castle?" Julie breathed. "Oden's castle?"

"Who's Oden?" I asked.

Lattie rolled her eyes as Moya replied, "Oden is the

Dark Lord of Nightmares. He rules the Territory of Nightmares, and no one, I mean no one, dares go there. Let alone brave the horrors of the forest he uses to protect his home." She shook her head in disbelief, staring at me. "How did you ever...."

"When I ran from Tess, I found an exit and went outside," I began. "I just needed some air, y'know?" My friends nodded in understanding. "I mean, holy shit. My entire life was turned upside down in the last twenty-four hours. Everything I ever knew was revealed to be lies. Everything. I feel bad for just running out like that, for leaving you guys to deal with her, but I just...I just couldn't. Not after everything else I've dealt with since moving to the city. I never get a moment's peace, no time to settle or digest anything before something else comes along." Julie took my hand, her crystal eyes glossed with concern. "But Evaine was there. Almost as if she knew. Before I could call for help, she took me and wisped away. She dragged me to the Dark Lord's castle and—" I flexed my shaky hands in front of my eyes. "My magic exploded from me; I was so pissed. Everything began to crumble and fall, the ceiling and walls caved in on us, but I somehow got out onto the lawn just before it all came crashing down." I gazed distantly as I recalled everything. "They...it fell on them."

No one said anything for a long moment. Julie and Moya exchanged a worried glance before my best friend squeezed my hand. "Well, that confirms who hired Evaine to follow you."

"It was stupid," I said. "I shouldn't have run like that. What's wrong with me?"

"Nothing," Julie replied. "You're going through some serious stuff here, Av'. Take some time to digest it all, and figure some things out. In the meantime, stay home. It's safe here."

"Yes," Moya agreed. "Evaine can only follow you in Ironworld, not take you. Tessana made sure of it. And the wards around the apartment are a bonus."

"I can't believe it," Julie blew out. "All this time. Tess, the Lady of Summer, was right next door to me. And you…"

I raised my brows. "I can't believe she lied to me," I muttered, refusing to let Julie continue where she was going. I didn't want to discuss who or what I truly was. Who my real mother was.

"She would have done it for a good reason," Moya said defensively. "Tessana would never… There's not a bad bone in her body."

"Protecting the heir to the Seelie throne is a pretty good reason," Lattie chimed in as she fluttered about the living room.

I chewed at my lip and caught Moya's gaze. "How do you two know each other?"

She sucked in a deep breath. "It was Tessana who took me and my sisters in when we first came to land. Gave us a home at her family's estate on the beaches of Summer."

I nodded. "Sounds like a good ruler."

Moya shook her head. "No, it goes beyond that. Tessana comes from one of the oldest families in Faerie's history, and her parents had long arranged a union with Kheelan before she was even born. She saw duty in her position by his side, a duty she couldn't ignore. We grew apart. The night of their union, I was on my way to the Summer castle to make amends, but…she'd disappeared. I wager that was the night she fled Faerie with you in her arms."

Guilt slammed down on me, and I stifled a whimper in my chest as I curled my knees to it.

"Not to worry," Moya said and patted my leg. "What's done is done. All that matters now is that everyone is where they belong, including you. Stay put in Ironworld. You'll be safe here."

"Only from being taken," I replied. "Evaine can still hurt me here. She can hurt all of you. She proved that with Max."

God, the whole Max situation felt like a lifetime ago.

Julie chortled and crossed her arms as she leaned back. "That's if they even survived what you did."

My eyes widened. "You think I…*killed* them?" A dry tightness formed in my throat.

"It'll take more than a bit of rubble to kill the likes of the Dark Lord and his assassin," Moya said with a chuckle. "But keep practicing your magic, stay close to home, and assume your normal life during the day. Evaine only lurks in the shadows and darkness." She tossed a dusty rose peacoat over her jumper and locked her eyes on mine. "You are the single most precious thing in our world right now. Keep yourself safe." She gave Julie a firming look, and Julie nodded dutifully.

With that, Moya wisped into thin air, taking Lattie with her. I stretched my legs out on the sofa, surprised by how little they hurt. In fact, my whole body felt far better than it should have, considering the injuries I'd had.

"Moya healed most of your serious injuries," Julie said quietly as if reading my mind.

She just stared at me in awe, and I hated every second of it. I didn't want her to look at me any differently now that I was some sort of prodigal heir. She opened her mouth to speak, but I beat her to it.

"Did you know?" I asked curtly. "Did you suspect it at all?"

"No, Av', I swear," she replied sincerely. "I had no idea who you really were or that Tess was otherworldly. She covered it well." Julie paused to swallow nervously, and her cheeks flushed with guilt.

I managed to stand up from the sofa. "I'm tired. I think

I'm gonna go to bed."

I walked toward my room, and Julie followed.

"But I knew there was something about you." Her voice was a pitch higher and soaked with worry. "At best, I assumed you were just a normal mortal with the Sight. But I'm sorry that I kept even that much from you. Moreso now." I half turned to face her as I touched the doorknob. She smiled, but her glistening eyes begged for forgiveness.

"It's okay," I told her and turned the knob.

Everyone I love lies to me.

Chapter Seven

enial was bliss.

I spent days moving through the motions of my life with a smile because I had to. I had to block it out, count my breaths, and completely forget that a Dark Lord kidnapped me, and I may or may not have killed him…and Faerie's assassin.

Moya scouted the borders, listening for whispers of movement from the Territory of Nightmares. There was nothing, not a word, from them…or from Cillian.

I hadn't seen him since our spat before my already chaotic life turned into a mess, and it pained me every time I thought about it. Celadine said he was away for work, but I didn't buy it.

I need to talk to him, to hear his voice and feel his steady chest beneath my palms. I'd told Celadine everything that had happened, and if she were appalled, she hid it well. She just sat in her gothic garden under the moonlight and listened intently, nodding where needed, and offered nothing but kind and wise words. I knew she'd pass the message to her brother through their psychic, mental connection.

That was three days ago, and there was still no word from Cillian. I felt anxious and unsettled, incomplete.

Max hadn't been to class, either, which only fueled the nervousness building inside me. Maxine Carmichael was a werewolf, an ancient Therian shapeshifter from Faerie. From the very world that birthed me.

And rejected me.

I wished I could talk to her to see if she was okay. God, I had so many questions and blank pages in my journal of collected Faerie history and facts. The little I knew about Therians came from Lattie and biased bits from my friends. But I would give anything to hear things from the side of a Therian. Like why they gave up the fight and their homeland and what caused the Great War.

I allowed these questions to burn into my brain because the alternative was so much worse. To wonder about everything else, to have my thoughts consumed by all the what-ifs that plagued my dreams.

And my nightmares.

Why did the Dark Lord chase me? What did he want? Did it have something to do with my unfortunate lineage?

Was he gearing to take my life and prevent the possibility of me taking my mother's throne? I wanted no part in it. She could rot there for all I cared.

But to entertain these possibilities meant he knew who I truly was and *what* I was. Not the distant ancestor from a Summer Fae, but as direct as I could ever be. Very few seemed to know these answers, answers I rightly should have.

"Avery?"

I shook my head, forcing the scattered thoughts back into their places, to the burrows and nooks of my mind. Tomas stared at me from the other end of the counter, eyebrows raised in concern.

"What?" I replied as the last of the brain fog dissipated.

He motioned to my hands. "I think that spot's clean."

I glanced down at the countertop where I'd been mindlessly scrubbing a washcloth in circles, and my face warmed. I tossed the rag in the utility sink and managed an empty chuckle as I busied myself with refilling the chocolate baked goods display, all the while feeling Tomas' worried glances.

After a few minutes, he sidled up to me. "Everything alright?"

I nodded as I added another row of fresh chocolate croissants. "Yeah, just a lot on my plate with work and school."

"Are we still meeting this weekend to work on the project?" His little half-smile was so endearing. How oblivious Tomas was to the tragic world hidden around him. I envied him.

"Of course," I replied. "Wouldn't miss it for the world. I gotta get some good headway done before it's too late." I closed the sliding glass door on the display and straightened, wiping my hands on my apron. "Unless you and Jules have plans?"

Tomas looked away and rubbed the back of his neck. "Yeah, I dunno. Probably not."

My heart sank. "Are you guys…I thought…aren't you two like a thing?"

Those soft brown eyes looked at me with kindness, sincerity, and worry. "I thought we were. I mean, I'd kind of hoped it was heading that way. She seemed really into it, but now…." He blew out an exasperated breath and shrugged. "I'm not sure. She's always busy, always has a reason—no, I'm not doing this. I'm not going to be that guy."

I placed my hand on his arm. "Be that guy, Tomas. You care about her. It's obvious. And I know she cares for you. Don't worry." I thought about our lives, my own mess, and how it's spilled into Julie's life, too, and guilt filled me. "But she is busy. I can vouch for that. But I'll talk to her." Panic lit up his expression, and I laughed. "Very casually, promise. She won't even know this conversation happened."

Tomas tipped his head to the side, and one of his deep brown waves fell across his forehead. "If you say so." He scooped up two garbage bags and motioned to the back. "I'm just going to toss these out and flat pack some recycling. You good here for a bit?"

I glanced around at the near-empty café. Only two patrons sat in the back in our comfy leather sofa chairs, headphones on, books in hand. A couple of students, no doubt. "Yeah, I think I'll manage."

I busied myself with stocking more baked goods, refilling cups and utensils, and topping up the dairy jugs while Tomas was gone. I almost loathed the quiet, though. It made it harder to hang on to that blissful denial. My over-active, overthinking brain was almost too much to stand.

My back faced the door when I felt it. I felt…*him.*

The little brass bell jingled over the door, and the air changed, like the calm before a brewing storm, dense and cool from sucking all the heat to build power. Something tugged at my chest, like a little string, prompting me to turn around, but I already knew what I'd find.

I slowly spun in place, dragging my gaze across the old tiles to the toes of his leather boots, and a cane touched the floor. My heart clenched in my chest, and I swallowed nervously as I stared into the stormy gaze of the Dark Lord of Nightmares. His snow-white hair was tucked back in a ponytail at the nape of his neck, showing off his gem-cut features and slightly pointed ears. A charcoal trench coat hung just an inch from the floor and mostly covered his immaculate matching vest suit beneath.

I silently prayed the two mortals would get up and leave, begged the universe to keep Tomas out back. My hands balled at my sides, and I stepped up the counter.

"What are you doing here?"

His sly grin made my teeth grit together as he sauntered up to the other side of the countertop and clucked his tongue. "Do you welcome all your patrons in that manner?"

"Only the ones who want to kill me."

He feigned offense. "My dear, I'm not here to kill you. Quite the opposite, in fact." He trailed a finger along the butcherblock with distaste as if touching anything in the mortal realm was beneath him. Then he shot me an exaggerated smile that didn't reach his eyes. "If anything, it should be me who's worried after the stunt you pulled."

"How did you survive?" I asked as I made a mental map of where the knives were and listened for any sounds of Tomas returning. "I destroyed an entire wing of your castle. It crushed you both."

Oden brought his cane front and center and rested both gloved hands atop its dragon head as he looked at me with unsettling admiration. "As impressive as that was, it would take a lot more than a bit of falling rubble to end my life, I'm afraid."

"So I hear."

He cocked his head with a look of surprise.

"And Evaine?"

Oden gave a raspy chuckle. "My sweet Evaine is death itself, Avery."

The sound of my name on his lips made my skin crawl. "So, she can't die?"

He sucked on his teeth. "I didn't say that."

"So, what do you want then?" I eyed the oblivious people over his shoulder and swallowed the lump in my throat. "Revenge? You want to destroy my home as payback? There are innocent people here."

He glanced around as if looking at ants beneath his feet. "These mortals? Innocent might be too loose a term for what they truly are." He pursed his lips and snapped his fingers. The air deadened and all sound muffled. "Such tiny lives. How do you do it? Live knowing your days are so numbered."

Panic rose in my chest. "What did you just do?"

"Just a little cloaking trick," he replied nonchalantly. "No one can see or hear us now."

My heart raced. I wasn't sure if that was a good or bad thing. But I wouldn't give him the satisfaction of seeing me fret. I crossed my arms tightly. "And...I can't answer your question. I'm sure your little spy has already told you by now. I'm not exactly mortal."

Oden purposefully set his cane against the counter and gripped the edges as he leaned forward, bringing with him a whiff of cigars and cherries. Those eyes snared me, like turning around to find a tornado at your back and nowhere to run. They raked over me, examining for what, I had no idea.

"Yes, that's a little detail I was particularly delighted to hear. How clever of the Summer Lady to hide you with humanity. No one even thought to look for a human child all these years. Even I must admit it was a good move."

"Why? What the hell do you want?"

He watched how my mouth cursed, and his cheek tugged at a grin. "I have a proposition for you."

"You can't be serious?" I leaned away from him. "You had me kidnapped and dragged to your castle like some wild game and thrown at your feet. I'm not some prized doe to be fetched by your minions. I'm a fucking *person*."

The sudden burst of inner rage came out of nowhere. I'd reached my limit for Faerie bullshit.

The Dark Lord inhaled deeply through his perfectly straight nose. "Yes, a mistake I seek to rectify."

"Why the hell would I make any sort of deal with someone like you?"

His brows shot up. "Someone like *me*?"

I lowered my voice. "You had Evaine follow me for

weeks. She attacked my friend. You killed the Seelie king, tried to kill me as a baby, then drove my mother to be the mad queen she is today. You're a monster. *You're* the reason Faerie has fallen into ruin."

He gave me a coy look, but something like regret flashed in his eyes. "Is that what you think happened?"

"I have it on good authority, yeah," I replied. "How can you expect me to agree to anything from you? How can I trust you at all?"

He flexed a leather-gloved hand. "Care to tell me how I might gain your trust, then?"

"You could leave me alone."

"Not an option."

I gnawed at my lip, and his eyes watched with a predatorial stare. My palms were covered in sweat. When would this nightmare end?

As if sensing my unease, Oden shifted. His broad shoulders were relaxed as he straightened and gently grabbed his cane. The storm in his eyes almost seemed to calm.

"How about a gesture of good faith then?" he offered sincerely.

"Would it get you to leave?" When he nodded, I waited in silence, both of us set in a stare-down. "I'm listening."

"A favor of your choosing," he said. "Ask anything of me, and I shall deliver."

"Wait…what?"

"Anything."

"*Anything?* Like, even…*murder?*" I almost laughed, but his expression didn't falter. I swallowed loudly. "Okay, so a gesture of good faith. No strings attached?"

Oden held up open palms. "Not even a thread."

I tipped my chin up. "Call off the deal with the Therians. The whole thing with the Fae blood."

He seemed surprised and amused. "That's it? You could ask anything of me. You could demand my throne, and I'd have no choice but to hand it over to you."

"I don't want anything to do with your damn throne," I told him, and something like awe washed over his expression. "I just want the butchering of innocent Fae to stop."

He gave me a look that said he was surprised I knew about that. "Done."

I narrowed my eyes. "Just like that?"

He snapped his fingers and shot me a grin. "Just like that." He began raking me over again with an unnerving admiration. Like a wild cat watching its prey. "I have no use for it anymore, anyway."

I felt exposed and nervously fiddled with my apron; Tomas would be back any second. I took a quick breath. "Uh, so are we done here?"

"I still haven't told you about my proposition."

"Oh, no, no." I waggled a finger at him. "No deal. Trust is earned over time. Not given on a whim. And I have high doubts you can rise to the occasion."

Oden grinned like a fox. "Very well. In time then." He offered a hand to shake, and I hesitantly accepted it. "Gilded promises are a thing of beauty where I come from, and not often exchanged due to their permanence and the repercussion if broken." The words came out in a raspy purr that tickled my spine. A warning and a promise. Oden released my hand and spun around toward the exit. "It was a pleasure, Avery. I will be in touch."

When the door closed behind him, the air broke, and all sound came rushing back, including the thundering pulse of my heartbeat.

The next day went by in a blur. But my dreams and thoughts were consumed by my interaction with Oden. I dissected it, every word, every facial movement from him. Scouting for signs of deception or misdirection. Lattie once told me that Fae didn't often lie. They could, but they preferred to use words like weapons and forge them into works of art and manipulation. But another thought occurred to me.

How did he get past Tess's wards?

I leaned against the rough exterior of my school while I waited for Tomas and checked my phone again. No reply from Cillian. It'd been days since we last spoke, and my nerves were beginning to fray.

Was he mad that I kicked him out in favor of Max? Did he want space to think about whether he wanted to be with such a chaotic mess as me?

The late Autumn chill whipped around my face, and I zipped my winter jacket all the way to my chin before fetching mittens from my bag. The doors opened, and Tomas stepped out onto the frost-covered sidewalk.

"Sorry," he said. "Had to stay behind and talk to my prof."

"No worries," I replied with a genuine smile. Tomas's golden retriever energy was infectious, always easing the tightness in my chest. "I needed the fresh air anyway."

We began strolling down the street.

"You headed to the gallery tonight?"

My head turned to every fleeting shadow. This time of year in the Maritimes meant shorter days, and the sun was already half set. Evaine would soon be lurking.

"No, I have the night off." I chewed at my lip and tried not to think of Tomas in the hands of Faerie's assassin. "Celadine is renovating the artist's studio upstairs, and we're between showings right now. I'll probably pop in tomorrow evening and catch up on paperwork."

Tomas walked me to the apartment, engaging in general chit-chat about normal things like work and school and what we had for breakfast. It was so refreshing. All the while, I scanned every dark corner for Evaine.

When we got to the back-alley entrance, he said, "Hey, you okay? You seem, I dunno, cagey."

"What?" A nervous laugh rolled out of me. "No! I'm fine, totally fine. I just–" An unusual shadow skittered across the alley floor, and I pulled at his sleeve. "Hey, you want to come up? I think Julie's home. We could veg and watch a movie or three."

Tomas chuckled. "You sure you're okay?" He patted the back of my hand, and I released his arm. "As awesome as that sounds, I'm bound for duty at my parent's restaurant. But I'll take a rain check."

"You can't skip it?"

He eyed me curiously with unplaced worry. "Skip out on my Korean parents? No, I value my life."

The shadows cleared as twilight filled the alley, casting it in a silvery glow, and I let my lungs deflate a little. "Fine, but promise you'll go straight there? No stops? No short-cuts down dark streets?"

Tomas's face became awash with realization. "Oh, I get it. Is this about your parents?"

My heart jumped in my throat, but then I remembered he knew the lie about my parents being murdered here in the city. Not the far more tragic and twisted truth of who my real parents were. I sighed, my shoulders slumping.

"Yeah, it, uh, it happened right around this time of year. I just get nervous for the people I care about."

The corners of his eyes pinched with his wide smile. "I was gonna catch the bus, but I can grab a cab."

"Would you?" I practically jumped at the idea. "Go wait in the café?"

He nodded and pulled me in for a hug. I stood there and watched him walk to the mouth of the alley until he was safe inside the coffee shop—well, as safe as possible—before I ran up the stairs and entered my apartment.

I was wrong about Julie. She wasn't home. I turned on a few lamps, grabbed a banana from the basket on the table, and viscously ate it while pacing the living room. I was rarely alone. Between school and my many jobs, plus training… I hadn't realized how much I depended on it to keep up the blanket of denial I wrapped around myself.

I could hear every clock in the apartment ticking away. Outside, the city lived and breathed under the night sky. Inside, the silence was crippling.

I sucked the last of the banana from my teeth as I marched to my room and opened the door. Cillian leaned with one leg propped up on the window sill. A black v-neck teased at his chest; a fitted blazer hid his muscled arms. I wanted to rip it from his body…but also slap him in the face.

I sighed, crossed my arms, and kicked my hip to the

side. "I have a front door, you know."

Cillian swung around and put both feet on the floor. "Yeah, but where's the fun in that?"

We stared at one another, both waiting for the other to speak.

"I'm sorry for not being here," he said after a moment, mesmerizing me with those lips. "I was blocking Cellie out. When I finally checked in, the visuals came through. She told me everything, and I flew home immediately."

"Where were you?"

He smoothed back a rogue strand of hair. "England. Making a deal with another gallery. I tend to get lost in work when I need to…process things."

I nodded and stepped further into the room. "I get it. I do the same."

"How's Max?" He actually seemed sincere.

"She's… I'm not sure. She was alive and okay when she left here, but I hadn't seen her since. She hasn't even been to class."

"Are you worried Evaine took her again?"

I chewed at my lip and sat on my bed. Half a second later, he joined me. My knee brushed his leg, and a rush of goosebumps raced under my clothes.

"No, Evaine got what she needed from her." I wondered then if her job was done. Did Oden hire her to follow and kidnap me, and that's it? If so, her job would technically be done. Was Evaine even a threat anymore?

Something deep in my gut told me I was wrong. Evaine would always be a threat. I could see it in her eyes when she looked at me. Pure hatred. It went beyond anything anyone would hire her for. She wanted me dead.

"Maybe swing by her apartment tomorrow?" he suggested, his hand next to mine on the mattress. I nodded as he slipped his fingers into mine and brought my knuckles to his lips. "I missed you. Let's not do this again." When I quietly laughed, he added, "Be friends with whoever you want. It's not my call to make." He brought his other hand up and dragged a thumb across my mouth. "Just don't expect me to like her."

I snorted. "I barely like her myself."

Cillian released my hand, cupped my face in his palms, and stared into my eyes. "You're extraordinary."

Wetness brimmed around my eyes. "Cillian."

"I'm serious. Look at all you're facing, all that you're uncovering. My God, you've barely even *lived*." He put his forehead to mine and sighed. "I shouldn't be adding to that stress."

I slipped my fingers over his chest. "I can deal with everything else. The only thing that keeps me up at night is worrying I'll hurt you."

He stiffened slightly at my touch, and I witnessed him growing against the inside of his pants. I gripped his side, and he wrapped a hand around the back of my head, holding me close as his mouth hovered over mine.

"Don't worry about me."

"How can you say that? I can't control this. I think–" His other hand reached down and gripped my ass. He tugged me into his lap and dragged his fingers down my thigh in one swift movement. A shiver rolled through me. "I think it's because I'm mostly human."

His mouth smiled against mine, and he laid a gentle kiss there. "For a human, you're capable of far more than you know."

I immediately thought of the gilded promise Oden had made to me. I may have ended the problem with missing Fae and the illegal trade of their blood on the Black Market. But now wasn't the time to mention that to my boyfriend. If he was upset about me being friends with a Therian, he'd lose his damn mind if he knew I'd made some sort of deal with a High Fae Lord.

"Your powers were born in an immortal's body. We're still not sure of your mortality. You just need time to figure it all out. And I'll be right here every step of the way."

Cillian's fingertips slipped under my shirt and fanned over my back, pulling me closer to his lap. I gently rolled my hips once, skimming over him, and he moaned against my throat, eliciting a similar response from me as I wrapped my arms around his neck.

The nightly chill that lived in him met the constant low burn of my skin and wrapped us both in a thick blanket as Cillian cradled me in his arms. He turned his head and placed his ear to my chest, listening to a few heartbeats before dragging his lips over the crest of my cleavage. His fingers dug into the skin of my back, and I raked my hands through his hair.

I wanted him. All of him, everywhere. Call it what you will, a predatory lure, a vampire's charm; I didn't care. He was mine; I was his, and nothing else existed. Just two bodies writhing together as one, sharing a heartbeat—*my* heartbeat—breathing the same hormone-infused air.

Cillian slipped a hand between us, dipping inside the rim of my pants, and I shifted slightly to give him more room. Cool lips claimed my throat while able fingertips caressed my most sensitive place. My body responded to his touch like a starved animal, and I gave a little hip roll, encouraging him. But he didn't need it. Cillian molded me in his expert hands, and the world fell away as he worked to bring me closer and closer to climax.

I felt it building, like a boulder rolling downward, gaining speed and barrelling toward a messy end. I couldn't help but think that's all we were. Mortals and immortals; moments of pain and pleasure hurdling toward chaotic ends.

"Oh, God, Cillian…"

"I've had thousands of years to contemplate my death," he whispered warmly against my skin, never breaking his stride, and my skin shivered, desperate to be set free from the confines of my clothing. "Nothing or no one ever seemed worthy of it." The words spilled over me between consuming kisses, and I tossed my head back, giving full access to my throat. It was an offer of trust to expose myself to him–to a vampire–that way. "But to die by your flame…." His fingers quickened their pace, taunting my release. "I'd lay down and welcome it."

Cillian gripped the collar of my shirt and yanked it down over my shoulder, extending his kisses while the space between my legs grew warmer and wetter. I slowly rocked with the guidance of his strong fingers, chasing the high, reaching for that pinnacle of bliss.

A growl rumbled in his chest as he ripped my shirt entirely away, the shreds of it falling to the floor. It only took one hand and a quick flick to undo my bra, and my breasts bared to him. He took one in his mouth, and I cast my face to the unseen stars.

"Cilli–"

He sealed his name in my mouth with a kiss so hard I whimpered. We practically devoured one another, and nothing else was left in the world except us. And, for a moment, I didn't worry about the summer flame that lived deep inside me. Didn't even think about it.

We moved together like a single wave, and he held the cusp of my release in his hands. He glanced up at me, and that cerulean gaze latched onto mine. I could hardly stand the raw immortal beauty of the man beneath me, delivering pleasure like some unknown god.

I brought my mouth down on his, dragging my teeth across his bottom lip, and his entire body tensed in response, deepening the kiss. He knew exactly what to do and where to do it, and I relaxed into his touch, letting him possess my body.

Hot and rapid breaths entwined, I found my release, and Cillian held on until the very last drop. I melted in his arms, and everything sputtered out, but he wasn't done. I let out a yelp as he swiftly threw me down on the bed and hauled my pants off. His cool fingers slid down my bare thighs as he positioned himself, and I scrambled for his belt.

I couldn't get enough of him. I needed every inch of him inside me, and when he freed himself, I was reminded how many inches it was and swallowed dryly before he gently inserted the tip. Cillian looked into my eyes, and we took a deep breath before he plunged himself to the hilt. I cried out as pains of pleasure and bliss swarmed in my head.

Every thrust touched a part of me that had never been touched before, and I craved more. I didn't want it to end. And when his muscles pulled tautly and his back arched, I rode the wave with him, finding my release for the second time.

We fell asleep in one another's arms as a gentle winter breeze drifted in from the open window. But Cillian's touch couldn't chase away the nightmares. Inescapable darkness.

I lay atop a mountain of hot ash and pushed myself to my knees. I scooped my fingers through it, smoke billowed, bits of bone fell to the ground, and my friends' screams filled my ears.

***

Barren trees lined the streets downtown as I walked to Max's brownstone basement apartment. Her garden was dying, and the door was ajar. I pushed it open and stepped inside. Max laid face up on her green velvet sofa. A full head of black curls fanned out around her as puffy, tired eyes stared at the ceiling.

The kitchen was a disaster. Bowls and wooden spoons and herbs of all kinds were strewn about. I spotted several open books tossed in the mix, too.

"What do *you* want?" Max drawled drunkenly from the couch. That's when I noticed the floor littered with vodka bottles.

"You haven't been to class," I said and eyed the wrinkles

in her oversized black t-shirt. It looked like she'd had it on for days. "And I hadn't heard from you since–"

"Leave."

"What?" Her response was a glare so deadly my throat tightened at the sight of it. But I dared move closer to her. "Max, what's going on?" I knelt next to her. "What happened with Evaine, I can't even imagine how horrible it must have been. But I'm here. You can talk to me. I can help you through it."

"Help?" she spat and flew upright. "What could you possibly do to help?"

"I dunno," I replied, at a loss for words. "What do you need?"

She bolted to her feet and stomped over to the kitchen. She grabbed one of the books. "Do you have a spell to reverse it?"

I blinked through my surprise. "What–"

"How about a curse to stop the change?"

I shook my head, confused by the manic outburst and what she was asking.

Max tossed the book on the cluttered table. "Or an enchanted dagger to drive through my heart and put me out of my misery?"

"Jesus, Max, what are you *talking* about?"

Tears welled in her eyes, spilling out over the tired, puffy skin underneath. "Therians can change at any age, but they can only assume the form of their parents. They can choose their own form if they wait until they're twenty years old before their first change. Any being, any animal. But we've been wolves since we stepped foot in Ironworld because we've been forced to."

The words flew around in my mind, dropping into place like mad libs as I fought to understand. Max wiped the snot and tears from her face with the back of her hand.

"No Therian has chosen a form in centuries. Not since their fall from grace in Faerie," she continued, her voice finally settling. "I was going to be the first. I was waiting, stifling it with herbs and potions and spells. I learned witchcraft to keep it at bay, much to my mother's dismay."

"What were you going to choose?"

She shrugged carelessly and swiped a near-empty bottle of vodka from beside the sink. She swallowed the last of it. "I have no idea, but that's not the point. The point is that I *had* a choice."

Everything fell into place, and my heart sunk to the bottom of my gut. She was a wolf when we'd found her that night. Evaine must have given her no choice but to defend herself. "Oh my god, Max… I'm so sorry."

"Sorry?" she said with a teary laugh. "You're *sorry*?" She threw the bottle in the sink, where it smashed, and I flinched. Maybe coming here was a bad idea. "What does it matter now, anyway. I'm a wolf. It's done. My mother got what she wanted."

I'd done this. Everything that happened to her was my fault. Evaine attacked her to get to me, but it destroyed Max's life.

"Sorry is all I can say," I told her sincerely. "I know nothing else…no other words can make this better. But I'm here. I'm your friend, whether you like it or not. I'm not going anywhere." She shot me another death glare. "I mean in life. I can clearly see you want me to leave, and I will. But I just wanted to make sure you were okay."

"Get out."

"Max–"

"I said get out!" she growled, and her dark brown eyes glowed as two pointed teeth shot down. Her fingertips turned into claws, tearing through a chair like butter. "Get out, Quinn, before I gut you on my fucking floor!"

I turned and ran, slamming the door behind me.

I bolted all the way home under the twilight sky and collapsed on the bottom step of the alley stairway, heaving for breath. My nerves thrummed like static. The early winter chill couldn't touch the heat that blazed around me.

I'd ruined Max's life. My lungs burned, but I couldn't peel myself from the step. My feet felt like lead blocks. I'd ruined so many people's lives, and the more I thought about it, the deeper it cut. I was like poison. Tess, Kheelan, my mother, Max, and I constantly put my friends in danger just by my mere existence.

Cillian dropped from the sky in an inky blaze, his shadows trailing behind him. They tucked away as he walked over to me.

"What happened?"

"Max," I sobbed. "She had never changed before; she didn't want to. She spent her entire life preventing it, only for Evaine to force it, and now her life is ruined because of me."

He sighed and squatted down next to me. "Don't get mixed up in their world, Avery."

"How can you say that?"

Cillian pursed his lips and moved my hair away from my face with a single fingertip. "The further you distance yourself from the affairs of mythical creatures, the better off you'll be. They'll either reject you, use you, or get you killed."

My mouth gaped soundlessly as I fought for words. "I–I can't just walk away from this."

"Yes, you can. I have. Cellie has. Our world rejected us, and we just let it. We're better for it."

I looked him square in the eyes. "Cillian. I'm the missing heir to the Seelie throne. The Lady of Summer kidnapped me as a baby and made me human. I'm dating a vampire. His sister is my mentor, my best friends are fairies, and I just ruined the life of another friend who happens to be a werewolf. I'm smack dab in the middle of it."

He pushed to his feet and paced in front of me. "But you don't have to be! You can leave it all behind and live a normal life. I can take you anywhere you want in this world."

I found the strength to stand and balled my fists at my sides. "Are you suggesting I run away from this colossal mess I've made?"

"You didn't make anything, Avery." He took one long stride toward me and grabbed both my hands. "Everything that's happened and ever will happen is not your fault but the fault of ageless, petulant monsters who will never quench their thirst for power."

Emotions boiled inside me, and I fought back the wave of tears that pushed its way up. My skin crawled with heat as my dormant power awoke and searched for a way out. I tried to reign it in, but it was no use. Light burst from my hands, and Cillian leaped backward with a hiss.

I quickly hid my hands beneath my jacket and hunched over myself as I turned from him. The tears came then, and I let them.

"Avery," he said with surprising calm.

He reached for me, and I scrambled away. "Leave."

"You're crazy if you think I'm leaving you like—"

"*Leave*, Cillian!" I screamed, suddenly relating to Max. "Before I fucking *kill* you!"

Pain flashed across his face.

"Please, leave," I sobbed, my knees wobbling. "I—I don't

want you here." That wasn't true, but I knew that's what it would take to make him go.

He hesitated but said nothing else before he took off into the sky. I crumbled to the ground and curled my knees to my chest as I buried my face and wept.

I had no idea how long I sat there, but the well of tears had run dry when footsteps approached, sauntering toward me with a purposeful stride. I lifted my head just a little, enough to spot the shiny, black leather boots as they stopped at my feet. I knew who it was and buried my face again with a grumble.

"Are you ready to hear my proposition now?"

I slowly lifted my head, baring my puffy red, tear-stained face to the Dark Lord of Nightmares. He opened his mouth to speak but flexed his gloved hand instead.

"Why can't you all just leave me alone?"

Oden smacked his lips and glanced around the empty alley. "Look, Avery, I'm only going to offer this once."

"I don't want anything from you."

"What if I said I could teach you to harness and control your pesky powers?"

I wiped the half-frozen wetness from my eyes as I blinked at him. "You can do that?"

Oden tipped his head and gave me a look that said, *Oh, please.* "You know I can." He was right. He'd touched me just once, and the control I'd felt at that moment was intoxicating. "Come to my kingdom, spend time in my domain, and I promise to teach you to master your powers."

I grimaced. "You can't be serious."

"As serious as death, my dear Avery." He glanced about with a particular distaste. He must have genuinely hated the mortal realm. "The full moon is the apex of magic. It's when it's the strongest and most malleable. Spend each full moon with me in training. I'll show you the berth of your magic, how to wield it, control it, protect yourself." His mouth turned up with a half grin. "And your mongrel friends."

"First of all," I spat and stood up. "Don't call them that."

He gave a smug smile, and something like delight warmed his expression as if he enjoyed how I spoke to him. He was a Fae Lord. He was probably used to groveling and sniveling at his feet.

I thought about the offer. As much as I wanted to reject it, to throw it back in his face, it was far too tempting. Moya was getting nowhere with me. Julie was busy with her own stuff. And Tess…Tess wasn't even an option. Oden might be my only hope in hell of getting this thing under control.

He exhaled loudly through his nose and stuffed a hand in the pocket of his charcoal slacks. "I'm only offering this once, here and now. If I walk away, so does any chance you have."

I chewed at my lip. "What do you get in return?"

Oden chuckled under his breath. "I'll call in that

favor later."

"No, I demand to know before I agree to anything."

With an eye roll, he put a thumb to my forehead, and I was immediately transported to a vision of some kind. But not in my mind…in his. A battlefield of hot ash stretched for miles, bits, and pieces of bodies strewn about. Wolves gnawed at severed limbs and tore innards from the dying. I peered down at my feet and saw that I stood on a pile of hot ash, and as I bent down to scoop it through my fingers, I realized that perhaps the image was from my mind. I'd dreamed of this before.

As quickly as he'd shown me, I was ripped from the scene in a single gasp.

"If you want to prevent that," he said solemnly. "I'd say it's in your best interests to hone your powers. Regardless of what I ask of you."

Did I really have a choice here? I'd said I couldn't walk away from the mess I'd caused. I wanted to help. I wanted to fit into this magical world. To be useful, to…belong.

"You can't hurt me while I'm there," I said, and I could have sworn his shoulders relaxed.

"Not a single hair on that pretty head of yours."

"And I want your sworn promise that Evaine will leave my friends and me alone."

Oden quirked a brow and gripped the dragon's head on his cane with both hands. Was he mad that I added to the bargain? The grin of approval he failed to hide to me otherwise.

"Done," he replied and offered me his hand. I stared at it for a moment. "Unless there's something else you'd like to add?"

The sarcasm lacing his words told me I'd better not, and I squared my jaw. "No, I'm fine with the terms."

I slipped my hand into his, surprised by the warmth seeping through his glove. His fingers tightened, and he yanked me close. His breath warmed my face as he peered down at me, lightning flashing in his eyes.

Suddenly, the base of my spine burned, making my back arch and my knees buckle. It felt like someone pressed hot coals to it. A scream erupted from me, I could barely stay on my feet, but Oden gripped my hand as he watched me suffer, refusing to release me.

When the searing subsided, he finally let go, and I crumpled to the ground.

"Excellent, I'll see you in two days. Don't be late."

I flipped my hair back and whipped my head upward, gawking at the nearly full moon.

"Pleasure, as always, Avery dear," Oden added and snapped his fingers, disappearing in the blink of an eye.

I scrambled to my feet and ran up the stairs, bolting for my bedroom. I shut the door behind me and stood before the floor-length mirror. Something tugged at the skin around the base of my spine. With a deep breath, I removed my shirt and turned, peering over my shoulder to see my reflection, and a gasp froze in my throat.

My skin was tattooed with a full moon flanked by two halves. Three moons for three days. A gilded promise and a painful reminder of what I'd done.

I made a deal with the devil.

Chapter Eight

Sleep be damned, I raced to the Black Market. The mundane storefront was long closed like most businesses downtown, but I slipped around back and entered through a loading door reserved only for people like me.

The shop owner sat in an oversized chair, legs draped over one side as they read a book. They took one sweeping look at me and sniffed the air before giving a nod of approval. I could proceed. I didn't expect to feel relief, but there it was.

I parted the black beaded curtain and entered the real Black Market. Giant pots clanked, and steam billowed from the food vendors. Colors and sounds danced in the air as others mended broken wings and traded beautiful linens woven of materials I'd never seen before. I whipped past tables and booths offering trinkets and tools. But I didn't need any of it. I knew exactly where I was headed.

I stopped outside the fabric tent of The Blood Reader and steadied my breath before parting the drape and stepping into darkness. A candle sparked to life, illuminating a small table with two chairs. One was occupied by The Reader–his pale skin, gouged eye sockets, and russet-stained mouth not failing to elicit a cringe from me.

He grinned wildly. "You dare come empty-handed?"

Shit. I still needed to earn some of the Faerie coins my friends always had. "I need your help."

Those long fingers curled together on the table. "Not without payment."

"Can't you just do this one, like, pro bono or something? I'm desperate here."

He took a big, long whiff of the space between us. "You've done much since we last met." His hands moved through the air as if he were conducting a symphony. "Found your power, returned the lost Lady of Summer to her throne, even drove a wedge in the trade of innocent blood. Impressive, Avery Quinn."

I swallowed hard, ignoring the fact that he knew my full name. "That's not all I've done–"

He waved a hand to cut me off. "Payment."

I groaned in frustration and searched my body, patting down my pockets and inspecting my hands. My thumb ring. A simple but thick gold band that Tess gave me for my birthday a few years ago. I plucked it off my thumb and tossed it on the table.

"There," I said. "It's solid gold. Will that do?"

The Reader pinched it between his fingers and ran it under his nose. "Yes. This will do just fine." He motioned to the other chair. "Have a seat, child."

"I'm not a child," I said and sat down.

He chuckled quietly. "*A* child, no."

I shook my head, ignoring his gibberish nonsense. "Look, I made a deal with the Dark Lord of Nightmares, and I need to know if it was a mistake. Have I put myself or my friends in further danger? Is there a way out of the bargain?"

"Do you *want* out of the bargain?"

I thought for a moment. "I just want to know if there's a way out if I wanted one."

The Reader held out his palm on the table and gestured for my hand. I placed it in his, and he flicked a fingernail across my skin so fast I hardly saw it. With a gentle squeeze, blood oozed to the surface, and I fought against my rising stomach as he dabbed a little on his fingertip and wiped it on his tongue.

He rolled it around his mouth for a moment, humming and hawing at whatever he saw; however it came to him. I wondered if things came to him as they did for me. As visions and dreams invade my mind. Or was it more of a feeling? Maybe it was a whisper only he could hear.

"The Dark Lord promises to help you."

"Yes."

"With something no one else can."

"Correct."

"Are you afraid of him, or do you fear what you might become if he succeeds in helping you?"

I hadn't really thought about it. "I…I'm not afraid of him."

A wicked half-grin spoiled his mouth. "Nor should you be."

I leaned forward. "So, I'm not in danger by spending time in his domain?"

"The bargain you made states that no harm can come to you while there, no?"

How he knew those details gave me an unsettling feeling. "Well, yeah, but–"

"What is it you truly seek, then, child?"

I leaned back in the chair and crossed my arms as I stewed my thoughts.

The Reader's chin lifted as he seemed to see something else. "Oh, you worry for your vampire. That he won't love you when he finds out."

"That's just part of it," I replied honestly. "I guess I'm wondering about the uncertain. I've been having these dreams, these…visions. Flashes, really, of a massacre. I'm worried that maybe I'm the cause of it. If I go to his domain and learn to harness my magic…."

"You fear what you might become."

I just nodded.

He turned my ring in his fingers and stared at it with those dark pits as if he could see beyond it, this tent, even this world. Something made him smile endearingly, and he plunked the ring down on the table just inches in front of me. I gave him a puzzling look.

"You are in no danger from the Lord," the Blood Reader assured. "I can't say the same for his domain, but you must uphold your end of the bargain. Just be careful. Your friends will understand. Your vampire might take a while to warm up to the idea, but he ultimately knows it's unavoidable. As for who or what you might become…that's in your hands, child."

I slipped my ring back on my thumb as I mulled over his words. Even though he told me what I already suspected, the words gave me a sense of calm and assurance I never realized I needed until I heard them. My breathing slowed, and my heart settled. I'd made a bargain with a Dark Lord, but I don't think it was a mistake.

I stood up from the chair. "Thank you for your time."

As I walked toward the slit in the curtain, the Reader cleared his throat. "Avery." The way he spoke my name almost sounded human, and I looked over my shoulder.

"Everything you're about to face in the coming weeks is nothing compared to what your mother has planned for you." He may as well have kicked me in the gut. No one knew who my real mother was except me, Julie, Moya, and Tess. "Learn all you can from the Dark Lord. You'll need it."

I opened my mouth to demand an explanation, but the Blood Reader disappeared. I fled the Black Market for home, making sure to be as quiet as possible when I arrived to not wake Julie. I had no idea what time of night it was, but I felt the downward pull of sleep call.

I cringed as my bedroom door creaked and sighed as I locked it behind me.

"Where have you been?"

I yelped and threw my back up against the door. Cillian sat on the edge of my bed, twiddling his phone in his hands. Those blue eyes cut deep as he lifted his gaze to me.

I stole a glance at my phone. It sat on my dresser where I'd left it. "Sorry. I didn't even think to take my cell."

"Where the hell did you run off to in such a hurry that you didn't even take your phone?" His voice bogged down with worry and exhaustion. "At two in the morning."

"The Blood Reader."

Cillian's dark brows rose beneath the curtain of black hair.

My feet were leaden as I shuffled to the bed and sat

next to him. "After we…after you left…The Dark Lord of Nightmares came to me. He offered to help me learn to control my magic. I agreed out of desperation. The panic came later when I lay in bed, staring at the ceiling. I needed some kind of assurance and answers, so I went to see The Blood Reader."

"In exchange for what?"

I gave him a puzzled look. "What?"

"The Dark Lord offered you something. Fae never offer anything willingly. What did he demand in exchange?"

I swallowed nervously, and my throat tightened. "He said he'd call in that favor later."

"What?" Cillian shot up from the bed. "Are you insane?"

Somehow, I found the strength to stand. "I don't need your permission to make my own decisions, Cillian."

"No, clearly not." His arms slapped at his sides before running his fingers through his hair, pulling it taut as his eyes glossed over. "God, what have you done?"

"He's the only one who can help me."

Cillian took one long stride toward me and gripped my arms, holding them tightly. I had to look away from the pain I found in his eyes. "He can literally ask anything of you, Avery. Anything. Do you understand that? He could ask you to slit your own throat, and the bargain would bind you. You'd drop to your knees without hesitation and cut *deeply*."

"I don't think he'd do that."

"Yeah?" He pursed his lips. "You guys besties now? You think someone named *The Dark Lord of Nightmares* is on your side?"

I shrugged out of his grip. "What's done is done. The bargain also binds him to help me. If he taught me how to control this, then it wouldn't matter what he asks of me. I'd turn him to ash before he muttered a word."

Cillian turned toward the window, shaking his head as he chuckled madly. "I can't believe you did this."

"I did it for us," I replied.

"For us?"

Rage boiled in my gut as it fought for space with the heartache I felt. "So, I don't fucking *kill* you, Cillian!" I held out my hands, palms up, and stared at them in disgust. "I'm almost afraid to touch you now."

His shoulders sank, and he tipped his head to the side. "I'm not afraid of you." His voice was calm. "You can't hurt me."

Tears brimmed my eyes. "Then you're a fool to think that because I've already proved I can. And I will again, and again…and again." I tried to swallow, but my throat was too dry. "Until I don't."

The grim weight of my words fell over us, and the room became silent. Only our labored breaths, wrought with emotion, filled the air.

When the painful silence became too much, I said quietly, "Just let me do this. Let me get better so we can be together, and I don't have to worry about turning you to ash every time I get upset. You've been alive for thousands of years, don't get taken out now. Not by me." I reached and took his hand, and his returning squeeze relaxed my heart. "You don't have to worry about me. The bargain will protect me. I made sure of it." Something like guilt flashed in his eyes as I peered up at him. "Unless that's not what you're worried about."

"No, it is. I swear. It's just–"

"You don't trust me."

"I trust you," he said firmly, and I believed him. "I think it's pretty evident how I blatantly disregard my life to be with you. I just don't trust *him*."

"Don't turn this into a pissing contest."

"How can I not, Avery? Think about it. The Dark Lord of Nightmares hired the world's most dangerous spy and assassin to find you. *You*. He wants you, whether for your power, body, or heart. Oden wants you, needs *you* for something. And you've just rolled out the red carpet right to his door."

I hadn't thought it all through, but Cillian was right. I'd never admit it, though. He released my hand and let it fall to my side as he turned for the window. Crouched over the sill, ready to leap, he threw half a glance over his shoulder.

"When you're not too proud to admit it, come find me."

***

Julie took a shot and sunk one of her balls as I rounded the corner of the pool table. Lattie fluttered about, cloaked to mundanes, stealing their fries and chicken fingers. Whispers and low chatter filled the old Irish pub we frequented, complaints about missing food.

"No Tomas tonight?" I asked her and checked my phone. "I texted him earlier."

Julie's cheeks flushed as she readied for another shot. "No, he's busy."

"You were talking to him?

She took the shot a little stiff and missed. "No, I just figured."

I sighed and gripped my pool stick in both hands as I put my weight on it. "Okay, look, are you guys fighting or something? I thought you were together."

"We were–are…." Julie pinched the bridge of her nose. "I'm…I don't know right now."

"Hey," I said calmly and smoothed her arm. "Talk to me. What's going on? I feel like we haven't had a moment to ourselves in weeks."

She shrugged. "We both have shit going on."

Lattie must have ventured into the kitchen. Sounds of metal and glass clanking erupted from the back and shouts of something about a bat. Spotted her fluttering back to our table with some raw chicken wings in her grip.

Julie rolled her eyes. "Get your pet in order, or she can't come to mundane spots like this."

"She's not my pet," I replied and crooked my finger at Lattie. She narrowed her eyes and buzzed over to me. "Look, you can't be bothering the humans, okay? If you're hungry, go outside and hunt."

A low hiss rasped in her tiny throat. "Don't chase the cats, Lattie. Don't bring rats home, Lattie. Don't pester the humans, Lattie." She tore off a giant chunk of fleshy chicken with those pointed teeth. "I grow tired of this bind, Avery Quinn."

"You and me both. If I knew how to sever it without killing one of us, I would do it in a heartbeat, you little mongrel." She hissed at me, but I smiled and threw her a wink. She was a nightmare sometimes, but I secretly adored her. I turned back to Julie. "So, Tomas?"

She groaned. "He might be avoiding me."

"What? Why? That doesn't make any sense," I said. "The last time I spoke to him, he seemed worried about you."

"Okay, fine. Maybe I'm avoiding him."

"Jules."

She took a long swig of her drink. "He told me he loved me."

I gasped. "What did you say?"

"I wanted to say it back," she replied sadly, staring off. "But then I thought of everything happening, all the danger constantly surrounding us, and then what happened to Max…."

Guilt hit the bottom of my stomach like an anvil. "You don't want to put him in danger."

She nodded.

"Jules, I'm sorry." Before she could object, I added, "None of this would be happening if it weren't for me."

"Av', you have nothing to be sorry for. None of this is your fault. The Fae and Therians have been fickle and viscous since the beginning of time." Lattie picked at gum underneath one of the tables, and Julie sighed as she grabbed her jacket. "Come on, let's get home."

We stepped out into the frosty evening, and I zipped my jacket up to my chin.

"Are you ready for tomorrow?"

I crossed my arms as we walked and pressed my lips together in thought. "As ready as one could be for going to a place literally called Nightmares."

"I still can't believe you made a bargain with the Dark Lord without at least talking to me first." I knew she was kidding, but when I didn't so much as chuckle, she added,

"Are you nervous?"

"The Blood Reader told me I had nothing to fear from Oden," I said. "And…I believe him. He just said to watch out for the domain. I'm guessing the Dark Fae are as bad as they sound." I failed to mention the bit he'd told me about my mother.

"Yeah, think Club Umbra but, like, times ten."

We rounded a corner and wove in and out of a crowd headed to the bars.

"So, you're really going through with it, then?"

"I have to, Jules. It's literally marked on my skin in melted gold. If this is how a promise with High Fae is sealed, I don't even want to know what would happen if I broke my word."

"Not pretty things."

Lattie fluttered around my head. "To cleave a bargain is to cleave part of your soul. Part of you would die. At best, your skin might slough from your bones. You could go deaf and blind or spew innards whenever you spoke."

"Geez, thanks for the traumatizing mental image," I grumbled.

Julie threw an arm around my shoulders as we headed for home. "Bring me back a souvenir?"

Chapter Nine

The next evening came too fast. That morning I'd received a fire message from Oden that simply said, *Waterfront. Seven o'clock.*

I left my apartment around six and headed for Celadine's in hopes I'd find Cillian and get to say goodbye. He hadn't responded to any of my texts. Maybe he was off in another foreign country again, blowing off steam. Perhaps I wouldn't even get to say goodbye.

I pushed open the heavy black iron gate and walked along the old paver stones embedded in the ground as I gripped both straps of my backpack. I had no idea what to bring for a three-day trip to the Domain of Nightmares, so I just brought the essentials; a few pairs of jeans, a couple t-shirts, underwear, socks, deodorant, and a toothbrush.

"Avery, what a pleasant surprise," Celadine greeted me from the solarium door. Even on the cusp of winter, she found a way to grow her garden of black dahlias, irises, and various foliage. She was draped from head to toe in violet silk, tied at her waist with a black sash. Only the hint of her stunning tattoos peeked up from her neckline. "I thought you had other arrangements this evening?"

I stuffed my hands in my jacket pockets. "I had some time to kill before I go."

She tipped her head to the side, her heap of braids and dreads shifting slightly. "He's not here." I nodded and pretended something across the private yard caught my attention. "I'm not sure where he is, actually. He's blocking me out again."

"Figures."

"Do you have time for tea?"

I smiled. "Yeah, that sounds nice."

I followed her inside the modest Victorian mansion and sat on one of the pristine white chaises while she prepared tea in the kitchen. I never saw staff here, not so much as a random cleaner. I wondered how Celadine kept this place so neat and tidy. The dark wainscotting never had a speck of dust on it. The place was like something ripped straight out of a story about a Victorian witch. Fitting.

She entered from the kitchen with a silver tray in her hands; mugs and a teapot, tiny jugs for milk and sugar, and a strange rectangular black box. Celadine set the tray on the table closest to me and took a seat at my side.

I peered inside my mug and saw a glob of honey. "Earl Grey?"

She grinned. "Of course."

"Are you okay at the gallery without me around for a few days?"

"Oh please," she guffawed, her bracelets jingling as she waved her hand at me. "We don't have a showing booked for weeks. This is always a downtime for the gallery. Use it to your advantage." She crossed one leg over the other, and the purple kimono slipped one down her thigh, revealing even more cool tattoos. "And I told you to take time to learn your magic. You have a–"

"Grand existence," I said with her, and we both laughed. "Yeah, yeah, I know." My lungs filled with a sigh, and I wrought my hands together. "I guess we'll see, won't we?"

She leaned over and grabbed the black box. "This is for you."

I slowly took it from her and ran my fingers over the suede-like surface. "What is this? Is this a *gift*? Celadine, you didn't have to get me a gift."

"Just open it," she insisted, flashing those violet eyes.

I plucked the top off. A small knife sat in black satin with a hilt wrapped in leather and a dark, shiny metal for the blade. I picked it up. "Why is it so heavy?"

"Most swords and daggers are forged of steel," Celadine told me. "That one dagger is made of iron."

"Oh…" Iron could harm, sometimes even kill, Fae. I rubbed my finger over the side of the blade. "It feels staticy."

"I figured you could withstand it, being mostly human." She gestured to the box. "There's a sheath for it underneath."

I pulled away the silky fabric and found a brown leather sheath. The blade slipped in perfectly, nice and snug, and I stood up to attach it to my belt.

"Thank you," I said sincerely. "I love it."

She smiled up at me. "I'm glad." She patted the couch for me to sit down again and leaned over to pour the tea.

The dagger fit perfectly, hidden beneath my jacket, and didn't dig into my side when I sat. Like it was made for me.

I got to the boardwalk by seven but had no idea what part Oden would be waiting at. The thing stretched on forever around the downtown coast of the Halifax harbor. So, I just waltzed along. The November full moon was like a bright medallion beaming down at me.

"Are you ready?" Oden said from behind, and I spun around with a startle.

I tugged at my backpack straps and glanced around, hoping to see Cillian. It didn't feel right to leave without saying goodbye.

"Avery?" Oden said and held out a gloved hand.

I stole one more look around and heaved a sigh as I

slipped my hand in his just as Cillian dropped from the sky in a dark, inky blaze.

"Avery!"

I took a step for him, but Oden gripped my hand tightly, and the world fell away as his hollow, raspy cackle echoed in my mind.

In only a moment, we stepped through the fabric of space and time, and I stepped foot on the dirt path that led to a castle in the distance. Oden slowly spun to face me, and I slapped his cheek with everything I had. He barely flinched but gawked at me with mock pain.

"You could have let me say goodbye!"

He put a hand to my throat, just enough to keep me in place, and I shuddered at the raging storm I witnessed in his eyes. "Let me make one thing very clear, right here, right now. I will not bend nor yield to anyone, much less a vampire. You made the bargain, Miss Quinn. We're on my time now. And I am Lord of this Domain. You will treat me as such."

And I would not bend or yield to *him*. I slapped his hand away and squared my jaw. "As long as we're making up rules, don't fucking touch me again."

We engaged in a stare-down heightened with stubbornness and rage on both ends. Finally, he turned from me in a huff.

"Come," he said curtly. I hesitated but sped after him.

"You're free to roam the mansion. The courtyard outside, as well. Use the grounds as you wish, ride our horses, explore the libraries, employ my staff to your needs." He stopped abruptly and glared down at me. "But stay away from the Dark Forest. You'll find nothing but death in there."

I pursed my lips, trying to hide the tremble I felt in my knees. "Noted."

Oden continued up the path. "There are no water sources around the mansion, so don't even think about traveling in or out or inviting friends. No one can wisp to the main house. Only I can."

That explains why I've always been brought to the edge of the property. "Anything else I should be aware of? Should I start writing this down?"

"You could watch the sarcasm."

"Nope."

He grumbled under his breath. "I'll show you to your quarters. There's a fully stocked wardrobe. Choose something appropriate and join us for dinner. I have guests, so I expect you to look presentable."

"I didn't come here for dinner parties, Oden."

He swung a large wooden door hanging on creaky hinges and stepped inside. "Yes, while I'd love nothing more than to take three days off from my duties to teach some wayward human magic, I'm a Lord." I followed him through the winding corridors and the lower-level rooms. "I have meetings and duties that simply can't be pushed aside." He touched my arm, and, in a blink, we stood outside a beautiful door covered in ornate carvings of vines. "This is where you'll be staying. Dress. I'll have someone come and assist you. Meet us downstairs in an hour."

"I don't need help—"

He snapped his fingers and disappeared.

Fuming, I pushed open the heavy door and let it fall closed behind me as I stood and took in the enormity of my room. It was like a studio apartment nestled in a wing made of stone with a giant canopy bed to the right draped in black silks, a giant, gothic-style wardrobe to the left, flanked by a beautiful matching vanity and writing desk.

To the back, a set of massive glass doors open onto a balcony. A quaint bistro table sat in the moonlight. I peeked inside the only other door to find a bathroom fit for royalty with dark stone, brass fixtures, and wooden finishes.

I tossed my backpack on the bed and flopped down on the plush mattress with a sigh. A muffled cry from my bag made me bolt upright. I scrambled for it and pulled back the zipper. Lattie poked her head out and blinked widely at the room.

"Lattie!" I exclaimed. "What the hell?"

She tumbled out onto the mattress and stretched her wings. "It was Julie's idea."

I rolled my eyes but laughed. A knock came at the door, and I shot a startled look at my stowaway. "Hide."

"I will not," she seethed as I hopped to my feet and opened the door.

A lithe fairy stood with a leather bag in her hands. Her green skin melted into her hair and swirled atop her head like soft-serve ice cream. Giant, black, almond-shaped eyes blinked at me as her tiny mouth opened.

"I'm Mags," she said softly but firmly, pushing her way inside. Two Fae, like Lattie, fluttered in behind her, carrying a pitcher of wine and a tray of snacks. She set her bag down and threw open the wardrobe doors. "I'm here to help you get ready for dinner."

"Oh, I really don't need help," I told her and swatted at Lattie to hush her hissing at the others. "I'm just going to wear this."

Her bean pole frame twisted halfway around, and she gestured at my outfit of torn jeans, brown leather jacket, and chipped red nail polish with her too-long arms. "Those cheap rags hanging from your body will not do. You're Lord Oden's guest. That comes with certain expectations."

"To hell with Oden."

Mags and the two sprites gasped in unison. "Entry to this castle and our Lord's time is a privilege bestowed onto no one. You are lucky to even be here. I would show some grace."

Lattie climbed onto my shoulder and bared her teeth at them. "And Avery could turn you all to heaping piles of charred flesh. I would watch how you speak to her."

Mags laughed. "I doubt that. Isn't she here because she doesn't know how to use her own magic?" She snapped her fingers, and an invisible force pulled me to my feet, holding me in place. "Now, what shall we wear for a first dinner?" She hummed to herself as she rifled through the dozens of garments made of tule, chiffon, and silk. Gemstones and glittered sheer sparkled, and I cringed. "Ah ha," she exclaimed and pulled out a floor-length gown made mostly of pink tulle. "Perfect."

My eyes widened at the gaudy thing. "Absolutely not."

Mags snapped her fingers again, and my clothes disappeared.

"What the hell!" I grabbed a blanket from the bed and covered myself.

Another snap, and my bathroom door swung open. With another snap, the tub was already half full. Steamed billowed into the air.

"Do I need to bathe you, as well?"

I grimaced and stalked toward the bathroom. "No."

After a few minutes in the giant, black, clawfoot tub, I wondered if I'd ever experienced something so lovely. Oils of all kinds were stacked on a wooden cart; bubbles tickled my chin as I sunk down. I closed my eyes and inhaled the heavy wafts of cherries and vanilla, then soaked until Mags banged on the door.

I wrapped a large black towel around myself and stepped into my room, my hair sopping all over the place. Mags snapped her fingers, and the vanity chair pulled out. She gestured to it, and I rolled my eyes as I sat.

Mags's long, boney fingers worked my wet hair with a mix of skill and magic as the two sprites fed me an assortment of cheeses and berries and a glass or two of something like champagne. Lattie hoarded all the meats and smoked bits of cheese.

My hair shone in long waves of red, soft like roses with half pinned back in cascades pinned with pink pearls, and I tried not to stare at myself in the vanity mirror. But I couldn't help it. Mags was making me look almost…Fae. When she finally stepped away, my makeup done, I couldn't believe the woman that stared back. Then Mags snapped again, and I was dressed in the pink dress.

"Oh, no, I'm not wearing this!" I said and jumped to my feet. "I look like a balled-up bubble gum wrapper!" The tulle ruffled and scratched at my skin as I moved.

She dug her fingers into the air, and I felt the invisible force shove me down into the seat again. Without another word, she plucked a sparkling pink tiara out of her bag and placed it on my head.

"Hell no." I immediately removed it and tossed it on the vanity. Mags swiftly placed it back, but it barely touched my hair before I ripped it off again. She went for it, but I glared at her as she pinched it between her fingers. "If you put that damn crown on my head one more time, I'll melt it to the floor."

"Lord Oden won't be pleased," she said.

"Let's get one thing very clear here, Mags," I said and smoothed out the ridiculous dress with as much dignity as I could muster. "I'm not here for your Lord's approval. We made a deal for him to help me. Once that's done, I'll never step foot in this place again."

Her dark green lips curved into a coy smile. "Very well." She snapped her fingers, and the door flew open. "Time to head down for dinner."

She shoved me towards the doorway. "Where do I go?"

"Just follow your nose."

Mags and her little team went left while I headed right down the long, winding hallways that seemed to never end. Lattie sat on my shoulder and curled into my hair.

"I can't believe you have to come here every month," Lattie hissed in my ear as we passed torches and statues and giant vases filled with plants I'd never seen before.

I groaned as my dress scraped along the stone floors. "As much as I hate to admit it, this might be my only option if I want to avoid turning everyone I love to…how did you describe it…heaping piles of charred flesh?"

Lattie let out a tiny harumph. "You're a god among ants."

I rolled my eyes as we took another turn. "I thought I was an annoying mortal who accidentally bound you to them."

"You can be both."

I laughed, grateful for how much it seemed to ease the tightness in my chest as I tried not to overthink what I was really doing. Wandering the gloomy halls of a castle in search of a dining room where a Dark Lord awaited to dine with me. I did as Mags said and followed my nose through a set of swinging doors, only it brought me to the giant kitchen.

Everyone in the room halted and turned to me with stunned expressions. Half a dozen Fae manned the kitchen; some with four arms, some stood on stools, while one towered almost to the ceiling. A stumpy, round Fae female with woody skin pointed a ladle at me.

"You lost, girl?"

Another moved toward me, licking their slimy lips as they gripped a giant cleaver dripping with yellow goo. "Have you come for dinner…or *for* dinner?"

He gestured to a giant boiling cauldron that hung over a fire in a stone wall. The others chuckled darkly as they all narrowed in on me, eliciting a violent hiss from Lattie and her tiny claws gripped my hair.

A hand touched my shoulder and spun me around. Sullivan, Oden's brother, gave me a smirk.

"Dining room's this way, Red," he said and motioned for me to follow.

I gathered up the many layers of my hideous dress with a huff of annoyance and struggled to keep up with him. We left the doors swinging closed, boxing in the riot of laughter that ensued with my absence.

"You guys could at least give me a map for this place or something," I said.

He chuckled lightly. "You'll get used to it."

His hair was tied back in a ponytail at the nape of his neck, but he wore what I'd always seen him in. Mundane black jeans and an old band T-shirt that looked like it'd been through the washer with rocks. His clunky leather boots echoed off the walls as we walked.

"I don't plan to stick around long enough to get comfortable."

He stopped outside two grand doors made of jade and etched with intricate black carvings and runes. "We'll see." He waggled his eyebrows and hauled open one of the doors.

I stood back and gawked at the gothic masterpiece that was the dining room. Like everything else in this castle, it was fit for a gothic king. Stone walls towered overhead, black chandeliers dangled from the ceiling at different heights, weighed down with a million candles. A long, rectangular table cut the middle of the space, made from dark, glossy wood. A centerpiece anchored the surface; a glorious mess of twisted branches and golden fruit with beautiful flowers I'd never seen before.

Oden sat at the head of the dining table. It was lined with black armchairs on either side, their backs done in a twisted design of black vines. A shadowy figure occupied one of the chairs to the right of Oden. No defining features to be seen, just pure, empty blackness. But two eyes blinked at me, and I knew where I'd seen it before.

In the Dark Forest.

"I brought a guest," Sullivan said cheekily as he motioned to me and sauntered around to his seat to the left of his brother.

I remained in the doorway, Lattie nestled beneath my hair at the back of my neck.

Oden's stormy gaze flashed across the room, almost… looking right *through* me. "It appears you're not the only one, brother." He gripped the air in front of him, and Lattie squealed as she was pulled from my neck and sucked right into his hand. He squeezed, and her little screeches made me cringe.

"Don't hurt her!" I yelled.

Oden brought her to his face with a snarl. "Come to make trouble?"

"I'm here to watch Avery." She chomped her teeth, narrowly missing his nose, then reared her head and bit down on his finger.

He shook her from his grasp, cursing under his breath, and she flew back to me at the far end of the table. Oden glared daggers at me as Sullivan snickered like a kid, and their guest sat unmovingly. I just narrowed my eyes at all of them.

"Why am I dressed like this?"

"You stay in my home; you're expected to dress accordingly."

"That wasn't part of the bargain."

Oden swiped a glass of red wine from the table and brought it to his grinning mouth. "You didn't ask."

I clenched my fists as my stomach twisted, that familiar and unwanted pressure of my power quickly growing. Sullivan had the right mind to look worried, but Oden clucked his tongue and waved his hand in the air in a pulling movement.

"We'll have none of that at the dinner table, Miss Quinn," he said with finality, and my magic snuffed out. "Now sit."

My breathing quickened with panic as I slowly took my seat as far from the three of them as I could. I couldn't control what lived in me, what belonged to me, but *he* could? That thought left me unnerved.

Oden and Sullivan engaged in conversation, just whispers from where I sat, while the kitchen staff brought out tray after tray and pitcher after pitcher, filling the table. Someone set a massive plate down in front of me, and I grimaced. Salmon? I grabbed a fluffy, buttery bun from a tray and lobbed off a bite while Lattie sniffed at my plate.

"You can have it," I told her. "I hate salmon."

Oden and Sullivan ignored me for the entirety of the meal. But not their guest. His insidious gaze was on me the whole time. An inky being swirling with whorls of utter blackness. The absence of everything. A void made into form.

I refused to show any fear in this place and just slumped in my chair as I ate bun after bun and engaged in a stare-down with it. Lattie shredded through my salmon, the smell enough to make me want to gag. But I kept my composure as I waited for this dinner to end so Oden could start teaching me magic.

But it never ended. It went on for hours as I filled my belly with bread and wine. Oden talked business and other things with his two guests, ignoring that I was even in the room. I couldn't even catch his gaze.

"Sullivan," Oden said a pitch louder, his plate long empty. "How goes operations at Umbra?"

Sullivan swiped a pitcher and filled his glass. "It's fine." He shot a look across the table at the dark entity. "If Misery kept his ilk in check, things would be much easier."

Misery? That was its name?

The dark form shifted as if stretching shoulders it didn't really have. "My *ilk*, as you call them, are not meant to be controlled. They are the deepest, darkest emotions of the living. They take, and they feed. What would you have me do?"

Sullivan took a long drink. "They're only permitted to feed on emotions in Ironworld, and you know it." He arched a bold brow at Misery. "If I find out any more of your kind have been feeding on human blood, I'll have them banned to the Dark Forest for eternity."

Misery slammed a shadowy fist on the table. "They're already banned to the forest!"

Sullivan shot to his feet. "I created Umbra to siphon the energy you and your ilk need. Consider it a privilege, you fucking monster. You're lucky my brother doesn't burn that forest to the ground with you lot in it."

Misery gave a harumph and a sly chuckle. "Our gracious *Lord* would never," he said with a lip-licking noise. "He needs us as much as we need him. Perhaps more."

My head swirled under the weight of all the wine, and I dragged my eyes across the table at Oden, expecting him to straighten out the discussion, but he was staring at me with a calculating look as he sipped from his chalice.

I quirked a brow, happy to finally have his attention. "Are we going to practice or not?"

He smirked and pulled a cigar from his jacket. I watched him bring it to his mouth, and he patiently lit it, puffing until the tip glowed red. I wanted to shoot from my chair and holler at him. But Lattie was asleep in my lap, and my head swirled with booze. So, I sat there all night while the three of them ate and talked more business I didn't care about.

I later woke in a cold sweat. It was well past the middle of the night, and I had no memory of returning to my room. *Or changing into pink silk pajamas.* I groaned as I tucked the blankets around my chin and rolled over, almost squishing Lattie. My stomach wanted to heave, but it came in waves, and I waited it out until I finally fell into a deep sleep.

The bedroom door flung open, ripping me from the dead sleep. The side of my mouth was sticky, and Lattie must have been awake for a while because half my head was twisted into dozens of tiny braids. I wiped my face with the back of my hand. I'd commit awful things for a glass of water.

"Time to get up," Mags declared and flung open the drapes. Sun barged into the room, blinding me. Lattie hissed and hid behind my back. "It smells like the cellar in here."

That wasn't early morning sun; it was definitely sometime in the afternoon. I'd already wasted an evening and a morning and learned absolutely nothing. I swung my legs over the side of the bed and waited out a wave of nausea.

Mags clucked her tongue at me. "Bastard."

My brows pinched together. "What?"

"Nothing," she replied and shook her head as she turned to the wardrobe. She rifled through the contents and pulled out a black dress that looked like it would choke me. "Go bathe."

Her two sprites flew in, carrying trays of breakfast snacks. Muffins and fruit and coffee. I could have kissed them. I quickly made a coffee and headed to the bathroom, leaving Lattie to the food.

There was nothing but crumbs when I returned, but she fluttered over to me and held a muffin out as she blinked those giant black eyes at me. I bit into it. Cherries. Coffee settled in my stomach, and the bath had done some good, so I sat at the vanity without a fuss.

I sipped a second coffee in silence while Mags worked on my hair. She yanked and twisted and pulled my blood-red mane into a beautiful, intricate updo of braids that held a giant bun in place.

"Lord Oden is away on business this afternoon," Mags told me. "But he'll return this evening."

I ripped my hair from her fingers and stood up. "*What?*"

"Lord Oden is away–"

"No, I heard you," I said impatiently. "What is this? What's happening here? Is this a trick of some kind?"

Mags steeled her expression and folded my dress over in her arms. "I don't know what you're talking about."

"I came here because Oden promised to teach me magic, to control my powers. It was *his* idea. It's the afternoon of day two, and all I've done is eat, drink, and sleep." I slapped my hands at my sides. "And let you dress me up like a damn fool."

"You have to trust our Lord has a plan," she replied. "He always does."

I scoffed. "Hard to trust a plan you're not privy to."

She took a few steps toward me and patted my arm with her long, green fingers. "I believe it's called faith, dearie."

I sulked while Mags finished my hair, then snapped her fingers to get me in the dress. A long matte black thing draped to the floor and swallowed my neck. The matching corset was so tight I could hardly breathe.

"Christ," I huffed as I tugged at the boning. "Can we maybe loosen this thing? I enjoy breathing from time to time."

Mags chortled and cleaned up her things, heading for the door as she beckoned her two minions. "Loosening a corset defeats the purpose of a corset, dearie." She tucked her leather bag under her arm and opened the door. "You're free to wander the castle until Lord Oden returns."

She left the door open, so I waited a moment before I turned to Lattie. "Come here and help me get out of this damn thing."

"The corset keeps the dress together," she replied. "What other options do you have to wear? The witch took your mundane clothes."

I fanned through the many garments in the wardrobe and realized they were all equally horrendous and constricting.

I bent over the back of the chair and groaned. "This place is going to be the death of me."

"Let me help." She flew behind me, and as her tiny but able fingers pulled and loosened the strings, I took a few deep breaths and made sure I could move without too much restraint. "Is that better?"

I twisted and turned my torso with ease, but the corset still held the dress in place. "Yeah, thanks."

With nothing else to do, we roamed the mansion for the afternoon. Checking out other quarters, peeking inside offices and sitting rooms. I dared a pass by the kitchen when our stomachs grew hungry, but the same terrifying kitchen staff manned the area, and I didn't want Lattie to end up on a platter.

We found a solarium that faced the courtyard, and we sat for a while with books we'd taken from one of the office bookshelves. I sat in a comfy oversized chair while Lattie rummaged every nook and cranny for bugs and mice with no luck.

The sun had begun to set over the distant horizon of forest tops, and candles automatically sprung to life with little flames around the room. I closed the book I'd been reading—something about the history of this region of Faerie and the various animal and plant life that thrived here.

Lattie flew over and ripped it from my grasp like a child in a tantrum. "I'm starving! Does this place not feed its guests?"

I rolled my eyes and laughed. "You ate my entire breakfast tray."

A low growl rumbled in her tiny chest but was cut short as she sensed something in the room. She crawled up my chest and stood on my shoulder, glancing around with narrowed eyes.

"What is it?

"Shhh," she hissed in my ear and sniffed the air. She lowered onto her haunches as her lips pulled back over her teeth and her narrowed eyes scanned the room like a hunting dog zeroing in on its find. "Something's in here."

Then I felt it. Swirling around my ankles, brushing against my leg. I dared a glance down. Black smoke crawled around the floor at my feet. Most of the candles blew out, leaving the room in the dank, orange glow of the slowly setting sun.

The black entity mixed with the dissipating smoke of the candles and crawled up my frozen body as Lattie swatted at it with her claws. The thing almost seemed to be… sniffing me. It reached my neck, and a yelp squeezed in my throat as it moved to my cheek and my ear, rustling in my hair, then coiled back down to the floor, where it slowly began to take form. It seemed to pull the darkness from the very shadows in the room, solidifying into some sort of strange shape. No, not a *strange* shape. A dog-like shape.

A jet-black dog sat at my feet, back straight, its giant paws tucked together as it blinked at me. One adorable, pointed ear twitched as it let out a little whine.

Shakily, I reached for its head. "Don't eat my hand." I smoothed my fingers over the silky fur between its ears, and the beast softened at my touch, inching closer and leaning into it. I chuckled and moved to the edge of my seat to scratch behind both ears. A warm tongue flicked out and left a slobbery kiss on my wrist. "Well, you're just adorable. Where did you come from?"

Lattie seemed unnerved. She jumped off my shoulder and fluttered over to the window, searching for her next prey. I couldn't tell if she were leery of the beast or just jealous. The dog put its whole weight against me as I pet it, its face nuzzling me, its hefty whip-like tail beating against the stone floor.

"What are you doing in here, Red?"

I spun and twisted in the chair. Sullivan stood in the doorway, glancing around as if he'd never seen the solarium before. No, more like he was seeing it for the first time in a long while.

"I was reading," I replied and sat back down as he inched further into the room. Lattie had flown out one of the open windows, and the dog was gone. "Hey! How did you do that?"

"Do what?" he gave me a puzzled look but chased it away with a smirk. "Enter the room? I'm told I do make quite the entrance. Want me to do it again? This time I can back my way in so you can check out my ass." He wiggled his hips, and I couldn't help but laugh.

"How are you so different from your brother?" I asked as he threw himself into the other oversized chair.

I liked Sullivan's style. Grungy and almost mundane. Thin black suspenders held tight, stretchy black pants tucked into the tops of his high combat boots. A black t-shirt showed off a few tattoos on his arms. Nothing compared to Celadine's artwork, but cool, nonetheless.

Sullivan kept glancing about the room as if studying an old friend. "Oden and I couldn't be more different because we've lived different lives."

"You spend a lot of time in Ironworld."

He blinked at me. "How did you know?"

I shrugged and set the book I'd been reading on the coffee table between us. "I can just tell."

"So, what have you done all day?" he asked as he took a cigarette from a metal tin and lit it with a match.

"You're looking at it," I said begrudgingly. "I wandered the castle for a bit, then sat here with some books for a few hours. Your brother is a terrible host and even worse teacher."

Sullivan took a long drag, and I fanned away the smoke. He waved his hand, and it began wafting out the window. Jealousy seethed in my veins. I wanted to be able to do that.

"Yeah, he'll be back later this evening. He had some pressing matters to tend to."

"More pressing than upholding his end of a gilded promise?"

He chuckled and tapped his cigarette on an ashtray that appeared on the table. "You have no idea, Red."

I raised my chin. "Enlighten me."

He took one more long puff and snuffed it out in an ashtray that appeared on the coffee table. "How about I feed you instead?"

Lattie suddenly appeared on the window sill like a dog that had just heard its food dish rattle, and I rolled my eyes. "Fine."

He brought us down to the kitchen, and I sighed in

relief when I saw that it was empty. The staff had long gone home, and everything was tidy and spotless. I lingered near the door as Sullivan raided the fridge and cupboard.

And something occurred to me. "How is it powered? I thought technology wasn't a thing here."

"It's not," he replied, his hands stacked with a tray of meats, cheeses, and fruits. A bottle of wine tucked under one arm. He tapped his boot against the side of the fridge, and it shimmered as though covered with a mirage. "It's magic that cools it. Some enchantment from the Winter Lord."

That perked my interest. I'd heard so little of the chilly domain we suspected Julie came from. "You know the Winter Lord?"

He shook his head and tucked a baguette under his chin. "I've never met the guy. Sounds like a real piece of work if you ask me. But my brother met him once." He paused for a moment, staring off. "It was my father who truly knew him. They were allies once upon a time."

"What happened?" I asked.

Sullivan rolled his eyes with a raspy chuckle. "That's a long story." He motioned to a cupboard near my head. "Grab two glasses, would ya?"

I exchanged a glance with Lattie, who never left my side, and plucked two large, stemless wine glasses from the cupboard before following Sullivan through the kitchen, the dining room, and a set of patio doors that opened onto an outdoor living room. I was grateful for the weather here. I didn't miss the bite of early winter in Ironworld.

The full moon shone bright and blaring, like a flashing neon sign of a reminder of what I'd gotten myself into. Sullivan set the food down on a coffee table between two black wicker chairs, and I sat in one of them.

"This was a waste of my time."

"I assure you it's not," he said and poured me a glass of wine before taking a swig from the bottle. "Whatever my brother is doing or planning, have some faith in him."

"Have some faith in him?" I guffawed as I picked at the cheeses. "Why should I even believe you? You tossed me at the feet of vampires and nearly got me killed. And your brother… He hired Evaine to hunt me down like a dog and somehow convinced me to let him train me, which he's yet to do."

His face paled, and he took another long swig. "I'm sorry about that. I had no idea who you were then."

I stuffed cheese and bread to the side of my mouth. "I'm not anyone."

"Sure, Red," he chuckled softly. "Sure."

Did they know who I really was? I didn't dare ask.

Lattie flew off with smoked sausage. "I don't want to wander the halls of a castle in a stupid dress, like a fucking extra on the Addams Family. I just want to learn to control my magic and get the hell out of here."

"Well, what can you do?"

I stuffed more cheese in my mouth and lobbed off a bite of ham. "I can call," I said between chewing and taking a sip of wine. "And I can travel through water." When he seemed impressed, I added, "I mean to a couple of locations…in Ironworld."

He laughed, but I didn't get the sense he was laughing *at* me. "Oden will help you master that burning sun, I promise. But it will take time. Be patient."

Cillian's face flashed through my mind. "I'm not sure how long I can keep coming here."

He drank some more and leaned down to swipe a handful of grapes. I'd already eaten half the cheese.

"Well, what else do you want to learn?" he asked.

I brightened. "Wisping. I want to learn to wisp. I've tried and failed miserably." And try as I might, I couldn't replicate what I'd done the other night.

He gave me a curious look. "You can water travel, and now you want to learn to wisp? I'm offering to teach you some real magic here. Why the need to be mobile, Red? You live in Ironworld. Just drive, take the bus, a cab."

"It's not that easy for me," I replied, my cheeks flushing with warmth. "I don't do so well in enclosed vehicles. Cars, buses, cabs, you name it. They make my head swim and my stomach heave. That's why I ride a bike."

He nodded. "That makes sense."

"What?"

"Cars, buses, trains," he said and paced in front of me. "They're iron cages. And you're–"

"Part Fae." The realization washed over me, nearly taking the breath from my lungs. All this time, all my life, that's why it affected me so much. I wasn't prone to motion sickness. Some dormant part of me knew they were magical traps. I steeled myself and set down my glass as I stood from the chair. "Teach me to wisp."

And so, he did. Or…tried, at least. Midnight was fully upon us when I collapsed on the ground with a groan, covered in sweat.

"It's hopeless," I muttered from beneath the arm I'd flung over my face as I lay on the grass.

Sullivan's boots toed my leg with a friendly nudge. "You're getting it, Red. You just wisped a whole ten feet."

I pushed against the cool grass and sat up, glaring at him. "Don't mock me."

He held up both hands. "I would never."

"What am I doing wrong?" I asked. "Is it because I'm not fully Fae?"

"Nah," he replied and offered me an arm. I grabbed it and pulled myself to my feet. "You can do it. You're just scared. You're not visualizing where to go."

"But I *am*."

"Yeah, but you're only visualizing what you can already see in front of you," he explained. "If you want to wisp to the other side of the castle, you have to *see* it, feel it, *smell* it. As if you're already there."

"But I don't know what it really looks like over there," I said. "Everything here is foreign to me."

"Try again. Visualize a room or place you *have* been here and can remember well. Feel it, smell it, hear it."

I sighed and closed my eyes as I rifled through the images in my mind. My quarters, the kitchen, the dining room, the solarium, the throne room… Flashes of the explosion made my heart race. Then the memory of being thrown from the rubble and landing on the grass. I tried to stop it, but it played in my mind like a movie. The feel of stone and dust against my face, the smooth grass sliding beneath me, the branches of the Dark Forest whipping at my skin as I ran. And then, that familiar feeling of being sucked through space and time.

No…no, no, no!

I peeled open my eyes to find myself surrounded by dense forest.

"Shit."

I'd wisped right into the heart of the Dark Forest, right to the very spot I ran to on that fateful night Evaine dragged me to the Domain of Nightmares.

How did I do that? I clenched my fists, closed my eyes, and concentrated on visualizing Sullivan standing on the patio. But nothing happened. I tried again. Nothing.

Emotions flooded my body—were *forced* into my body, and every ounce of happiness spewed from me. I wanted to die. And just as quickly as it came, it was gone.

I leaned against a tree and gasped for air.

"I don't recall inviting you to my home," a slick voice said as shadows moved around my feet. Misery. "Come to play with me and my friends, have you?"

"No," I replied and spun on my heel, but something held me in place. "I accidentally wisped here. I'm just leaving." Damn it, how did I *do* it? How did I wisp?

Inky whorls of darkness swirled up from my feet, wrapping me in shadows.

"Why the rush?" Misery asked with a fox-like sneer. He manifested in front of me, and those unearthly eyes blinked madly. He was like the boogeyman brought to life. "I wonder what our mighty Lord of Nightmares might do if his precious guest was returned with her eyeballs missing." I felt an invisible claw gently rake across my cheek. "Or her tongue." He put his mouth to my ear and purred darkly, sending a rush of unwanted goosebumps over my skin. Claws sliced my dress across the boning of my corset, nicking the skin of my stomach, and all I could do was let out a stifled wince. He chuckled evilly. "Or her fragile, mortal innards."

I couldn't figure out how to wisp, but I knew how to call upon my power. Controlling it was another story. But I didn't have a choice. I had to get away.

My magic yawned awake and blossomed in my hands, burning away the shadows. They absorbed into Misery, and he took on a more human form. He was still all black, even his eyes, but his features sharpened to that of a man, and he grabbed me by the throat.

My magic sputtered out as I gasped for breath and clawed at his wrist. He squeezed harder and harder, and a low and hollow chuckle floated out of him.

The sky cleaved with lightning, and something dropped from above. No, not something…*someone*. Oden. He roared and shook with anger as the ground rumbled. Misery let me go and shadows leaked from him like an oil spill, each one taking on a solid form and encircling the two of us.

Oden grabbed my arm and hauled me behind him. I wanted to protest, wanted to scream to let me help, but a bolt of light formed in his hand, and he held it out as it shaped into a white, glowing scythe. He took one giant swing and cut every single shadow being in half. Their unnatural screams pierced the sky, and Misery stood just a few feet back, hunched over in rage.

Oden pointed the scythe at him. "You have three seconds before I banish you to a sunny pasture somewhere."

Misery gestured to speak, and Oden slammed the bottom of the staff on the ground, shaking everything around us. The shadow creature fled, and the Dark Lord turned to me with an unreadable expression, his chest heaving under a half-opened black shirt and charcoal vest.

My mind raced with questions. "What are those things?"

The glowing weapon was gone, and he smoothed back a few stray white hairs as he towered over me. "Syphons. They can produce and feed on all the darkest emotions while dissolving all that makes you happy. Misery, Grief, Fear, Vengeance, Anger, Sorrow. The list goes on." Oden eyed me up and down. "You must have been a beacon for them. All those human emotions fluttering about."

"How—how did *you* find me?"

He wriggled his wrist, showing off golden rings, all gilded promises. "The bargain includes that no harm would come to you. So, when harm was coming, my wrist burned, and I followed the bargain to you."

I digested that as I thought of something else. The glowing scythe, he'd just made it out of thin air. No, out of light, just like I had once and haven't been able to replicate since.

The storm in his eyes began to settle, his breathing calm. "How did you end up so far into the forest?"

"I accidentally wisped."

"Accidentally?"

"How did you do it?" I asked, bypassing the amused look he was giving me.

"Do what?"

"The blade… You made a solid thing from nothing."

Oden grinned coyly. "Not nothing. It's my power, my darkness, my…I guess you could say it's moonlight, to be exact. It flows in me like a living thing and can be manipulated into whatever I want it to be. Just like your light."

He formed the scythe again, and I marveled at it. He was right. It was moonlight. I stepped back as it morphed into a sword, two swings and it was a lasso. He roped it over me, tightening it around my body, constricting my arms and lungs. The look in his eyes said one thing, *be afraid. I dare you.*

I only grinned up at him. "Show me."

Chapter Ten

He didn't show me. He wasn't even there for the rest of the night or the better part of the next day. I woke up early and searched for the least hideous garment from the wardrobe before Mags showed up, but my mundane clothes were cleaned, pressed, and stacked in an empty cupboard.

The last day. I was going home in a few hours and had long given up hope of learning anything at all from Oden. It was now well past lunchtime, and my stomach growled.

Lattie sniffed at the air from the solarium chair where we sat. "Think we can find something to eat?"

"I don't want to go anywhere near the kitchen."

She grumbled and tipped her head back. "I'll miss the view, but I'd rather stay in Ironworld, where I can *eat*."

"Thanks for coming, by the way," I said. "At least I didn't have to waste my time alone."

Lattie shot upright and hunched her shoulders with a low hiss. And I felt the soft, sifting shadow curling around my ankles, brushing against my legs. I smiled and leaned over, smoothing my hand over the black smear until a dog took form. The same midnight black hound as before. I scratched between his ears as he flopped that massive head on my lap.

"What's your name, I wonder?"

"Foul beast," Lattie muttered from my shoulder.

"Don't mind her," I told the dog and held his face in my hands. I kissed his head. He smelled like night air and new puppies. "She's just a curmudgeon."

His floppy ears perked, and he looked toward the door over the back of my chair. I stole a glance, and Sullivan stood in the archway. When I looked back, the dog had disappeared.

"Hungry, Red? Oden's back." He wore a black long-sleeved shirt, grey plaid pants tucked into his boots just below the knee, and a grin from ear to ear. "Or would you rather practice some more wisping?"

"I think I'll practice in Ironworld," I replied. "Where I won't end up in the middle of a murder forest."

He gave a soft chuckle as he shoved off the door frame and motioned for me to follow. "Come on."

I got up and stomped after him with Lattie in tow. He let me stew in silence as we walked. We were almost at the dining room when Sullivan looked at me from the corner of his eye.

"Mad?"

"You have no idea," I replied as we turned a corner and stepped into the dining room where Oden sat at the head of the table, which was already lined down the middle with an array of food. Sullivan took a seat, and I stormed over to Oden's side. He leaned back and glanced up at me with a look of surprise. "Are you going to teach me anything, or will I just keep coming here and wasting my time?"

"Have you not learned anything?" he said teasingly.

I wanted to slap the smug grin right off his Lordly face.

"No, I haven't!" I yelled at him, and he had the right mind to flinch. Somewhere over my shoulder, Sullivan stifled a laugh. "All I've done is hang around your stupid castle in ridiculous dresses, eating food I hate. All that spying on me, and you didn't learn a single damn thing."

He steeled his expression, and his chair screeched across the stone floor as he stood, towering over me with a glare full of an early morning storm. "You can't expect to learn everything in a single weekend, Avery, dear. You must first practice self-control. In *every* aspect of your life."

My eyes widened in rage. "What the hell is that supposed to mean? I don't want to wander the halls in a gown and read books under the sun like some hapless maiden! I'm not here on vacation!" My stomach tightened, and my fists clenched as the glow of the Summer sun seeped from my pores. I stepped toward him and poked a burning finger at his chest. "You promised to help me, and all you've done is *piss me off!*"

The sharp outline of his lips widened into a fox-like grin. "Yes, but look how much practice you've gotten."

I blinked, and my magic immediately tucked away. "What?"

He stepped toward me, forcing me to back up against the wall. "Your power becomes uncontrollable with your anger and fear. The only way to exercise control is to face it." He placed both hands on the wall at either side of my head, and my heart raced. "You think I can teach you to manifest weapons or wisp between worlds when you can't even control your temper?"

"You mean…" The weekend events played through my mind in a different light; the food, forcing me to sit through that wretched dinner, the dresses, Mags, and Oden ignoring me. "You've been *deliberately* pissing me off this whole time?"

Sunlight burned in my veins once again, building with my rising spite. It radiated from my skin, bursting through the fibers of my clothes, filling the dining room to the brim. The walls began to shake, and panic struck me right in the chest. *Please*, I begged it. *Please stop.*

The light ebbed in place. *Please*, I asked again. *I don't want to destroy another room. I don't want to bury us all.* With a sigh, my magic slowly retreated, seeping back into my body. But Oden grabbed my arm.

"There it is," he said, almost squeezing the sun from me. I marveled at how it poured over his skin, leaving him unharmed. How did he do that? His long fingers wrapped around my arm and gripped even harder. "That uncontrollable part of your magic. Let it out."

"What? No, I can't–"

"Let it out."

My back arched as my power seemed to obey him, and a cry forced up my throat. Sunlight filled the room, pure blinding light that pressed against the walls.

"That's it," he cooed. "Let go, take off that leash. Set it free."

And so, I did. I held back the fear I harbored for my own magic, fear that it would kill me and everyone I love, and let it expand beyond the room. The window shutters flung open, and the chandelier rattled above. Dust sprinkled down from the ceiling. Sunlight pried my mouth, expelling itself, stretching every part of me, and filling me simultaneously.

Oden grabbed my other arm. "Put an elastic on it." My panicked eyes darted to his. "You can do it. Just imagine an elastic band and place it over your power." When I shook my head, he added, "You want to save your friends? Do you want to learn what you can do? *Put the elastic on it!*"

Something in my core clenched. A sort of determination I never knew I had possessed me. My arms suddenly felt stronger, my legs sturdier. I imagined a rubber leash between my hands and tested its strength before closing my eyes and tossing it over all the light in the room. It stuck, and everything came to a halt as if the wildness of my power waited. For what…I had no idea.

Stop, I told it. *I'm in charge.*

It slowly poured back into my body without hesitation, and I felt it. The pure, utter control. Control that had always been there. I was just too afraid to see that I had it in my grasp.

"See?" Oden smirked and stalked back to his seat. "Your magic is a living thing, but you're in control. You just stunt it. You hold back." He tilted his head. "A scared little thing with too much power. All you had to do was let go completely. Now you know the bounds of your own magic. *Now* we can begin."

He sat down and began filling his plate.

Every inch of me hummed as I came down off the high. "So, that's it?"

He almost snorted as he filled his cup. "Goodness, no. You've got a lot to learn but overcoming the fear of your own magic was step number one." A wicked grin. "You say I didn't learn anything from spying on you. I learned *every-*

thing." His chair creaked as he leaned back and unfurled his hand in a sweep across the table. "Feel free to stay for dinner. Otherwise, go home and practice. I'll see you in a month."

My throat tightened at the realization that I wanted to stay. But I could never let Oden know that. I grabbed my bag and slung it over my shoulder as Lattie flew to my shoulder.

"Goodbye," was all I said and left.

I got halfway to the exit when I heard footsteps approaching from behind.

"It's the brother," Lattie hissed in my ear.

"Hey, Red!" he called and ran to a stop. "I'll make sure you get home."

"I can manage on my own."

He shrugged and stuffed both hands in his pockets. "Kinda part of the deal, though. Oden swore you'd be safe. I have to at least get you to Ironworld. From there, you're on your own."

"Fine, get me to water," I said and started walking. He fell in sync by my side. "You guys sure go to extremes with everything, don't you? Harvesting blood from your own kind. Teaching me magic with tactics I'll need therapy for." I didn't bother to hold back the venom in my voice.

"Hey, look, I made sure none of the Fae we captured were hurt. We only took small amounts of blood from them."

"What I saw, that was cruel."

His long, dark hair flopped about as he walked. "I know." Silence fell between us, and the only sounds to be heard were our breaths, the crunch of dirt, and the flutter of Lattie's wings. "I did what I had to do to keep ties with the Therians, to grant my brother enough time to—"

My head whipped to him. "To what?"

He gnawed at the corner of his mouth. "Find you. The heir."

I focused on the stone floor ahead. So, they *did* know my secret. "I don't know what you're talking about."

Sullivan let out a low, raspy laugh. "Don't worry, your secret's safe with us. Only my brother and I know."

"That doesn't exactly make me feel better."

He just shrugged. "I get it, though. Being thrust with a responsibility bigger than yourself."

"What responsibility do you have?" I scoffed.

"None, thank the gods," he countered and held a pause. "But my brother does. He took the throne when he was just eighteen years old."

Something in my gut went icy. Both of us were thrust with a responsibility bigger than ourselves at a young age. Perhaps the Dark Lord of Nightmares was more equipped to help me than I thought.

I still didn't like the idea that he knew who I really was.

We stepped outside. Crickets chirped in the dark wood that surrounded the property. Sullivan walked calmly by my side as we headed for the edge of Oden's wards.

"You know, we're not the bad guys in this whole thing, Red. Oden has a part to play for his domain, for the Dark Fae he's been tasked to rule. But we're not the villains. You'll see soon enough."

"Why should I believe you?"

The path turned and wound around a small garden. A pond glittered in the sunlight in the far distance.

"Oden made a deal with the Therians that he would supply them with Fae blood in exchange for their help killing Mabry and overthrowing the Seelie Court. If they succeeded, Oden would take the throne and grant the Therians a place in Faerie again. But now that we have you…."

"I am *not* taking any throne of any kind."

He shrugged and stopped a few feet away from the water. "You'll play a part either way. The throne and power automatically go to you if we kill your mother. You can keep it, share it with my brother, or bestow it fully onto him."

"He can have it fully," I said, reeling from the information. I hadn't considered the repercussions of being the mad queen's heir. Hadn't let myself.

He crossed his arms. "I think he wants to earn it by working with you."

I considered it and stared at the water. I thought that I'd doomed myself by making this deal with Oden, that I would be walking into a literal nightmare. But his home was lovely, despite being surrounded by a wretched forest and having a kitchen staff that wanted to eat me. Then again, was that also part of the plan to piss me off? Was everything an act this weekend?

"You know, you're not what I thought you were." I squat down.

"Is that good or bad?" he asked.

I glanced up at him, my hand hovering over the water. "I guess we'll have to see." I touched the water. "Oh, say bye to the dog for me." I closed my eyes and thought of home but could have sworn I caught a look of confusion on Sullivan's face.

Chapter Eleven

The sky was a different sort of brightness in Ironworld than it was in Faerie. There, summer was in full swing. Here, Halifax was on the cusp of winter. Fresh snow kissed the ground, and the air tickled my nose and throat. But time also flowed differently. I left the coming twilight of Nightmares just moments ago and stepped into the early morning of Ironworld. The city yawned awake as I left the Public Gardens and headed home.

"I can't wait to eat," Lattie said as I turned the key and pushed open the door.

"Lattie, you weren't starving there. You ate most of my food," I replied and left my shoes, jacket, and bag in the entryway. "I'm sure you hunted a few things on the grounds, too."

"You're back!" Julie chimed as she jumped from the couch and sped over to me. Lattie fluttered off for the kitchen in a huff. My best friend's eyes frantically raked me over. "Are you okay? How was it? Tell me everything."

I blew out an exasperated breath and wrangled my hair into a ponytail. "Let's sit."

"I wasn't expecting you back until tonight," she said and scooped up a steaming cup of coffee from the coffee table.

"It was almost evening when I left."

"Oh, that's right," Julie replied from the rim of her cup. "Time moves differently there. I just thought, with Oden's note–"

"Oden sent a note?"

She plucked it from the table and handed it to me. I opened the brown parchment to find a beautiful black scrawl.

Avery is here. She is safe. She'll return at the end of the third day.

Lattie flew over and perched on the back of the couch, her gangly arms full of bread and cookies. I nabbed a bagel, and she growled at me.

"Tess sent word a few times," Julie told me, unable to look me in the eye. "She was worried."

"She doesn't get the right to be."

We let a painful silence hang between us as she sipped her coffee and tightened her white robe over her jammies. I grabbed myself a coffee from the kitchen and sat back down.

"Did anyone else check in?" I dared ask.

She gave a tentative smile. "Everyone did, Av'. We were all worried about you."

"Who's everyone?"

She let her head tip to the side. "He didn't call, but his sister did."

I expected as much. Cillian was just as stubborn as me, but I knew he also wanted to give me space and show me trust, as much as it probably killed him. Celadine checked in; that was at least something. She would have updated him.

"Did you learn anything?" she asked.

I almost said no, but that would be a lie. He'd tested me the whole time, showing me the bounds of my power and emotions and how they're linked. Sullivan taught me to wisp. Sort of.

"Um, actually, yeah. It might take some time, but I think it'll work."

Julie failed to hide her look of surprise. "Well, just... be careful."

I smiled and tucked my feet under me as I turned toward her in a more comfortable position, holding my warm coffee to my chest as the steam billowed in my face. "I will." My lips were dry. "I'm gonna go work in the café."

She scrunched her face. "You're going to work? *Now?*"

I shrugged. "So much has happened and is *still* happening. I need to do something normal, so I can think."

"I get it," she said, chewing at her lip. Her crystal eyes glistened. "But I'm still here. We're all still here for each other."

"I think I just need some mundane time. No supernatural anything, just slinging coffee for four hours."

I could tell she wanted to say more, to convince me to stay and just talk it out with her. But that's not what I needed. I had to completely remove myself from everything to sort my thoughts. I'd always been that way.

"Hey," she said casually and leaned back into a few pillows with her coffee. "We all have our ways of coping with things. I'm just solidifying the fact that I'm he–"

"Here if I need to talk. I know." I gave her a genuine smile and patted her knee as I stood. "Head down later this afternoon, and we'll eat all the baked goods left at the end of the shift."

Julie tossed her head back with a laugh. "Sounds good."

I sent Cillian a quick *talk later?* text and changed into a clean pair of jeans and a navy sweater before heading downstairs. The other barista was working the same shift. Penny. Even better. I mindlessly held a minimal conversation with her while breaking down the past few days' events and my last interaction with Cillian.

Four hours flew by. The monotonous tasks were like a

type of therapy for me. I worked through everything but still had no clue what to say to Cillian when I did see him.

After my shift ended and I gorged on chocolate croissants with Julie, I headed to Celandine's quaint Victorian mansion. My two favorite vampires lived on one of the few streets of downtown Halifax lined with towering trees. They created a beautiful and almost eerie canopy of branches. I loved it.

The old metal gate creaked as I closed it behind me. A break in the trees showed a glowing crescent moon, forever a ticking clock for me now. As much a reminder as the gilded tattoo on my back.

Celadine halted on the front steps, cradling a large basket of black flowers to her chest. I knew where those were going. I'd seen them before in beautiful bouquets all around the gallery. I had no idea she grew them herself.

"Well, you made it back in one piece," she teased. Her violet eyes flashed with delight. Her glasses were perfectly balanced atop her head of braids and dreads where random metal beads and glass baubles gleamed in the moonlight.

"Barely," I quipped.

Celadine laughed and continued up the stairs. "Come in. Tell me all about it."

I followed her into the spacious front porch, where she dropped the basket. "You haven't seen my home studio, have you?"

"I didn't know you had one," I replied as I slipped my shoes off. "But I'm not surprised."

She led me through the house to a set of double sliding doors. She slid one open, and I followed her inside. The room was spacious, and the walls towered with shelves of art supplies. A pile of canvases sat in one corner, a bookshelf in the other with an easel in front.

Celadine leaned her bottom against a small wooden desk. "This is my space. No one else comes in here, nor do I share it with anyone. It's the most intimate part of me. Decades of emotions have been poured out in this room."

"Why show it to me?"

She turned. "I want you to see how important it is to have your own space. Your life is messy, and you've got ties in every corner. Find a place to pour those thoughts and emotions out, turn them into art, or turn them into ash. Whatever you need. But make it *yours*."

I gnawed at the corner of my mouth as I circled the studio, noting the specific tools and paints she used. Admiring the neatness of it all. "When I was in the Domain of Nightmares, I found myself in the middle of the woods, and these creatures flooded me with every dark emotion. Things I didn't even know I could feel." My breath jittered. "But Oden said it was my human emotions that attracted them. If Oden hadn't shown up when he did, the creatures would have… I don't know."

Yes, I did, but I didn't want to say it. Didn't want her to worry or her brother. Misery would have drained every ounce of happiness from my body and filled me to the brim with ugliness.

"Perhaps gaining control over your powers isn't the only thing to be learned."

But it wasn't enough. I wanted to be powerful and wield magic with confidence. But I also wanted to be strong, to defend myself. Things were coming and building over the horizon. I could feel it; my visions told me as much. I just couldn't make sense of them. But my mother was the mad queen of Faerie. Trouble was inevitable.

"Can…can you teach me self-defense?"

She balked. "What?"

"Just a few moves," I said. Grasping that ounce of control, how my magic finally listened to me, was addictive. I wanted to learn more and do more. I wanted to be strong. Capable. "I mean, you're practically Vikings, aren't you? You've got to know a thing or two."

"That's a hurtful stereotype," a raspy voice gently hollered from the doorway.

I spun around, but my heart sank at the half smile he seemed to struggle to keep. He could barely meet my eyes, but he did, and I witnessed just one thing. Remorse.

I played it off. "I mean, if you're not able to, I can just

enroll in karate classes across town–"

Cillian shoved off the doorway with an exaggerated eye roll and waved me to follow. "Come on."

Celadine laughed as I stalked across the studio and followed Cillian deeper into the house. After a moment too long of watching the stiff muscles of his back move beneath his thin, black shirt, I tugged at his sleeve.

"Hey, can we talk?" I asked as he half-turned with a hopeful look. I wrapped my fingers over his forearm and tried to ignore how his whole body seemed to relax at my touch. "Where are we? What's going on in that brain of yours?"

He sighed through his nose. "Too much."

I stepped closer, relishing the cool breath that kissed my face. "Tell me. I want to know what you're thinking."

Those striking blue eyes scanned my face as he weighed his words heavily. "I'm thinking that I hate this. I hate that I feel so deeply for you so soon, so much, so…*consuming*. That it might scare you away."

The last word came out with a loss of breath.

"I hate that there's nothing I can do or say to change your mind or get you out of this bargain. I hate that, for three days a month, I have no idea what you're doing, what's being done *to* you, if you're even alive–"

I put my finger to his lips. "I'm fine. More than fine. Yes, I entered this bargain with desperation, but I think it might have been the best choice. I've been practicing with everyone here for weeks now, with no improvement. I spent one weekend in Faerie, and I can see it. I can see the control; it's within reach."

His lips pressed into a thin line.

"I'm going back," I told him. "I know I can master this; I can get what I need there. Just a few more visits."

Cillian loosened a breath and put his forehead to mine. "I know. I won't tell you what to do or how to do it. If this is what you need, then go. Just make sure to come back to me each time." He pulled away and cupped my face in both hands, hooking my gaze with his. "But if you return to me with so much as a scratch, I'll kill him."

I chuckled through the kiss he laid on my mouth, but something touched the bottom of my stomach, a worry I never knew was there. I didn't feel threatened by Oden. Yes, I knew he was dangerous and powerful. I saw it for myself. He knew the secret of who I really was and apparently wanted to earn my trust by working with me to gain the throne. I knew he killed Orion. But part of me felt... *knew*...he'd never hurt me.

But would he hurt Cillian?

He took my hand and continued leading me down through the house until we got to a large wooden door. He pushed it open, and I followed him inside to find a massive gym with every exercise machine I could ever fathom.

Stacks of weights piled the corners, a wall of mirrors reflected the entire room, and a small bar area hugged the empty stretch next to the door.

"What is this?" I asked.

All worry had melted away, and he boasted that devilish grin I loved so much. "When you're immortal and never sleep, you find ways to fill the time." He crossed his arms, showing off the lithe muscles beneath his thin sleeves. "If he gets you three days a month, give me the rest. Every day with me down here."

"Every day?"

He laughed. "An hour each day. Learn your magic by whatever means you want, but I'll teach you to fight. We can do it in the morning before your classes or at night after you've finished working at one of your many jobs."

"Don't make fun," I warned mockingly. "Not everyone has centuries of wealth. What makes you so qualified to shape me into a fighter?" I teased.

"What was it you said?" His arms swayed easily at his sides. "I used to be a Viking?"

I shrugged. "Didn't you?"

Cillian laughed to himself as he seemed to recall a distant memory. "Yes, but I was more than that. Our mother was the village priestess, the healer, and the sorceress. But my uncle was a warrior. The best one, in fact. He led our people through battles and attacks and trained the young men in our village. After he died, the responsibility was left to me, but it wasn't long after that when Cellie and I… changed."

"And you were cast out."

Cillian nodded. "Anyway, enough doom and gloom. Are we training or not? You pick the time, and I'll be here every day. There might not be a Viking warrior in you, but I'll sure as hell whip you into shape."

I thought for a moment. There was no way I could work out after a long day of classes and slinging coffee. My mornings were pretty lax. My first class didn't even start until nine on most days.

I stuck out a hand to shake. "Mornings it is."

✳✳✳

After getting a feel for all the equipment, we headed to his apartment and made love. I lay contently in Cillian's arms, my still-hot body melded with his cool one without a layer of clothing between us. The cool wintery air breezed over the room, lulling me into a deep sleep. But only nightmares were there to greet me.

A black silk gown flowed down my body, pooling on the ground at my feet. The fabric seemed to have been threaded by a midnight storm, and thunder rattled my veins. I glanced up at a silver-framed mirror that suddenly appeared on the grass, and Oden stood behind me as he lowered a twisted black crown onto my head. But it wasn't any of that which rattled me.

A pure look of triumph smeared across my face in the reflection.

I awoke with a dying gasp, my entire body flinching, and Cillian's arms tightened from behind as he pulled me closer to him. I stared out the open window and silently focused on my breathing.

But I couldn't seem to settle. Not with the way the white moonlight reminded me of Oden's scythe, and the winter treetops looked like the treacherous landscape of the Dark Forest.

Cillian nuzzled my ear with a sleepy rasp. "Bad dream or vision?" The words were a whisper. He and his sister never fully slept, but they did rest, and I thanked the stars he was there to hold me through the emotions that slowly settled within me.

"Dream," I replied, but my throat tightened. *Or was it a vision?*

Rain began to trickle outside, falling through the deadened winter trees and frosty pavement below like drops of glass. A crescent moon stared back at me through the bramble of black branches like a constant ticking clock in the sky.

Cillian stirred and burrowed his face into my neck. I

could feel him growing against my bare behind, and something blossomed in my chest. A want—no…a *need*. I gently rolled my hips, and he hardened, eliciting a low moan from him that vibrated right through me.

His hand roamed up my stomach, leaving a trail of hot goosebumps, and cupped a breast. I slightly arched my back, giving him more access, and he pulled me closer. His fingers wandered downward, slipping between my thighs and gripping the meat of my leg as he pulled it back toward him and slung it over his hip.

Even though Cillian lay behind me, I was borne to him, and something awakened inside me. A growing hunger and need to cast a blanket of his scent over the fear and worry seeping from my pores. I wanted him all over me, inside and out.

Cillian's fingers slid over my warm core, igniting the most sensitive nerves. A hot gasp turned over in my throat, and I buried my face in the pillow, but it only encouraged him. Gentle, purposeful circles, fingertips dipping in and out of me. I reached down, joining my hand with his.

His teeth grazed my ear. "Oh, God, Avery…"

I reached for him, guiding him toward what I desperately wanted, and he teased my opening with his tip, refusing to go any further. He continued coaxing pleasure from me with his fingers, and I arched my back even further, practically begging him.

"Do you want me?" he whispered against my exposed neck, reminding me of what lay just beyond those lips. Teeth. Weapons. A means to an end if he ever so wished. But I knew Cillian would never hurt me, and I tipped my head back, pushing the skin of my neck against his open mouth.

"Yes," I replied as he drove himself inside of me.

I cried out with a mix of pain and pleasure, and Cillian's hand crawled up to my neck, wrapping his long fingers around it. With every thrust, every dip and roll of his hips, I wanted more. I wanted to get lost in him as he lost himself in me.

He quickened his pace, gripping my thigh, and I could feel his entire body tensing at my back. He spilled into me just as I found my own release, my eyes locked on the white crescent moon the whole time.

Chapter Twelve

As the weeks passed, I filled every second of my time with school, work, and training. Classes seemed so simple and trivial compared to my life's true chaos. I flew through lessons and easily compiled my portfolio. I poured hours each week into my big end-of-semester project and even took it to work with me some nights.

But Celadine had a show booked for New Year's, so I had to switch and spend most of my time at the gallery prepping for that after I peddled coffee for a couple hours.

Weekends and the witching hours were for training.

When I wasn't learning about poisons and sneaky weaponry from the twins, I practiced wisping with Julie, studied herbs and potions with Oliver, and control with Moya. But each day began with an hour in the gym with my vampire boyfriend. I wanted to learn to fight, to at least defend myself, but Cillian only had me building muscle. In other words, lots of cardio and weights.

But I wasn't the only one jamming every second of my time with things. When Julie wasn't practicing wisping with me or taking her own classes, she was helping at the Sanctuary. Since the gilded promise Oden made to me about ending his deal with the Therians, hoards of displaced Solitary Fae had flocked to the secret haven in the in-between, where Faerie and Ironworld overlapped. The same place Oliver's property was located.

Julie and I strolled up and down the never-ending aisles of the Black Market while she shopped for supplies to bring to the ever-growing Sanctuary. Pots and utensils, blankets, and tarps. I noted how most vendors had Yule décor hanging from the tent flaps and strung from the tops.

"Shit, Christmas is soon, isn't it?" I muttered.

Julie laughed as she fanned through a stack of linens. "Yeah, in like two weeks. Not excited this year?"

I chewed at the corner of my mouth and stared at the heap of things I carried. "Well, I've spent every Christmas of my life with Tess."

Something seemed to click, and Julie dropped the linens on the table and grabbed everything I was holding. She snapped her fingers and shoved it through a rip in the air, and it all disappeared.

"What—where did it go?" I asked.

"A closet we all share at Oliver's," she replied and slung an arm over my shoulder. "We've got some other shopping to do." Before I could mutter another question, she added, "This is our first Christmas on our own, and with everything that's happened…." She let out a groan and shook her head. "I should have planned something."

"Jules, you don't have to—"

"Yes, I do." She stopped at one of the larger vendor booths, filled with an array of crafted things. "You may not have Tess this year, but you still have me. And now we both have this new family of friends, plus your vampire duo." When I opened my mouth to protest, she shushed me. "Do you want presents or not?"

I laughed and agreed. What else could I do? Julie was an unstoppable force you could ever argue with. So, we spent the rest of the time shopping for Christmas presents. A few weeks back, I'd given Oliver a bunch of mundane cash to trade with some Fae he knew that used the currency and got me a small pouch of Faerie coins. Julie said she was more than happy to share hers with me, the coins she earned from odd jobs for Solitary Fae across the city. But I wanted my own.

When we both circled around and met up again, my backpack was stuffed with gifts for everyone. I'd find something for Tomas in Ironworld, but I got a pair of leather gardening gloves for Celadine that never wore out, a set of beautiful coral hair combs for Moya, a collection of cork-topped vials for Oliver, and an enchanted picture frame for Julie filled with a moving image that the old, wrinkled, hunched over vendor pulled from my memory.

It was of Julie and me, but she was in her Fae form, the one she hid from the world. I wanted her to know how I saw her.

I'd planned on gifting part of my art project to Cillian, a three-dimensional picture of him crafted from the many images and sketches I'd scribbled in my book. A picture of himself, surely, he'd love it. I laughed as Julie stopped at my side.

"What's so funny?" she asked.

"Nothing, just thinking about Cillian."

She narrowed her eyes. Julie still wasn't convinced about my choice of boyfriend, and I didn't blame her. I mean, he *was* a vampire. To her, his food source ran in my veins, and he could overpower me with a single finger. Fae were biologically programmed to sense the danger of a vampire. It was in their nature to hate them.

But not Cillian and Celadine.

I inhaled deeply through my nose. "What did you get for Tomas?"

Her cheeks reddened. "Nothing. I wasn't sure... I haven't seen him in a while."

"You guys haven't talked at all?"

"No," she replied and turned to the exit. "I figured he would have told you how horrible I am for avoiding him."

We strolled. "He's a gentleman, you know that. He's only ever asked how you're doing. But I figured you guys would have at least talked about things by now." Tears welled in her eyes, and I pulled her into a hug. "If you love him, just tell him. To hell with this secret identity garbage."

"I can't, Av'," she said with strain and wiped the tears from her cheeks. "I can't do that to him. It just feels so wrong to let him get so close to our world when everything is on the edge of imploding. I don't want him to get hurt."

I pursed my lips in thought. "Are you sure that's it, though?"

She sniffled. "What do you mean?"

"I know you're scared to let anyone get too close. To *see* you."

Her crystal eyes sparkled with disbelief and denial. She backed away. "I, uh, I forgot something."

"Jules—"

"I'll be right back," she rushed, "Wait for me."

I didn't want to argue with her, and she clearly didn't want to talk about it. I nodded and folded my arms as she ran off and disappeared deep into the Black Market.

***

We'd walked home in silence, and I tossed and turned all night. Lattie hadn't come home, and I was left alone with all my thoughts, my never-ending circle of thoughts.

I turned my alarm off when the sun rose and got ready for class. I took my time and kept quiet, then headed down to the café just as Penny opened. It was a cold, calm, early winter morning, and I shook off a chill as I helped myself to a coffee.

I killed some time chatting with Penny, then headed off for class. I figured the walk would do me some good, and maybe I'd come home after class and actually sleep. I stepped onto the deafeningly quiet street, and the cool air iced my throat.

A black van screeched to a stop, and I stood between its side and the entrance to the coffee shop. It had me blocked in. As the van door rolled open, I stepped to the side, and two men in dark clothes lunged for me.

"What the hell?"

My coffee splattered over the cold concrete, and I jumped back, but they grabbed my arms and dragged me toward the awaiting van. My kicking did nothing. I took a deep breath as my foot met the edge of the van door, and sunlight burned in my hands.

And then there was darkness.

I struggled to open my eyes as if my brain couldn't find them. *Arms, legs.* The world blinked into existence, and the slow drag on my mind told me I'd been out for hours. I wiggled my fingers, but they were filled with pins and needles.

Finally, my eyes peeled open to a cloudy film, and I waited for the room to come into view. Stone surrounded me as if the room were hewn from the earth. I counted my heartbeats. No…not a *room* but a *cell*. Iron caged me in, and my naked limbs were pinned down with leather straps.

Everything fell into place, and the world snapped back to me.

I awoke with a gasp and strained against the straps, cold metal biting against my bare back. And that's when I noticed needles sticking out of my limbs in several areas. Six in total. And two more from my neck. Each one with a dark red hose that led to blood collection bags.

"What the shit!" The words took so much energy to mutter, energy I barely had. *How long have they been draining my blood? Who grabbed me off the street?*

My head was free, and I craned my neck to take in my surroundings. Nothing but a large iron cage wedged into a hole cut from the earth. But inside the cage, around the medical bed I lay on, were metal cabinets and stacks of crates. Crates with the Therian insignia.

"Fuck," I hissed slowly and assessed my restraints once again.

It took every ounce of energy, but I wiggled my arms

and legs, hoping to find a weak spot in the straps. The one pinning down my left wrist was a little loose, but not loose enough. I pulled, but my thumb wouldn't fit through.

My body deflated against the surgical bed as I fought to catch my breath. Every single movement caused great discomfort and wrung out my energy. They must have been draining my blood for hours.

I waited a moment, breathing in and out in long, slow breaths, and yanked at the strap again. My thumb almost fit, but I could feel the pressure at the joint near my wrist, threatening to pop it out of place. My heart sank as I realized that's what had to be done if I wanted to escape.

I steeled my nerves and filled my lungs, wishing I had something to bite down on. But I didn't have time to wait. I had to do this now before someone came along. I counted to three and yanked my hand away from the strap as hard as possible. The unnerving sensation of bones and flesh moving unnaturally made my stomach twirl, and I failed to stifle the sound of agony that erupted from my throat.

But my hand was free.

I wasted no time freeing my limbs from the leather restraints and didn't think twice as I ripped the needles from my limbs and neck. Each one had its own sort of agony, tugging at my skin. A warm sensation trickled down the right side of my neck, the blood refusing to stop. Frantically, I searched the cabinets for anything to wrap it with. I found a gauze roll and hastily wrapped it around my neck with as much pressure as I could manage.

Now to find a way out of this cage.

The iron-barred door was bolted shut with a giant black padlock. *Would they be dumb enough to leave a key in here?* I glanced around, my eyes landing on the old metal hinges that held the door in place, and I laughed. *No, but they're stupid enough to use the same old hinges as the Summer dungeons.*

I grabbed a chunk of stone from the corner of the cage and quickly beat it against the bottom of the pins, popping them up and out of the hinges. Footsteps sounded in the distance, growing quicker and louder with every second. My heart jumped into my throat, but I pulled at the cell door, and it flung to the side with an ear-piercing clang.

Voices now mixed with the footsteps.

I slipped out and ran in the opposite direction, my legs threatening to buckle with every step. Wherever I was, it seemed to be a series of underground tunnels and different rooms. Some were cells like the one I was in; others were almost like offices. I passed a small library full of old, dusty tomes and a larger room with a giant rectangular table in the center covered in papers and random objects.

My mind raced with so many panicked thoughts. Get out, hide, and get clothes. The footsteps and clamor of angry voices told me they'd reached the cell I was held in and realized I had escaped. I couldn't stop, couldn't even hide. If these really were Therians—*wolves*—then they'd sniff me out in no time.

I scanned every hallway, every room, for an exit. A window, at the very least. But I must have been so far underground. There was nothing but endless stone and torchlit tunnels.

My energy was down to the dregs, and my legs wobbled with every step. I leaned against the rough walls for support as I walked. Running was out of the question now; I could barely stand. The jagged architecture tore at my exposed skin as I fumbled and fell my way along. The footsteps echoed, and I knew they were on my heels. I had to get out of sight before they rounded the last corner.

My heart raced, and my throat tightened. I slipped into a dark room just as their voices touched my ears, and I held my breath in the shadows while I waited for them to pass, silently praying that they wouldn't pick up my scent. My lungs burned as I counted each second, one after another, as the sounds of my pursuers slowly fazed out. I sobbed and clumsily fell to the floor.

"Quinn?"

I yelped and peered into the darkness as I scrambled back across the dirt floor.

"Christ, Quinn! What are you doing here?" Max said as she stepped out of the shadows, her arms full of vials, velvet satchels, and tiny boxes. She stuffed everything into an empty shoulder bag and crouched down. Her big brown eyes were alive with a panic I couldn't place. "*What. Are. You. Doing. Here?*"

"You tell me!" I exclaimed and then quickly lowered my voice. "One moment I'm stepping out of The Chocolate Kettle, the next I'm being thrown into a van. I woke up down here, naked, strapped to some gurney with needles sticking out of my body."

She sighed through her nose and pinched the space between her eyebrows. "Fuck."

"What?" I asked and curled my knees to my chest. "Did you have anything to do with this?"

"No," she replied, removing her long black jacket. "My mother did."

Max scooped her hand under my arm and helped me to my feet with ease. I wondered just how strong she was, even in her human form. She fed my arms through the sleeves as I let my weight fall against the wall and waited while her fingers fiddled with the buttons that, thankfully, lined the whole length, covering my naked body.

"Thank you," I said.

Max grabbed my hand and peeked out the door. "Thank me when I get you out of here." I let her lead me down the hallway. She moved as if every inch of this place was second nature, and perhaps it was. "You have no idea what you've gotten yourself into, Quinn."

Why *would* Max's mother kidnap me and take my blood? Then it hit me. "I think I do," I replied, and she yanked me around yet another winding corner. "I made a deal with the Dark Lord of Nightmares."

Max came to a screeching halt. "You did *what?*"

"I made a deal with him–actually, no. I *forced* him into a promise. To stop the illegal harvest and trade of Fae blood with the Therians. I guess your mom wasn't too happy about that."

She narrowed her eyes. "You're even dumber than I thought."

"Excuse me?"

She turned to me and slung a hood over her head. "I told you not to catch my mother's attention. She'll take whatever you have and leave you for dead. Instead, you do something even worse by making some bargain with the Dark Lord?"

"A promise," I corrected. "I gave nothing in return."

Max's shoulders shook. "Why? Why would he do that? He must have known the blowback it'd get from Vivian."

"He's trying to gain my trust."

"Why?" she begged. "You told me you were no one."

"I'm…" Damn it. Did I trust Max? "I may be the long-lost daughter of Queen Mabry."

Max's eyes went as wide as saucers. "Jesus fucking Christ." The words were barely a whisper. "You need to get out of here now." She grabbed my hand and pulled me along.

"What's wrong?" I struggled to keep up. My bare feet scuffed along the scratchy floor.

Max stopped and turned again, her chest heaving. "If you think Oden's little promise to you did anything, you're dead fucking wrong. Vivian Carmichael has been planning things long before you or I were born."

"What kind of things?"

"Like taking the Seelie throne from Mabry," she replied regretfully. "My mother had a deal with Oden to help him overthrow Mabry. He'd supply Fae blood, and the Therians would fight with his army. But you just roll up, the literal fucking *heir* to Mabry's throne. Do you realize the target on your back?"

I swallowed dryly. "Yeah, but then it'd just be a fight between your mother and Oden for the throne."

Max opened her mouth to say something but folded her arms as she looked into the distance.

"Unless there's something I don't know," I said, and Max refused to look me in the eye. I dodged into her line of sight, forcing her to look at me. "What's going on?"

She sucked in a long, exaggerated breath. "Fuck it. Come with me," she said in a hard exhale.

I followed her down a narrow wing where fewer torches lit the way. Both of us cast careful glances over our shoulders. We stopped outside a set of metal doors with a small window. Max stepped aside and nodded toward them.

Slowly, I peered inside, and my heart sank. Six beds in a line, all like the one I'd been strapped to. Only these held down various Fae. Ones I'd never seen before. Two were humanoid but with distinctive features. The almond eyes, the pointed ears, long limbs. But four were of the smaller variety with snouts, floppy ears, and curling tails. Each no bigger than a cat.

And all with hoses draining blood from their bodies.

"My mother is building an army of vampires with Fae blood in their veins. She's going to use them to invade Faerie and take the throne with or without your Dark Lord."

I reached for the handle. "We have to get them out!" Max grabbed my arm, and I stared at it. "Are you seriously going to stop me?"

She considered it for a moment. "No. I just needed a moment to be sure."

"Sure of what?"

"That this is worth putting the final nail in the coffin of my relationship with my mother." The corners of her mouth twitched, and I realized how very little I'd ever seen Max smile. She let go of my arm. "It is."

We opened the doors and wasted no time detaching the Fae from the needles. We started with the two larger ones.

"Can you walk?" Max asked one of them, and they slowly nodded.

I moved over to the smaller Fae, the ones that looked drained of all life. I stuffed two in Max's arms and cradled the other two in mine.

My pulse thundered. "If we can get above ground, I think…I think I can wisp us to safety." That was a lie. Five minutes ago, I barely had the energy to stand. But something ran through me, a compulsion to help these creatures. "Or maybe one by one. I don't know. I-I'll try."

Who was I kidding? I could barely wisp myself.

"I know a way we can sneak out," Max said.

We followed her from the room and down several hallways, with me in the rear. I breathed heavily as the air changed from hot and damp to cool and crisp. I quickened my pace, knowing we were close to an exit. A set of concrete stairs led us to a small crypt, and Max pushed open the stained-glass door.

We all fumbled onto the cool grass, and I fell to my knees. Rather than help me up, Max dropped to her knees beside me, and then the two larger Fae after her. We all passed around and held one of the smaller Fae.

I held my free hand to the middle space in front of us. "We have to be touching. I-I don't even know if this is going to work." My insides brimmed with determination.

But everyone put their hand on mine, and I closed my

eyes. I conjured a picture of the Sanctuary and locked it in my mind with such precision it almost scared me. The fabric of space and time pulled at me from all sides for a fleeting second, and I opened my eyes.

It worked.

Several familiar faces stared down at us as a few others approached. One was Julie. A sob broke through me, and she fell to the ground beside me. Her hands hovering, frantically searching over me.

"What the hell happened?" she shrieked as some larger Fae encircled Max.

A dark, fuzzy ring began to close in and narrow my vision. "We're going to need…more…tents," I managed to say before passing out in her lap.

Chapter Thirteen

A familiar smell roused me from some of the deepest sleep I'd ever had. My senses noted a crackling fire, some stew brewing, and herbs drying in another room. All mixed with a lovely earthy tinge. Something tugged at my hand, and my eyes peeled open.

Oliver sat next to the bed I lay in, wrapping my hand. His eyes darted to my face, and he grunted approvingly. "You're awake."

"Unfortunately," I groaned and attempted to shift in place. But my body felt like a deflated balloon.

He gave a slight chortle and leaned back on the rickety wooden stool he sat on. "Thank the stars you're even alive, girl. You looked like a corpse when they dragged your body here last night. I couldn't even tap a vein to start a blood infusion until a few hours ago."

My head was heavy as a stone as I checked my other arm and noted the needle taped to the inside of my elbow.

Panic flooded my body, and I wanted to bolt from the bed and rip the thing out of my arm. Oliver took my hand and covered it with one of his, patting it slowly, comfortingly.

"Hush now, you're safe," he said calmly. "It's putting blood in, not out."

"How did you know—" I glanced around the tiny bedroom. "Where's Max?"

"She's being held in another room," he replied.

"Held? What do you mean?"

"Aya and Brie made sure she didn't leave until you woke up and could verify her story. They're watching over her."

"She saved me," I rushed out. "Max saved me. She's not the enemy—can I speak with her? Can you bring her in here?"

His large troll lips mulled together. "Very well."

Oliver stood and ducked through the doorway. I lay there and stared at the ceiling, willing my poor heart to calm down. Oliver returned after a minute with a disgruntled Max in tow. Her hands were bound with a simple rope. Did they seriously think that would hold her? She was a werewolf, for crying out loud. If Max wanted to escape, she could have. Easily. The fact that she was still here, allowing herself to be tied up, spoke volumes. To me, anyway.

"Are you okay?" I asked her.

She seemed puzzled at the question but shrugged.

"Better than you."

"Thank you," I said. "For saving me and for helping me free those Fae." I looked at Oliver. "I think you can remove the ropes."

But before he could, Max pried her wrists apart with ease, and the rope ripped in half, falling to the floor. Oliver grumbled something under his breath and walked away as Max entered the room, her back pressed against the wall.

"When can I leave?" she asked me.

"You're not a prisoner," I told her, and she gave me a look. "Max, we both know you could have left at any time. Why did you stay?"

She stared at the floor in thought. "I don't know."

Even after running around underground, saving those fairies, and spending the night at Oliver's cabin, every inch of her was immaculate. From her unwrinkled leather pants to the long-sleeved black shirt she wore. Not a single braid was out of place. Not a speck of dirt on her ebony skin.

On the other hand, I looked like someone stripped me of my clothes and dragged me across a field of shit. I pulled the handmade quilt up further over my body. I still wore Max's peacoat, but the sleeves had been ripped off where Oliver had been working on me.

"Shit, sorry about your jacket," I said. "I'll pay you back."

A grin tugged at the corner of her mouth. "Don't

bother. It's my mother's."

"Why were you wearing your mother's jacket?"

She seemed to question the words that wanted to be said. "Fuck it, may as well jump all in." She shoved off the wall, and her chest rose as she filled her lungs. "I wasn't supposed to be down there in the coombs, and wearing my mother's jacket helped me slip by the guards."

"Coombs?"

"What you saw was a tiny part of an elaborate underground system of catacombs that spans the entire city. Maybe even more. It's where the Therians first took refuge five hundred years ago when the Seelie king forced them all from Faerie. At first, it was just a simple underground space, maybe an abandoned sewer system or something. And, over hundreds of years, they expanded and transformed it into what it is today. Cells, laboratories, offices, meeting rooms, treasure troves, and catacombs to bury our dead."

"You bury your dead down there?"

"Well, the important ones, anyway," she replied. "Leaders, fighters, heroes."

"Why weren't you supposed to be down there?" I asked. "Aren't you the daughter of the leader or alpha or whatever?"

She unfurled her fingers with a look of disdain and crossed her arms. "I've been known to steal a thing or two from down there."

"Like what?"

Max tensed but never rose to anger. I was getting the gist that she didn't like oversharing. "Supplies…for witchcraft."

That made sense. I thought of Max's apartment, the herbs, bottles, and bowls that looked like they were plucked from the set of The Craft. And the Therians eradicated the witch population after coming to Ironworld. Of course, they'd have supplies.

"Max, I have to tell them."

Her dark eyes fleeted to mine and stayed there, a sort of understanding passing between us. It wasn't the witchcraft or the existence of the underground network that I needed to tell my friends about. It was Vivian's plan to use vampires and invade Faerie.

She nodded. "I know."

I chewed at my lip. "Are you…will you stop me? Are you going to tell your mother?"

"That woman has been dead to me for years." Still, a nervousness came over her, and Max steeled herself. "Do whatever you have to do. Just leave me out of it."

"I promise."

She arched a brow. "Aren't you part Fae in some way or another?"

My throat was dry and tight. "Yeah, or another."

Max grinned and turned to the door. "Be careful. Your

promises are dangerous."

She turned the knob, yanked it open, and motioned for everyone to enter the room. I wondered about gilded promises and what weight they held. The power they had.

Julie, Moya, and Oliver filed inside, lingering around the doorway. All eyes were on me.

"I'm completely fine," I said honestly. "But there's something you all need to know." I glanced at Max, who crossed her arms tightly. "Vivian Carmichael, Max's mother, is the alpha of the Therians, and she's using the Fae blood to feed vampires so they can invade Faerie and kill Mabry."

"But I thought she had that deal with Oden to help him overthrow the Seelie queen?" Julie said as she rolled up the sleeves of the long white shirt she wore over matching leggings.

I nodded. "Yeah, I don't think Oden knows of her plans to do it herself and take Faerie for the Therians."

"When is she planning to do this?" Moya asked with an unnerving look.

Max shrugged. "I have no idea. I haven't talked to my mother in a while."

Moya paced in place. "Avery, you need to tell Oden. Find out what he knows and what he plans to do. I'll head to the Summer domain and see if I can talk to Tess and Kheelan. I'll get my sisters to do some recon on Therian hot spots we know of."

Max shifted from side to side and looked at me uncomfortably. "Why do you all care?"

I blinked at her. "We all belong to both worlds and don't want to see them crumble. Are you going to help or not?"

She had a calculating look on her face as she looked from me to all my friends. "Screw this," she said and pushed through the doorway. No one dared follow her, and I didn't blame them. Max was a bomb just waiting to happen.

I didn't want to be there when it did.

***

Cillian cradled me in his lap while we looked up at the stars from my balcony. One arm around my back, the other hung over my waist, rubbing the skin beneath my olive-green sweater; I nestled my head against his chest, breathed in his soothing scent of night and leather, and told him everything that had happened.

I felt him tense beneath me. "I want to rip Vivian's throat out."

"Don't risk your life like that," I said and shifted in his lap so I could face him. "She has an army of vampires and werewolves, Cillian. Jesus. You might be immortal, but you're not invincible."

Those cerulean eyes sparkled in the moonlight, and he pushed my hair over my shoulder with a sad and distant look. "I know."

"Why do you do that?"

"Do what?"

I dragged my fingers across the stubble on his jaw and stared at it. "It's so subtle, most people wouldn't even see it. Both you and your sister do it. Sometimes you just… I don't know. It's like you'd *welcome* death or something."

"Maybe we're just not afraid of anything," he replied cheekily.

I wrapped both arms around his neck. "We're all afraid of something."

I meant it lightly, but his eyes darkened, and wetness filmed over them as he stared at me. I wondered what he truly feared. Was it losing me or hurting me? Because it was both for me. My biggest fear was accidentally killing my boyfriend and losing him all at the same time. I thought about it constantly.

The pain I sensed in his gaze made me look away, and I cleared my throat. "So, when will you actually start teaching me to fight? There's only so much cardio I can take."

"Cardio, weight training, endurance, and stamina," he corrected. "You have to make your body strong first. Then you fight."

"Then teach me one thing for now," I pleaded. "Anything. I just want something I can use to defend myself." When he went to argue, I quickly added. "The Therians will use the vampires to betray Oden and take over Faerie. And I'm going to get roped into it. I can *feel* it. I need to be able to protect myself."

"You've only been working out a few weeks," Cillian said consideringly, his cool hand caressing the skin of my lower back. "But I might be able to teach you a defense move or two in the morning."

A few weeks? Oh, shit. I hadn't noticed how much time had gone by. I looked up at the moon, and it was nearly full. I headed back to the Domain of Nightmares tomorrow night. But I didn't want to think about that.

Cillian picked up my shift in mood and brushed his fingers across my neck, over the vein that throbbed when my pulse quickened and demanded my attention.

"Hey," he whispered. "Stay with me."

I pressed my lips together, and his eyes fell to my mouth as he smeared his thumb across it.

He slipped the tip in, and I swirled my tongue around it, eliciting a deep moan from his chest as he pulled me closer. I could already feel him growing beneath my leg.

"Julie's inside," I said.

His eyes flashed with deviousness. "Then you best not make a sound."

My legs slightly parted across his lap, a silent invitation, and he took it. His fingers slipped inside the waist of my pants and slowly worked magic as they passed over my most sensitive spot. Warmth pulsed there and spread outward. My mouth gaped with a moan, and Cillian capped it with his own, dragging his teeth over my bottom lip as he pulled away.

Those fingers massaged slow, sensual circles, coaxing a building climax that ebbed within me. When I dared make a sound, he stopped and quietly chuckled under his breath at the glare I shot him.

I curled my hand over his forearm, begging him to proceed, and he obeyed. My body responded, writhing in his lap as we exchanged heated moans of pleasure.

"Oh, God…" The words were no more than a whimper in my throat.

His other hand, the one at my back, smoothed up my spine and grabbed the hair at the nape of my neck. He gave it a gentle tug, pulling my head back, and my face tipped to the night sky where stars watched as my body trembled and I spilled my release into his hand. He kissed my exposed neck, sending goosebumps racing over my skin.

We sat motionless as statues, his hand still nestled between my thighs. My rampant heart beat between us as I waited for my lungs to calm. Finally, I turned my face to his, and he kissed the tip of my nose.

I gripped the back of his head and planted a hard, consuming kiss on his mouth. He protested with a groan when I leaned away, but his eyes widened as I slid from his lap and nestled on the balcony between his legs.

It was my turn.

***

It was lunchtime when I got a fire message from the Domain of Nightmares. It just said, *Harbour at Noon.* I'd hoped he wouldn't summon me until the evening, like last time, so I could spend the day with Cillian. But my vampire boyfriend did manage to teach me a couple of defensive moves before I got called away.

I walked down to the waterfront and strolled back and forth the long boardwalk that skirted this side of the harbor, searching for a tall, brooding, white-haired man. God, I hoped he at least saw fit to hide his pointed ears or leave behind the gaudy cane. The people of Ironworld weren't ready to witness a Dark Fairy Lord in all his glory.

The mid-December chill seeped between the layers of my clothes, and I flexed my gloved fingers, wishing I wore an enchanted pair that Aya and Brie gave me, ones that kept my hands nice and toasty. But I wouldn't need them where I was going.

I considered wearing a ring the twins also gave me, though. One made of a puzzle that could turn into iron knuckles. But my thumb and half my hand still swelled from escaping my binds down in the Therian coombs. I couldn't bear to let anything touch my hand at all. It just ebbed with a nagging ache.

After an hour of walking, I finally sat on a bench and waited. If Oden refused to be more specific with times and locations, he could just come to me.

Sullivan appeared on the bench next to me without a sound, sipping a Timmies hot chocolate, one leg crossed over his knee. His usual thin leather jacket was replaced by a dark brown parka and a hood lined with fur. He grinned at me, the tiny piece of metal in his lip gleaming under the winter sun.

"Afternoon, Red."

"He can't even meet me himself?"

"Oden's busy," Sullivan replied and took a sip from the red to-go cup. "So, I offered."

I leaned back, stretched, and crossed one ankle over the other. "Your brother isn't holding up his end of all this very well."

"What do you mean?"

"I'll reserve my wrath for him if you don't mind."

He regarded me for a moment, then fetched a pack of cigarettes from his pocket. I watched as he stuck the butt end of one in his mouth and lit it. He took a long drag and let out a slow breath of smoke. "Just tell me."

"Vivian kidnapped me and drained a shit ton of my blood," I said, my breath turning white in front of me. I'd save the part about her backstabbing his brother and building her own army of vampires for when I saw Oden. "Plus, Evaine still lurks around."

"Fuck." He took another long drag. "Oden's gonna be pissed."

I guffawed. "Doubt it."

He grinned knowingly to himself. "Still a skeptic?"

"I've yet to learn *anything*."

Sullivan half turned to me; eyebrows pinched together. "You haven't been practicing what he told you?"

"Well–" I took a steadying breath. "I mean, yes, I have, but–"

"Show me."

"What?"

He rolled his eyes and chuckled. "Show me how much you've practiced, Red."

I blinked a few times and adjusted how I sat, sitting up and staring at my open hands. I summoned my light, pooling in my palms like a tiny spark. I let it grow and grow, cascading over my fingers and pouring down to the snowy ground, melting everything around the bench. And just like the snap of an elastic band, I reined it in, and we sat in regular sunlight again.

Sullivan gave me a cheeky smirk and a wink as he stood

and snuffed out the cigarette with his boot. "I'd say you've learned something." He offered a heavily ringed hand to me, fingernails chipped with dark polish. "Shall we?"

I stood, slipped my hand into his, and took a deep breath. We stood at the edge of the castle's property line when I let it out. Well, the wisping line, anyway. I shuddered with a glance toward the Dark Forest, remembering the way Misery and all his friends made me feel. I breathed in through my nose. The air was different here. Denser, sweeter. More alive.

"How'd you get away?" Sullivan asked as we strolled up the long dirt path.

I subconsciously tucked my arm to my side, trying to hide my injured hand. "I managed to wiggle free of the straps and took the pins out of the door hinges."

Sullivan threw his head back with a deep, raspy, guttural laugh.

"What?"

"I'm gonna like havin' you around, Red."

"Don't get used to it," I warned him. "I don't plan on sticking around long."

He didn't reply and kept quiet as we strolled through the castle and right to the door of my temporary quarters.

"Oden will be back for dinner," he said and spun on his heel. "Relax. Get ready. See you in an hour," he called over his shoulder and disappeared around a corner.

I opened the thick wooden door with a huff and realized it didn't feel as heavy as before. My arms and body were stronger just from working out for a month. Nothing major, just a sense of might. I grinned as I shut the door behind me. Maybe Cillian knew what he was doing after all.

The room was different. The furniture and décor still mocked a dark castle vibe with emerald silk sheets and warm walnut furniture. But a desk had been added, its surface covered in art supplies. Coloring pencils, paints, pastels, charcoal, a stack of paper, and a few flat canvases.

I flung open the giant wardrobe, expecting to find an assortment of god-awful dresses. "What the hell?" The words were a whisper. Pants and shirts and sneakers and boots.

I reached inside and dragged my hand through the fabrics. All silks and gorgeous linens, but no more dresses. My fingers fished through my favorite jewel tones of navy, crimson, and jade. All mixed with black garments. Gold jewelry and accessories hung from inside the doors.

A knock came at the door, and Mags burst in before I could reach it, her two minion fairies in tow. They carried trays of snacks and a pitcher of wine and set it on the vanity as Mags gawked at me.

"Don't you Ironworlders have any sense of self-care?" she asked, gesturing to my hair and general appearance.

"Don't you fairies know how to properly knock?" I retorted and slipped out of my coat. "You're supposed to wait for permission to enter."

Her large, black eyes narrowed, but I caught a hint of a grin creasing the sides of her mouth, pulling at the lovely green color of her skin. She shooed me toward the bathroom, where I could already hear the giant bathtub filling. Mags followed me inside.

"I can get undressed and bathe myself–"

My clothes disappeared with another snap of her long, green fingers, and I'd forgotten the brown and blue bruises that peppered my body from the blood-sucking needles the Therians had jabbed into me.

Mags' eyes widened. "What in the world...." She grabbed my wrist to hold out my arm, but it was my injured hand, and I winced as I hauled it back from her grasp. She noted me nursing it to my chest. "What in the gods' name happened to you?"

"I had an unfortunate run-in with some werewolves." It didn't even bother me that I stood bare-naked in front of this woman, this Fae. She didn't look at me any differently than if I were fully clothed. This was her job.

"Is the hand broken?"

"I don't think so," I replied and tried to rotate my wrist. A sharp sensation bolted up my arm, and I seethed. "Just...hurt."

She turned off the tub, filled to the brim with hot, soapy bubbles and oils. "Why didn't you have it healed?"

"It *is* healed. I didn't want to worry anyone. I'm fine, I just—"

"You're in cahoots with a circle of capable Fae, a healer being one of them." How did she know that? "There's no reason for you to walk around with injuries like that."

"Can you heal them?"

"I'm skilled at many things, Miss Quinn, but a healer, I am not." She helped me step into the deep tub, and I almost moaned at the instant relief on my muscles. "Bathe. I'll pick out something for you to wear," she said as she turned for the door.

"Mags?" I said, and she glanced over her shoulder. "Something…with long sleeves?"

Her mouth pressed into a thin line, and she nodded before shutting the door behind her.

I soaked for half an hour before I let Mags and her helpers have at me. She dressed me in gorgeous navy, wide-legged silk pants and a matching long-sleeved top that snugged my upper body. My red curls bounced and shone in the mirror as she helped me add gold hoops to my ears and bangles on my good hand. Her two Fae carried a pair of blue velvet flats and placed them at my feet. I slipped them on. A perfect fit.

I strolled through the castle, taking the time to observe the art on the walls. All beautiful and abstract. Dark, just like the property, but somehow still warm and inviting.

I entered the dining room and stopped, thinking I had the wrong room. Gone was the long, gaudy table, replaced with a smaller, more intimate round one made of dark stained wood. A gorgeous bouquet of black and silver flowers anchored the center. I eyed Oden sitting in a grey wingback chair, two matching ones equally spaced around the table, and he gestured for me to sit.

"You look lovely," he said without really looking at me and placed a napkin on his lap. He unbuttoned the charcoal vest he wore over a light grey shirt.

I scooted my chair in and forced back the wince that came with the use of my wrist. "Where's Sullivan?"

"He'll join us shortly." He brought a glass of bourbon to his lips and inhaled before taking a sip.

The kitchen door swung open, and a server—one of the creatures from the kitchen—sauntered over and placed bowls of soup in front of us.

"Enjoy, Milord," the horned Fae said to Oden and tipped its head. They turned to me with a genuine smile. No malice, no I'm-going-to-put-you-in-a-stew threats. "And Miss Quinn."

So, it was all an act before. I managed a nod and a crooked half-smile. "Uh, thanks."

They returned to the kitchen, and I stared down at the soup as I dragged a spoon through it. Butternut squash. One of my favorites. Trays of side dishes appeared; toasted baguettes with avocado, freshly baked buns, and steamed veggies soaked in butter.

"No theatrics this time?" I asked, licking a smear of avocado from my thumb.

Oden grabbed a fresh rosemary bun and tore it open, ignoring me. "Sullivan tells me you have news."

I reached for another piece of baguette, and a small shot of pain lanced my wrist. "Yeah, buckle up because–"

"What's wrong with your hand?"

"What?"

Those stormy eyes watched me like a hawk. "Your hand. You nurse it."

"It's fine." I slipped it beneath the table.

A sense of boredom overcame him, and he focused on his soup. "How about a trade?"

"More deals? You can't think I'm that stupid."

His hand quietly clenched into a fist. "No deal, a *trade.* And that smart mouth of yours will get you into trouble."

I raised a challenging brow. "With whom?" His eyes darkened as he chewed. I cradled my wrist in my lap, and my stomach tightened. "What sort of trade?"

"I'll heal your injury and show you how to do it your-self." He grinned like a cat at the little show of interest in my eyes.

But I didn't reply. Not yet. Let the bastard wait like he's made me wait so many times. With my good hand, I poured a glass of wine. Lightning fast, Oden tossed a bun at me, and I instinctively reached with my only free hand. I dropped the bun and winced as my back hunched over in the chair.

"Christ! Alright!" I stuck out my arm toward him. "Show me."

Without hesitation, he cupped my hand in both of his. His hands were cold and firm. Not like Cillian's, where the night lived in his skin, but like a cool, airy breeze. Magic thrummed from where we touched.

"Close your eyes." He waited until I did. "Imagine your body like a fleshy machine, everything moving and working in motion. Feel for the wound, how it's broken, and see what's missing. Piece it back together."

As he spoke, I drifted deep into the recesses of my mind, imagining everything he said in that soft, raspy voice, like the sexy villain in pretty much…*everything*. I focused on the working parts of my body, how the blood flowed, the heart pumped, and the lungs breathed.

I followed the blood down my arm and to my wrist, where I could sense how the bones weren't placed right. I struggled, and Oden clenched my hand just a little, enough to push me forward, and I imagined it mirrored to my other hand.

A cold, tingly sensation brushed over my wrist, and I opened my eyes as Oden let go and leaned back in his chair. I blinked a few times and lifted my hand. It was completely healed.

"I did that?"

He took a spoonful of soup. "Didn't you?"

I wanted to kick him. Sullivan came strutting in and shrugged out of his jacket. He passed it off to one of the servants. I hadn't noticed just how defined he was; lithe muscles and cordage flexed beneath a tight shirt he wore over black jeans. His dirty combat boots were at least laced up. That long dark hair was swept back in a knot, and he gleamed at me.

"Get a good look, Red?" he said cheekily and took a seat. A bowl of soup was placed before him.

I shook my head and laughed. "I never realized how much you look like an Ironsider."

Sullivan slurped his soup. "I get that a lot."

"Why don't you dress like them?" I asked. "Like a Lord, or whatever."

"I spend a lot of time in Ironworld," was his only reply. But I could tell he wanted to say more. The fleeting look he threw his brother told me so. "But you already knew that."

After a weird moment of silence, Oden finally said, "Umbra is Sullivan's pet project."

My brows pinched together. "The club?" Sullivan nodded with a mouthful of food. "That atrocity is your doing?"

"Hey, now!" Crumbs fell from his mouth. "You came on a bad night. You got it all wrong, Red."

"Umbra is a safe place for my people in Ironworld, and the energy it generates fuels back to the Dark Forest to keep the ilk satiated."

I made a mental note to add these details to my book. "Ilk, like your friend Misery?"

"Misery is not a friend nor foe," Oden clarified. "But one of many creatures birthed of darkness to balance all that is good. I do what I can to keep the darkest of my Fae contained within the forest. They can leave but at a great cost. They wreak havoc on one another, which feeds them. The pain, the sin, the desire. Every dark emotion or need haunts those woods. But it's an essential part of my domain, of Faerie even. A…necessary evil, if you will."

I opened my mouth to ask more questions, but Oden cleared his throat, stopping me.

"So, this news," he said with an air of finality that told me that was the end of the other conversation.

I cut to the chase. "Vivian kidnapped me, drained my blood, and nearly killed me."

He paled, and those eyes turned murky with thunder. "What?"

"Yeah, and that's not the worst part," I added. He exchanged an alarmed look with his brother, who only shrugged. "You may have ended your deal with her. But she never stopped harvesting Fae blood or trading with the vampires. She's building her own army and plans to overthrow Mabry herself." I grabbed another piece of avocado toast. "Maybe that was her plan all along."

Oden gave me an incredulous look, one filled with calculation, as he realized just what the leader of the Therians had been up to.

"Did you seriously have no idea?" I asked.

He blinked away the storm in his eyes until they simmered to a soft bluish grey and rolled his shoulders as he took the last mouthful of bourbon. "I had inklings for months, but I needed a good reason to break the deal I had with her. I'm just surprised you were able to figure it out."

I couldn't tell him I was friends with Vivian's daughter. That might put Max in more trouble than I've already dragged her into. I cleared my throat and turned my attention to Sullivan, who tapped the rim of his glass. I watched as it magically refilled with liquor. I looked to Oden and caught him filling his in the same manner.

"Can you teach me that?"

He and his brother exchanged a grin. "I'll add it to the list."

"There's a running list?" I quipped and took a spoonful of soup. I wanted to moan at the soft, velvety taste. "Here, I thought your plan was to torture me slowly with boredom."

"You were expecting torture?" he teased. Sullivan stifled a chuckle under his breath as Oden leaned closer, the darks of his eyes boring into me. "I can delve out whatever torture you like, Avery dear. But I assure you, you'll be far from bored."

"Alright then." I pushed my bowl away. "What are we learning tonight? I've got limited time to do this, and I don't want to waste a minute of it."

Oden grabbed a napkin from the table and wiped his mouth. "Tomorrow, we train. Tonight, you learn." He pushed out his chair and stood next to me. "I've got some reading material for you. Follow me."

I grabbed another piece of baguette and hurried after him.

"See ya, Red!" Sullivan called.

I just nodded, mouth full of bread and avocado. I followed Oden down the torchlit corridor. A gentle breeze filled the castle, probably blowing in from whatever verandas and open arches there were. I still hadn't seen the whole expanse of the property, but I knew it was massive.

Servants tipped their heads with genuine smiles as we passed. No fear, no trembling slaves, no scurrying away. I thought of helpful Mags, as rough around the edges as she was. And the kitchen staff, how they toyed with me that first night but were clearly just pulling my leg. His staff loved him dearly, respected him, even. They seemed to enjoy the work they did here.

I watched him as we walked. Studied the width of his shoulders under perfectly fitted clothes, how they moved with each step. The grace and power he exuded.

Finally, we stopped outside two beautifully ornate walnut doors. Oden pushed them open, and I hurried inside after him. It was an office. Bookshelves stocked with beautiful tomes reached the ceiling and lined half the room. A dark wooden desk anchored the space, topped with papers and maps and a small globe that clearly wasn't the same Earth I knew.

Warmth radiated from a roaring fire nestled in a rock bed wall, and I stepped toward it as Oden plucked a book from the shelves.

"Here," he said and thrust it toward me. I barely caught it. "Read that tonight."

"What's it about?" I asked, examining the worn black leather binding and thick, weathered parchment.

"It touches on the origins of magic and some history. Knowing *how* goes hand in hand with knowing *what* lies inside you." He pointed at my chest.

The dark lord stood not a foot in front of me, those stormy eyes locking a firm grasp on me. I averted my gaze over his shoulder and did a double take at the painting above the fireplace.

I stepped around him, staring up at it. "That's mine."

It was the missing painting from Tess's house. The one with the distant castle tops and flying creatures in the sky. Evaine must have stolen it after all.

"Is that so?" Oden grinned next to me.

"Yeah!" I reached for the painting, but he grabbed my wrist with lightning speed. I flashed him a heated look.

"Well, seeing as it's a portrait of my home, I say we share." When I refused to look away, he chuckled deeply under his breath. "I can pay you whatever sum you name."

My throat suddenly tightened at one thought. I'd painted this place before I ever saw it. What did that mean? Was I meant to meet Oden and come here for help? Or was it a warning…an early vision before I knew what they were?

As much as I wanted to believe Oden was a good guy in all this, I had to remind myself that this man murdered the Seelie king and had me spied on and kidnapped. And, as if he could sense or smell my thoughts, Oden's face tensed, and he released my arm as he took a step back.

A figure moved in the corner, and a soft shadow lurked across the floor. My heart tightened as I stared in horror for just a split second. A dog formed and galloped across the room for me, tongue hanging off to the side. I knelt with a smile and scratched his ears with both hands.

"Hey, boy!" I said and kissed his smooth forehead. His mighty tail beat against the floor. I glanced at Oden with a chuckle, but he gawked at the sight of us with a mask of awe.

"Kol," he whispered unblinkingly.

I gave an exaggerated look of surprise to the dog and smoothed his fur. "So, you do have a name?" He licked my face. "This guy's been keeping me company when you ignore me."

Oden shook his head, a bewildered and unsure look about him.

I stood up. "What's the matter? Afraid your dog will like me better than you?"

"It's not my dog. It was my mother's. We…haven't seen him since her death."

"Oh." The word was dry in my mouth. I held the book tightly. "Well, I'm glad he decided to show up. I'm going to head up to my room and read."

Oden seemed to snap out of the daze. "Oh, yes, of course." He cleared his throat and busied with some papers on his desk. "I'll see you in the morning for training."

I left it at that, and Kol followed me back to my room. I sat in bed for hours, surrounded by dark silks and endless pillows. A warm night breeze sifted in through the open window as I slowly stroked Kol's fur with one hand and read the book with my other. I didn't know what to expect from the pages, but I inhaled the information.

It began with the origins of Faerie. Explained with passages and ancient sketches that told the tale of a sleeping world that was suddenly cleaved in two; Faerie and Ironworld born from it. Only Ironworld had only adopted the name in recent centuries. Before that, it was just the mortal realm. A world of non-magic, and then Faerie, a world that simply *was* magic. Everything here was made or birthed from it.

Other chapters explained how magic worked and how it's almost a living thing and deserves to be used with respect. It touched on balance and how both worlds needed it. Good and bad, dark and light, happy and sad. One couldn't exist without the other.

Other chapters were like history lessons detailing past kings and queens, lords, and ladies and how Faerie wasn't always headed by a single court. The world was once divided equally for balance. But somewhere along the way, greed and power paved the path for thrones, and the Seelie court was formed. But the fighting never stopped and eventually led to the Great War, a magical civil war that drove the Therians into the mortal realm.

A yawn forced open my jaw, and I set the open book down on the bed as I stretched my arm and rolled my shoulders. Kol gave a low moan of disapproval at the absence of my fingers in his fur and nudged my arm with his cold, wet nose.

The breeze picked up and coaxed through the room, flipping the pages of my book until it landed on a later section, bookmarked with an elaborate chapter heading drawn of symbols and whorls I didn't recognize. But the title I could read.

Origins of Witchcraft

What was anything to do with witches doing in a dark Fae lord's personal library? As far as I knew, it was a mortal race that had long been taken out by the Therians. No one talked about it. As I read, I pulled the book toward me and propped my elbows on my lap.

Thousands of years ago, the Fae tried to share their world with humans and gifted them a spark of magic. It bled into nature for them to use; thus, witches and sorcerers were born. The rulers of Faerie adored their creation, and they knew extensions of their world that pulsed into the mortal realm were to be protected.

This information was lost and buried. Julie once told me that humans experimented with Fae blood to force magic into their bodies. But according to this, it was a gift.

Another yawn rocked through me, and Kol snuggled closer, resting his giant, heavy head in my lap.

I chuckled quietly and scratched behind one of his soft ears. "Is that a hint for me to go to sleep?"

He breathed a nasal sigh in response. I set the book aside and shimmied further into the bed, the heaps of blankets and pillows hugging me. I drifted off in a matter of minutes, only to wander right into a vivid dreamscape of a roaring sea. I stood on a wet, sandy beach of smooth black granules and watched as waves of jade crashed into jagged rocks, catching flecks of moonlight.

To my left, and far down the beach, stood a figure draped in red. Her long crimson hair cascaded down her body and bled into her gown. Her back was turned, and I yearned to run to her.

"Do you want it?"

I spun around, and Tess was there. She smiled warmly and held out a golden crown embedded with yellow jewels. Words evaded me, and I glanced back to the woman in red. She was gone. And when I turned back to my aunt, Oden stood in her place, holding out a dark crown molded with sharp peaks and obsidian gems.

"Do you want it?" His deep, raspy tone vibrated through me, and I stood there, speechless. Thoughtless. I didn't know what I wanted. But it certainly wasn't a crown of any kind.

I opened my mouth to speak, and something sucked me out of the dream. I blinked at the dark canopy overhead, the dewy morning sun filtering through the fibers. Kol was nowhere to be seen. Someone banged on the door, and I begrudgingly slipped out of the blankets, letting all the warmth escape.

I opened the door a few inches to see Oden standing there.

"Did you read the book?"

I rubbed at my sleepy eyes. "What? Oh, yeah, I did, but—"

"Good. Meet me in the front courtyard in ten minutes." He spun on his heel and disappeared before I could even reply.

I grabbed the first thing I touched in the wardrobe and hauled it on; a pair of silky black slacks and a tank top with a sheer golden blouse. I didn't bother tying my boots, just tucked the laces inside and hastily brushed my teeth before wrangling my hair into a ponytail.

My fists clenched as I stood in the middle of the room, eyes closed tightly. But I didn't need to focus as hard as I usually did to wisp, the magic flowed through me with ease, and I stepped through the fabric of space and time into the courtyard in front of Oden's castle.

He stood waiting, hands tucked behind him, the neck of his grey tunic left unbuttoned. It was the first time I'd seen him outside his usual formal attire.

"You're late," he said, and I couldn't tell if he was serious.

I just gave him a look. "Listen, you woke me up less than half an hour ago, and I haven't had coffee. Be thankful I'm not chewing you a new ass."

The horror on his face made me smile with delight. "It's just an expression, chill."

"You sound like my brother sometimes." He gestured for me to join him on a nearby bench. A large one carved of marble. I crossed one leg over the other, and he handed me a cup of steaming coffee he seemed to pull out of thin air.

I accepted it with a moan, letting the warmth seep into my hands, and the coffee soothed my insides with just one sip. "So, what am I learning today?"

"Did you read anything about magic of the mind?"

I thought for a moment. "Yeah, there's certain Fae, a select few, who can wield powers of the mind. Dreams, nightmares. Can manifest them as well as walk through them."

"Yes, and others have abilities to see moments in time. Past, present, and even future."

I nodded and took another delicious sip. It had a sweet aftertaste. "The Oracle."

Oden casually began rolling up his sleeves. "The only one I knew of was part human, but somewhere along the line, was clearly a Fae ancestor."

"Because he'd lived so long?"

Oden gave me a look of surprise. "That wasn't in the book."

"I've been researching you guys and your world for months," I replied, my mouth suddenly dry. "Especially after I learned that I might be some mortal Oracle, too. I want to know what my mind's capable of instead of this mess of visions and weird bits of dreams I can't make sense of."

He leaned forward on his thighs, the thick cordage of his arms flexing in the sunlight as he wove his long fingers together. A curtain of white hair fell over his shoulder.

"Think of the mind as a series of never-ending doors, and behind each is a memory, a thought. But the same applies to the universe. To time itself. Everything is reachable by someone like you."

A sort of coldness took hold of my chest. "I don't want that kind of power."

He chortled and leaned back on the bench. "Well, whether you want it or not, you've got a gift for magic of the mind. It wouldn't hurt to learn as much as you can."

"So, where do I start?"

He spent the rest of the day teaching me. I learned to search my own mind and feel for the strings of power. I visited memories I'd long forgotten about, rooted in my childhood and my life with Tess. Smells and sounds and feelings…mostly happy, carefree. Simple. A stark contrast to the life I now lived.

For hours I surfed my mind, then even more hours practicing how to home in on my visions, on the part of my brain that somehow tapped into the fate of others. It was simple, really. Almost too simple. Magic came so easily here in Faerie, unlike the struggle I felt when trying to maintain control over it at home.

Oden slipped away a couple times to deal with lordly duties and left me to practice on my own, and, honestly, it was almost better. I didn't have to worry about his scrutinizing face, and those dauntless eyes fixated on my every move.

The sun had long set when he finally returned the second time, the curved handle of a wicker basket clutched in his hand.

"Hungry?" he asked, dangling it. His smile wasn't enough to distract me from the bags under his eyes. I wondered what sort of things he'd been dealing with all day.

I rolled over on the grass and closed the book I'd been reading. More histories of Faerie and tales of great leaders before our time. Oden joined me on the ground, and we sat across from one another. It looked strange; a dark lord of Faerie perched on the dewy evening grass with a basket of food.

I pressed my lips together to keep from laughing. "What's on the menu?' I asked and peered inside the basket.

"Freshly baked buns, cheeses, fruits, and nuts," he replied as he took each item out and lay on the grass between us. He snapped his fingers, and a cozy blanket suddenly appeared beneath us. "And Freya's homemade meatballs," he added and scooped up a tiny ceramic pot. He removed the lid, and a cloud of delicious smells wafted out.

My stomach growled. "I hadn't even realized I was hungry until now."

"Apologies," Oden said and handed me a fork. "I forget that normal people eat several times a day. I work so much; I barely get time for a single meal most days. Having you stay with us has given the kitchen staff some reprieve from my usual coffee and whatever I can stuff in my pocket on my way out." He chuckled under his breath. "Usually, a muffin or a piece of fruit."

"I get it. My diet consists of whatever I can nab from the bakery as I leave for school or work." I speared a giant meatball and took a bite. It was heavenly. "Or leftovers from the occasional dinner Julie makes. But that's usually a pre-made lasagna or something. At best."

He shoved a piece of cheese to the side of his mouth. "Pre-made?"

"Yeah, like store-bought boxed lasagna? Haven't you ever seen it?" His look of confusion told me otherwise. "Haven't you ever spent time in Ironworld?"

Oden inhaled deeply through his nose as he stared off thoughtfully. "It's been a while since I last visited the mortal realm in person, aside from our few meetings."

How he said *in person* made me wonder how many dreams he'd invaded over the years. How many nightmares did he manifest for Fae and mortals alike? Could the Dark Lord of Nightmares tap into the mind of a Therian? I knew nothing about the person sitting across from me and sharing his supper.

In a blink, the world vanished, and I sat on the castle's cold stone floor of some wing. As I stood, a woman's scream pierced the hazy air, and I followed the sound to an open doorway. A man–Fae–lay on the floor, his long silvery hair soaking up a pool of fresh blood as another Fae male stood over him, holding a bloody heart in his hand. In the corner, a beautiful young woman cried. Her rounded ears told me she was human, and they widened when her soft brown eyes saw me.

"Oden!"

A gasp rocked my chest, and I stumbled backward into another vision. Or was it a memory? I cradled the same human woman, only she was much older. She reached up and caressed my cheek, and tears streamed down my face as she faded away. The moonlight blanketed her lifeless expression, and I hugged her frail body tightly as I wept.

Something grabbed my shoulder and hauled me from the dreamscape. I sucked in a fresh breath of air and planted both hands on the ground to steady myself.

"What the hell are you doing?"

"What?" I panted and looked sideways at Oden. He was furious.

He bolted to his feet. "How dare you pry inside my mind uninvited!"

I scrambled up. "I didn't mean to! You think I *want* to be roaming around in *there*? One minute I was eating a meatball, and the next—"

"Enough!" He poked my shoulder with enough force to make me wince. "Don't ever go inside my mind again."

"Or what?" His answering look sent a shiver down my spine. I almost didn't want to know how that would end. I stomped down the fear that chilled my insides. "Screw you!"

He grabbed his jacket with a low growl and stormed off for the mansion. Rage festered in my gut, and I kicked over the croc of meatballs. Oden spun on his heel, but I clenched my fist and wisped back to my quarters. Kol appeared in a spiral of black smoke and sat waiting on the bed, but I couldn't sit down, couldn't stop from pacing the floor.

I wasn't just upset. A range of emotions flooded my veins and sent my heart racing. What I'd seen in Oden's mind, in his memories… was awful. He witnessed his father's murder when he was just a boy and his mother's eventual death. I felt what he'd felt.

I slipped out of my clothes and took a bath. The steam, bubbles, and oils soaked the tension from my body, and the water was barely room temperature by the time I got out. I wrapped my body in a navy silk robe and crawled over the mattress toward Kol. His tail whipped against the blankets.

A piece of parchment appeared on the bed. With a sigh, I flicked it open.

Apologies once again.

The period was so large as if he'd let the pen sit there a moment, and the ink bled into a big black dot, followed by the words, *good wisping.*

A smug smile pinched my cheeks, and I set the message on fire. I watched it burn and turn to ash in my hands before blowing it onto the floor. The mattress groaned under my weight as I snuggled in and wrapped an arm around Kol.

"It was *great* wisping."

***

The following day, Mags brought me a tray of breakfast foods and some coffee. Apparently, Oden had ordered me to meet him in the stables first thing.

"You don't have time for a bath," she said as she fussed my hair into a thick braid.

"I had one before I went to bed," I replied, feeling like a child. "Do you personally make sure all the guests are bathed?"

Mags put her hands on her hips. "What guests? You're the only one Lord Oden has ever permitted. I haven't tended to guests since his father's rule."

"What?" I nearly choked on a grape.

"And it's my job as waiting-maid, especially with female guests, to ensure they're prepared to navigate their days in the kingdom and to be presentable for my lord."

I finished getting ready in silence, my mind full of thoughts and questions about how long these halls were empty, aside from Oden, his brother, and the staff. Did he not throw events? Have family that came for the holidays? Did Fae have holidays?

Mags gave me an outfit of comfortable black pants, almost like denim, and a long-sleeved navy blouse under an ankle-length black jacket that nearly covered the wine-colored boots I wore.

"Here," she said and shoved a brown leather shoulder bag at me. "For the trip."

"Trip?"

She chuckled and began scooping up her things. "That bugger. He really loves to leave you in the dark, doesn't he?"

I shrugged and slung the long strap over my shoulder as I rolled my eyes. "He's the lord of darkness. I'd expect nothing less."

Mags gently but firmly gripped my arm, her big black eyes wide and fixed on me. "He's the lord of many things, Avery Quinn, but the kind of darkness you think isn't one of them." She released my arm and gestured for the door. "You'll see. Stables are off the North wing. Just head down across the lawn and follow your nose."

Her words left me unsettled, and the way her face pinched at that last part told me she wasn't a fan of the stables. But I'd be fine. I grew up in the country riding our neighbor's horses and helping tend them every summer.

I wove through the castle until I found the North wing, thanks to the help of one of the staff. I'd never been to this part of the massive property before and took my time admiring the artwork of maps and gardens and strange symbols I didn't know how to read. Even though the mansion had a library, stocked bookshelves were tucked in every nook and cranny; empty hallways, spacious corners, and even built-in to furniture.

I wondered if it was for show, for the whole castle-vibe aesthetic, or did Oden truly read that much? When you could live forever, I guess you had to find never-ending hobbies. I wanted to stop and read some of the titles, but I knew he was waiting for me.

I found the stables easily. As Mags said, I just followed the scent of hay and manure, a smell that rustled up memories of summers passed. I'd worked for Mr. Dempsey for three summers on top of my other odd jobs to save for my Vespa. I laughed at how I didn't even need the bike now that I could wisp where I wanted to go.

Two silky black horses whinnied as I entered the stables. Oden stood between them, reins in each hand.

"What took you so long?"

I stifled a grumble. "Look, you may be able to snap your fingers and get ready, but I'm a lowly mortal who actually has to put their pants on one leg at a time."

He wouldn't look at me. "I hope you can ride; I don't have time to teach you."

The way he said it with such a snark made me want to kick him in the leg. It was almost as if he wanted me to be ill-equipped to ride. Was he still pissed about last night?

I held out a palm with a smug look. "Actually, I've been riding for years." With a raised brow, he placed the reins in my hand, and I hopped into the saddle with ease. I stared down at him. "Hope you can keep up."

His face was blank as he mounted the other black beast. He halted and tied his hair back.

"Do they have names?" I asked as I stroked the mane.

Something tugged at the corner of his mouth. "No, I just call them my night mares."

It took me a second, but I laughed. "Did you just tell a joke?"

"If you're lucky, you might get another." He left the stable.

I made my horse follow and sidle up to Oden's left. We fell into an easy trot, and silence let the sounds of nature surround us as we went. The crunch of dirt beneath hooves, the rustle of wind in the cherry trees.

An hour must have passed before the silence became too much for me. I tipped my chin toward the cherry trees lining the land to our left.

"So, what's with all the cherry trees?"

"My mother had them planted when I was establishing the boundaries for the Dark Fae. They're not allowed to pass them, and, on this side, we harvest the fruit each year for my people. In fact, that's where we're going, to one of the towns to discuss matters of the upcoming cherry festival."

"Cherry festival?" I balked. "That sounds like something from a kid's book, not the land of nightmares."

He pinched the bridge of his nose. "Let's get one thing clear here, Avery. My land is vast and diverse. I've done my best to keep the darkest of Fae contained and satiated so the rest of my people, people no different than you in terms of morality, can thrive. Yes, I may have been tasked with leading the dark, but it's just a small part of my job. This is not the land of nightmares you think it to be."

My throat tightened. "Sorry."

We moved along the wide dirt path for another half an hour in more silence. I scanned the forests, admired the clearing, and was awed at all the different animal life that passed us. Blackbirds with golden wings, deer with twisted horns of obsidian. I sketched them all into my mind.

"Apologies for my behavior last night," Oden finally spoke with a strained rasp. He stared straight ahead.

"Thanks," I said, gripping the saddle. "I'm learning. I'm going to make mistakes. So, if you ever talk to me like that again, I'll singe your pretty hair until you're bald."

He let out a guttural laugh and seemed just as surprised as me at the outburst. As if he hadn't truly laughed in years. "Noted." He glanced down at his horse and then at mine before bringing those stormy eyes to me. He arched a brow. "Care to race?"

"Are you up to the challenge, milord?" Mocking him brought me a sense of joy I never knew I needed.

With his hair pinned back, more of those pointed ears showed and added to the sharp features of his face. He looked at me like a devious cat and kicked his horse into gear. I watched as he took off, leaving me in little dust clouds. I squeezed my legs, and my horse raced after them.

It'd been a while since I last rode, especially this hard. I almost forgot how it made my heart soar. My limbs pulsed as my veins burned with adrenaline, and I gripped the reins, leaning forward as I approached Oden. He glanced over his shoulder and lowered himself closer to the horse as it sped up, and I laughed through the rush that burst through my chest as I did the same.

We laughed together as I finally passed him and came

to a screeching halt where a creek cut across the path. His horse skidded to a stop next to me, and he dismounted it before tying the rein around a tree. He turned to me with an extended hand, but I quickly swung my leg and hopped down before he could offer help.

"Impressive." He removed his black leather gloves.

"You can turn moonlight into solid objects, and you think riding a horse is impressive?"

Oden gave me an exasperated look and shook his head with a half smile as he glanced up at the sun with a sigh. "I was going to teach you more magic of the mind as we rode today since you're still so ill-prepared." He ignored my eye roll. "But it seems a perfect time to show you how to wield."

"Wield?"

"Turning the light into things, as you say."

I clapped my hands together. "Awesome, this is what I've been waiting for."

"You can summon the light with ease now?"

I nodded and turned my palms up, letting a pulsing ball of sunlight fill them.

Oden slowly paced in front of me, one hand tucked behind his back. "Now, close your eyes and picture an object in your mind. Note the lines, the curves, and the space it takes up. Feel that in your hands. Mold the light."

I pictured a dagger as I did once before and hadn't been

able to replicate since. But now, I was more in control of my power and could wield it more confidently. It didn't own me; it was *part* of me. I couldn't be afraid of it. I learned that embracing the great power that lived in me was the key to controlling it because the moment I hesitated and the second I relinquished control, things would fall apart.

"There we go," Oden said hesitantly. "Hold it."

I opened my eyes. A dagger of golden light rested in my hands, and my heart danced a little. I slowly gripped the rounded end, and it solidified even more. It was like holding metal and stone and glass all at once.

The blade flickered and shot out from both ends, becoming a sword instantly, and I dropped it to the ground, where it disappeared.

"Shit," I grumbled.

Oden chuckled, fetched two beautifully wrapped sandwiches from his saddle bag, and handed one to me. "You'll get it. Just keep practicing what I showed you."

"Thanks." I unwrapped the carefully folded brown paper and remembered the bag that Mags gave me that dangled at my side. I fished out a small tin of brownies and two apples.

We walked off to the side of the path where two large flat rocks were and sat down with our spread. We ate our sandwiches—the most delicious deli-like sandwich I'd ever had—in comfortable silence. Half the brownies disappeared before either of us spoke.

"Do you like being the Lord of Nightmares?" I asked.

He gave me a look that said he'd never been asked such a question before, and it took him a moment to respond. "I enjoy my role in the lives of my people." He sighed deeply. "But sometimes, a part of me wishes I could just hand it all over."

"Where would you go?"

He took the last brownie and tore it down the middle. "My domain is vast, even bigger than the Seelie Court when you account for the unclaimed land," he replied and handed me half the brownie.

I plopped it in my mouth and shoved it to the side as I chewed. "So, what would you choose to be if not a lord?"

Oden gave me a sideways grin. "King has a nice ring to it."

So, he wanted the Seelie throne after all.

The horses whinnied to go, and Oden stood up from the rock. "We should get going if we want to make it back by dark."

I stuffed the tin and apples in my bag and hopped on my horse.

It took about another hour to get to the village from there. But I used that time to practice wielding. Oden just watched from the side, careful, curious, but never hovering. By the time the rooftops breached the hilltops, I could easily form the dagger, and I breathed a sigh of relief as I tucked my magic away.

It was a quaint and surprisingly modern little place, bustling with life as Fae busied about. Some stood on ladders, hanging red garlands. Others used magic to turn the flowers in planters and beds from blue to red and black. At the far end of a spacious town square, vendors set up wooden stands and a giant stone fire pit with grills.

Oden pulled up to a larger building made of pale rock, the same rock used for most structures, even the stone-laid streets. Carvings of winged creatures marked the entrance, where we dismounted and tied up the horses.

"This is the closest town to the castle," Oden told me as I continued to take in the beauty of the modern village. Kids played in the distance, restaurants opened their windows to let out billows of steam, and jewels glistened in storefronts. "Welcome to Haven."

"Aptly named," I replied and turned to the building we stood outside of.

"I'll just be a few minutes in here," he said. "You're welcome to join me, or you can wait here."

"All this way just for a quick visit?"

He grinned. "I have many stops to make, Avery dear."

"And what was the point of bringing me along?" I gestured for him to walk toward the entrance, and I followed.

"Like I said, my duties as lord of this domain don't stop just because you're here. But I also have a duty to uphold our bargain. I thought I would teach you some things along the way." There was a glistening in the corner of his eye. "Gods forbid I waste your precious time."

I wanted to slap his arm, but with all those eyes on us, I wasn't sure if casually assaulting their lord was a good idea. I crossed my arms and walked with him to the double door entrance as it swung open, revealing a beautiful Fae woman with long chestnut hair swept back from her face with wooden combs.

"Milord!" she greeted. "You're just in time!"

"Now, now, Misaldri," he said with a chuckle as he embraced her. "I've told you to call me Oden. When will you learn?"

"Perhaps another hundred years," she replied and winked at me. "And who is this?"

"Misaldri, this is my friend, Avery Quinn." The word friend almost seemed hard for him to say. "Avery, dear, this is Misaldri Leester, the mayor of Haven."

"*Mayor*?" My eyes widened in disbelief, and I shook her hand.

"Yes," she answered for him. "Someone's got to run this place for him while he's off–" Oden loudly cleared his throat, and she gave him a look that said *oh, please*. "Come," she said, holding a gentle hand at my back. "We could use the extra set of hands."

Oden almost looked panicked. "Oh, I'm only here–"

"Come, now," she said and yanked him along.

The kitchen brimmed with people in aprons, each tending to a task on one of the many surfaces. It was the most enormous kitchen I'd ever seen, even more so than the one in Oden's castle. Cream-colored cabinetry reached the ceiling, fronted with glass to show off the beautiful dishes inside. White marble veined with gold stretched as far as the eye could see, bending in an L on each end, anchored by a giant island in the center.

Heads turned toward us, lending smiles and greetings. Oden soaked it up as he began shaking hands, and I noted the scattered items. Flour, sugar, eggs, and bowls and bowls of cherries. Rolling pins and spoons clanked, steamed billowed from bubbling pots.

Pies? They were making cherry pies.

"Here you go." Misaldri held out both hands, each offering a cream-colored apron. I exchanged a look of surprise with Oden, but his was fake. He chuckled softly and strung the apron over his head. Misaldri shook the one in front of me and smiled widely, her perfect teeth gleaming. "You don't want to ruin your clothes."

I took it and leaned toward Oden. "I-I don't bake."

Those steely eyes raked over every line of my face with delight. "Racing horses is easy, but you draw the line at baking?"

I shrugged. "I'm just not great at it. At all."

Oden half turned toward a giant table with benches on either side. He fetched a large bowl of fresh cherries and ushered me to sit down.

"You can still help," he said, setting the bowl in front of me. Misaldri handed him an empty one, and he put it on the table next to it. "Pit the cherries."

I stared at everything but couldn't bring myself to be mad about it. I sat in the kitchen of a Fae mayor, escorted by the Dark Lord of Nightmares, and got to pit cherries for pies as I glanced out an open window at people preparing for a festival. It was like a scene from a movie.

"Are we seriously doing this?" I asked.

He handed me a thin wooden skewer. "Yes."

Oden went to help make crusts as I started shoving the skewer through the cherries and dropping them into the bowl. After a few minutes, three kids no older than ten sat with me and began pitting their own cherries. The mayor laughed and smiled at me, and I found Oden's delighted stare from across the room.

I widened my eyes. "You gave me the kid's job?"

His laugh got lost with the others as everyone chuckled at my expense, but I couldn't help but laugh, too. I never expected to have fun today. Honestly, I'd pictured another fight with Mister Moody. I was beginning to learn just how tumultuous he was. Like the storm I often saw in his eyes, his behavior was unpredictable. One minute he's aloof; the next, he's brooding. And I witnessed firsthand how he could go from partially bored to pissed and raging in half a second.

"Why are you staring at Oden?" one dark-haired kid asked a little too loudly.

I snapped out of my daze and realized he was right. "I wasn't," I replied, focusing on my cherries. "I was just admiring the kitchen."

They were adorable with their large almond eyes and slightly pointed ears sticking out from their chestnut hair. Siblings, clearly, and definitely Misaldri's kids. I could see her in their features the more I looked at them.

"You're not Fae," another one asked.

"Nope," I said. "Well, I'm partially Fae."

"Can you do magic?" the one next to me added.

I nodded and held out a red-stained palm. A spark of sunshine formed, and their eyes widened with glee. I noticed a few heads turn discreetly in my direction, so I quickly tucked it away.

One of the triplets across from me shrugged as he pitted his cherries. "That's pretty good, I guess. For a mortal."

"Half mortal," his brother corrected, which warranted an eye roll from the other.

Kids were so brutally honest and straight to the point.

I like them for it. I'd babysat enough over the years to get a taste of their cut-and-dry ways. These Fae boys were no different.

I spent hours sitting at that table and pitted endless bowls of delicious dark cherries. I learned the boys' names were Simon, Valdri, and Theon, and they learned just about every detail of my existence as they drilled me question after question.

Eventually, they grew bored and ran off to play somewhere, leaving me to pit by myself while Oden crafted surprisingly perfect pie crusts. I lost count after a hundred. Just how many pies did this festival need?

Eventually, I nabbed some extra dough from the center island and molded a slew of pastry flowers. I placed them on a tray and handed them to one of the staff.

"My word," they said, admiring my work. "These will go on the pies for the auction."

"Yes," an older Fae woman agreed with a nod as she peered over his shoulder. "Far too pretty for the eating contest."

"And much too delicate for transport to the other towns," another chimed in.

So that's why we made so many; other cherry festivals were happening. I wondered if those towns were like Haven or did they differ in look and size? Were they also making pies or contributing to the festivals in some other way?

Was it a massive group effort throughout the land?

I sat at the table and spotted Oden at the far end of the kitchen near an open back door as he helped haul in giant bags of flour and stack them on the floor. The sleeves of his tunic were rolled up as far as they could go, showing off the corded muscles of his arms. His apron was splattered with flour and red juice. For a moment, I forgot he was the dark ruler of a Faerie domain and someone capable of killing the Seelie king.

Something soured at the bottom of my stomach, and I forced myself to look away just as Misaldri sat across from me and slid a whole pie in my direction.

"It's chocolate pecan," she said and picked off a bite with a fork. "Figured you're sick of cherries."

I cautiously took a bite, ignoring how she watched my every movement. A creamy, nutty, chocolatey flavor burst into my mouth, and the mayor chuckled at my widened eyes.

"It's one of my favorites, too," she said and ate more.

I couldn't resist. It was the best pie I'd ever tasted, and soon a quarter of it was gone. Oden was still helping the staff move things around and get pies in a giant oven.

"His mother used to do this," Misaldri told me as she watched him with me. "The cherry festivals were actually her creation. After she died, Oden took it upon himself to keep it going."

I poked at a large piece of pecan with the tip of my fork. "Seems a bit out of character for someone like him."

Misaldri seemed to want to say something but held her tongue instead. We continued sharing the pie in silence for a few moments before she asked, "So, where did you learn to make pastry flowers like that?"

I shoved a bunch of pie to the side of my cheek. "Oh, uh, I've used clay as a medium many times." I shrugged. "It's basically the same idea, just more delicate."

"You're an artist?"

"Sort of," I replied. "I mean, yes, I am. I've created my whole life in some way or another, and I'm taking classes in Ironworld right now."

She perked up in her seat. "Then you must come to the festival! It's all about art and dance and good food. All the best artists in the lands will be there." She glanced at Oden. "His mother adored art, you see. She wanted to celebrate it."

I set the fork down and leaned back. "I can't. I…I only come during each full moon."

The space between her eyebrows pinched. "You can't come any other time?"

I thought for a moment. I mean, I could if I wanted to. I was free to do whatever I pleased. But the idea of telling Cillian I was staying a few more days to enjoy a festival might fracture the delicate understanding between us. He knew I needed to come here to gain control over the magic that resided in me, for my sake and his. But coming here for pleasure…

I gave her a genuine smile. "Thank you for the invitation, Misaldri. But I'm afraid I have obligations in Ironworld that I can't ignore."

She reached across the table and took both my hands in hers. "Well, the invitation stands. Come any time. You'll always have a place to stay here." She gently squeezed my hands and patted them before letting go and sitting back with a quiet sigh. "But, if you can't come for the festival, at least stay for a cup of creamy cider."

"Creamy cider?"

She snapped her fingers and two steaming cups, practically bowls, appeared in front of us. I inhaled the warm aroma of cinnamon and spice mixed with thick, creamy milk.

"Well, how can I say no to that?" I said, and we shared a laugh as we sipped.

It was like drinking Christmas and Halloween from a cup, and I relished the thick, creamy cider filling my insides. It was the most fantastic thing I'd ever tasted, and I pondered how I might get the recipe for the café back home.

"So, if you can just make things appear with the snap of your fingers, why go through all this trouble to handmake pies and prep for the festivals?"

She gave me a look that seemed to ask *you don't know,* but she took a moment to reply. Her long Fae fingers wrapped around the massive mug as she thought. "When you can live forever, it's easy to let life pass you by without actually touching it. If we snapped our fingers and used magic for everything, how would we appreciate the little things? How would we know the feeling of reaping the rewards of hard work?"

"That makes sense," I said and took another long sip.

Oden walked up to our table as he removed his soiled apron. Not a spec touched him outside of where the apron covered, and I wondered if he protected his skin and fine clothes with magic.

"It's time to go," he told me, his face unreadable as he unrolled the sleeves of his tunic.

Misaldri stood up from her seat. "Thank you for all your help today, milord." She glanced at me. "And apologies for monopolizing your guest."

"Not at all," he replied, the corner of his mouth twitching slightly. "You're actually saving me a headache."

I rolled my eyes and smiled at the mayor. "Thanks for having me, and best of luck with the festivals."

She nodded. "Of course. And my offer still stands." She snapped her fingers, and a thermos appeared in her hands. "Some creamy cider for the road."

I accepted it and said goodbye to the rest of the staff before following Oden outside. The sun dipped in the sky, and ribbons of orange and purple danced over the tree tops.

We walked to the horses, and I untied the reins of my mare. "So, Dark Lord of Nightmares, pain in my ass, and…pie maker? You've got quite the roster of skills."

Oden untied his horse with a blank and distant expression. "The pain in your rear end I do for free." I muttered a playful curse under my breath as I hopped in the saddle and adjusted myself. The fact that I'd been enjoying myself here all day rather than learning magic suddenly hit me, and self-loathing set in like poison. "The pies, however–"

"You do for your mother, I get it," I said quickly and chewed at my lip as I scanned the beautiful town. I could feel Oden's eyes on me, but I didn't dare look at him. I just wanted to leave before I fell even more in love with Haven.

"Lord Oden," someone said quietly from a line of thick bushes that trimmed the edge of the property. An older female Fae. She wore thick brown denim, and her hands showed signs of hard work. "May I have a word?"

"Of course," the dutiful lord replied and handed me the reins of his horse.

He took a few steps to the side to speak privately with her. She told him something with a lowered voice and eyes full of concern. Oden's back stiffened as his stormy gaze turned dark, and his brows rose. I couldn't hear them, but I could plainly see the one word that moved his mouth.

Where?

The woman gave him some more details, and he nodded with thanks before sending her on her way. He paused before he walked back to me and took the leather straps from my hands without a word.

"What was that all about?" I asked.

He threw himself into the saddle with artful ease, flinging his long white hair over his shoulder as he stared at me with those storm-filled eyes. I swear, I saw lightning flash in them as he blinked. So quick that I almost missed it. His expression was riddled with thought and calculation. Was he going to tell me the truth or hand me lies, just like everyone else in my life?

Finally, his broad shoulders rolled with a sigh that rocked through him, and he leaned forward on his horse. "There was a body found at the edge of the Dark Forest near a logging road. A group of loggers found it. That was one of them."

Something cold filled my chest. "A-are you going to call off the festivals?"

"No," he replied quickly but seemed to be considering it. "That would only cause a riot. The loggers are keeping it quiet until I get to the bottom of it." He flicked the reins, and his horse trotted back down the trail we came from, and I followed close behind.

It wasn't the Dark Forest that lined the path, but the darkness between the trees looked different going back, and I had to remind myself to take full breaths as we rode. My eyes were locked on the shadows, watching for signs of movement. As if my horse could sense my worry, she sidled next to Oden's.

"Do you think it was Misery or some other dark Fae from the forest?" I asked.

He grumbled deeply. "It's possible, but I don't think they're that brazen. I'll find out once we get back."

The way he spoke made me think he suspected who or what might have done it, but he wasn't going to tell me, so I didn't bother to ask. I didn't blame him for wanting a moment's peace to think through everything. Between training me, running a domain, dealing with the ilk of the Dark Forest, the threat from Ironworld, and now this mysterious murder…I got it. I understood the need to think in peace. He carried the burden of being a leader, even a dark one, on his shoulders; I couldn't do it.

We rode in silence until we reached the same creek that cleaved the path, and we dismounted to give the horses a break. I took my thermos of creamy cider and walked down to a set of large stones. I sat on a rock and sipped my new favorite beverage, and the ground crunched beneath Oden's boots as he neared.

I gnawed at the inside of my cheek. "Can I ask you something?"

He stuffed his hands in his pockets and fixed his gaze on the horizon. "I know you will, regardless of what I say."

"Did you know what Vivian was up to?"

He inhaled deeply through his nose, eyes still distant and unblinking. "I expected some kind of backstabbing or betrayal. It's just their nature. But not like this." He guffawed and stared down at his feet. "But they're not bound by gilded promises, not like I am. I never thought I'd see the day when Therians and vampires work togeth-er. They've been enemies since the day the shapeshifters moved to Ironworld."

"Do you think she can do it? You think she can win?"

"Her plan only works in theory," he replied. "We have no idea if drinking Fae blood will grant the vampires ac-cess to Faerie. They may very well turn to ash the moment they step foot here. But if it works…."

I swallowed dryly. "We're all fucked?"

He looked at me with such a gleam in his eye. "Not if my plan works."

"And what plan is that?" I asked and offered my cider without thinking.

He came closer, and his fingertips brushed mine as he took the thermos, and I saw it. The deep longing in his eyes. The sense of purpose, drive, and determination to save not just the world he ruled but the one he loved.

A flash of guilt flicked over him, and he stiffened as he brought the rim to his lips and drank. He handed it back to me. "You're learning fast. With the magic."

I sighed as I twisted the top back on. "It's actually easier here." I stood up and took a few steps to the water's edge, peering into it. "Like I walked through some kind of fog. But it's exhausting most days. Like I'm using double the energy to do everything."

"You're living an immortal life inside a semi-mortal body, Avery. It's unnatural."

I didn't reply because the weight of his words rang true in my mind. I knew, deep down, I couldn't stay this way forever. I just didn't want to face that fact yet.

I heard him approach, and his face appeared in the water beside mine. We stared at one another's reflections. "I can fix it, you know? I can lift the bind, take away all that makes you human." I stilled. "You'd be as you were born." He waved a hand in front of my face, and my reflection changed; a slightly longer neck and more prominent eyes, my hair glowed like liquid embers, and two pointed ears peeked out from it. "Fae."

I allowed myself to stare at it for a moment before turning away. "No. I value my humanity."

"But it's a lie."

I shrugged as I spun back around. "My whole life is

a lie. But I'm used to this one." His eyes were like two moons beaming back at me. Sadness rimmed them. "Besides, I already have a way to do that. Oliver saved all that he took and kept it in an orb."

"Use it, take it back," he almost pleaded, but his face remained neutral. "Become Fae and have complete and utter control over your powers. Who knows what you could do if you shed that human skin."

I backed away, slowly shaking my head. "I can't do that. I'm not…." My throat tightened with a dry swallow. "I'm not ready."

Oden took one long step toward me. "You need to get ready. Soon."

"What's the urgency?" I stuffed my hands in my jacket pockets as I tried to read his face.

He thought for a second. "If we can get you to where you need to be if you can learn to fully use that Summer sun, then not only could you be Faerie's savior, but you'd be mine."

It all fell into place, the pieces clicking in my mind like a countdown. Oden hired Evaine to watch me, then kidnap me. Then insisted on helping me control my magic, my Summer sun before Vivian invaded Faerie.

With vampires.

I narrowed my eyes. "You son of a bitch."

His expression told me he didn't expect me to get mad,

and he came toward me with open palms, his brows raised. "Now listen. Yes, I made a deal with Vivian to use vampires to overthrow Mabry and take the throne in exchange for letting the Therians back into Faerie. But not like this. Vivian had secretly been building an even bigger army of vampires to take the throne for herself. Now all the world's bloodsuckers will come here and destroy everything, killing *everyone*. Vivian won't leave a single Fae alive. I *need* to fix this; I *need* to stop her."

I squared my jaw, my eyes stinging with wetness. "And you're going to use me to do it."

Oden's gaze darkened. "No, not use. *Beg* for your help. Work with me. Help me stop this."

"You mean clean up *your* mess and risk my *life* doing so." The words cracked over my voice.

He shook his head. "No, that's not–"

"You never wanted to help me, did you?" I wrung my hands at my sides. "You just wanted a way to fix your mess. You really are a monster, aren't you?"

I couldn't tell if anger or shame filled his eyes and his chest rose. "I was desperate to dethrone Mabry, and now it's grown beyond my control. Vivian *will* invade, and she's using vampires as her way in."

"And I should stop them." I meant it as a question, but it came out empty. The words carried no meaning because I wasn't sure what they meant to me. I knew he wanted me to; I knew I should.

I felt numb.

Oden grabbed my upper arms and forced me to look him in the eyes. He was so close; I could feel his warm breath on my face. I could feel the stormy rage emanating from every inch of his body, but his face remained staid. "No, Avery. I want you to *destroy* them."

Everything about the situation made my head spin. The enormity of what he was asking me to do, the burden and responsibility he put on my shoulders, the weight of it all pushed down on me, and I became locked in his grip, lost in those ancient eyes.

I brought my knee up to his groin, and he reeled back.

"I am not a weapon to be wielded!" I yelled as the Dark Lord of Nightmares backed away, hunched over himself as he bit through curses. "And what was today? Parading me around like some toy. You wanted people to see the mortal girl you're going to use to save them. And what did you plan to do after you use me like some atomic bomb?" I flapped my hands at my sides. "Kill me like you did the Seelie King—"

The words stifled in my mouth as Oden's lips crushed down on mine, his fingers digging into the flesh of my arms and sending electric shocks through me. But it wasn't a gentle kiss. It was a desperate means to shut me up.

I screamed against his mouth, and light exploded from

me, sending him skidding twenty feet across the ground. The forest rustled and slowly settled as Oden grinned at me like a sly cat. "You'll do fine indeed."

I took a deep breath as I hopped back on my horse, and I glared down at him in spite. "I hope Vivian shreds you to pieces."

✳✳✳

I took off back to the mansion and left Oden in my dust. He never pursued, but I knew the moment he arrived. I paced my quarters, still stewing in anger, as a dark cloud gobbled up the sky and thunder rolled in.

The Dark Lord was home.

He never came to my door, never sent word for supper. The moon was barely visible through the thick grey clouds, and I grew bored in my room. The art supplies held no appeal to me here, where my only goal was to learn magic and go home.

I wandered the castle for a while, my footsteps echoing off hollow corridors. Torchlight chased away the shadows, and the wood crackled in my ears, startling me every now and then. I had no idea what time it was, but the staff had long retired for the night. Even Kol was nowhere to be found.

Maybe I should have gone to bed, but I couldn't sleep.

Not when my blood still seethed, and Oden's words still rang in my ears. All this time, from the moment I'd moved to the city, he'd been watching and scheming to use me as a weapon to wipe out Vivian's plan and clean up his colossal mess. I felt like a fool because deep down in my gut, I thought he wasn't as horrible as the rumors stated. But he never wanted to help me.

I was nothing but a means to an end.

A pair of ornate patio doors hung open near the end of a random wing, and a figure with long dark hair sat casually in a wide chair. Smoke billowed up from the tip of a cigarette. I loosed a sigh, letting tension roll off my shoulders, and stepped onto the beautiful stone-laid patio.

"Evening, Red," Sullivan said without looking up at me. He took another long drag of his cigarette. "Can't sleep?"

"That's a vast understatement." I took the chair next to him and tipped my heavy head back.

He wore a pair of old denim jeans and a loose black t-shirt with holes around the hem. His boots laid tumbled off to the side. "Learn anything today?"

I chortled. "You mean besides the fact that your brother is a selfish piece of shit?"

Sullivan looked at me, the full moon sparkling in his deep, brown eyes, and clucked his tongue mockingly. "Only I get to talk about him like that."

"Did you know?" I asked, and his immediate sigh and

shifting in his seat told me the answer. "Did you know what he planned to do with me?"

He carefully considered his words as he snuffed out his cigarette in an onyx tray. "I know what's coming, what needs to be done, and I understand his reasoning for his actions. I may disagree with them most of the time, but I get it. An incredible burden has been placed on his shoulders, and it doesn't matter what he decides; someone will always get the butt end of it."

"And you think I deserve that sort of fate?" The words were barely a whisper as I stared at the perfectly laid stones.

Sullivan leaned forward as much as he could and lowered his face, catching my gaze. "I didn't say that'd be you, Red. No, I'm afraid your fate is greater than all ours combined."

Bile burned at the back of my throat. "I don't believe in fate."

A low, raspy chuckle turned over in his throat as he lit another cigarette. "That's too bad."

I didn't reply. Didn't want to. Sullivan's carefree ways made it easy to talk to him, easy to like him, even. But underneath it all, he was no better than Oden. They were the sons of rulers past, and both did things to further their agenda for domination. Oden wanted to use me as a weapon, to risk my life, and Sullivan clearly agreed.

He glanced to the right, where a quaint greenhouse

sat near the hedges. Black roses and silver flowers pushed against the transparent walls and spilled out the open door. I immediately recognized them from the fresh bowls and vases I'd seen around the castle.

"You see that greenhouse?" he asked, and I just nodded. "It was my mother's, Serene. When she was alive, there used to be pink ones, too."

The sudden flip in conversation ruffled my mind, but I welcomed the change in topic. I recalled the tidbits I'd picked up about their late mother.

"What a beautiful name," I said. "She sounds like she was wonderful."

He inhaled sharply through his nose as he stared longingly at the flowers. "She was."

I picked at my chipping nail polish. "How…how did she die?"

"Old age."

"What? I thought you guys lived forever?"

"A long time, yes. But not forever." He guffawed. "Fucking kill me now if I have to roam this place for eternity." He took a long drag. "But, no, my mother was mortal. A human woman, a witch, actually. Gods, my father loved her fiercely."

Something in my stomach tightened. "But…that means…"

He grinned coyly, flashing his teeth which were

surprisingly white for a smoker. "My brother and I are part human."

Just like me.

Sullivan stood from his chair, the metal legs scraping across the rocks. He turned to the doors behind us and patted my shoulder. "I'll let that sit with you for a bit, Red. Night."

He left me on the patio, where I sat until a pale bluish glow stained the sky and dew formed on the chair beneath me, seeping moisture into my clothes. I didn't bother heading inside. I just wanted to go home. I ventured across the grounds and down the winding dirt path that led to the water and did just that.

Julie was still asleep when I entered the apartment, and I quietly went to my room. The window was open, letting in a crisp winter morning breeze, and Lattie was nowhere to be found. The mattress sagged with my weight, and I realized just how tired I was.

The very air in Ironworld buzzed with sounds and electricity; such a stark, exhausting difference from Faerie. But before I could lay down and sleep, a folded piece of parchment fluttered in through the window like a butterfly, and I pinched it between my fingers with a sigh. I already knew who it was from.

I opened the note, black ink scrawled beautifully across the paper.

Apologies for everything. I would understand if you wished to never return, given my behavior and your impressive grasp on your magic. But your lips have touched mine. Should you ever need me, simply call my name, and I'll be there.

I brought the paper to my nose and inhaled the subtle scent of black cherries before setting it aflame.

Chapter Fourteen

All the answers. Promise.

I sat on my bed, knees bunched to my chest, and rested my chin atop them. I'd stared at a leafy green invitation for hours. They'd come earlier today, invites to Tess and Kheelan's upcoming vow renewal. One for Julie and one for me, but hers was an actual invitation with dates and times. Mine was just a piece of paper with Tess's handwriting.

All the answers. Promise.

She knew me so well and knew that a basic invitation written by someone else wouldn't be enough to convince me. But those four simple words were exactly what I wanted to hear.

I stared at it as my heart thwomped in my ears, beat after beat. I couldn't drown it out. My chest tightened, and I wrapped my arms around my legs, demanding my lungs to relax, and a long sigh escaped from me as I reached for the paper again. I scrawled one simple word in reply.

Fine.

The note dissipated before my eyes, and the dust blew out the window.

***

The sun glinted off the pond by Oliver's, glaring in my eyes.

"Y'know, I've never spent more than a few hours in Faerie," Julie said as she stared unblinking at the water. "Most of it in Dreams, roaming the libraries and archives."

I turned to her. She'd torn through half her wardrobe before deciding on jeans and a white tank top, muttering something like Tess would have outfits for us to wear. Anxiety rippled off her. But I understood why she felt that way, returning to a place that rejected you, a place you longed for.

"Hey, Jules," I said, and she finally looked at me. "You don't have to go if you don't want to."

She sucked in a deep breath of air and smiled. "No, I want to." Her eyebrow arched at my leather jacket. "You're gonna want to lose the heavy clothes, though."

"Why—"

Julie grabbed my hand and touched the water. We wisped right to an open field, half surrounded by wooded forest, the other half opened to a vast valley and distant hills over the crashing shores of the sea. Luscious, citrusy scents wafted in the air, mixed with saltwater and apple blossoms.

A lovely wooden carriage awaited, the driver standing near the door.

"Ladies," he greeted and bowed at the waist of his golden tunic. "Lady Summer has requested I deliver you safely to the castle for this evening's ceremony."

Julie just waggled her eyebrows at me.

Sweat already coated my skin, locked in by the insane humidity. Summer was in full swing here. I slipped out of my leather jacket and rolled up my sleeves as I followed her to the carriage and let the driver help us step inside. Two benches faced each other, flanked by small open windows.

He cracked the reins, and we headed down the narrow mouth of a path that cut through the beautiful forest. I stared out one of the windows, relishing the gentle breeze on my clammy face. Giant bees the size of squirrels buzzed alongside pixies of every color, catching the sun's rays that pierced the forest canopy.

"So, what does Cillian think of you coming here?" Julie asked me.

I chewed at the side of my lip. "Less than enthused."

I glanced back at the passing scenery. A deer with golden antlers galloped by. "I think he feels the more time I spend in this world, even amongst Fae kind in Ironworld, draws me further away from him. He wants nothing to do with the magical realm and thinks I will get hurt."

"I get it," she replied. A sort of understanding in her crystal blue eyes. "He doesn't want to be part of a world that rejected him." She shrugged and shook her head, and I could see the mixed feelings wrought on her face. If anyone could relate, it was Julie. "And he loves you. Whether he's said it yet or not, he does. I can tell. And he probably feels helpless having to watch you head off to a world he can't even step foot in, worried if you'll even return."

I crossed my arms and leaned back. "I hadn't even considered...."

The carriage jostled over bumps as Julie swiftly moved to my bench. "Don't beat yourself up, though. I trust you; we all do. I don't believe you'd put yourself in danger just to learn magic. If you think Oden can help, and he clearly has been, then you do what you feel is right. Cillian must know that, deep down."

I thought about my last encounter with Oden, how I spat on him with hate in my eyes. I never wanted to see him again. Julie was wrong; I'd made a bad decision, I'd entered a bargain with the Dark Lord of Nightmares in the trust he only wanted to help me, but it was all part of his plan to use me.

Shame filled my chest, pressing on my lungs, but I forced a smile for her. "Well, you'll all be happy to hear that I'm not going back. I think I've learned enough."

Her eyes widened. "So, the bargain's done?"

The golden mark of three moons pulled at the skin of my lower back, a constant reminder that it wasn't over. I shrugged and peered out the window. The swirling tops of a castle appeared in the distance. "I made it pretty clear during my last visit."

I knew she could tell there was more I wasn't saying, but, like the friend she was, Julie straightened and wiggled in her seat. "Good. I could use your help at the Sanctuary."

I laughed. "It's been a while since I visited. How are things going there?"

"Things are okay now," she replied, braiding her fingers together in her lap. "But more and more Fae are fleeing the Seelie lands and spilling into Ironworld in search of refuge. We're taking in as many as possible, but space and supplies are running low."

"Maybe Tess could help," I suggested.

"You think she would?"

"I think if she wants any hope of repairing our relationship, it's the least she can do."

This woman, this Fae ruler that swept me away in the dead of night to an unknown world and lied to me my entire life…yeah, she owed me an explanation, but she also had the means to help those poor Fae, and I wanted to hold on to the idea that the Tess I knew was real. The kind-hearted, loving, helpful woman that raised me.

The carriage rolled to a stop inside a courtyard, and Julie looked at me. "Well, let's see how today goes before we ask for favors."

The door swung open, and we stepped into the sunlight that seemed to radiate from everywhere. The Summer castle loomed overhead and stretched as far left and right as I could see. It was made of pale sandstone with open arches and canopies of flowers. The courtyard was filled with blooming gardens and trickling fountains where fish jumped and splashed. Below our feet, a path set with shells and stones led the way to the front gates and beyond.

We followed an usher into the castle, where servants and staff bustled about, carrying fabrics, trays, and endless décor in preparation for the ceremony. Everyone seemed to be in good spirits, excited for the return of their Lady. The vibe was infectious, and I smiled at those who passed us by as our guide led us through winding corridors and up curling staircases to our quarters.

"Here we are," the woman said, a delicate Fae with skin the color of wet sand and pink hair that cascaded to her waist and shimmered like pearls. She turned the giant golden knob on the wooden door, letting it swing open. "This will be your shared quarters for your stay."

"I'd like to speak with Tes—with the Lady of Summer before the ceremony," I said.

The woman blinked. "I'm afraid that's not possible. The Lady is busy with preparations. You may speak with her after the festivities."

"Oh." Disappointment fettered in my chest, and I exchanged a glance with Julie.

The woman motioned for us to step inside. "Everything you need is already in the room. A team will be by shortly to get you both ready."

She turned on her heel and sped off down the corridor before we could answer.

Julie shrugged. "Shall we check it out?"

I smiled and released the tight breath held captive in my chest as I followed her inside. The shared room was more like an apartment. A common room with luxurious coral couches and golden accents sat in the center, flanked by a quaint kitchenette, towering bookcases stuffed with leatherbound titles, and a curved patio overlooking the courtyard. Three doors lined the back wall, and we poked our heads in each one. Two bedrooms and the biggest bathroom I'd ever seen, even more than the one I used at Oden's.

Sweat pooled in all my unsightly areas, and I shed the loose shirt I wore over a tank top. "Is it always this hot here? I almost jumped in the fountain downstairs."

Julie chuckled as she poked around the books, tilting her head to read the spines. "I'm not sure. This is my first real trip to Summer aside from our stint in the dungeons. And it wasn't that hot then."

I wanted to ask her more and talk about how she felt being there. And Tomas. I never got the chance in the carriage ride, but I'd meant to speak to her about him. The poor guy was heartbroken and confused. If she was going to break it off completely, she had to tell him rather than avoid him.

But a prep team showed up and divided us. Trays of food and wine were constantly refilled as we ate. I took one into the bath with me while Julie picked out fabrics and welcomed the warm buzz of the wine while I let a trio of rainbow-skinned Fae poke and prod at me.

After hours of prepping, I stood before a golden-framed mirror and stared in disbelief. My pale skin glowed against the scanty teal sheer dress that looped around my neck and hung down my body, only covering what was needed. The thin fabric bunched at my waist, held by a stunning golden belt.

They pulled my long, red curls back with a clip and the ponytail trailed down my bare back, touching the gilded bargain embedded there. Chunky gold jewelry bedecked my wrists, fingers, and ears, catching the glint of gold dust blown onto my skin. I just stood and stared at my reflection. If I had pointed ears, I'd pass as Fae.

Julie was dressed in a similar fashion, but her dress was shell-white and adorned with mother-of-pearl accessories. Her stark blonde hair was left in soft waves, a simple coral barrette pinning it back behind one pointed ear.

"You look amazing," she told me with wide eyes.

I gestured up and down at her. "You look like a sexy angel." We shared a laugh as we were passed new flutes of wine. "Why are you holding on to your glamour, though?" I asked, noting how her skin still resembled that peachy, human tone and her blue eyes didn't hold the depths of the sky.

Her cheeks reddened. "I don't know. I'm just…used to it, I guess. Like a reflex."

I walked toward her and gently took her hand in mine. "Just let it go. Of all the places in the world, this is one where you can definitely be yourself."

She searched my eyes for any sign of doubt and sucked in a long, deep breath. As she released it, the last of her glamour faded, and the radiant, ethereal, snow-white goddess blossomed. The sun seemed to soak into her snowy skin, making it glow like diamond dust, refracting off every strand of alabaster hair. Her blue eyes now held the vastness of the skies, captivating me, almost making my knees buckle and send me to the ground at the sight of them.

I'd seen her in her full Fae form, but not like this. Perhaps being here, in her homeland, away from the stifle of Ironworld, revealed even more of her eternal beauty.

"What?" she said, her face unreadable.

I shook my head and blinked away the daze. "You have no idea how absolutely breathtaking you are, Jules. If this is what Winter Fae look like in Summer, I don't think I'd be able to handle seeing them in their own realm of Winter."

She rolled her eyes and shoved at my arm. "Oh, my gods, shut up." She downed her entire glass of wine and turned to one of the waiting maids. "Is it time to go yet?"

"No, not quite yet. The ceremony starts in an hour." The older Fae gestured to one of the staff waiting by the door. A smaller, much younger Fae with an auburn pixie cut and big green eyes. "Ginny would be happy to take you both on a tour of the castle and grounds if you like."

"Lead the way, Ginny," I said. If we stayed in the room for another hour, Julie would be wasted on Summer wine before the ceremony even began.

I knew she was nervous, unsettled even. Being here was just as strange for Julie as it was for me. But I wondered if she felt the same thing I did, the little inkling in the bottom of my stomach, tied to an invisible string that undoubtedly pulled me to Faerie. It was an ancient thing; the feeling of belonging and unbelonging and the magic and emotion festered inside me.

Ginny sped through the castle, eager to show us every nook and cranny. Several wings made up the building, each filled with various quarters, libraries, meeting rooms, halls, and more. We saw everything there was to see, from the ornate ocean details that touched every part to the massive kitchen filled with foods of every nature. Tiers of mini cakes and pies, trays of sausages and meats, cheeses, and at least four different types of bread that I could count.

Julie and I joked about several aspects; the gaudy vases and paintings of half-naked Fae, some with the lower half of a sea creature. There was a mix of them. Whale tails, flowy ribbons, fish fins, and more. I wondered if real mermaids looked like that, not the cartoons I grew up watching.

We swiped a couple of cheesy buns from the kitchen and happily accepted a few flutes of wine from passing staff. We eventually made our way outside, but at the back of the property where the ceremony was being assembled. A vast, never-ending mass of gardens and fruit trees and flowing fountains. Canopies of white flowers hung overhead with butterflies fluttering about.

White chairs lined and filled the sides of a wide path, trodden with the same white flowers as above. The sun beaming down made the setting seem like a dream. Julie fit right in as Fae began filing in and taking seats. But, when I glanced down at myself, I realized…I did, too, even in my human form.

The image of what Oden showed me in the lake that day flashed across my mind, and I blinked away the memory of what I'd truly look like as Fae. If I ever decided to accept the orb that Oliver kept for me.

It was almost cruel to have shown me because…deep down…I did want to be like them. Beautiful and eternal and special. But to give up my humanity now, when it was the only thing I clung to, the only thing that hasn't changed in my life…

It was overwhelming to even think about it.

Once the seats were full, Kheelan and Tess walked to the altar from each side and faced one another. Kheelan's tall, lithe frame was covered in a white suit with gold embroidery, his long blonde hair pulled back in a pony at the nape of his neck. A golden sword, thin and seemingly useless, dangled from his side. An accessory, really.

It took me a moment to drag my eyes to Tess because some weird part of me *knew* I'd find her staring right back. And she was. She stood across from her husband, a golden bouquet in her hands, and gazed over the crowd at me. Her blue eyes glistened with gratitude and remorse, and I had to look away.

I glanced up only when the priest began reciting the words, relieved to find her looking at Kheelan. I finally noted her dress, a flowing train of white and gold silk, draped around her neck and gathered at the waist with a belt. Her waves were swept back from her face with combs, and she was crowned in gold.

The vow renewal was lovely and nothing like what I expected. I thought it'd be grander and more impactful. For an event that took nearly twenty years to complete and one that would give their domain the power to rise to a court, I figured there'd at least be more people.

But it was quaint and intimate with soft melodies of harps and violins. The food began appearing on white-dressed tables surrounding the seating area in a semi-circle. Once everyone was standing, the chairs disappeared, and round table sets took their place.

Julie and I made a beeline for the food and loaded our plates with everything we'd seen in the kitchens earlier. We found a spot to sit and made it about halfway through our spoils before one of the servants approached the table.

"The Lord and Lady of Summer request your presence in a private hall," he said with gloved hands tucked behind his back.

I dropped everything immediately and shot to my feet, desperate to speak to Tess, although Julie seemed reluctant to leave behind her meat pie. The Fae led us from the celebration and back into the castle to a set of double doors. Two others opened them for us, and inside, the

Lord and Lady of Summer awaited on thrones carved of giant conch shells.

They'd already changed from their ceremonial garb into more casual attire. Kheelan in loose white pants and tunic, Tess sporting a similar sheer contraption to what Julie and I wore. Only hers was as bright as the sun on the sea.

She straightened and moved forward at the sight of me, but Kheelan's steady hand swiftly moved over top of hers on the arm of her throne, signaling her to remain seated. My heart raced, and I wiped my sweaty palms against my dress as we approached them. Julie gave a respectful curtsey-like bow, and I tried to copy her. I could have sworn I heard Tess stifle a snicker.

"Congratulations," Julie said to them.

Kheelan just nodded. I couldn't tell if he looked bored or if that was just his face. But Tess beamed with hesitant excitement, her eyes never leaving me.

"Thank you for coming," she said to both of us. "I wasn't sure you would."

"How can one refuse such an honor?" Julie replied, and I wanted to kick her at the weird formal tone. But, then again, she knew more about the royal protocols of Fae than I did. I knew nothing. I was probably offending Oden and his entire domain regularly when I was there.

Tess exchanged a look with Kheelan. "Yes, well, I must admit my intentions for inviting you here are layered. I wanted you both to be part of this day—my day—*our*…day," she fumbled over her words. I'd never seen her like this before. "But I also needed to clear up a few things."

I crossed my arms, but they almost slipped from their place at how clammy my skin was. "I'd like that, too."

Tess's cheeks flushed pink as she stared at me with eyes full of emotions, unspoken words, secrets, and a life lived long before I was born. "I was telling Kheelan the story, the *whole* story, of the night I ran away. The why…and the how." She cleared her throat. "And the details about where exactly I took you from."

I chortled. "Some creepy nursery in the Seelie castle, I presume?"

Kheelan shifted in his seat. "Yes, our world assumes as much since the news of your existence has spread."

So my secret wasn't really a secret anymore.

Tess wrought her hands together in her lap. "No, I took you from the loving family I'd hidden you with since your birth."

"What?" Julie and I replied in unison.

"How much do you know about Fae gestation periods?" Tess asked.

I cringed and rifled through my thoughts. "Uh, Lattie once mentioned something about it. That it's short?"

"A mere three months," Kheelan confirmed. "From conception to birth."

"So, what does that have to do with me?" I asked. "So what? My mother got off easier because she's Fae?" I almost laughed.

"No," Tess said, struggling for words. "You ran off so soon the last time we spoke. I never got the chance to explain everything. And…I…" She guiltily looked away from her husband's stare. "I wasn't speaking much upon my return to Summer. I never explained the entire story to anyone until a few days ago. When Kheelan and I finally…talked."

I was the lowest of lows. I hadn't even considered how all this might be affecting Tess. The transition back home, having to answer to so many people. But she leaned forward.

"You see, Mabry is my sister."

A sort of cold quiet filled the hall, reminding me that it was just the four of us. No guards stood by, only outside the doors. When no one answered, and Kheelan nodded at her encouragingly, Tess continued.

"I was a Summer elf, living alone in my family's estate by the water on the Summer beaches. Kheelan had been courting me for months, and I knew he would ask for my hand in marriage any day." She slipped her hand into her husband's and smiled at him. But something felt off. Forced. "One night, Mab came frantic to my home. Pregnant." Tess's eyes glossed over. "I'd no idea. I hadn't seen my sister in years. We, um, never really saw eye to eye in life. She refused to tell me who the father was. I-I helped her give birth right on my kitchen floor." She smiled—a genuine one—at me. "A baby girl."

"Me?" The word was nothing more than a dry whisper in my mouth.

"Yes. And Mab was delirious, wrought with fear and anger and spite. My gods, she wanted me to get rid of the babe. Said it was an abomination, a painful reminder." She tilted her head, still staring at me. "But I couldn't do it, my gods. You were an innocent baby. So, I hid you with a family in a nearby village. The Quinns. When I returned home, my sister was gone. A few weeks later, days after Kheelan asked for my hand, I'd gotten word that the Seelie King had taken a bride. The first one ever, and it was my sister, which was one of many red flags."

Kheelan cleared his throat, shifting in his seat. "You see, the king has never taken a bride in his entire existence. Very few knew of my Lady's relation to her. Mabry made no claim to a family line. No one knew where she even came from. Even to this day."

"But we're from a long line of old Fae with great power," Tess added and gestured at me. "Your sunlight runs in our veins, but only a few have wielded it. I think the last was over a thousand years ago."

I flexed my hands, knowing it was there just below the

surface of my skin, running through my veins, pulsing through my entire body. It was a part of me now, maybe always had been. But now I was in control.

Julie crossed her arms, her face pinched in thought. "So, that doesn't explain what happened the night you ran away."

Tess's shoulders widened as she sucked in a deep breath. "My sister was mad; I'd known it my whole life. When I discovered the–when…I began to fear what she'd do to any heirs–I did what I had to do to protect you."

It all fell on me like a heavy blanket. "So, I'm not the missing Seelie heir?"

"No, sweetheart. You're not."

"But, as her offspring, you do have a claim to the throne," Kheelan butt in and immediately slunk back at the look Tess shot him. "If you wanted it, of course. In her death."

"Why would I want that?"

Kheelan looked guilty but riddled with a sense of duty. "If you won't take the throne, then we need you to keep acting as if you believe yourself to be the heir. It's the only leg-up we have against Mabry. She hasn't thought twice about her first-born daughter since that night on your aunt's floor. But, if she believes the heir has been found, she'll be distracted, and it might buy us the time to find a crack and infiltrate her court."

"But it's a lie," I cried out. "And puts a target on my back!"

Tess pressed her lips together. "And we also need you to keep spending time in Nightmares."

"How do you–" She looked away. I narrowed my eyes, but Julie took my hand. "You've been *spying* on me?"

"It's for your own good–"

"But it's putting my life in danger! I don't want any of this!" Julie wrapped her arms around me to keep me still. "I'm not a tool for you to use in this fight. I'm not a weapon to be wielded!"

I had uttered the exact words to Oden. Is that all I was to them?

"I swear," Tess said and shot to her feet. "We've got guards all over Ironworld, wards around your home, school, the gallery. Everything. We'll overthrow Mabry but need time to garner forces, make plans, and find allies."

Allies. Oden had an entire army and fought for the same cause, it only made sense for them to work together, and I was the bridge between Summer and Nightmares.

But Oden wanted the throne for himself.

I chewed at my lip. "What does Mabry do that makes her so bad? Aside from being a horrendous mother."

"She taxes her people to the brink of breaking," Kheelan said. "And won't let anyone come or go from her lands. Her people are trapped, beaten, and worked to death. And no one is allowed in to help."

"She's been known to torture, even murder, those who cross her," Tess added.

Julie turned her head and looked at me. "The Seelie is supposed to keep everything in check. Balanced. The right in all the wrong. With her on the throne, Faerie crumbles."

"Why can't you become a court now and challenge her throne?" I asked Kheelan and his brows shot up.

"Well, I would love nothing more," he said. "But it would be a suicide attempt at this point. I need time to build my forces, get people in, and collect information." He fixed his stare on me, eyes wide as he slightly lowered his head. "Time I'm hoping you can give me."

My stomach burned. I turned to my best friend for a sign of what to do or even say. But her hapless expression gave me nothing.

I rubbed my hands over my arms. Goosebumps scaled my skin despite the hot, humid weather. "Can I think about it?"

"Of course," Tess replied before Kheelan could. Would he have persisted that I decide? Demand I do it regardless? I couldn't read the Lord of Summer the way I could read his wife. "Whatever you need."

"We do have some news for you," Julie said with reluctance, perking Kheelan's interest. "What do you know of the coming Therian threat?"

His hands curled into fists on the arms of his throne. "We're…aware."

"How aware?" Julie asked. "Because her plans have shifted." I'd told her the few details I gathered from my last trip to Nightmares. "She's building a vampire army and plans to use them to invade Faerie."

Kheelan's brow lowered; Tess moved her hand over her mouth as she stared at me with worry. "We're aware," he repeated. It was clearly all we were going to get from him. "We're not worried. We've been watching Vivian Carmichael's movements for some time. The Therians will not break my borders. Their eternal punishment for the uprising in the Great War is death upon arrival."

"You're fools to think that," Julie exclaimed, and Kheelan's entire demeanor changed from blank calm to quiet rage. I bet no one talked to him like that.

"Not even Oden knew of her plans to betray him," I added, distracting the Summer Lord from my friend.

"Enough!" Kheelan shot to his feet. The double doors behind us immediately swung open, and two guards stomped inside. He motioned for them to come closer. "I will not discuss private domain matters with a few lowly Ironsiders."

Julie balked. "*Lowly—*"

"You're free to roam the castle grounds," he said sternly. Tess looked like she was fending off a sudden headache.

"But your welcome expires in the morning."

***

I let my white silk robe fall open over my matching pajamas and welcomed the cool midnight breeze that coaxed off the nearby ocean. It wove through the halls of the Summer castle as I wandered quietly. Everyone had long gone to bed, but I couldn't sleep. I could barely sit still.

My brain ached with the pressure of all the thoughts that occupied it. Thoughts and worries that had no solutions. I'd tossed and turned in the heap of silks that dressed the bed, even found myself wishing Kol was there to snuggle and distract myself enough to fall asleep.

But I was alone here.

The dead quiet enveloped me as I sat on the deep sill of an open arch, and I peered down at the glorious courtyard below. It transformed at night. Lovely pinks and yellows became darkened versions of themselves and reached for the moonlight as the sounds of fountains bubbled in the distance.

"Can't sleep?" Tess asked, suddenly appearing at my side. There were no footsteps on the soft sandstone, so she must have wisped.

I didn't move my gaze from the gardens below. "I hardly do these days."

"Do you want to talk about it?"

I finally looked at her, and she pressed her lips together, eyes wet. "There's not enough time in the world to talk about it, Tess." I bunched my knees to my chest, and she sat in the empty space on the sill. "I feel lost, spinning in circles, passing all these stops, but I don't know where to go. All I wanted was to move to the city with Julie, try art school, and live on my own. That's it. I never expected to get mixed up with vampires and werewolves, never thought there was anything wrong with me—"

"There is *nothing* wrong with you," she said and moved her hand over mine. I just gave her a look that said *oh please*, but she squeezed my hand. "Nothing. Do you hear me?"

"Fine," I replied and cleared my throat of the tightness building there. "But still. I've been shown a different life, a life I was robbed of, and I'm not sure if I should mourn it or be thankful I dodged a bullet. But then again, the bullet is also staring me right in the face, and I don't know what the right move is."

I tore my gaze from her and returned to admiring the courtyard. Silence filled the space between us.

Tess sniffled. "I'm sorry."

Just two words, but what else could she say? Convince me to help murder my own mother? Beg me to keep spending time in the Domain of Nightmares, where the ruler wanted to use me like a weapon, too? Help stop a race of angry, jaded werewolves from invading a world I was stolen from?

I was too young to face these possibilities and inexperienced with magic and life.

"What does your boyfriend think of it all?" she asked.

Cillian. Gods, that was another cog in the constantly moving parts of my life. "He…isn't on board with any of it, aside from me learning to control my magic. He thinks I don't owe you guys anything."

A ghost of a smile moved her lips. "He's not wrong. You owe this world nothing. If anything, you're the one who's owed something."

"I'd settle for proof."

"Proof?"

I inhaled deeply. "I need proof that I'm not the missing heir because part of me feels connected to Faerie on some deeper level, and I don't know why. In Ironworld, everything is…hard. Here, my magic flows freely and is easy for me to control. My thoughts and dreams are plagued with ties to this world. Gods," I guffawed. "Even the food tastes better to me." I capped my hand over hers atop my knee. "I feel connected to this world, and it goes beyond the simple fact that I was born here. Something…calls to me."

She waited for a beat and then let out a sigh that ended with a slight moan. "I know why." My blood stilled, and I straightened, removing my hand from hers. She glanced around cautiously and stood up, holding out her hand for me to take. "Come. It's easier if I show you."

Tess took me by the hand and wove through the castle, pausing every now and then to get her bearings before we finally emerged outside at the backend courtyard that stretched toward the sea. I realized then how she barely knew her way around because she hadn't spent much time here before fleeing to Ironworld with me. This was all as new to her as it was to me on some level. I admired her bravery for returning and facing all she left behind.

She took me to a massive fountain, an octagonal stone basin with a statue of some valiant knight on horseback in the middle. The circulating water was enough to drown out any sound we might make.

Tess sat on the edge of the fountain. I joined her as she leaned forward and tiredly raked her hands through her hair, revealing those slightly pointed ears.

"Are you okay?" I asked.

She straightened and gave me a warm, tired smile. "I'm fine." She patted my leg. "Don't worry about me. You've got your own battles to face. And…I'm sorry I didn't prepare you for any of it. I thought–I'd hoped we would live in the country forever, just you and I, away from the harsh reality of both worlds. I just–" she chuckled sadly. "I just never accounted for you growing up."

I had no choice but to grow up at a blinding speed in the months since moving to the city. School, two jobs, being responsible for myself, getting into a serious relationship with a vampire, then discovering an entire world of mythical creatures right under my nose, one that I belonged to but…didn't belong to.

My heart sank, and I picked at my gold nail polish. "So, what do you need to show me?"

Her face was pensive, but I didn't want to talk about the past and what could have been. I slowly forgave my aunt for what she did because I know now that she did it to protect me.

"I want to show you the night of my wedding," she said. "After the ceremony, and I knew my sister wasn't going to come, I snuck out in the middle of the night and went to the Seelie castle hoping to talk to her."

"And did you find her?"

"Yes, and someone else." Tess turned to face me and touched her fingertips to the water in the basin. "I'm going to show you a memory. I need you to stay still, calm, and quiet. Okay?"

I just nodded as she pressed a wet finger to my forehead, and I closed my eyes. And, just like my strange visions, I was in a dreamscape. The edges blurred and disappeared, focusing on small details. The warmth of a hearth and darkened windows in a lovely, quaint estate. In the distance, I could hear the ocean crashing against rocks. I moved further into the home, and a woman–a Fae–with hair red as blood lay screaming on the wood floor. Tess's blonde head blocked my view of the Fae's face, but I knew who it was.

My mother.

She screamed as she birthed a child. Her white cotton dress was soiled with blood. Tess helped coax the infant from her sister's body and took it in her arms, wrapping it in a blanket as she peered lovingly at its face.

"Kill it," Mabry said, her voice strained and defeated as she collapsed on the floor completely.

"Mab, you can't be serious–"

"I said get rid of it!" she screamed madly. "It's an abomination! I don't need any painful reminders of what was done." She sat up and grabbed my aunt's sleeve desperately. "Please, sister. Just get rid of it, do this for me, and I'll never ask of you another thing. I cannot be tied to the father; I cannot bear to even look at the babe's face. Do this for me."

Tess's young face paled as she cradled the baby close to her, shielding every inch from the monster that lay on the floor. She slowly nodded, a calculated look in her distant eyes, and stood.

"Stay here," Tess said. "I'll be back soon."

The memory vanished, and I was transported to the

cover of a forest's edge, watching as Tess peered out at something in the distance. No, not something...*someone*. Two someones, to be exact; my mother, draped in a deep red robe, her beautiful hair hung messily around her arms. She argued with a man in a black hooded cape, but I knew who it was by the berth of his shoulders and the stance of his gait.

Oden.

"I had a son," Mabry insisted, eyes alight with madness. "Our bargain is invalid."

"I can smell the lie on your lips!" he replied angrily. "Need I remind you that *you* came to *me*, you wanted this bargain, and you happily agreed to it. Your first-born daughter in exchange for the potion. Now I'm here to collect what is mine."

"You said I could raise her until eighteen."

Oden chuckled darkly. "So, you admit it is a daughter, then?"

"No, I gave birth to Orion's son," she argued, and I noticed her hands dripped with blood. "I just want to remind *you* of the terms of our bargain, Dark Lord."

"You lie, Mabry," Oden said. "And not very well." He pushed past her and headed for the door she had left open behind her. "What are you up to?"

Mabry jumped to stop him, her hands leaving sticky blood all over his cloak. They argued and struggled, but their sounds drifted from my ears as my attention turned to Tess with me in the trees. Her eyes were wide with terror. Breath heaved rapidly in her chest as she backed away, mumbling something to herself.

And she was gone.

Something cold touched my forehead, and I opened my eyes as I was sucked back to reality and stared at my aunt on the fountain's edge.

"Now you see," she told me quietly. "Why I did everything, and why you feel so drawn to this world."

My mouth gaped soundlessly for a moment. "I… She promised me to Oden?" I thought of the gold rings around his arm. One of them was for my mother, for the bargain she'd made on my life.

Tess nodded, her lips tight. "She must have done so blindly because she believed you were dead. I'm so sorry, sweetheart."

Tears brimmed my eyes. "Why are you sorry? You did everything you could to protect me." My shaky hand took hers. "But why? Why would you do that? You gave up your entire life and your duty to this place."

She beamed proudly, her blue eyes glistening as they searched in mine. "That's the only answer I've ever known with all my heart. Because the first moment I held you in my arms, I knew I loved you. My blood ran in your veins just as my sister's did, and I *loved* you. The Quinns knew that. They were my mother's old friends, and I told them I'd return to get you one day. My original plan was to raise you with Kheelan when the time was safe, but…well…."

The tears poured over and streamed down my face. I didn't know how much I needed to hear her story. I'd made up my mind about everything, convinced myself that those I loved were a bunch of selfish liars and didn't care about me at all. But I saw it now, the ultimate sacrifices Tess made for me. I wasn't robbed of life; I was given one.

I flung my arms around her, and she embraced me tightly. "I love you."

We sat for a while, wrapped in one another's trembling arms under a blanket of stars, tears soaking our shoulders. Eventually, I pulled away and wiped my face.

"Thank you."

Tess smiled. "I just want you to know that I have no regrets. I would do it all again if given a chance. Again and again. Because you're what matters most to me in this world, Avery. No duty, no title will ever change that."

A teary laugh gurgled in my throat. "I think your husband might have something to say about that."

She rolled her eyes. "You let me worry about Kheelan."

I always admired my aunt. She was brave and funny and raised me all on her own. I grew up wanting to be just like her because she was everything I thought a person should be. But I had a new level of respect, even love, for her now that I knew the full story, knew all that she had done and would still do in the name of what she loved.

A strange sense of purpose rose within me.

"I want to help," I blurted without thinking, and she looked at me curiously. "With the Therians, with Nightmares. I'll do what I can, but I can't make any promises. Oden's like a vault. He doesn't share things with me."

"If you spend enough time there, he will. Trust me."

"Well, our bargain is only good until I've learned enough," I told her. "And I've already got a good handle on my powers." I flexed my hands, my magic purring in response as I thought of the other bargain. The one he'd made with my mother.

"I'm glad to see." Something like regret flashed in her eyes, but her smile whisked it away. She patted my lap as she stood. "Well, I should be getting back before I have the whole guard out here looking for me."

I grabbed her hand. "Tess, are…are you okay here?"

She tilted her head and laughed, squeezing my fingers. "I'm where I'm needed now. I've done all I can for you. Those years, those precious days we spent together, it was a gift. For both of us." She let go of my hand. "And now it's time for us to decide which path our lives will take. Regardless, mine will always be entwined with yours. Never forget that."

I stared up at her with glossy eyes. "I love you."

"I love you, too. Goodnight."

"Night," I replied as she turned and headed back to the castle. Her robe trailed behind her.

I sat outside all night with a blanket of the brightest stars I'd ever seen as I thought of the heir. It wasn't me, but I had a sibling out there somewhere. A brother. Did he look like me? Did he know who he was? If no one else had been able to find him, what hope did I ever have?

And I thought of Oden's bargain with my mother for her first-born daughter. Would she have made it if she knew I was alive? Did it mean I belonged to him in some way? Is that why he could manipulate my own magic?

When the sun cracked the horizon, I headed back to my quarters and woke Julie up before we headed back home. My mind was filled with questions that would never have answers.

Chapter Fifteen

"But it doesn't make any sense!" Cillian paced my room. He was thrilled when I told him I wasn't the missing heir, but I couldn't say the same for the bomb I dropped about spending more time in Nightmares. He wrung his fingers through his dark, silky waves as his muscles flexed beneath his long-sleeved black shirt. "You owe these people *nothing*."

"I promised Tess," I said from the edge of my bed. I was so tired. Between work and school and my trip to Faerie, sleep was few and far. My voice strained with exhaustion. I just didn't have it in me to fight with him. "The Therians want to invade Faerie and use vampires to do so. They'll kill everyone. It'll be a massacre. An extinction for both our people."

"They're *not* our people!"

But they were. "The least I can do is get some information

for Tess."

"Just stay out of it. Let the Therians invade and claim back their land. Let them leave Ironworld. Good riddance. What duty do you have to a place that never knew you? To a mother who wanted you dead? What do you expect to do, Avery? Help *kill* her? Because that's what it'll take to get rid of the mad queen."

I squared my jaw, my eyes stinging all around the edges, burning with the need to sleep. "I could."

"It's suicide."

I couldn't tell him about the first-born bargain my mother made with Oden. I didn't want anything to stop me from going to Faerie and learning magic while getting any information about Oden's side in this fight. Because that's what was coming, a war, and I could help stop it.

But keeping that from him felt wrong. The secret festered in my gut.

Cillian sat next to me with a long exhale. "Look, I removed myself from that world a long time ago. I refuse to step a toe closer. If you dive deeper into your roots, get involved in their ancient politics and wars, I can't follow you."

"What are you saying?"

He shoved off the bed and sauntered over to the open window. The cold winter breeze crawled across the room and bit my skin.

"I'm not sure," he replied. "I need time to think about everything. You're moving closer and closer to everything I've been distancing myself from for thousands of years, and it's killing me to watch you do it."

I rubbed my hands over my face. "Then don't." I closed my eyes for a moment, and when I opened them, he was gone.

Sleep never came that night.

***

With just five days left until Christmas, I sat on my bed and wrapped all the presents I got for my friends. Lattie tinkered about on my dresser, opening jewelry boxes, and spying inside books.

"So, your vampire lover isn't as valiant as the ones in your stories," she noted as she held up my old copy of Twilight. I'd told her everything that had happened over the last few days.

My shoulders slumped as I secured another gift with a final piece of tape. "He's just scared. I'm heading right into the face of everything he's been running away from. He just needs time."

Lattie chortled as she held one of my fake gemstone rings up to the light. "Time is something none of us have right now."

"What's that supposed to mean?"

She left a mess on my dresser and fluttered over to me, her big black almond-shaped eyes blinking with a skim of light blue. "Maybe you can't feel it, but I can. Things are in motion and coming to a point. Events, tensions, plans. Any day now, our lives—your life—will change beyond recognition." I just stared at her as her words sank in. "Whether the Therians succeed or not, things will change forever, and I'm not even sure what that will look like."

I chewed at the inside of my lip. She was right; the Therians could invade Faerie any day. We don't know the exact details of Vivian's plan, the where, and the when. We only know the how. And, if they succeed, Oden, Tess and Kheelan, and the rest of the free domains will engage in an all-out war.

In the best-case scenario, Faerie wins at a significant cost and drives the Therians and vampires out. But that still leaves them fighting amongst each other for Mabry's throne. Worst case…the Therians win and take over a land I've come to fall in love with, where people I care about reside.

And I sat here wrapping presents.

I tossed everything aside and fished my green jacket from the back of my door. My hand hesitated over the doorknob. I couldn't tell Julie where I was going; she was just as unenthused as Cillian about Tess's plea for me to spend more time in Nightmares.

But I had to do something.

I steadied my breath and closed my eyes as I slowly clenched my fist and wisped right from my room to the waterfront. With a quick look around to ensure no one was looking, I crouched down, touched my fingertips to the frigid harbor water, and pictured the border of cherry trees, inhaling their sweet and bitter scent.

The deep bellow of music pulsated in my ears, and I opened my eyes to find Oden's castle thrumming with life. Night had already fallen, and the windows cut the darkness like arched-shaped cookies, light pouring and spilling over the lawns.

Was he having a party?

I didn't need my thick jacket here where winter had yet to arrive, so I shrugged out of my coat and slung it over my arm as I made the long trek up the winding dirt path. The ground vibrated with the base of music with each step I took. Two guards stood outside the back door I usually used. I held my breath as I approached, expecting them to block me from entering, but they just nodded with recognition as I reached for the handle.

Soon, smells of roasted meats and fruity wine filled my nose, and I followed the mix of scents and sounds through the castle. It led me to the grand dining room, where tables heaping with food lined the walls and people danced.

I recognized some faces from Haven, even Mayor Mis-aldri, who waved at me from across the room where she stood amongst a group near the band. Fiddles, flutes, and other instruments played, reminding me of times I spent at the Sanctuary.

"What are you doing here?"

I spun around at the sound of his voice. "I had some free time."

Oden arched a suspicious brow as he swirled his glass of amber in circles, eyeing me curiously. "And you chose to come *here*?"

He wore his usual slacks and fitted shirt, but the sleeves were rolled up, and the top few buttons hung open. His stark white hair kissed his shoulders, slightly shorter than before. He must have gotten a haircut.

I placed my jacket on the back of a chair. "No, I thought I would spend any time I could learning more magic and building my strength." I gave him an impatient look. "Y'know, with the impending war looming over us? I need to be prepared, and we have a bargain."

He watched me for a moment, and I brushed away the urge to slip inside his mind again. "That we do. For each full moon."

I swung my arms and took in the party happening around us. "So, I'm not allowed to come to your party then?"

A ghost of a grin tugged at his mouth as he brought his

glass to his lips. Those stormy eyes never left my face. "It's not my party. It's my brother's."

And that's when I noticed him sitting amongst the band, strumming away on a lute like a damn fool. The biggest smile on his face. Sullivan was so different from his brother that I almost found it hard to believe they were even related.

"Shouldn't you guys be in meetings and making war plans?" I asked.

"Why the sudden interest?" he asked and tipped back the dregs of his drink. "The last time we spoke, you wished Vivian would tear me to shreds."

"I had time to think."

"And?" He tapped his glass, and it magically refilled.

I sighed. "And I realized it would be wrong to turn my back on this. I have people I care about here–in Summer," I quickly added, and he grinned like a cat. "If I can help in any way, I should. I *will*." I pointed at his glass. "You were supposed to show me how to do that, by the way."

Oden chuckled under his breath and took two strides toward a nearby table. He swiped a bottle of wine and an empty glass from a stack and handed them to me.

"It's a lot like wisping," he told me. "You have to see it; you have to know where it's coming from."

"You mean it doesn't just magically appear?"

"No." He set the bottle down. "Imagine the wine in

your glass."

I closed my eyes and thought of the bottle, its fullness, the deep purple shade of the liquid inside, and the smell of fermented cherries. I opened my eyes and tapped the empty glass, picturing it filling with wine.

And it did.

"Quick learner," Oden said and turned toward the party. He stuffed a hand in one pocket. "Go enjoy the party."

"Where are you going?"

"Off to make plans of war."

I rolled my eyes at the sarcasm in his tone.

He left the room, and I wanted to run after him, to drill him with questions about the first-born bargain and get any info I could for Tess, but someone grabbed my arm and spun me around.

"Red!" Sullivan bellowed and stumbled as he yanked me close, his lute in one hand, his heavy boots stomping against the floor. "Come to dance with me?"

"No, I–"

Sullivan spun me around and around until we mixed with the crowd and the other musicians struck up a new festive tune. I tried to tell him I wasn't there to party, but the music was loud and infectious, and people's cheer filled the room.

So, I danced.

I let Sullivan take me by the hand as we twirled and

pranced to song after song. Drinks were never-ending, as was the glorious food floating on trays held by staff. Baked cheese delicacies and perfect pastries stuffed with minced meats, trays of nuts and dried fruits, and bowls of strange dips.

Misaldri found me again, and we moved to a quiet corner to sit and catch our breaths.

"How was the cherry festival?"

"Wonderful!" she replied and accepted a tray of finger foods from a passing servant. "The turnout was great; people from neighboring villages came. I heard several other festivals across the domain had similar results. It's always a fun time. I'm sorry you had to miss it."

"Maybe next year," I told her, surprised by the honesty in my voice. I wanted to go.

She regarded me with a curious brow, but her eyes were prideful and certain.

"Where are the boys?" I asked her.

She stuffed a pastry to the side of her mouth and smiled. "It's my night off. They're with their father while I spend the evening here. It's the first time the Dark Lord has opened the doors to his home in many years."

"Apparently, it's Sullivan's party," I replied and chugged back a large glass of water.

"Yes, but Oden approved it. Seems his mood has shifted."

"Mood?"

"While I've been blessed with his quiet friendship over the years–something I think carried over from his mother–he's been fairly…prickly since his mother's passing many years ago and has since become a bit of a recluse. Burying himself with work and duties. Keeping his people at arm's length."

I thought of how he'd opened his home to me, how I could waltz in here without an invitation. Even had my own room, however temporary. I glanced around the hall where people celebrated solstice under his roof for the first time in who knew how long, and he was nowhere to be found. He wasn't even here enjoying the party.

Maybe he really was making war plans.

"Excuse me," I told my new friend and stood up. "I have to find the restroom."

"Of course," she replied and stood with me, scanning the crowd. "I'm going to find that devilishly handsome brother of Oden's and employ him to dance with me."

I laughed. "You won't have any trouble there."

The castle's hallways were a welcome refuge from the clamor of sounds within the dining hall. My ears boomed with the reverb of music and laughter long after I left. I checked the library, the kitchen, the throne room, and even the courtyards out front, but Oden was nowhere to be found. I couldn't wisp within the castle grounds, so I continued my search, hoping to stumble upon him eventually.

I rounded one of many dimly lit corridors, and the end glowed with firelight. It danced on the stone, and I followed it toward the scent of cigars and sweet liquor. I stepped inside, knowing he was there before I even saw him. His power, that ever-building storm, was like a silent beacon, constantly pulsing, sending waves through the air.

He sat behind a massive desk heaped with papers and books, ankles crossed over one another on the edge as he leaned back and gazed out an open window. A hearth was nestled in the wall to the side with a cozy fire crackling, and bookshelves flanked it, towering to the ceiling.

"Don't like parties?" I asked him.

He didn't flinch at my presence, and I wondered if he sensed me coming the whole time. He once told me nothing happens in his castle without him knowing.

"I've got more important things to tend to." He took a sip of amber from a crystal glass and swished it in his mouth before swallowing.

I slowly walked through the massive study, noting different books laid open and what information I could discreetly absorb. It was just old maps and things written in languages I couldn't read.

"Did you ever find out who killed that Fae?" I asked, suddenly remembering the worried look on that woman's face.

Oden set his feet on the floor and turned in his seat, looking me up and down. I just stood and stared back, expecting him to lie or tell me to leave at best. But he inhaled deeply through his nose.

"Yes, it was Evaine."

The sound of her name sent blood searing through my veins.

"She's upset with me and wanted to send a message." He downed the rest of his drink and as he stood up. "Or a warning. I'm not sure yet." He leaned back against the front of the desk and crossed his arms.

"For what?" The words were dry in my throat.

Oden pinched the bridge of his nose. "When I hired her to help me find the heir, she had plans to take over my domain once I took the Seelie throne."

I nodded once. "Ah, I see. And I ruined all that."

He chuckled sadly, tiredly. "That you did. And more."

Good. Some part of me delighted in the fact that I caused that bitch any amount of inconvenience. "What do you know about the mad queen?"

"More than most, less than some."

"I didn't come here for vague riddles, Oden."

"Then why *did* you come here?" He gave me a heated look laced with anger.

My heart nearly stopped at the clipped tone. Even I didn't really know the answer to that. For Tess? For myself? To get away from my crumbling life in Ironworld?

"Why did you lie?" I dared ask, and the truth of my visit reared its ugly head. I hadn't even realized it until now. Oden was the only one who could give me the answers I needed. "Why didn't you tell me about your bargain with my mother?"

His mouth gaped, and his eyes flashed with realization. "Who told you?"

"My aunt."

Oden glanced thoughtfully at the golden rings that circled the skin on his wrist. One of them for the very bargain I spoke of. "That bargain is my life's biggest regret. I had been so alone, lost for so many decades. I'd been planning to overthrow Orion since he murdered my father, but I didn't have the means or the power to do so." He regarded me with a head tilt. "But a queen made for me would have been the solution. I acted blindly, only focused on one thing. But I never should have bargained with an innocent life. When I learned you'd had no knowledge of it, I saw my chance to set it right."

I willed myself not to grind my teeth together. "But you still had Evaine spy on me and drag me here."

"To beg for your help," he noted. "I thought if I brought you here, the power of the bargain would sway you at the very least. But that first visit—she can be violent in her ways—it shouldn't have gone like that."

"Show me."

"What?"

"Show me what happened that night."

The look on his face told me he knew exactly what night I spoke of. He pushed off the desk and dragged two armchairs over. We sat knees to knees as he wrung his hands together in his lap.

"Open your mind to me," he said with a gentle rasp.

I closed my eyes, and he pressed a cool thumb to my forehead. The touch immediately let in a rush of images, spinning like a Rolodex of memories. Suddenly, everything stopped, and I stood just outside the castle under a midnight sky, watching the thicket of cherry trees as if waiting for something.

The trees rustled, and a woman emerged, stumbling and panting for breath. Her long red hair fell in tangles around her, matching the stains on her familiar cotton dress. It was my mother; I could see it in the face that stared back at me, the memory crisper than the one Tess had shown me. And that dress…it was the same.

She'd given birth to me the same night she made the bargain with Oden.

I watched as she dragged a blade across her palm and let the blood trickle to the earth below. She demanded Oden's favor, and I realized what he was showing me—trust. He trusted me with the knowledge of how I could gain control over him, to ask any one thing he couldn't refuse.

I pushed him from my mind and gasped for air as I braced my sweaty hands around the arms of the chair. "That's enough. I can't–I don't want to see her face anymore."

"I imagine you know how the rest went," he said with a drip of remorse. "She begged me for a potion to make the king fall in love with her, and I saw my chance spread wide open before me. It didn't matter if she was successful in her quest to wed the Seelie King. I knew I could take them both down with a queen at *my* side. My father's domain was powerful under his and my mother's rule. If I had made it a court, I would have been equally powerful as the Seelie kingdom. Maybe more." He looked at me, at the tears that brimmed my eyes. "I'm…sorry I never told you. At first, I'd hoped the bargain would just bring you to me when you turned of age. But when I learned I had to track you down, when I had to watch you, learn from you…I saw something else. Something I never knew I needed. A second chance to make it right." He sighed nervously. "I wish I never made that bargain with your wretched mother."

"But does this mean I *belong* to you in some way?"

He waited for a beat. "No."

But we both knew it was a lie.

"I can't be your queen, Oden." I needed to clarify because I realized the glimmer I often found in his stormy gaze was hope. He looked at me with the hope of fixing more than his bargain with Vivian. He wanted me to help him take the Seelie throne.

"I know," he replied honestly. He circled a long narrow table opposite the fireplace, filled with even more books and papers than his desk. "But, how about a job offer?"

"A job offer?" I scoffed but wiped the laughable smile off my face when I realized he was serious.

"Yes, be my business partner," Oden insisted.

I approached the table. "And what's the business?"

He tilted his head, his white hair falling like a curtain on the side of his face as he gave me an unreadable look. "Saving the world."

Something warmed in my belly at the idea I could be that important, that I had something to offer this world and the next. I wanted to save it, both sides. My home was in Ironworld, but part of me was falling in love with Faerie and all it had to give.

But my chest squeezed with anxiety. I was just a girl. A few months ago, I thought I was no more than a human college student.

But Oden thought I was the heir to the Seelie throne. I couldn't help him, and he deserved to know that. The clock was ticking on the coming war between Therians and Fae. He needed every moment possible to find the true heir if he wanted any hope of taking that throne.

I opened my mouth to tell him my secret, but a loose piece of paper atop an open book caught my eye at the same time as his, and I grabbed it. He followed me around the study as I examined the handwritten list.

"Uses for…*the girl?*"

"Avery, let me explain–"

My eyes widened at the paper.

"Those were from Evaine, from her…observations of you."

He reached for the note, but I held it away as I stepped back. "Woo her and wed her. Use her magic to build my court." I glared at him. "*My* Court? If you forced me into some kind of marriage, wouldn't it be *our* Court?"

"Avery–"

"Baring my offspring," I continued with a crack in my voice. Tears filled my eyes at the last line. "Kill her and take her power for my own… Oden, what is this?"

He hung his head in shame.

"Oden!" The crumpled list bounced off his chest.

"That was before."

"Before *what?*" I hastily wiped the tears from my face. "I will *not* be used as a pawn in this war. I will *not* be taken advantage of. My power is *mine* and mine alone, to use as I see fit, to decide for *myself*." I walked toward him, and he had the good sense to back up. Rage built within me, igniting my magic as it readied to defend me. "You will *never* have my power, and I will *never* be your queen. You can take the bogus job offer and shove it up your ass."

I swung a fist toward him, but he caught my wrist with lightning speed, and my skin burned under his grip. His eyes widened with a heated stare. Anger burned through me, and I swung my other fist at him, but he caught that one, too, and crossed my arms over my chest as the table slammed into the back of my legs.

I could feel his breath on my face, spilling over the sharp lines of his lips, and his jaw ticked to the side. Contained anger simmered all around him. God, what have I done? Was he going to kill me?

"Go back to your vampire, Avery," he said flatly and released my wrists to pull my jacket from thin air. "He might soon be the last one left."

He shoved it at me, and I side-stepped toward the door, holding it to my chest as I fled the room. He never pursued. Not when I ran through the castle, not even as I stormed down the dirt path that led to the water. But someone's quickened footsteps approached from behind.

"Red!" Sullivan called as he ran to catch up with me. He fell into step at my side. "Going home so soon?"

"I shouldn't have come here," I spat.

"Well, I'll walk you home." He lit a cigarette between his lips before taking a long draw.

"No, don't leave your party."

We came to a stop at the water's edge. "I'm bound to ensure your safety. I was just being nice about it."

"Oh, shit, I forgot he told you to do that." I slipped my coat on. "You seriously don't have to. I can make it back to my house without getting killed."

We exchanged a skeptical look.

"Fine," I replied. "Just make it quick. Once we cross, wisp right to my back door."

Sullivan took one more long drag of his cigarette and tossed it to the ground before taking my hand. Calloused fingers gripped mine, and we crossed over to Ironworld in the blink of an eye. He squeezed my hand, and we stood outside the door behind the café.

Max sat on the step.

"What are you doing here," I asked.

She only glared up at Sullivan, whose eyes were as wide as saucers, like he'd just found a pot of gold.

"I need to speak to you," she said in a way that told me that was all she'd say around Sullivan.

I turned to him. "I'm home now. Go back to your party."

"Are you sure you don't need me to stay?" he asked, his eyes flitting to Max.

I just shook my head and nudged his shoulder. "Listen, don't go there. For your own sake." I glanced down at Max, who looked like she killed people for fun. "Trust me."

Sullivan backed away, one arm behind his back, the other throwing me a mocking salute. "See ya, Red." He tipped his head to Max. "Goddess."

A growl turned over in her chest as she slowly stood, her maroon leather jacket groaning in the cold. He just laughed and disappeared in a blip.

"Faerie trash," she muttered under her breath, her curls bouncing.

"Hey!"

She rolled her eyes. "Sorry."

I stuffed my hands in my pockets and shook my head. "So, what's up?"

"I need to hide out from my mom for a bit. She somehow discovered I helped you escape." She looked bored, but I knew it was a front. "And that I was stealing that night."

I saw her differently now that I knew what she really was. Long legs built with lithe muscles, fingers with claws hidden beneath, a lethal body made for killing. I only witnessed her wolf form once, when she was limping and injured, and it still terrified me. Max was a creature of the night and one to be feared. I couldn't imagine her running from anyone.

"What will she do if she finds you?"

Pain flashed in her deep brown eyes. "Nothing humane."

I fished my keys out. "Well, you're welcome to crash at

our place for a bit."

She closed in, her arms crossed. A confused look contorted on her face. "Thank you."

I passed her on the steps and laughed. "Jesus, it doesn't have to be that painful to say, Max."

She just groaned from behind as we climbed the rickety wooden staircase. Moya and the twins lounged in the living room while Julie made margaritas in the kitchen. It was one of the rare times I saw Aya and Brie in casual attire, grey leggings, and teal-colored sweaters. Everyone came to a halt and stiffened at the sight of Max, and Lattie hissed from atop the kitchen cabinets.

"Woah, chill," I said. "She's a friend. She's proved as much, don't you think? And she needs to hide out from her mom."

Moya arched a perfect pink brow, her hair thrown into a massive messy bun. "And what does your mother have to say about the missing Fae she's been harvesting blood from?"

"I made a deal with Oden," I told them. "You guys know that. He can't break it. And we saved those Fae from the coombs."

Julie walked into the living room carrying a jug of yellow slush. "Deal or no deal, Av'. There's still Fae going missing."

"What?"

Moya folded one silk-clad leg over the other. "I just got word. There are some missing from the Sanctuary. They left days ago and never came back."

Max grimaced at my side. "Nothing you do will stop her. Those few Fae we took from the coombs are probably just a fraction of what she has tucked away."

I thought for a moment. "If that's true, then we have no idea how large Vivian's army really is."

Silence coated the room, so heavy my heart pounded in my ears. Was Vivian kidnapping Fae in masses and continuing to grow her vampire army that could cross the border?

"We have to know," I said to my friends. "At least an estimate of what Faerie's up against. Tess and Kheelan should know. They're the only other ones with an army besides Oden."

Julie came close. "We'll figure it out, Av'."

Max was like a statue next to me. How could she be so still? I secretly admired everything about her. She was like a beautiful bomb, just waiting to go off, and I couldn't look away.

"I may have someone I can call for information," Max said. "Just give me a day."

Moya eyed her cautiously. "Thank you."

"Max, you don't have to help if it's putting you in danger." I slipped my boots off.

She gave me a look that said, *don't tell me what to do*, so I wove around the coffee table and sat on the couch. "You can take my room." I pointed at my closed door. "I'll crash on the couch."

Max paused before stalking off toward my room, ignoring the looks of my friends. She closed the door behind her.

"What's that all about?" Julie asked and handed me a frozen margarita.

I shrugged. "Just shit with her mom. I can't imagine having Vivian for a mother would make for an easy life." I thought of Mabry and what my life would have looked like if she'd raised me. Would I be a tyrant like her or subject to her wrath?

They nodded and moaned quietly in agreement.

Julie perched on the arm of the sofa. "So, where were you all night?"

Blood flushed my cheeks, and I stared into the sour slush in my glass. "I, uh, went to Oden's. I was there to find info for Tess, but it was a bust."

The space between her delicate brows pinched. "Yeah?"

I downed a big gulp of my drink. "Hmm, hmm. Sullivan was having a solstice party."

Brie perked up and set both feet on the floor. "We should have a solstice party!"

"Where?" Aya added, just as excited.

It felt like the worst time to throw a party, but I didn't have the heart to say it. The excitement on my friend's faces at the mention of it…they deserved it. I deserved it.

We flew into planning mode for a last-minute Christmas party, and all the while, I could feel Julie's cautious, wondering stare. We decided on the Chocolate Kettle for a location after hours, and I couldn't help but think–despite all the chaos–how this was exactly what we needed.

***

The morning sun warmed the early crispy chill. I waited for the coffee to perk as I wrapped my uber-thick wool sweater tight across my chest. Tess had knitted it for me one year; it was big and chunky with soft olive wool. I loved it.

Julie was already out practicing wisping, according to the note she left. I poured a cup of coffee as my bedroom door opened, and Max, looking just as she did the night before, crept out. Her eyes met mine, and I lifted my cup.

"Coffee?"

"Yes, please," she replied and sat at the table. I poured her one and set it in front of her. "Are you going to class today?"

I swallowed dryly, hugging my cup to my chest. "Yeah, I should probably make an appearance. I've…missed a few classes."

"A few? You haven't been there in days."

"I know, I know." I stared out the window, yearning to reach out and touch the sunlight pouring in. "I just have a lot going on." She rolled her eyes. "I've been working on the end-of-semester showcase, but I think…I think after the holidays, I might take a break. Maybe resume classes next Fall."

Her eyes flashed. "Are you fucking serious?"

"Max."

"Quinn, if I can do it, so can you. Don't give me that shit."

Someone knocked at the door, and I sighed in relief as I went to open it. Tomas stood there, bouncing with anxiety. He burst past me and paced in the porch area.

"I'm losing her, aren't I?" he said in a broken tone.

I loosed a sigh. "It's more complicated than that. And it's not my place to–"

Something white shot across the living room, and Julie came to a screeching halt, her face alit with vindication.

"I did it!" she said excitedly. "I finally wisped through our wards from across the city! It's the furthest I'd–" She stilled, her crystal blue eyes locked on a stunned Tomas.

Julie was in her full Fae form.

"Tomas…" she barely whispered and took a step for him, her unblinking stare filled with tears. She changed to her usual human form.

Max sipped her coffee. "Little late for that, don't you think?"

Tomas was silent, unreadable.

I touched his shoulder, and he flinched. "We're all Fae. Well, I'm part Fae, part human. Made human." I shook my head. "It's complicated."

I glanced at Max, and she grimaced. "I'm not involved in this." My eyes widened at her. "Fine. I'm a witch."

I cleared my throat.

"And a shapeshifter."

Tomas paled and backed away. "I'm dreaming."

"No," I said calmly. "You're not."

I knew exactly what he was feeling. Like a rug you never knew you were standing on is pulled out from beneath you. You don't even know where to stand, let alone what to say or do.

"I-I need to go."

We watched Tomas turn and run out the door he came in. No words to even call after him. Julie was crushed; her pained expression cut me in half, and my heart broke for her. She ran to her room and slammed the door.

Max peered up at me from the table. "What's that all about?"

I just stared at Julie's bedroom door. "Her biggest fear is not being accepted for what she is. She's faced a lot of rejection from people she thought loved her. And the man she loves just ran away at first sight of her."

Chapter Sixteen

Fat snowflakes drifted to the ground as I sat on my bed and stared out the window. Christmas was in just a couple days, and I couldn't help but think of Tess. I pulled the blanket closer, hugged my knees to my chest, and tipped my head back against the headboard. A blank sketchpad lay open on the bed. A painful reminder that I was too overwhelmed to concentrate on art.

I thought about my conversation with Max. School, work…it all seemed so pointless. No, just expendable in the grand scheme of things. An ancient race of werewolves was about to use an army of Fae blood-fueled vampires to cross the Faerie border and kill anyone that stood in the way of Vivian taking Mabry's throne.

My *mother's* throne.

What a wretched creature she was. Ordering her baby to die. Did she kill the true heir, too? Was that the reason no one could find him? If he really was dead, what did that mean for me? Maybe I did have some claim to the throne. Not that I wanted it.

Everything was such high stakes and uncertainty, and it sent my heart racing with anxiety just thinking about it. I didn't know what to expect in the coming days, maybe weeks, but I did know one thing for sure.

It'd be a massacre if the vampires managed to cross the border. They'll have a taste for Fae blood and a smorgasbord before them. And when the Therians somehow get through, there'll be no stopping them.

I bolted out of bed, not bothering to change out of my navy flannel pajamas, and failed to settle my breathing as I gripped the fabric of space and time. I opened my eyes, my feet firmly planted on Cillian's apartment balcony. Blackout blinds covered the windows.

I stormed inside, and Cillian jumped up from the leather sofa at the sight of me. His deep blue eyes were wide.

"Avery," he panted and stopped a breath away from me, his hands hovering over my body, unsure where to touch. "What's the matter?"

The tension between us was gone. I didn't want to fight with him anymore. I slung my arms around his neck and slammed my mouth over his, desperate for touch. "Make love to me, Cillian. Tell me everything's going to be alright."

His arms wrapped around my torso and crushed me to

him, devouring my kisses. "I can't promise you that." He put his forehead to mine.

A slight whimper squeezed from me, and I bit back the tears that threatened to rise. I dragged my lips across his with a feathered touch. "Then lie to me," I whispered. The words barely escaped before a sob broke through.

Cillian smoothed my hair away and held my face in both hands, his eyes searching mine for answers I couldn't give him. "I would never lie to you."

My tears ran down over his hands. He was right. Cillian was always brutally honest, even when it broke my heart. I couldn't fault him for it.

I kissed him again, and his hands slid to my thighs and hoisted me into his arms. I wrapped my legs around his waist, never breaking my hold on his mouth. It was a kiss that pounded deep, clutching my insides and claiming everything. I never wanted to let go. I was falling apart, and Cillian was the only one who could hold the pieces together.

I leaned back for just a moment, long enough to pull free the drawstring that held up my pajama pants. He backed up and sat on the couch, and I slipped my pants off at his feet, revealing a scanty pair of black lacey underwear.

I put one foot on the couch at his side, my knee almost touching his head, and a moan turned over in his throat as he dragged his mouth over my inner thigh. I began unbuttoning my flannel shirt, taking my time as he stared up, and our gazes locked, his lips still pressed against the skin of my leg.

"If you wish to wear this shirt again, I'd suggest you hurry up before I destroy those buttons."

Goosebumps scoured over me, and a roguish grin spread across his soft pink lips. He hooked a finger through the waist of my underwear and yanked them free, eliciting a slight gasp from me. It left my skin smarting, but I relished in pain. I wanted more.

"Bite me," I told him.

The sensual haze in his eyes vanished, and his fingers stilled around my thigh. "What?"

I nudged my leg closer to his face. "I want you to bite me."

"I can't–you don't know what you're asking, Avery," he said, but I could hear the desire in his voice. I wondered how long it'd been since he drank fresh human blood. "A bite–to drink from you and not kill, it creates a bond–"

I gripped his chin in my fingers. "So, create it. I belong to you; in every way a person can belong to someone." Thoughts of the first-born bargain filled my mind, and I desperately needed to douse them. I released his chin and raked my hand through his silky black waves, grabbing the back of his head. "Now claim what's yours, Cillian."

My heart raced, sending blood coursing through my

veins, and, I swear, he seemed to almost sense it. I stood before him, bared and naked, as he caressed my bent leg, bringing his nose and lips to the tender skin of the inner most part of my thigh. He glanced up at me, those cerulean eyes asking silent permission, and I nodded, squeezing the hair at the back of his head, urging him forward.

His lips parted, and he clamped his mouth down over my skin. I held my breath, waiting for the pain, but there was only a slight pinch as his teeth punctured my skin. Immediately, some force rushed through me—life, throbbing and pulsing in my veins as Cillian coaxed the blood from my body. There was no pain, only a deep pool of ecstasy. I wanted nothing more than to fall into it completely, to get lost and never resurface as my life force funneled into him.

A moan rumbled from me, and Cillian's eyes shot open, his mouth clamped around my leg. Gone was the blue I loved so much, replaced by the fully blackened stare of a predator. But he didn't scare me. Every part of him was beautiful to me. I reached for his face, my thumb brushed the blackened skin beneath his eye, and he released his hold on my leg to shrink away from my touch.

Blood dripped down my thigh as I took his face in both hands, placed my mouth over his, and pushed him down on the couch. I climbed over him and straddled his waist; I could feel his impressive length pressing against my warm center, rubbing against the hot bundle of nerves there.

The black in his eyes slowly began to fade. His fingers dug into the flesh of my back as I rolled my hips, dragging myself up and down the length of him until the sounds of his desire, his need for me, escaped.

"Holy fuck, Avery," he hissed as his tip teased my opening.

I mounted him, sliding my body down over the rock-hard member, and immediately withdrew with a wicked grin. Cillian's hands grabbed my hips, demanding I return, and I slipped back in place, letting him fill me. I relished the sensation, the connection. My blood flowed in him, and now he pulsed within me with every buck and dip I made.

Our labored breaths entwined as I rode him, each thrust passionate and final. I could feel his release building, scouring his entire body as his muscles tensed. My back arched, readying my own blissful release, but Cillian grabbed my waist and flipped me over with blinding speed.

I gripped the couch cushions in a blink as his fingers rubbed hot circles over the wetness between my legs. He positioned himself from behind and thrust himself deep inside.

I cried out as Cillian filled me, and my insides stretched and throbbed around him. He smoothed the skin of my back, his thumb brushing over every little curve of my spine. I felt his soft lips follow and whisper against my skin.

"Come for me, Avery."

I buried my face in the couch cushion as he pounded hard, thrust after thrust, reaching the deepest parts of me. My climax built again, like a coming storm darkening the sky, and I gave myself to it as the ecstasy of release exploded from me, entwining with his own, and our cries of pleasure filled the room.

***

As I dragged it into place, the white cube pedestal groaned, echoing off the gallery walls. Celadine carried a pile of white cloth napkins and set them on the banquet table near the back.

"Anything else I can get you?" she asked, braiding her pale, tattooed hands at the waist of her stark white pants suit, the collar high around her neck.

She wanted to match the aesthetic of my showing. Everything was pure white; the marble floors, the tables of refreshments, and the backdrop behind the three pedestals that displayed my art. Her braids and locks were neatly swept up into a massive bun.

"No," I replied, setting the final art piece in place. "I'm all done." I rubbed my hands against my white jumper and loosed a nervous breath. I couldn't think about the fact that people were coming any minute to see *my* art. "Oh, I wanted to apologize for missing a few shifts. I just–"

"I understand." Celadine waved it off with a kind smile. "But just know, I want an apprentice, but I also want someone who can run this place with me one day. I want it to be you, Avery. When you're ready."

I gave her a dumbfounded look. "Oh, Celadine…"

She shook her head. "But I don't want you to feel obligated. When the dust settles after this war, I'd love to sit down and discuss your future at the gallery."

I chewed at the inside of my lip. "What if the dust never settles? What if…" I couldn't say it, but the words burned at the back of my throat. What if we all died?

Celadine's violet stare locked on mine with a heavy dose of confidence. "I've roamed this earth for thousands of years. I've seen countless wars, natural disasters, and horrors you could never imagine. Horrors I hope you never have to. But I can assure you that the dust always settles, and we move on."

I wanted to say yes, but my life was so scattered and uncertain. "Can I think about it?" I swallowed dryly and quickly added, "I'm honored and want to, yes. I mean, I'd be crazy not to want that. But I can't commit to anything right now, not until this is over."

"Of course," she replied, no sign of doubt or hurt in her tone.

She was like a rock on a crashing shoreline. Steady and

solid, she never wavered in her purpose or belief. Her confidence in me constantly inspired me to keep moving forward in every sense of my chaotic life.

She glanced over her shoulder toward the doors and giant windows that faced the gallery, now covered in blackout blinds to block the late afternoon sun that drained her energy.

She handed me a small white remote. "Here. People will arrive any moment, so I'll make myself scarce until the sun goes down."

"Thank you for everything, Celadine."

She threw me a wink as she turned toward the back of the gallery where her office was. A few seconds later, the gallery door swung open, and Tomas walked in, dragging a trolley of equipment with him. I ran over to help.

"I didn't think you'd come," I said, hiding my relief.

Tomas smoothed out the white hoodie he wore, and I smiled. He remembered the theme. But he gave me a weary look and noted where my hands hung at my sides like he was unsure what I might do.

"It's my project, too." He shrugged nervously. "I'll just set up and go, then come back when it's over."

He grabbed the handle on the trolly, and I reached for his arm. "Tomas, it doesn't have to be like this. You have nothing to fear from Julie and me. We're still *us*."

He tilted his head with a sigh. "Yeah, but…you're *not*."

I had no reply. I knew just how hard a pill it was to swallow, finding out the world around you was nothing like you thought it was and discovering the person you cared for wasn't even human. I wanted to tell him, wanted to share that with my friend. I could help because I was there once.

But the doors opened again, and one of my instructors from school walked in. I showed them around the gallery as Tomas set up the lighting and audio. I opened the blinds, and people began filing in. Some from school, some off the street. All the while, even after he was done, Tomas lingered. Julie arrived, and he immediately busied himself with wires, but I caught him stealing glances at her.

She didn't look his way once.

"This looks amazing, Av'," she said with a drink in hand as she stared at my work. "You're incredible."

I sucked in a deep breath as I turned and faced the tree pedestals with her. "It's a wonder I even finished them. You know, with everything we have going on."

"It's a lot," she replied. "How are you coping, by the way?"

I chortled and pressed my lips together as I glanced across the room. Tomas blushed when I caught him staring at Julie. "I'm fine because I have people in my life who love me and understand on a level no one else can." I subtly tipped my chin in Tomas's direction. "But Tomas has no one, not one single person he can turn to with this. You should talk to him."

"I-I can't."

"Jules…"

"How can I face him, Avery? He saw what I was and looked at me like I was a monster. I'm mortified. He'll never see me the same again, never talk to me like he once did. There'll always be this invisible thing between us."

"I think he's just scared."

She downed the rest of her champagne. "That makes two of us," she said with spite and headed off to a group of people that waved at her.

I spotted Max in the crowd, a long white maxi dress hugging her body as her perfect braids cascaded down her back. She eyed my work with an unreadable expression. God, she was like a brick wall. But I sometimes saw through the cracks, saw the emotions she kept so guarded.

I sidled up next to her.

"Good work," she said flatly, not breaking her gaze at the pieces.

"Thanks for coming," I replied and handed her a drink. "You left the apartment."

"I got my hands on some wards," she replied stonily. "Thanks for letting me crash."

"Anytime," I said. "That's what friends do."

She finally looked at me and opened her mouth to speak, but something over my shoulder caught her attention, and she narrowed her eyes, a deep growl turning over in her chest. She handed me back the flute of champagne and stormed across the room where her mother stood.

"What are you doing here?"

Vivian smoothed a hand over the white fur shawl that hugged her neck. "I've come to appreciate some art. I hear the artist is to *die* for." Her red lips turned up in a wicked grin.

"How dare you come here after what you did," Max told Vivian, who looked at her daughter like a wild cat turning its nose down at rotten meat.

"After what *I* did?" she scoffed. "What about the things you've done, dear daughter of mine? Stealing, lying, conspiring against your own family, rejecting your gods given birth right."

Max simmered with rage; her fists clenched at her sides. "Leave."

People noticed the nearly silent, passive-aggressive fight unfolding and casually moved away. The air in my lungs turned cold as I held my breath, and flashes of being held down on that surgical bed came flooding back. Images and memories I'd apparently blocked out.

Vivian Carmichael, the alpha of North American Therians, flicked her deadly gaze to me with a look that said, *I'm coming for you.* Without even thinking, my lips parted, and a whisper of a name spilled out.

Oden.

Within moments, the gallery door swung open, and he was there, draped in a slick charcoal dress coat. His human form didn't fool me but clearly worked for everyone else, as no one even glanced his way. Part of me didn't think it would work, that'd he'd hear my call, and I begged my lungs to relax as he scanned the crowd and found me. Sullivan appeared at his side, and the two strode across the gallery for me.

"You called?" Oden said with a coy smirk.

He clearly knew I'd do it. *Your lips have touched mine…* The words on that note whispered in my head. But I didn't care. At that moment, I needed him there for so many reasons. That woman wanted me dead, at best, and my friends were here. Not to mention innocent people. Nerves rattled under my skin. Seeing Vivian did something to me.

"I-I…"

Oden noted where my eyes unblinkingly stared, at my friend and her mother, as Sullivan clamped a hand atop his shoulder.

"Brother," he said quietly. "Look who's here."

Oden's eyes widened at the sight of Vivian and then shot at me with nothing but remorse. He turned and stormed toward her, eliciting a deadly snarl from Max, who at least had the good sense to step aside. I sped over to her, Sullivan hot on my heels.

"Vivian, I told you to stay away from these people," Oden warned. The winter sky outside darkened and rumbled in the distance.

"I'm an investor at this gallery. I have every right to be here," she replied.

Something bubbled up inside me. A dose of confidence suddenly formed. "We're actually running this show after hours. So, technically, you don't have a right to be here."

Oden towered over her. "I know what you're up to, so I'd suggest you leave before this ends badly for you."

Her perfectly shaped brows rose, testing his audacity. "And what exactly do you think I'm up to?"

My throat squeezed. "The Fae will fight with everything they have, Vivian. We know everything. You're building an army and sending them to their deaths."

"They're already dead."

"And do they know how little you value them?" Oden countered.

A sly chuckle turned over in her chest as she regarded every one of us, her daughter last. "It doesn't matter. Soon, I'll have what I want while taking care of two birds with one stone. And there's nothing you can do to stop me."

Before we could utter another word, she turned on her heel and left.

Max stared after the void of her mother's absence, her dark eyes glistening with tears of rage and betrayal. Part of me understood that feeling but not quite in the same way. I never knew my mother, but she rejected me, nonetheless. I placed a comforting hand on my friend's back, and she stiffened at the touch but didn't shy away.

Sullivan chuckled. "That bitch is all talk."

Max shot him a look that could set fire. "If you think Vivian Carmichael will give up her chance to reclaim what was taken from us so long ago, then you're a fool." She glanced at Oden. "The Therians have been planning this since before you were Lord."

She shook off my touch. "Max–"

"I have to go," she said and slipped out the door.

Sullivan trailed after her with a cheeky look on his face, and I sighed as I hugged my arms tightly around my torso. I took stock of the gallery; no one seemed to notice the interaction that had just unfolded. Where ancient, powerful beings had a heated discussion about the fates of both worlds.

I wished for such bliss.

"Well, she's as much a delight as her mother," Oden finally said.

My lungs deflated with a heavy sigh. "She's really not that bad."

"No?" He quirked a silver brow as he peered down at me. There was a hint of hope in his stormy eyes, and I knew he wasn't talking about Max.

I gave it a second thought and knew I had to let go of the anger in my heart. It already harbored too much, and I needed to keep the peace with him for Tess's sake. I promised her I'd find out anything I could about Oden's plans. But also…I didn't want to be mad at him anymore. He was my teacher, who helped break through my mind and gave me the confidence to accept my magic.

"No, not so bad at all," I replied. "Once you get through that thick exterior and sheer idiocy, I mean."

He let out a raspy chuckle.

"But I need something from you," I added, and he didn't retort. "I can't trust you if I worry you will use me."

"I would never–"

"And I can't be your queen," I said quickly. "Or business partner, or whatever you want to call it. I have a life here in Ironworld, which I hope to return to once this is all over." His expression fell with disappointment. "But I want to help. Let's forget the full moon rule. Train me as much as you can until the eleventh hour, and I swear, I'll use every ounce of my power to stop Vivian."

He seemed to mull it over and then held out a gloved hand. "A promise then. Help me, and I swear to never betray your friendship."

Without thinking, I slipped my hand into his and shook it. "Deal."

A slight burning circled my wrist, and I seethed at the

pain. It only lasted a moment, and I knew, from the warm look in his eyes, that a similar gold band must have formed around his wrist. A gilded bargain to stop this war and never betray one another's friendship.

I decided then and there to stop spying for Tess. I wasn't finding out anything, anyway, and I couldn't break the gilded promise. I'd use my time with Oden to train and prepare as much as possible. If he willingly gave me information that I could share, then yes, I'd tell Tess. But this meant I'd spend even more time in Faerie, and my heart sank at one thought.

Cillian.

Chapter Seventeen

I couldn't believe it was already Christmas Eve. I gathered my few belongings from school; no one left anything over the holiday break. The campus bustled with eager students, excited to go home and see their families.

I submitted my written report on the gallery showing and spoke with a few of my profs about taking a break after the holidays. They all protested, but I assured them I was okay and needed some time for personal matters. There were summer classes I could take to catch up. When I was done, I stopped at the coffee cat outside.

"Large hot chocolate, please," I told the guy bundled up in a parka and wool gloves. He quickly poured it, and I handed him a five. "Thanks."

Tomas stepped outside, and I waved at him. I expected a grimace and a nod, but he smiled and came over.

"Can we talk?" he asked.

I picked up my bag and slung the leather strap over my head. "Yeah, of course. What's up?"

Tomas began walking down the sidewalk, away from prying ears, and I followed.

"I just wanted to talk to you because you're like me. You're human."

"I'm really not, though."

"Yeah, but you're human enough for me to relate to."

"Look, Tomas, you really should be talking to Julie about this." I didn't want to get in the middle of anything, but he *was* my friend.

"Why did she lie to me?" And there it was. He wasn't upset about what she was. He was hurt because she kept such a big secret from him.

"She had a good reason," I told him sincerely. "We all did. There are certain dangers that come with being in our lives right now, and I think she was trying to shield you from it because, trust me, she's absolutely torn up about it. She cares about you a lot."

His brow pinched together. "What kind of dangers?"

I stopped and glanced up and down the sidewalk. "The world isn't what you think it is. Vampires, shapeshifters, and Fae walk among us every day. Some use glamours, others just blend in easily."

"Like Max," he said.

I nodded. "There are two realms. Here, Ironworld, and a place called Faerie where more magical creatures live. Time moves differently there, beings live for thousands of years, and it's where shapeshifters, Therians, like Max, first came from. Hundreds of years ago, they were forced into Ironworld after a massive war with the fairies. And now? Therians plan to use an army of vampires to invade Faerie and reclaim their land."

Tomas's eyes were wide as he stared into the space behind me, where my breath turned white in the cold. He was listening, I could tell, but the weight of it all was a lot to process. I knew the feeling. I continued on, telling him every single detail about how my estranged mother rules Faerie, how so many people want to take her throne, how I had the power of the sun inside me, and that Julie was an orphaned changeling Fae left in Ironworld, but the rest of her story was hers to tell.

"Look, Tomas, I won't tell you what you should do." I sipped my hot chocolate. "I wasn't given many choices when I fell into all this, and I don't want that for you. Choose whether you want to risk your life to be in Julie's. Trust your gut."

He guffawed, finally focusing his gaze. "Trust my gut? That thing can't even handle milk."

We shared a laugh.

"Look," he said, stuffing his hands in his pocket. "I just

needed some time."

"I get it." I took another long sip. "We're having a Christmas party tomorrow night at the cafe. You should come."

He gave a lopsided smile. "I'll think about it."

***

Julie and I spent the whole day decorating The Chocolate Kettle. Customers stopped to admire the beautiful garlands, candles, wreaths of berries and pinecones, and fresh linens over tables. Julie said trees weren't part of the Faerie solstice traditions, but we were also rooted in Ironworld, so I had the twins bring a small evergreen and place it in the corner of the café. I gave them a box of bulbs and sparkly tinsel I grabbed from the dollar store, and they were like two excited cats trying to figure out how to decorate it.

The sun began to set, and Julie finished filling the carafes with fresh coffee, hot chocolate, and tea. "People should be here soon," she said and pulled two giant flasks of liquor from a canvas bag with a waggle of her brows.

I laughed. "Everything's ready. I'm just going to run up and change."

I slipped into a comfortable outfit of black leggings, wool socks, and my favorite olive sweater. I scooped up the gifts I got for everyone and headed back down. Moya,

Lattie, and Oliver were already there, along with a few Fae I recognized from the Sanctuary.

Aya and Brie turned to me, proud of their job on the tree. "Are those the presents you put beneath it?" Aya asked. I loved how in awe they always were with simple mundane concepts.

"Yes," I replied and handed them my small stack. Brie took them and set them around the bottom where other gifts waited.

I chuckled as the sisters poked and picked at every package, noting the glitter, bows, and tags on each. Their eyes lit up when they found their names. I took a moment to admire their ability to be so happy, despite all that's happened to them. Cursed, removed from their bodies, and banished to a foreign land. Moya once told me that the sea screamed in their heads, and I wondered how much of that was metaphorical or did the ocean call to them, begging for their return.

Lattie flew over to me, carrying a small burlap bag closed with a drawstring. It was half the length of her body, so I relieved her of it.

"What's this?"

"It's for you," she said. "As a thank you for everything. Happy Solstice, Avery Quinn."

"Oh, Lattie…" I opened the bag to find three large, unusual red berries I'd never seen before, like a mix between a raspberry and a kiwi. I dumped them into my hand with a curious look. "Uh, thanks."

"They're a rare berry only found in the hills beyond the Seelie Court," she explained, and then her toothy grin turned into a grimace. "I didn't think you'd appreciate a fresh kill left on your bed."

"That would be correct," I said with a laugh and put the berries back in the bag. "Thank you, Lattie. I love them. I have something for you, too, but it's upstairs in the apartment by the patio door." I cocked my head toward the stairs. "Go check."

She flew off, and I knew, in a few moments, she'd be squealing with delight. I'd found a giant wooden dollhouse in the classifieds and tweaked it to be an actual place for her with a bed and storage. A home.

I sat on the old leather sofa between Aya and Brie as they showed me how to use the gift they got me when Lattie finally returned. She went right for the food, but the swollen blue skin around her bulbous black eyes told me she'd shed a tear.

"The thigh holsters are lightweight," Brie said. "You won't even feel them."

I glanced down at the pair of tiny daggers they gave me and admired the intricate metalwork and dark wood handles. They were no bigger than my palm, but the twins said they were the perfect weapon for me because they were enchanted to never miss the target.

"Enchanted them myself," Oliver assured me with a twinkle in his beady brown eyes. He was curmudgeon most of the time, but Solstice seemed to bring out the joy in all of us.

The music switched back and forth between classic Christmas tunes and beautiful Solstice melodies as all my friends gathered and enjoyed the party. Food and drinks were bountiful, as was the cheer. No one spoke of the dark cloud of war looming over us.

The evening carried on, and I constantly looked at the door whenever it opened, hoping to see Cillian. His sister was out of town for work but sent me a text to wish me a happy Solstice. It was crickets from my boyfriend, though.

I'd considered inviting Oden and Sullivan but decided against it as I wasn't sure how it would make the others feel. They weren't as acquainted with the Dark Lord as I was. And I invited Max, but she just texted back a GIF of someone shaking their head.

The little bell above the café door jungled again, and I turned to see Tomas standing there, an unmarked box in his hands. Julie stood and stared at him from across the room, an unreadable expression on her face. I hopped up from the couch.

"Hey!" I greeted. "You made it."

"Yeah," he said, unsure, and handed me the box. "It's

dalgona, a Korean candy. My mom made it."

I opened the box to find individually wrapped gift bags tied with red ribbons. I closed it and smiled at my friend. "I'm glad you came." He eyed Julie over my shoulder. "Just go talk to her."

I watched as he walked toward her, her face blank and unsure. But he only said a few words, and I could see her expression morph. Tomas took her hand, placed a kiss across her fingers, and she slung her arms around his neck before they retreated upstairs.

The bell chimed again, and I spun around, hoping to see my holiday date. It wasn't Cillian, but my heart still leaped out of my chest at the sight. She stood near the door and glanced around as many stopped and respectfully bowed their heads in greeting.

Tess blushed and waved them off as she spotted me and headed right over, a large dark green package under her arm. She wore no queen-like garb, no crown, just a pair of jeans and a lovely rose-colored jacket.

"How did you know?" I asked.

"Julie told me," she replied and gently punched my shoulder. "Thanks for the invite."

I laughed. "I'm sorry, I didn't think you could come."

Her blue eyes sparkled with nothing but love. "I wouldn't miss Christmas with you for the world. It was always your favorite holiday."

"And yours."

"Well, I mean, the food."

We shared a laugh, and she handed me the package. "Merry Christmas, Avery."

"Thank you," I replied. "You didn't have to get me anything."

"Sure I did." She walked over to the counter where the carafes of warm beverages were. "You got *me* something."

I raised my brows. "Awfully bold of you to assume."

She gave me a look that said *oh please* and held out her hand.

I rolled my eyes but couldn't help laughing at my aunt. The one person who knew me more than anyone in this world. I set the box she gave me on the counter and pulled a gift bag from the pocket in the space I shared with my bedroom closet.

Tess gawked at me in disbelief. "That's an impressive trick."

My cheeks warmed. "I have a good teacher."

She didn't comment on that as I handed her the bag. She pulled out the tissue paper and the small canvas held inside. Tears glistened as she admired the painting of our home in the country, the house we had shared my whole life. The home she made for us.

"I love it." The words came out broken and wet as she wiped a stray tear from her cheek. I placed a gentle kiss there, and another tear took its place. Tess stuffed the painting back in the bag and forced out a laugh. "Open yours."

I tugged at the green ribbon and lifted the lid. Some sort of garment lay folded neatly inside. A mix of leather and some other material I couldn't place, patches and strips of a deep teal woven with brown braided leather. I stared at it curiously and pulled it out. It was a jacket of some kind.

"It's armor," Tess said, and I set it down. "Dainty and light, but practically impenetrable. I had it custom-made from a special material found in the Summer kingdom."

My heart sank. "Do you think I'll need it?"

My aunt gave me a weak smile. "I won't beat around the bush. War is coming, whether Kheelan believes it or not. I have eyes and ears in Ironworld. You're inexplicably tied to both realms, Avery. I just…I just want you to be safe."

"I will be," I assured her. "I'm not alone."

Tess peered around the café, her gaze landing on Moya, who was already staring right at her. Some kind of longing in her deep, sea-green eyes. I desperately wanted to ask what the deal was with that. There was obviously some history there, but I decided it could wait. This wasn't the time or place.

"I should get going," Tess said and held her gift close to her chest. "Thank you for this. I love you, sweetheart."

"Love you, too, Tess."

When the party began dying, and almost everyone was gone, I headed upstairs. Tomas and Julie were locked away in her room, and a small part of me settled, knowing they'd be okay. I needed a win in all this, and I'm glad it was for my friend.

I set all my gifts on my dresser and turned to find a black shoebox tied with a black ribbon on my bed. I sat down and slid it into my lap as a dark billow of smoke poured in through the open window. It slowly dissipated, leaving Cillian leaning against the sill. Even after all this time, he still took my breath away. No matter how angry I was with him, the distance we constantly threw between us, the sight of his blue eyes and pale skin, cut with the blackness of his hair, never failed to make my heart skip a beat.

"Open it," he said softly.

It was a music box. A wooden treasure intricately designed with whorls of gold and black. I lifted the lid, and it played You Are My Sunshine. My tired eyes stung with wetness.

"It's beautiful." I wiped my cheek and smiled at him. "I've never gotten so many gifts in my life."

He crossed his ankles and gripped the window sill, looking like he belonged on the cover of a magazine with his black trench and cashmere scarf. All black, as were the clothes he wore underneath. I didn't want this weird rift between us anymore.

We hadn't spoken since he bit me, but I think he wanted

to give me space after I'd gone to him on the brink of a breakdown. And before that, something had shifted and cracked when I told him I would spend more time in Faerie. But I didn't want space anymore.

"Isn't that what Christmas is all about?"

"No." I shook my head and set the jewelry box on my bedside table. "Even though I have something for you. It's at the gallery."

"Yeah?" He gave me a coy look.

"A portrait of yourself." I shot him a wicked grin, and he pushed off the window and sat on the bed with me. "You'll love it."

His dark brows shot up. "Is that so?"

"Yes." I crawled into his lap. "And Christmas is about being with the ones you love." His hands splayed over my back as I grazed his lips with mine. "I love you, Cillian."

His arms tightened around me, crushing me to him. He swept my hair away and claimed my mouth with an all-encompassing kiss, leaving me breathless as he pulled back.

"I love you, too."

✳✳✳

Weeks flew by. I filled my time with preparing in every which way I could. I took a break from school and went down to one shift a week at the gallery and café because

I was chasing the high of strength and magic and my ever-growing control over both.

Cillian made my body strong in the gym, pushing and testing the limits of how far I could go. I spent hours there every week. The twins taught me stealth, and how to use the daggers they gifted me. I never knew there were so many uses for two small knives.

I spent any spare time I could in Faerie while Sullivan taught me to use a sword, and Oden continued to test my powers, both physical and mental. I gained a new kind of control over my own mind, chasing away unwanted dreams and visions.

But the most impressive was the complete control of my magic, the sunlight that burned in my veins. Well, what I thought was total control. Oden constantly teased the idea of getting back what was taken from me so long ago. Everything that made me Fae. He said it would turn my magic into something bigger, better, and more beautiful.

I often thought of the orb that sat on Oliver's shelf. He said it was mine, to claim when I was ready. But I wasn't. I didn't think I ever would be.

All that aside, something loomed over all of us. The utter silence from the Therian world. No one's heard a word about Vivian's movements. I checked in daily with Max, who claimed her contact was solid and could be trusted. When something moves, she'll know immediately. All we could do was wait, so I filled every second of my waking hours with training.

But I needed a break, so I headed to the Sanctuary with Julie to drop off supplies for the Solitary Fae. It had been so long since I last visited and helped. Guilt ate away at me as I walked the lakeside park hidden in a secret pocket in the folds of the border.

Displaced Fae gathered in groups, setting up tents, cooking and serving food, and washing clothes in barrels. They had what they could carry and not much more, but they still had smiles as we passed.

What did that say about my mother? These people would rather leave their homes and live in a world with nothing than stay under her rule. A new sense of guilt mixed in my stomach, a sort of responsibility to these Fae.

"I can't believe how many new faces there are," I said.

Julie handed a stack of tent canvases to an organizer. "At this rate, we'll run out of room and supplies in a week. Whispers of war can really ruffle some feathers."

I thought about Haven and how spacious they were, how they worked together to grow gardens and share everything.

"I'll be right back," I told Julie and jogged down to the lake.

The firelight didn't reach the water, and I knelt, sticking my fingers in the cold, dark lake. In seconds I was a few yards away from Oden's castle. I pulled out one of my little daggers and imagined him as I whispered his name.

I held my breath for a moment, and he appeared, his smile faltering as his eyes slid to the dagger I had against my open palm. This was the place my mother once stood and forced his hand with the ancient ritual.

But I didn't draw blood. Yet.

Oden said nothing.

"Can I trust you?" I asked, the question holding so much weight.

Without hesitation, he nodded. "Yes."

I put the dagger away as he tilted his head with a curious look. "Is there room in Haven?"

"Room for what?"

"People."

He searched my face, and I could see the cogs of questions working in his pointed gaze. "How many people?"

My shoulders rolled as I inhaled deeply and glanced at the water. "I can show you, but you have to swear never to reveal the location."

He slightly bent at the waist. "You have my word as Lord of this domain and by my oath to never betray your friendship."

I held out my hand. "Then come with me."

Oden stared at my upright palm with an unreadable expression, so I grabbed his hand, his long and sturdy fingers wrapping around mine. I closed my eyes, and in a second, we wisped to the Sanctuary. It was the first time I ever did it with another person. But, then again, everything was so much easier for me in Faerie.

I released Oden's hand as he took in the scene around him and Fae of every shape, color, and size, stared at us. The Dark Lord of Nightmares never left his domain. Somewhere in the crowd, a baby cried, and he turned to me.

"Help them pack up. I'll speak with Misaldri immediately."

"All of them?"

"Yes," Oden replied. "And any more that need refuge. I have other towns that can take them in."

"Thank you," I said sincerely.

He just tipped his head and vanished.

Chapter Eighteen

Sweat covered my body as I flew upright in my bed of dark silk. Kol rustled at my side and let out a disgruntled moan that I woke him up. I swung my legs off the side, resting my feet on the cold stone floor, desperate to feel something real.

Oden had taught me to keep my visions and dreams at bay, but the vivid nightmares still seeped through. Always the same. As I walked over bodies, nothing but miles of ash fell to the bloodied ground. But tonight, something was different. A sound, a distant cackle tainted the dark skies, a voice I'd only ever heard in my mind.

My mother's.

More weeks had gone by with no word on Vivian's movements. We couldn't even tell how she was communicating with her people. So, I continued to fill my time, dividing it between training and helping the displaced Fae settle in Haven. But it meant I was spending more and more time in Faerie.

Cillian and I worked on our communication. I was as open and honest as possible about my desire to be here in my homeland. Yes, my mother rejected me, but Faerie didn't. I loved being here; something in the land, in the very dirt beneath my feet, called to me and only settled when I was here.

I enjoyed my work with the Fae, helping them find homes and roles in the communities Oden opened to them. It gave me a sense of purpose, which I never knew I needed.

But today was for training.

Mags drew me a bath as I nibbled on the tray of breakfast foods her team brought. Kol nudged my leg with his cold, wet nose, and I scratched the space between his ears with a laugh before tossing him the last of my bacon. Since spending more time here, the dog never left my side. He came with me to Haven, sat on the sidelines, watched me train, and followed me through the halls of Oden's mansion.

I guess I was a dog owner now.

After my bath, I got dressed and headed to the front courtyard, where I knew Oden was waiting. He stood with a sword in each hand, their tips to the ground, and wore more casual attire than his usual Lordly suits. The neck of his grey tunic hung open, revealing the smooth, pale skin of his chest. The rolled-up sleeves prominently showed the corded muscles of his arms, and they flexed as he swung the two swords around.

"Showing off?" I teased.

"I'm a High Lord. I don't need to show off," he replied cheekily and handed me one of the blades. "Stance."

I widened my feet and bent my knees, my sword held out across my body.

"Today, we'll practice sword fighting while wisping," he said.

I blinked quickly. "Why? That just sounds like a recipe to get stabbed."

"Are you still adamant about fighting in Vivian's war?"

"Yes."

He turned his wrist and bent his knees, readying to fight me. "Then it's a necessary skill that could save your life. Now, on guard."

The sun moved across the sky while we sparred, and my arms begged for relief as sweat pooled in all my unsightly areas. But I couldn't stop. Learning both physically and magically was addicting on a level I couldn't even describe. The more I mastered, the more I wanted.

And Oden knew that. He didn't stop until I could expertly wisp and dodge every one of his attacks and use the skill to take him down. I appeared behind him and kicked the back of his knee, then wisped to his front and knocked him flat on his back as I jumped atop him and held my sword to his neck.

"I win," I said in a huff.

His grey eyes beamed with pride as they locked on mine, our labored breaths mixing in the short space between our faces. But I found something in his heated gaze I'd never seen before. A sort of longing, a wanting that shouldn't be there.

I quickly scrambled off him.

"You're learning at such a fast rate," he said as he peeled himself off the grass. "And the work you've done in Haven is incredible. Misaldri sings your praises often."

I couldn't look at him, didn't want to see that look in his eye again. "Yeah, I enjoy the work. It feels good to help."

He loosed a quiet sigh. "Would you reconsider my job offer?"

"What?" I swallowed nervously. "Oden, I–"

"It's honestly just a role, Avery, nothing more," he assured. "The work you've done in Haven, in the Sanctuary, the determination I see growing in you each day, you'd make a fine partner. I'd be honored to work with you–"

"Oden, I'm not the Seelie heir," I blurted out. His face twisted in confusion. "I was born before Mabry took the throne. So, I'm not actually the one to fulfill your bargain. I...I can't give you the power you want."

He searched my face, his stormy eyes slowly raking over every line as he approached me. "The deal I made wasn't for the Seelie heir. It was for her first-born daughter. I just assumed it would be their heir, what with your mother's intentions for the king. Like the rest of Faerie, I had no idea of your existence."

My throat tightened. "Oh…"

The corner of his mouth crooked upward. "So, if you'd like the job, it's yours. I could use the help, especially now that you've grown the population of my domain."

"I'm happy to help where I'm needed," I told him sincerely. "But I can't be your partner, Oden. You know that. I have–"

"A life in Ironworld, yes, I know. You've said." He inhaled long and deep through his nose and looked toward the castle. "Well, I'm going to get ready for supper. See you there?"

I shrugged playfully. "Maybe."

He snapped his fingers and disappeared. But I stayed outside, practicing the combination of wisping and swordplay some more. When the sun finally set, I wandered inside to change. Supper was over, and everything was cleared, but I managed to steal an apple from the kitchen before one of the cooks bit my fingers off.

I roamed the mansion and ended up in the massive library I'd come to love. I had learned so much during my stay in Oden's domain and absorbed any information and histories I could find. But this time, without my nose in a book, I noticed something I'd never seen before. A painting on the floor, partly covered by the furniture scattered about.

Curious, I moved a few chairs and realized it was a map of some kind with pictures and words that told a story. It was a map of Faerie in its entirety, so different from the one I created based on the info Lattie once gave me.

"It's how Faerie once was," Sullivan said from the doorway. "Before the Great War."

I stared down at the ancient painting and noted all the different territories. Summer, Winter, Dreams, and Nightmares. Each one offered something that Faerie needed to make it whole. Balance. And then my mother's court—Orion's back then—near the top, taking up a considerable amount of land. Beyond it, a range of giant mountains skirted the continent. The hand-painted script said it was called Dragon's Pass.

"Were there actually dragons there?"

He stuffed both hands in his pockets as he came further inside the room. "Oh yeah, giants in the sky. Beautiful." He peered down with a distant memory clouding his gaze.

"What happened to them?"

"Orion had them killed," he replied sadly. "For fear someone might use them against him."

"Geez, sounds like he was a smidge insecure," I kidded, but, for once, Sullivan didn't laugh.

He knelt and pointed a black painted nail to a river that cut through the continent from the Eternal Sea and poured into the lake at the heart of Faerie. It divided Summer and Seelie.

"I used to go to this river as a boy and watch the dragons land for a drink. After the Great War, this is where Orion placed the wards to keep out the Therians. He worked with Kheelan's father to construct a tower that held a device to keep the wards in place. No one is allowed near it now."

Something cold seared through my limbs, tingling my fingertips as I stared at the spot on the map. "What did you just say?"

Sullivan stood. "No one's allowed to go near the river?"

"No, about the tower and the wards."

He looked down at the map again. "It's used to…keep out the Therians." I could tell the exact moment his mind caught up with mine, and his warm brown eyes shot at me with panic.

"I bet my life that's where Vivian plans to have the vampires cross over," I said. "If the Therians can't come with that tower in place, it'll be the first thing they take out."

"Holy fuck…" He stepped away, raking his hands through his hair as he stared at the painted river.

"We need to talk to your brother."

***

Oden sent his brother back to Ironworld with me, and I texted Julie the moment I stepped foot on concrete to get everyone and meet at home. I sent a message to Max, too.

Sullivan waited with me in the living room as everyone showed up, one by one until people filled the apartment. Julie, Lattie, Moya, the twins, Oliver, and even a reluctant Max stood leaning against the wall in the back.

"I won't beat around the bush," I said to them. "I think we discovered where Vivian will strike first and how."

Oliver grunted from the loveseat. "How so?"

Moya cleared her throat. "We've had eyes all over. There's been no sign or word of any movements."

I nudged Sullivan, who was staring at Max. He blinked and focused. "Uh, an ancient river cleaves the land, connecting the Eternal Sea to the heart of Faerie."

Lattie hissed from atop her little house. "It's also a direct gateway to Ironworld."

"But there are gateways all over Faerie," Julie said.

I wrung my fingers together in front of me. "A nearby tower protects the device keeping the wards in place." I turned my head in Max's direction. Her face was stone. "The wards that ban the Therians."

"Of course," Max seethed. "Why didn't I think of it

before? She's using the vampires to take out the tower so *she* can cross over with her Therian forces and go straight for the Seelie throne." She rolled her eyes and pulled out her cell phone as she slipped into my room.

We all hovered around in silence, each deep in thought. It was the most information we had in weeks. I was beginning to think perhaps the war wouldn't happen, that Vivian's plan wouldn't work.

The loveseat groaned as Oliver shoved off it. "How big is Oden's army?"

Sullivan's throat bobbed. "Ten thousand."

"Summer has a little more than that," Moya added. "It might be enough."

Max slowly stepped out. She only looked at me and gave a slight shake of her head. "No, it won't be." Blankly, she glanced at her phone and slowly returned it to her pocket. "My mother has nearly fifty thousand vampires ready to go from all over the world. Waiting to be summoned here."

I screwed up my face. "Christ, that means she's been shipping Fae blood all over the *world*?"

"Did you ask your contact about the tower?" Aya asked Max.

Another solemn nod.

Not just a confirmation that she asked but a verification that it was true. We'd put together all the pieces of Vivian's plan.

A gasp tingled my throat. "I have to tell Tess. Kheelan needs to be prepared, or they won't stand a chance once the vampires cross the border."

"We can't send word," Moya chimed in. "Can't risk it falling into the hands of the wrong people."

"Then we'll go in person," I said.

Oliver's chunky boots stomped across the hardwood as he paced in thought. "We need to know if Vivian's plan will even work before we alarm the Summer army. She's only banking on the theory that vampires can cross with Fae blood in their system. If it doesn't work, this war will end before it begins."

"What are you suggesting?" I asked, already on his trail of thoughts. But I didn't want to believe it.

The thick wrinkles of his face softened. "We need to test it first."

Julie shot to her feet. "What vampire would be will-ing to try? It's a suicide mission." She looked at me, and I swallowed nervously. Her blue eyes widened in disbelief. "You're not thinking of asking Cillian, are you?"

I shook my head. "No, I could never ask. He already risks too much just by being with me. I couldn't bear to be responsible for whatever happens if Vivian's theory is wrong."

"My mother is many things, Quinn, but a fool isn't one. If she's steamrolling with this idea, it means she's sure it works."

"But we have to know for certain," Oliver persisted.

A blanket of silence fell over the room.

Finally, Moya spoke up. "Max is correct. Vivian wouldn't risk looking like a fool. She only has one chance to pull off something like this. But we do need to make sure. Alerting Kheelan…it could ignite a war regardless of what happens."

The blood drained from my face as all heads turned to me. "I-I can't ask Cillian to do this."

"Yes, you can." His voice sent a warm shiver down my spine, and I glanced up to find him lounging in the open patio door. "But you don't have to. I'll do it. I'll test the theory."

I sped across the room. "You do understand the risk, right?" He steeled his face. "Cillian, it could kill you."

He tipped his chin toward Max. "As much as it pains me to admit it, the wolf witch is right. Her mother wouldn't go this far on hope alone. My guess is she's already tested it, so I'll do the same." He reached out and cupped my face in his hand. "For you."

I pushed him into my room and shut the door behind me. My heart raced, pounding against its cage as I paced. So many thoughts ran through my mind. This war was about to happen any day, and we had to warn the Summer kingdom. But we needed proof.

"Avery."

"I can't right now." I waved him off as I continued pacing anxiously, gnawing at my thumbnail. "This is too much to ask of you. I spent months worrying that I might kill you, and here you are asking me to let you just waltz right to your death."

"Possible death," he corrected.

I shot him a look. "This isn't the time for sarcasm."

Cillian grabbed my arms, pulling me to him. "Avery, I've pushed back against your life's path because…it scared me. I worried it would lead away from me, and that was selfish. I want to be part of the solution. I want to help you, be there for you in whatever choices you make in life." He let go and shrugged. "And if that means helping the people—the world that's rejected me for so long, then so be it. My place is with *you*."

Tears stung the rims of my eyes as I stared at his perfect face. I took in every line, every crook, and cranny; the softness of his seemingly pore-less skin. I ran my thumb over his pink lips. Storing it all to memory.

He was right.

So, I took a deep breath and backed away as I pulled down at the collar of my shirt. "Then drink."

***

I sent a fire message to Oden with sparse details of my plan. His reply came in seconds and in just four words.

My domain is yours.

Cillian wrapped me in his arms and shadows as we flew to the waterfront, where we suspected Vivian would have the vampires cross over, and he set me down in the moonlight. I didn't want to think about it too much or give myself a chance to let in the doubt again because part of me wanted to haul Cillian away and run off to the other side of the world until this whole thing blew over.

But I couldn't do that. I made promises, and people were counting on me. I had to warn Tess but couldn't do it without proof Vivian's plan would work. And I swore to Oden that I'd use my powers to help in any way I could.

I grabbed his hand and bent over, sticking my fingertips in the frigid harbor. It only took a second, but my heart beat a thousand times. My fingers ached as I clenched Cillian's with all my might. And, when I opened my eyes…

He was there.

It worked. We turned to one another with almost giddy faces. Vampires can enter Faerie with Fae blood in their veins. But reality pressed in, and my joy at Cillian's survival faded away as we both realized the weight of what that meant.

Vivian's plan definitely works, and there will be a fight for the Seelie throne. Now it was just a matter of who claimed it.

"So, this is where you've been going?" Cillian asked, glancing around at the sprawling acres of forest and perfectly manicured lawns flanking the long dirt path to Oden's home. The Faerie moonlight filtered down over him as if it were studying him, sniffing, looking for a way to settle over this foreign being.

"Yes," my throat tightened as I swallowed. "This is the Domain of Nightmares." I gestured toward the Dark Forest. "Well, in there is. Oden considers the rest of his land to be free. Fae of any kind are welcome to come and live peacefully."

His brows pinched together. "So, it's just a front? The whole evil nightmares bit?"

"Well, I wouldn't say that," Oden's raspy purr spoke from behind. "More like a necessary evil."

Cillian spun around and faced the Dark Lord of Nightmares, and my chest tightened. Will this be a fight? To my surprise, my vampire boyfriend offered his hand.

"So, we formally meet at last. Cillian Danes."

Oden quirked a silver brow at me and tilted his head as he dragged his gaze back to Cillian's face. He shook his hand firmly.

"Indeed. Oden Whitlock."

It was the first time I'd ever heard his full name. Lattie once told me you could hold power over any Fae should you know their full name, and I wondered if Oden was telling the truth.

"So, you're the vampire who holds the heart of my dear friend." His smile was perfectly polite, but there was a hint of sarcasm that only I could pick up on.

"Yes, and the vampire who will fight in this war for you."

Oden tucked a hand behind his back. "Oh, I assure you, it's not just for me." He turned on his heel. "Come, dinner's waiting."

I took one step. "Oh, we don't have–"

He glanced at me over his shoulder with a look that said we couldn't refuse, so I sighed and took Cillian's hand as we followed the Dark Lord to his castle.

Sullivan was there waiting, and he looked like he might burst at the sight of the three of us strutting in. But whatever smart-ass retort sat on his tongue, he kept it in, even as we sat and feasted.

We talked of Cillian's past as a Viking, my foibles with learning magic–but mostly my clumsy swordsmanship. I argued that it vastly improved over the last few weeks. Only Sullivan agreed.

Not one word was uttered about the coming war. Although it was all at the forefront of our minds, none of us dared mention it. It felt like a last supper of sorts, and I soaked it in. The ease with which conversation flowed, the glorious taste of food, and the sweet warmth of wine on my tongue.

I freshened up in the bathroom before we left. But when I returned to the dining room, Sullivan was gone, and Oden and Cillian sat in a strange but seemingly comfortable silence.

"Ready to go?" I asked hesitantly.

Cillian exchanged a single nod with Oden and stood up. "Thank you for the meal."

"We'll have another when this is all over," Oden replied. But there was a sliver of sadness there.

They were wishful words. Any day now, one of us could be dead.

We said our goodbyes and slipped away to the water in silence.

Chapter Nineteen

It was the cusp of dawn when we returned, and my body begged for sleep. I couldn't remember the last time I got a whole night's rest. Cillian refused to leave my side, so I closed my curtains and crawled into bed, where I drifted off in his arms. When I finally opened my eyes again, the sky was still a murky navy.

"What time is it?" I groaned, my mouth parched.

Cillian shifted next to me. "Six thirty," he replied softly. "You slept all day."

I bolted up. "What? How could you let me do that? We have things to do–"

He pressed his palm to my chest. "Settle down. You're mostly human, Avery. You can't run on fumes, especially if you're adamant about fighting in this fucking war." He took a moment to steel himself. "I spoke with everyone while you slept. They're all up to speed."

There was a *but* that lingered in his tone.

I placed my hand over his, and my heartbeat pulsed through both. "What's wrong?"

He looked at me through his dark lashes. "Max just called and said she has what we need. Everyone's meeting here in a few minutes."

What we need?

I said nothing. Cillian waited on my bed while I got changed into fresh clothes and wrestled my hair into a ponytail. I could hardly stand to look at my reflection in the mirror over my dresser; sleep deprivation wasn't a good look. My red hair seemed duller, lifeless, my already pale skin a deathly white. Perhaps Oden was right. Living an immortal life in a semi-mortal body was draining me.

When everyone gathered around, Max finally showed up. Cillian called Celadine, and Julie brought Tomas, who sat beside her on the couch, her hand firmly clamped between both of his. I guess he decided to risk it after all.

Max remained standing. "My mother has begun summoning vampires to the city."

"Are you certain?" Moya asked.

She nodded. "My contact is solid. He confirmed it a few hours ago. Over half have already arrived."

Panic set in. But Cillian laced his fingers through mine, willing me to calm.

"We're out of time," Oliver grumbled.

"I have to go to Tess now," I announced, and I caught Celadine throwing her brother a worried glance. "We know Vivian's plan will work, and now we know things are in motion. Kheelan needs to prepare as many soldiers as he can."

"I'll go home and enchant some weapons for us all," Oliver said and snapped his fingers, disappearing in a blink.

Aya and Brie tightened the harnesses and bandoliers that strapped their chests. "We'll head to the Seelie Court and see if there's movement there."

"I doubt my mother plans to defend her people," I warned them. "If she knows of any of this, then she'd be wise to sit back and let all the threats surrounding her throne take themselves out."

I stomped over to the porch and grabbed my jacket from a hook.

"I'm coming with you," Julie said, her face solid with determination. "To help convince Kheelan this is really happening."

Moya chortled. "It'll take more than the two of you to sway the Summer Lord's pride. He won't take orders from a couple of girls."

"What's his deal?" I asked. "For someone obsessed with protecting his borders and showing off his men, you'd think he'd take action at the word of any possible threat."

Moya pursed her lips. "He's a dick."

We all gawked at her blatancy, so out of character for the ethereal sea maiden. But before I could say anything, Max piped up.

"Is there a way to bring them here? I can attest to my mother's plan; I can be the thing that convinces him."

Moya's face lit up. "No, but I can cloak you. Possibly."

"Cloak me as what?"

"I can put a glamour over your Therian signature and maybe cloak you to pass as Fae, at least long enough to get over the border."

Max guffawed and crossed her arms. "Don't let my mother know you can do that. If this attempt fails, she'll hunt you down and milk you for every ounce of magic you have."

Silent Celadine in the back stepped closer. "You'll need cover on this side until you cross over in case Vivian has eyes on us. I can perform a spell, but I'll need someone to maintain it while you move."

"I can do it," Max says dutifully. "Show me."

Julie looked at me with eyes wrought with concern. "What if we're wrong about the time? What if the Therians…" She ran a nervous hand over her face and glanced at Tomas. "What if we're too late?"

"We're not," I assured her.

Cillian leaned in. "I'll be at the border. I'll cross over at the first sign of trouble on this side."

She turned to Celadine. "Can Tomas stay with you until this is over?"

"Of course," she replied and smiled at Tomas, who seemed to be struggling to keep up with everything.

"I don't need a babysitter," he chimed in.

Julie took his face in both her hands, tears barely held back. "They know you're connected to us; you mean something to Avery and me. You could be used against us, or worse…."

None of us wanted to utter the words.

Tomas nodded solemnly. "I get it. I'll go with the vampire lady."

Celadine gave a slight chuckle. "I promise I don't bite."

The plans were in place; we all had jobs and raced against the clock. After Celadine showed Max how to maintain the cover, and Moya cloaked her to be Fae, the three of us wisped to the water and then traveled to the river near the Summer kingdom.

Max shielded her eyes from the blaring sun setting over the horizon with one hand and covered her stomach with the other. "Moya's cloak barely works; I can feel the wards pushing against me."

"Are you okay?" I asked her.

She took a few deep breaths, her dark eyes full of determination. "I'll be fine."

Something caught her attention, and she sniffed at the

air just as a dozen Summer soldiers appeared. Their golden armor was blinding in the sun, and the swift sound of their swords unsheathing clanged in my ears.

"You're trespassing," one of them warned.

"We need to speak with Lady Tessana," I said loud enough for all to hear. "We have pressing news."

He tipped his sword in Max's direction. "You'll be going nowhere with that Therian spy."

"*Spy?*" she spat. "Do you have any idea who the fuck I am?"

"Frankly, we do not care," he replied. "You broke the wards, which is an offense that warrants death."

Julie jumped in the middle, arms out. "Woah, hold on. This is Lady Summer's niece. We were just here for the wedding. Surely some of you remember us? How would the Lady react to you killing her only niece?" She held her chin high as grumbles and whispers moved through the soldiers. "We have news that the Therians will cross the border any day. We need to speak with the Lord and Lady. *Now.*"

Her words were enough to dodge a death sentence but not enough to go free. They bound our hands and wisped us to a nearby city, where they locked us in a cell made of stone and guarded with metal bars. No door. Wisp in, wisp out.

I screamed for them to get my aunt as they walked

away without a word. I could only hope they would. I knew Moya would eventually find us, but we didn't have the luxury of time.

We paced the dirt floor impatiently for what felt like an eternity. Through a tiny barred window, I could see the sky turning deep shades of blue with the coming night. Max tried to pry the bars, but they burned her skin on contact. Her roar was deafening as it bounced off the walls, a deep guttural sound that shook my insides.

"They must be warded," I said as calmly as I could.

Julie's feet scuffed over the floor. "This is the town with no name. It was built temporarily while the Seelie king had the tower constructed and the wards put in place. But over the years, Kheelan has employed it as a watch station. Everything here is meant to hold Therians."

"Do you think they'll get Tess?" I asked.

Something rumbled the ground under our feet, and the three of us froze.

Max sniffed the air. "What the hell–"

The back wall exploded with a deafening crack of crumbling stone, and two Summer soldiers tumbled to the floor as I screamed and Max pulled us both out of the way. As the dust settled, the view outside sharpened, matching the sounds of swords clanging and magic exploding everywhere.

The vampires were here. We were out of time.

"Wisp us back home!" I screamed to Julie. I couldn't wisp across the border yet.

"I can't do it that far! Not with the three of us!"

"Then take Max!" I pushed her toward my best friend.

Max swatted at me. "Absolutely fucking not!"

I buried my rising fear and grabbed the armored jacket Tess gave me from the pocket in the space where I kept it. I shoved my arms through the sleeves and zipped it to my chin. "Then we'll wisp to the border."

I grabbed both their hands, readying to wisp the great distance. Another explosion crashed through the cell, and a giant block of stone knocked into Julie. She crumpled to the floor as blood leaked from her head.

Chapter Twenty

Vampires poured into the nameless city like a wave, crashing through things and ripping out throats. Summer soldiers engaged, fighting them off with swords and magic. They were definitely stronger, but the vampires far outnumbered them.

Max and I sat on the floor in the corner of the cell, Julie's head in my lap, my hand firmly pressed over her wound. I couldn't heal her; the injuries were too severe. She needed Oliver.

"We have to get out of here!" I yelled at Max through the chaos that ensued. Another blast took out more of the building, and we huddled together over Julie's body.

Max flipped her head up. Her dark brown eyes were different. Something otherworldly and ancient and fierce. She scooped up Julie's legs. "Come on. Watch my back. I'll watch yours."

I followed her lead and secured Julie's shoulders in my arms as we slipped out of the cell. We hugged what was left to the wall outside, frantically watching for vampires. I fumbled a few times and cursed my own mortality, but I knew I wouldn't have been able to carry my friend at all two months ago. I tapped into every ounce of strength I had while Max led us away from the stream of vampires coming in. We darted behind a smaller building, and she stopped. Julie flattened on the grass.

"Okay, we have to get to water, right?" Max asked, panting.

I thought about the map I once saw of this area. "The river is the only one I know of," I said. "Unless we move toward the heart of Faerie where there's a lake. But I'm not sure which is further. I-I don't know where we are, exactly."

"Can you wisp us somewhere?"

I shook my head. "Not this many people, not without help."

"I saw you do it before!" she yelled. "In the coombs!"

I shook my head, panicked. "I haven't been able to do it since, not like that."

Max spun in the dirt, struggling not to scream. She kicked a large rock, and it cracked in half. I tried not to look so stunned when she turned and faced me.

A vampire appeared from the alley between us and the

next building. He lunged for Max, but she grabbed him by the throat and slammed him to the ground. She pounded her fist into his ribs, and I let out a yelp as she ripped his heart right from his chest.

Footsteps echoed to my left, and I hopped to my feet, ready to protect my unconscious friend. The vamp was a smaller woman, but her face contorted with a hungry snarl as she leaped for me.

Faster than ever, a dagger of sunlight formed in my hand, and I thrust it toward the vampire. It slid through her chest like butter, and I nearly lost my grip as I felt the tip puncture the heart, like stabbing a stress ball.

Her body crumpled at my feet, and I stared at it in frozen horror. Max touched my shoulder, and I stifled the scream that burped from my chest.

"I take it you've never killed one before?"

I thought of the ring of ashes that surrounded me in that warehouse. It was nothing like this. Before, I hadn't known what I did, hadn't seen it. I didn't even mean to do it.

But this…

Julie moaned from the ground.

"Jules!" I exclaimed and fell to her side. "Are you okay?"

She sat up, rubbing her head. The blood already beginning to clot around the wound. "Just a bit dizzy. What happened?"

"The vamps are here," Max hissed and glanced about. "We need to get to water. How far is this place from the river?"

Julie thought a moment. "It's not far. Maybe a couple of kilometers West of here. But we can't leave!"

"Jules, you're injured."

She shook her head. "I'm fine. Here, help me up." I hauled her to her feet. "If the vampires are here, they're going for the tower. We have to stop them."

"She's right," Max said. "If that tower goes down, the Therians come, and it's game over."

"Av', you go, wisp to the tower, and use your sunlight to help." Julie was focused and determined.

"By myself?"

"You won't be alone. Kheelan's men have to be there by now. Max and I will make our way toward you until I'm strong enough to wisp us both."

I looked back and forth between them, unsure of what to do. I didn't want to leave Julie when she was injured, but I did trust Max to protect her.

"Quinn, if my mother's army gets through, we're all fucked. And not just temporarily fucked, I mean point of no return *fucked*." She shoved at my arm. "*Go!*"

A couple more vampires came around the corner, and Julie threw up a cloudy forcefield around us as Max spun her fingers and muttered something in another language.

The vampires' necks cracked, and their heads flopped to the sides, followed by their bodies as they crumpled to the ground.

Julie held the protective shield in place. "Go, Av'! We've got this! We'll meet you there!"

I reached for the fabric of reality around me and clenched my fists, imagining the hill I saw near the river. The wind changed, and a cool breeze wove through my hair as I opened my eyes and peered down. With the river to my right, a tower erected from the ground in the distance, maybe a few kilometers away. But a sea of vampires and golden armor stood in the way.

I focused on the tower and wisped there in a blink, my breath heaving in my chest. Adrenaline coursed through my limbs, and every inch of my body was on high alert as a few dozen Summer soldiers skirted the tower with me and fended off hoards of vampires. The noise of swords and metal clashing with ripping flesh and violent screams clanged in my ears.

It was a massacre.

I tried not to look down at the blood and other bits I knew littered the ground, but I could feel it beneath my boots, slippery and threatening to take my feet out from under me.

One of the soldiers noticed me. "What are you doing here, girl?"

A tall, muscular, bald vampire lunged for him from behind, and I moved swiftly, forming a dagger of sunlight in my hand. I jumped forward and narrowly missed the soldier's neck as I used both hands to drive it into the vampire's heart.

"I'm here to help," I said and backed away, steeling my nerves as the vampire hit the ground like a sack of potatoes.

I took a deep breath, and the depths of my magic stirred in my belly. I flung my arms out and pushed, sending a wave of sunlight cutting the air. Dozens of vampires turned to ash, but it wasn't enough. It barely made a dent.

But it seemed to spark some hope in the soldiers. The one I saved, his eyes went wide at what I could do, and he yelled over the chaos, "Protect the girl! *Form*!" Suddenly, several Summer soldiers moved and formed a barrier around me. "Can you do that again?"

"I can try," I said. "It takes a lot of energy, and I'm… mortal." I wigged my hand "Sort of."

Breathily, he handed me a dagger from his side. "For when you run out of energy."

I accepted the weapon, and we exchanged a knowing nod. Two strangers, instantly bound by duty and purpose. He turned and faced the hoards, blade in one hand, golden magic crackling over it like lightning.

In that moment, I became someone else. I had to; it was

the only way I knew to get through it. I stomped down my nerves and locked away the voice in my head. My magic was already regenerating inside me, and I summoned it, forming a slew of sun daggers.

With a mighty push, I flung them outward, sending dozens of tiny sharp objects soaring toward the vampires that closed in. It took a bunch of them down, but there was no end to them in sight.

I moved with the soldiers, using them as my shield as I threw glowing spikes for what felt like hours, but I knew only minutes had passed. My heart thrummed in my chest, excited by the danger but terrified of it. I didn't let it stop me, though. The high of winning—or at least keeping the vamps at bay—fueled my every move. The tower remained intact, and that's all that mattered.

Two thick, beefy vampires came barreling into the side of my shield of bodies, knocking them to the ground as others came running right for me. I gasped and fumbled backward. In a blink, one of them was on top of me, his bloodied mouth baring chomping teeth that went for my neck. His teeth grazed my skin. I kicked and squirmed beneath him, my armored jacket riding up.

"Get off me, you piece of shit!"

A strange pressure pierced my stomach, and I gasped for air. With a sickening scraping sensation, he pulled a dirty knife from the flesh next to my belly button, and I cried out.

Shakily, I pressed my hand over his face and burned it with sunlight. We screamed together as his elbow dug into my wound, my power searing his immortal skin. The world threatened to go dark, but I hung on until he finally retreated, and I rolled over, desperate to catch my breath. My soldier friend appeared, speared the vamp's chest with the tip of his blade, and then hauled me to my feet.

"Are you alright?" he yelled.

I leaned against him and shook my head. My hand slid under my jacket and clamped over the gushing hole in my side. I couldn't speak, the edges of my vision darkened, and my legs drained of all strength.

He tucked one armored arm around my back, hooking under my armpit to stabilize me. Working quickly, he un-zipped my armored coat and ripped his one metal glove off with his teeth. He placed his bare hand over my dirty, jagged wound and a pleasant warmth filled it, threading my flesh back together.

"The Stonemaker has arrived!" someone called out, alerting everyone and eliciting cries of triumph.

The soldier still held me with one arm while his other slashed away at the undead as we made our way back toward the tower. My energy came back with every step I took.

A troll, the only other one I'd seen besides Oliver, stood

at the base, protected by six soldiers. With his thick arms held out, he worked magic to pull rocks from the earth and cover the tower in a protective case of stone.

Soldiers hollered and threw their arms in the air at the win. No one was getting through a wall of boulders. The vamps kept coming anyway, but now the soldiers advanced, creating a berth of space around the tower and fending off the hoards.

"You need to get out of here," my friend told me as we stood behind a solid line of defense.

I shook my head, already feeling my strength and magic returning. "No, I can't. My friends are here. They're coming from the unnamed city; I need to find them!"

Undecided, he raised his head to glance over the crowd. "Okay, what is your name, girl?"

"Avery," I replied. "Avery Quinn."

His eyes widened. "By the gods, you're Lady Summer's niece!" He seethed a few curse words under his breath like someone had just handed him an unwanted baby. "My name is Gideon," he said breathily, sweat dripping down his face beneath his helmet. "I'll help find your friends, but then you must leave!"

"Gladly!" I said, and he yanked at my arm, insisting I stay close as we fought through the sea of vampires.

It was like cutting through impossibly thick grass. Grass that swiped and bit at you. Gideon slayed vampires to our right while I stabbed chest after chest and slit flesh as it neared. With every step, my powers grew like a battery recharging.

But I wanted to save it. My physical energy was staid, and I relished how my muscles burned with purpose and how my weapon almost searched for the next target before it was even done with the last. Sticky, wet blood coated my face and body, matting my hair and drenching my clothes.

We emerged from one hoard and stumbled right into a pond of thick mud, immediately losing our footing. But I looked up and saw a nearby hill, empty of anyone, that was high enough to give a view of the entire fight.

"There!" I pointed. "We need to get up there so I can search for my friends."

"Come on, then!" Gideon huffed, his armor clanking as he stood and helped me to my feet.

The mud was up to our knees, but we finally crossed the massive puddle and climbed the foot hill that looked out over everything. My heart nearly stopped in my chest.

"My gods…" Gideon removed his helmet and blew out in a whisper as we gawked at the horrific sea of blood and bone and flesh littered with golden armor that glittered in the moonlight.

"There!" I pointed to a scene on the far end of the battle where vamps circled two figures; a massive black wolf and something so white it looked like fresh snow under the moon. Julie. "Those are my friends!"

Gideon saw Max and whipped his head to the tower. It was still intact. But the hoard pressed so hard that the soldiers backed up against the stone.

"She's a good Therian, and we used magic to get her here," I clarified and reached out to my powers. I was still too weak to wisp. "Can you wisp to them?" He looked like he might protest. "Please! I'm not strong enough to get that far yet. I'll stay here where I'm safe. *Please*, Gideon!"

He wavered, seemingly weighing it all. The soldier leaned close and clasped his hands over mine that held the dagger. "Keep this ready and stay low."

I nodded, and he slipped his helmet back on before wisping off across the battlefield. I squinted, searching for him, and saw him appear at my friends' sides. Within seconds, the swarm of vampires pushed outward, and I finally took a breath.

I scanned the field and spotted a large cluster of soldiers and blasts of golden magic. Thick vines and roots ripped from the earth, ensnaring vampires by the neck and beheading them. Kheelan and Tess had arrived.

I watched in stunned awe as my aunt—my gentle, loving, caring landscaper of an aunt—manipulated the earthy elements to fight through the masses, working with her husband to keep the bulk of the hoard from advancing toward the tower. She wore a rose pink jacket of the same material as mine, but hers hung to her knees. An ethereal glow hummed around her and Kheelan, making them both easy for their guards to protect but also making them targets.

Footsteps crunched behind me, and I spun around just as a fist met my jaw. The ground slammed into my body.

"Well, well, well," the female vampire taunted over me. I recognized her face. "What are the chances I'd find *you* here?" It was one of the vampires from the council that night when I'd accidentally reduced her people to ash.

I never took my eyes off her but discreetly hid my dagger beneath my leg, waiting for the right moment.

"Botwood will be pleased when I bring him your pretty little head." Her blackened predator eyes deepened, the darkness spreading outward as she hovered over me and blocked out the moon. Her hair was tucked back in one long black braid. "Did you know his brother was among those you burned that night?"

"It was either him or me," I spat, refusing to show fear even though I was flooded with it.

An evil chuckle rolled over in her chest as she sauntered a few more steps closer, her boot toeing mine. Even in shadow, her pointed teeth flashed. Paired with the dark pits for eyes, she looked like a demon, like the worst vampire myth made real.

"I've never tasted one with sunlight before." She ran a pale hand over her stomach in an oddly sensual way.

She leaned closer, and my sweaty hand lost its grip on the knife under my leg. I inched away, buying time as I firmed my grasp on the wooden hilt. I'd drive the blade through her chest if she jumped on me.

Thunder boomed in the distance, and something moved in the sky, catching the vampire's attention. A massive shadow loomed, expanding and blocking out the stars and moon. Tension built in the air like a coming storm, and she didn't even notice as I scrambled away a few more feet.

The blanket of darkness fell to the ground, covering hundreds of vampires and instantly drowning them in nightmares. I could tell as much by how they all clawed at their own faces and screamed in horror until their bodies plunged to the ground with a sickening, wet sound.

In the middle of it stood Oden and part of his army. They began hacking through vampires like a field of grass, but Oden was as still as a statue. Clad in thin black armor with charcoal-colored details, sword in hand, he slowly turned, dragged his gaze across the battlefield, and looked right at me.

In this chaos…he knew exactly where I was?

He saw the figure next to me, and his shoulders tightened. But I couldn't risk him wisping here and exposing my spot on the hill. If I were going to use my sunlight to stop these vampires, I needed time for my energy to replenish.

I moved, and the vampire turned her attention back to me, but she wasn't quick enough. I rolled and slashed the back of her knees. She keeled over from the instant pain as I jumped up and drove the blade through her back with all my might until the squish of her heart pushed back. She choked as blood spewed from her mouth and finally collapsed on the ground.

Panting, I searched for Oden, but he was gone. I stood on the hill alone–my powers slowly growing and refueling–and looked out over the noise and bloody chaos that stretched to the horizon. Vampires tore into Fae; Fae swung blades and swords, limbing and dismembering vamps.

Oden was one of them.

I found him again amid the battle, hacking away at vampires with a painful grace. His weapons of choice were a long sword and a round shield made of pure moonlight. It illuminated the dark battlefield, blinding the vampires so his men could take them down. More of his dark army poured in over the foothills, taking out troves of snarling vampires in their wake.

I kept searching until I spotted the only wolf; a dark, viscous spot amongst the red carpet of earth. Max shredded through every vamp that came near. Around her, something white and ethereal bounced from place to place as it danced through the enemy, wisping and swinging a thin blade when she appeared. Oden was right. It was a great skill, one I'd only mentioned in passing to Julie.

She and I weren't experienced fighters. We couldn't stand off against an enemy like the rest, but we were clever and able. Still, I watched her struggling as the hoards increased, and I almost took off running for my friends, but Gideon appeared again and quickly created a space around them.

I took a steadying breath.

I could see the river from this vantage point in the far distance. A metal line glistened in the moonlight from the Seelie side, and vampires continued appearing out of thin air on this side. They were coming from Ironworld in droves, swarm after swarm.

The Fae held the line, refusing to relent as the vamps attempted to push their way into the Seelie lands. But, at the rate they crossed the border, the Fae wouldn't be able to hold the line for much longer.

On the opposite end of the battle, a thundering sound boomed through the earth, and I watched in horror as a wave of vampires cleared out a section of Fae soldiers from the tower base. Oden shouted over the chaos and ordered his men to run there, but it wouldn't be enough.

The tower would fall, and the Therians would arrive soon.

My chest tightened, unable to contain the sharp, rapid breaths that pounded in my lungs. I searched within myself, frantically combing for my magic, but it wasn't ready.

I needed more, I needed to wipe out as many vampires as I could with my sunlight, and if I used it now, it wouldn't be enough and would only prolong the Therian's arrival.

A scream pierced the air, louder than any cries of battle, and my head shot in the direction it came from. Tess screamed for help just a few yards away as a group of vampires held her down, one on each of her limbs.

"Tess!" I took off running, slicing my blade through anything in my way.

Roots and vines tore from the ground and swiped at the vamps attacking her, but another group hacked away, shredding Tess's attempt to save herself.

"*Tess!*" I cried again, but I couldn't get through the hoard.

Elbows and fists pushed me back, striking my face and knocking me down again and again. My aunt's screams turned wet and gurgled, igniting something in me. A drive to save her, the woman who raised me—*saved* me—the only mother I ever knew.

I pushed to my feet, and a long whip made of pure sunlight formed in my hand. I knew the cost; this would set me back and use what little reserve of magic had been building within me. But I had to save Tess.

I cracked the whip back and forth, sunlight burning the air where it went, and sliced through the wave of vampires keeping me from my aunt. *Whip, crack, whip, crack.* Blood splattered my hands and face, coating me in fresh layers of sticky crimson. Heads and arms and flesh fell around me. I didn't stop. Tess's screams pulled me toward her, and when the sea of vamps thinned, I saw her.

Four vampires had her pinned to the ground while another crouched over her. The muscles in my arm strained as I used every ounce of strength to fling the whip from side to side, and sunlight sliced through them, leaving steaming chunks of bodies on the ground.

I ran and hauled away the dead vampire that collapsed on top of her, and words gurgled from her mouth with blood. Her neck was torn apart, flesh and arteries dangling from it. She grasped at my jacket with frantic hands, unable to voice the words she wanted to tell me. And then I realized…she wanted me to zipper the coat.

Tears streamed down my face, and my throat tingled as I grabbed her hand and placed a shaky kiss across her fingers. "No, Tess. Don't worry about me." I slid an arm under her back as the other futilely covered her grotesque wound. "Come on, let's get you out of here."

She was deadweight, unable to stand, and I collapsed on the ground with her. She moaned in pain. Frantic, I searched for help in the chaos, refusing to let go of her.

Another, much more profound, cry of pain cut through the noise of war, and I watched in horror as vampires held Kheelan in the air and a swarm circled them, keeping Kheelan's men at bay. Tess grappled at me, desperately pulling at my clothes. Her beautiful eyes were full of pain, and it gutted me to even look at her.

"He…lp…him…" she managed to say in a choppy, strained whisper.

My eyes widened. What could I possibly do to help Kheelan? He was surrounded by dozens of vampires. "I-I can't leave you!"

"P…leeease…"

Her pain was mine, and I held my aunt's hand tight to my heaving chest as I fought with what to do. I had seconds to decide. I couldn't save him, but I might be able to slow them down enough to create an opening for his soldiers. I kissed Tess's hand once more and rested it on her stomach.

I pushed to my feet, ready to throw my whip, but a vampire came barreling toward me and knocked me to the ground. It was a dead body, and I shoved it off as I struggled to my feet.

Kheelan's roar of pain filled my ears, and I had no choice but to stand there and witness the beasts of Ironworld rip his armored body in half. Metal clinked to the ground, followed by his innards, and a surge of great power cleaved the air, combing over the battlefield. The force threw me back, and I slammed into the bloodied earth, knocking the wind from my lungs.

A High Lord had been killed.

Chapter Twenty-One

I crawled in the mud toward Tess. She couldn't move aside from gasping for air. With each attempt, blood spurted from her open neck. But still, tears rolled down her face. She knew her husband was dead.

Someone fell to their knees at my side, and I reached for my dagger, but Oliver's voice anchored me.

"By the gods," he said, quickly examining Tess. "We need to get her out of here!"

A second later, Moya appeared, holding my aunt's face in both hands. "Tessana! *Tessana!* No, *no!* You can't leave me! *Don't leave me!*"

"Can you save her?" I asked Oliver as he worked magic to secure what was left of her neck with bandages.

"I won't know until I get her to my cottage," he replied and stopped to clap his hands together.

A spear appeared, and he fired it at a vampire that was

too close. Moya was only focused on one thing. Tess. I cracked my whip at two more vamps, and their heads rolled across the ground. Oliver looked me up and down.

"You're hurt," he noted, reaching for the bloodied spot on my shirt as my jacket fell open. "Come with us. I'll tend to it."

I shook my head. "No, I'm fine. A Summer soldier healed me." He finished the thick bandage around Tess's neck. She was utterly unconscious. "Take her. Get out of here. This is a battle we never had a chance of winning."

Oliver stood and hauled me to my feet. "There is always a chance, Avery. As long as we're still alive, there's always a chance."

"*Avery!*"

My heart jumped in my chest at the sound, and I perked up, searching over the heads of others. Cillian's voice called again, "*Avery!*"

I spotted him a few yards away, fighting his way through vampires and dodging swings from unknowing Fae. Quickly, I looked at Oliver.

"Take Tess, save her, please. I'll be fine. Cillian's here." He seemed to want to protest, but we didn't have time. Not with the hoards of vampires working to take down the stone protecting the tower. Not when Moya was falling apart as my aunt drifted closer to death. "Please, Oliver! Save my aunt. She's the only family I have." I swallowed dryly. "And she's all Summer has left."

He gave me a grave nod and wisped the three of them away in a flash. Part of me was relieved knowing at least two of my friends and Tess were away from this nightmare. I took one deep breath, turned to where Cillian was and began making my way to him.

We both fought and sliced and pushed our way toward each other. Every vampire I left on the ground bloomed hope in my chest with every step closer. Cillian's blue eyes never left me, and a manic smile spread across my face. Just a few more yards and his arms would be around me. Safety. He was my safety. I just had to get to him, and then we could leave this place to the great beings who started it all.

The blackened tips of leathery wings and a set of bloodied, curled horns caught my eye over Cillian's shoulder, and my innards went cold. Through the chaos of flying swords and tumbling bodies, flashes of Evaine's sinister face stared back at me, locking my feet in place. Fear gripped me, squeezing around my heart, and all I could do was heave frantic breaths in and out of my lungs.

She lifted a long wooden spear in her clawed hand, and an evil cackle crawled through the air, circling my ears. Her tar-black eyes slowly moved to the back of Cillian's head—he had no idea.

"Cillian!" I screamed as Evaine's shoulder pulled back,

readying to send the spear right for the man I loved.

My fingers curled into fists, and I ripped at the fabric of space and time, clawing my way to him. I appeared in a blink and slammed into his chest just as another force knocked him into me and slammed us to the ground. A foreign pain bloomed in my shoulder, and I gasped for air as the weight of Cillian's body crushed me.

"Cillian!"

I tried to move him, but he groaned against my neck. The spear stuck out of his back. I grabbed his face and pushed his head up, sending me a blinding shock of pain. I dared a glance down, and a panicked scream erupted from me at the sight of the wooden spear lodged in my flesh.

I couldn't move him. We were pinned to the ground together.

Vampires still came in troves. Magic blasted all around like powerful bombs, shattering in my ears. The cries of the injured and dying layered between the deafening sounds of weapons crashing together. And all I could do was lay there as Cillian's dying body deflated on top of me.

A cry choked in my throat.

"Let go," he muttered with strain, struggling to move his head and look up at me. The blue of his eyes had faded to grey, and my heart broke in two. I thought he was telling me to let go of him, but he repeated, "Let…go… the elastic."

The elastic. The part of me that kept my powers in check. I thought I'd let go of it ages ago, but it was there. I could feel it, stifling my abilities and keeping them in a corner.

"I can't," I told him, tears and sweat and snot coating my face as I held his. "It'll kill you."

He gave me a ghostly look that said what we were both thinking, what I didn't want to utter out loud or even admit. He was already dead. The spear must have pierced part of his heart—not entirely. He would have been dead instantly if it did. No, Cillian was slowly dying in my arms, and there was absolutely nothing I could do.

A crumbling stone boomed in the distance, shaking the ground. The tower was down. In a matter of a few heartbeats, the roar of wolves sounded in the air, igniting victorious cheers from the vampires. Thunder and lightning crashed in the sky as darkness moved like a living thing overhead. Oden must have cast another blanket of nightmares.

It began to rain hard and fast and out of nowhere. Heavy droplets quickened, and a torrential downpour drenched the battlefield as three races of ancient beings continued killing each other for power. Max and Julie were still out there somewhere.

Cillian didn't move, and his eyes clouded over. I shook his shoulder.

"Cillian!" I cried. "Throw up your shadows! It might

save you!"

There was no response.

My heart stopped. "No! Cillian! Cillian!" I shook him harder, crying. *"Cillian…"* The word pushed from my lungs in a whimper.

Rain washed over us, diluting the caked carnage on my face. The salty, earthy taste of blood and dirt coated my mouth as I cried and wrapped my arms around him. The pain in my shoulder was a scratch compared to the ache of death in my heart.

"I love you," I whispered against his cheek and trembled as I wrapped my arms around him.

My silent sobs became violent cries, and I sucked in one deep breath before letting go. My pain cleaved the air, and a supernova of sunlight surged from my body, combing and raking over the land, burning up every vampire for miles. I felt every one of them, every immortal life I took, until the weight on my chest lessened, and I knew he was gone.

I couldn't bear to open my eyes.

But the battle still raged, and I lay in the middle of it. The vampires were gone, but wolves still ravaged the ash-ridden land. I could hear their determined cries as they fought against their enemy.

I wanted to roll over and die there where Cillian's ashes coated the earth, but it would only be a matter of time before some Therian came and tore me to shreds. I didn't want to die like that.

I gripped the thick spear still lodged in my shoulder and ripped it out, tearing the flesh even more and forcing my eyes open. Blood leached from the gaping hole, and I placed a shaky hand over it as I struggled to roll onto my knees. Warm crimson oozed between my fingers, staining the ground. I fought to catch my breath and pushed myself to stand.

Thick flakes of ash coated the land as far as the eye could see. The rain continued to belt down over us as Fae gained the upper hand, mixing with blood, bone, and ash to create a horrific carpet of carnage. My breath heaved and burned in my chest as I peered around and noted that the vampires were gone. In the distance, the tower was surrounded by Summer and Dark soldiers. Therians retreated, heading back to the river.

It was over.

I wandered mindlessly, tripping over bodies and armor. I didn't know what to do or where to go. My powers didn't respond to my weak call; I couldn't even wisp. I was a shell.

Fields of carnage stretch all around. Blood leaked from my body, soaking my clothes and running down into my boots. Darkness closed in, eating away at the edges of my vision. I clumsily stumbled to the right and slipped in the mud, but I didn't bother to catch myself as

I dropped into a shallow pit where a huge rock had been pulled from the earth.

Kheelan. Tess. Julie. Max…*Cillian*. I held their faces in my mind as I drifted. A strange sense of peace washed over me, coaxing me along, beckoning me to follow it. Rain filled the hole I lay in, mixing with mud and blood. I stayed there, unmoving, as the pit slowly became my grave, burying me. I took one last breath just before the water covered my face.

Silence.

I said my goodbyes to everyone I loved and handed myself over to the pure, undiluted promise of death. I waited for my heart to stop beating, for my lungs to burn up what air was left in them.

I was ready to go.

After everything I had just witnessed, I didn't have what it took to stay in this world. I couldn't bear having Oliver look at me with a broken expression to deliver the news that he couldn't save Tess. Didn't want to find out that Julie and Max died fighting for their lives.

And I couldn't face Celadine.

I knew it was weak and cowardly of me, but I'd already given enough. There was nothing left. My heart slowed, and I continued to fade away. I welcomed the cold end; it was just within my grasp. My dying mind wandered, reaching for the promise of death to take me away from here, to wipe away all that I'd just endured. It was too much for one person to bear, and I only hoped that my memories would die with my beaten body and that my soul could leave it all behind.

The muffled sounds above the water that covered my ears began to fade even more, the world becoming nothing more than a distant place as I drifted. The cold beyond beckoned, and the fingertips of my mind stretched toward it.

Hello, sweet death.

Something broke the surface of my watery grave and grabbed my arm, yanking me away from the end within my grasp. They hauled me up, and I crumpled lifelessly on the ground as the painful sound of the world came rushing back.

"Is she dead?" I heard Julie gasp.

Max's wet curls splattered across my face as she put her ear to my chest. "No, there's a heartbeat. It's faint, but it's there."

Strong hands yanked at the collar of my jacket, jostling my pending corpse. "Gods above." It was Oden's voice. "How did she survive such a blow?"

Smaller fingers delicately examined the wound. "Fuck. It's laced with something." I heard sniffing, and Max's breath warmed my cold flesh.

"What is it?" Julie asked.

"Belladonna," Max replied, unsure. "But—" She sniffed again. "It's mixed with something else. I can't place it."

"She needs a healer," Oden said with desperation and slipped his arms underneath me.

"No," Max told him. "This was made with witchcraft. She needs a witch."

"Celadine?" Julie suggested.

"No." She released a defeated sigh. "Someone with more experience."

"What do you *mean*?" Julie sounded exhausted and panicked, her shaking hands cupped around mine. "There are no other witches, Max! They're all long dead, remember?"

Oden's chest rumbled with a helpless groan as he held me close. My body hung in his arms like dough. I couldn't move, couldn't even tell my eyes to open. It was like I was paralyzed.

"I know someone who can save her," he told them reluctantly. "But I have to take her alone."

"Are you fucking crazy?" Max chewed him.

"There's no way in hell we're leaving her side, Oden."

"Then she shall die here on this bloody battlefield! Is that what you wish?" The desperation that broke through his voice was raw and unyielding.

There was silence for a moment, aside from Oden's rampant heartbeat pulsing through my body. Then I felt Julie's hand in mine once more.

"Go then. Do whatever it takes to save her and keep us updated *every* moment of the way."

She barely finished her sentence before the air tightened and changed as Oden wisped me away. I still couldn't move; my eyes remained closed as I lay limp across Oden's capable arms. Everything inside me wanted to let go, to drift away again, but his voice whispered in my ear.

"Stay with me."

A new smell filled my nose—sweet and smoky—and the sea crashed in the distance, adding a tinge of salt to the aroma.

"Lord Oden!" a woman exclaimed, and footsteps quickly approached. "Who is this?" A gasp. "My word! Why are you in armor—is that *blood?* What's *happened?*"

"There was a war," he told her breathily as he walked and carried me somewhere. "The Therians tried to invade Faerie; they killed thousands."

"So your suspicions were true then?"

He held me tighter, closer. "This girl saved us all, and now she's dying. I need your help. She's been poisoned with belladonna and some other concoction. Call your sisters immediately."

"Of course," she replied without hesitation. "Bring her inside and put her down on the bed. I'll be right back."

"Bring all the antidotes for poisons you have!" he called after her, and his words trailed off with a tearful crack.

Within minutes, what sounded like a team of people arrived. Metal tools and glass jars, cork tops popping, liquids bubbling. My mind tried to follow all the sounds and sensations, but it was too much. They ripped away most of my clothing to assess the damage.

Apparently, the poison Evaine had on the spear was belladonna mixed with something that had gone extinct in Ironworld centuries ago, but they recognized it and had the means to make the cure.

Something cold and wet poured over my wound, and my eyes flew open with blinding, searing pain. If they told me they'd set fire to my shoulder, I would have believed them. Another dose of the substance sent me bolting upward, screaming, and clawing to escape.

"*Just let me die!*" I screamed, my voice not my own.

Oden stood helplessly near the back of the room, a wide-open balcony behind him. Strong hands slammed me back down on the bed, and another dose of the antidote poured over the wound. I shot up again, desperate and manic.

This time I spotted the sprawling rooftops of a foreign city in the distance before they shoved me back down again. The faces above me were strangers, but parts of them struck a familiar chord in the recesses of my mind. Beautiful women, some with braids in their hair, others bald or had neatly pinned curls, but all with tattoos on their skin.

Tattoos like Celadine's.

Finally, the burning subsided, and my body deflated on the bed. I became leaden as the women worked to clean my wounds and stitch my skin in various places. I hadn't realized I had other injuries that serious.

One of them hovered over my face with a warm, motherly smile and gently put a cup to my mouth as she cradled my head with one hand. I drank the contents, some kind of sweet milky substance, and let my head fall back on the pillow.

"We've given her something to help her sleep while we work on her," the first woman told Oden as he came to my side. "Her wounds are extensive, and the poison was crafted with magic. We'll have to undo whatever's been woven to ensure every drop is gone from her system."

"Of course, Valdri," Oden spoke so softly it almost didn't sound like him. He stepped to my side. "Do what you must."

The edges of my vision began to darken as sleep dragged me under the sedative. But I grabbed his sleeve, and he glanced at me with pain in his grey eyes. The skin around them taught with exhaustion and splattered with still-fresh blood.

"W-where am I?" I mumbled, every word dragging like lead on my tongue.

A ghost of a smile tugged at his mouth but didn't reach those stormy eyes. "The only place that could save you," he said. "A secret place where witches thrive." The world faded away as he smoothed the hair from my face and muttered a few last words.

"Welcome to the Isle of Serene, Avery."

Continue Avery and Cillian's dark and epic love story in book two of *The Ironworld Series, A Throne of Burning Embers!*

Be sure to follow Candace online or subscribe to her reader newsletter for updates on the release!

Other Titles by Author Candace Osmond

Dark Tides Series

Kingdom of Sand & Stars Series

Silently Into the Night

A Touch of Darkness Series

About the Author

Candace Osmond is a **#1 International & USA TODAY Bestselling Author** and **Award-Winning Screenwriter**. She currently resides on the rocky East Coast of Canada with her husband, two kids, and bulldog.

Connect with Candace online! She LOVES to hear from readers!

www.AuthorCandaceOsmond.com

Check out all of Candace's book merch and signed paperbacks in her reader merch shoppe, Death by Reading on Etsy!

www.ingramcontent.com/pod-product-compliance
Lightning Source LLC
Chambersburg PA
CBHW020346220726

48290CB00014B/1108

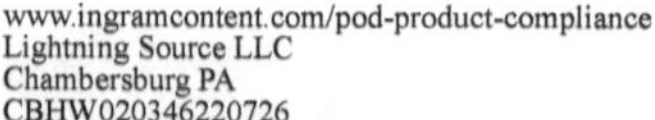